# "Let me see you to your car."

She flicked her eyes back to his, her expression carrying a hint of question but not the suspicion that had been there earlier. "That's not necessary."

"Yes, it is. I need to know you're safe. I couldn't live with myself if I just walked away and something happened to you."

She raised her chin as if she'd figured him out. "Because I'm the new boss's sister and an executive at Kendall?"

"No. I suppose that's a good reason, but it's not my primary one." Of course, technically, protecting the boss's sister *was* his reason for being there, but the words felt good on his tongue.

She tilted her head to the side and arched her eyebrows as if waiting for him to come clean.

"Let's just say I'll be thinking about you all night. I don't want those thoughts to be laced with worry." It sounded like a line, and as soon as he'd said it he'd wanted it back. The ironic thing was, it was one of the first honest things he'd said to her.

First published in Great Britain 2012
by Mills & Boon, an imprint of Harlequin (UK) Limited,
Eton House, 18-24 Paradise Road, Richmond, Surrey TW9 1SR

Special thanks and acknowledgement to Ann Voss Peterson for her contribution to the SITUATION: CHRISTMAS series.

© Harlequin Books S.A. 2011

ISBN: 978 0 263 89583 4
ebook ISBN: 978 1 408 97753 8

46-1212

Harlequin (UK) policy is to use papers that are natural, renewable and recyclable products and made from wood grown in sustainable forests. The logging and manufacturing processes conform to the legal environmental regulations of the country of origin.

Printed and bound in Spain
by Blackprint CPI, Barcelona

# SECRET PROTECTOR

## BY
## ANN VOSS PETERSON

Ever since she was a little girl making her own books out of construction paper, **Ann Voss Peterson** wanted to write. So when it came time to choose a major at the University of Wisconsin, creative writing was her only choice. Of course, writing wasn't a *practical* choice—one needs to earn a living. So Ann found jobs, including proofreading legal transcripts, working with quarter horses and washing windows. But no matter how she earned her paycheck, she continued to write the type of stories that captured her heart and imagination: romantic suspense. Ann lives near Madison, Wisconsin, with her husband, her two young sons, her border collie and her quarter horse mare. Ann loves to hear from readers. E-mail her at ann@annvosspeterson.com or visit her website at www.annvosspeterson.com.

To those who put others before themselves.
The definition of a hero.

# *Chapter One*

If Natalie didn't need an infusion of caffeine so badly she could barely see straight, she'd walk out of the coffee shop right now, despite already having paid for her latte.

She checked her watch and tried to resist the urge to tap the toe of her pump on the tile floor. She could feel the man next to her give her a once-over. Dressed in jeans, with shirttails hanging out and shoes that looked more like slippers than street wear, he was probably thinking she was uptight.

He was probably right.

Six foot, thin build, he was also kind of cute, at least in an ordinary sort of way.

What the heck? She was usually drawn to the good-looking ones. Maybe it was past time to shake things up. Taking a deep breath and curving her lips into a smile, she gave him a glance.

He looked away.

Figures. Natalie's luck with men was right up there with her talent for finding short lines.

She peered at the darkness outside the coffee shop's glass doors. Jolie would be finished trying on brides-maids' dresses before Natalie even reached the bridal shop. And Rachel would surely be finished with the fitting for her wedding dress. Natalie wouldn't even get a glimpse. She was on schedule to let down both her future sisters-in-law and disappoint herself, and for what?

Caffeine was a horrible addiction.

"Double shot, low-fat latte?" The barista raised a pierced brow and plunked the cup on the counter.

Natalie flashed her best imitation of a grateful smile, picked up the coffee. She dodged her fellow addicts and pushed out the door, chimes jingling in her ear.

A chill wind hit her face. November in St. Louis was unpredictable, but one bit of weather that she could count on was that winter would eventually arrive. Apparently it had sometime in the past half hour. Using her free hand to wrap her trench more tightly around her, she made a mental note to dig out her wool coat before work tomorrow.

Her heels clacked hollow on the sidewalk. Dark windows stared down at her from all angles. City noises drifted on the breeze, sounding as if they were coming from the riverfront, blocks away. The temperature wasn't the only thing to have changed in the time she'd been stuck in the coffee shop. Since she'd last walked the three blocks from the office, the business district seemed to have vacated for the night.

The bell on the coffee shop's door jingled, as someone followed her into the cold.

She crossed the side street midblock and headed back toward Kendall Communications and the executive parking garage. The drive to the bridal shop wouldn't take long. And Jolie would try her dress on again, if need be. The night was looking up.

The sound of footsteps shuffled behind her.

She glanced back. The silhouette of a man strode along the sidewalk. Tall, thin, shirttails flapping in the breeze. Must be the guy from the coffee shop, although on second glance, his hands were empty. Shouldn't he be carrying a cup?

She quickened her pace.

She was being silly. She knew it. But there was something about the dark and the quiet and the cold that set her nerves on edge. She just needed to get to the Kendall building. There she could duck into the parking garage and the guy behind her would continue down the sidewalk to wherever it was he was headed.

She turned the corner, half expecting her follower to walk right past.

He made the turn, as well.

She forced herself to breathe slowly, in and out, countering the patter of her heartbeat. People walked down the same streets all the time. She was being silly. Here she hadn't even had a sip of coffee and every nerve in her body felt like it was buzzing. Maybe she didn't need the extra jolt of caffeine after all. Maybe tonight she was twitchy enough without it.

The darkened tower of her family business loomed ahead. She walked a little faster in spite of herself. With any luck, the parking attendant would still be at his post. He would smile his usual friendly smile, and she would chuckle to herself about how paranoid she was being. She didn't know why she felt so afraid of a guy that just a moment ago she'd thought was kind of cute.

Sure, when it came to choosing men, she was a horrible failure. But that didn't mean just because she glanced this guy's way he would turn out to be a mugger.

She passed the stairwell leading to the parking garage's lower level and made for the car entrance and the attendant. She turned the corner and looked to the booth.

It was empty.

Natalie's mouth went dry. She spun around, certain the man would be behind her, a gun in his fist or maybe a knife, his lips pulling back in a sinister smile.

The sidewalk was empty, as well.

She waited. Ten seconds. Twenty. No one appeared.

He must have turned off. He must not have been following her after all.

She was obviously losing her mind. Understandable, she supposed. Ever since Rick Campbell had been exonerated in her parents' murders two months ago and then was killed himself, the entire Kendall clan had been on edge. Murder did that. If any family knew that, it was theirs.

On top of that, two of her three brothers, Ash and Devin, had lived through horrors of their own in the past two months. Horrors they'd thankfully overcome. Both now engaged to women they loved, her two oldest brothers had been blessed as well as challenged. But the deaths of their parents continued to hang over the entire Kendall family like a shroud.

She shook her head to dislodge shadowy thoughts she'd been trying to banish for twenty years. As if a mere shake of the head would do that. The only thing that worked was painting. Turning her childhood fears and guilt into images. Getting them out of her head, onto canvas and shutting them away in her studio where no one could see them.

She ripped open the flap on her coffee and took a long sip. Already her heartbeat was slowing. Already she was starting to feel normal again. But despite her earlier promise to herself, she didn't feel much like laughing. All she felt was grateful no one else had witnessed her ridiculousness.

Replacing the coffee flap in order to keep her latte hot, she continued down the ramp to the garage's lower level. A lowered garage door and smaller human-size door nestled side by side at the bottom of the ramp. The executive parking filled the whole lower level. Besides being security locked, this part of the garage also had the advantage of being heated in the winter. And it had both a street entrance and an elevator that led directly to the offices on the upper floors.

Balancing her coffee in one hand, she groped in her bag for her keys.

The door behind her clicked open.

She whirled around.

Emerging from the stairwell was the man with the untucked shirt. The door slammed with a loud clang.

The sound shuddered up Natalie's spine and echoed off the concrete. For a moment, she couldn't focus. She couldn't move. All she could do was think about how alone the two of them were—no other cars, no one to come to her aid. Even if she screamed, would anyone hear?

Her phone. Instead of grabbing her keys, she pulled

out her cell. She stared at the screen. Underground garage. Surrounded by concrete.

No service.

She held the phone to her ear anyway. If he thought she was calling someone, he would leave her alone. Wouldn't he? The shuffling sound of those god-awful loafers moved toward her.

A high whistle of panic rose in her ears. Oil and concrete and old exhaust clogged her throat.

"No reception down here, I bet," he said in a quiet voice.

He wasn't fooled by the phone. All she could do was make a run for it. Get through the door and slam it before he could follow. She dropped the useless phone back in her bag and groped for her keys. Her fingers hit steel. She pulled the key chain out, jingling in shaking fingers. She tried to fit her key into the lock.

"Need help with that?"

His voice was right behind her shoulder. The faint mint scent of mouthwash fanned her neck.

She turned her head to look at him.

He stared at her with sharp brown eyes. His dark blond hair was mussed, blown by the wind. He looked like a regular guy. Perfectly ordinary.

Then why was she so frightened?

She turned back to the door. He hadn't hurt her yet. Hadn't even touched her. All he'd done was ask if he could help. That had to mean something. Right? Maybe she was doing all this panicking for nothing. Maybe she really was going crazy after all. "No, thanks. I can get it."

"You seem…scared."

She didn't know what to say. Admit she was frightened out of her mind? Or just play it cool. "I was just startled."

"Startled? That's not what I had in mind."

His voice sounded low, calm. Everything Natalie wasn't. Everything she didn't think a mugger should be, either. "I'm…I'm okay now." She fibbed, feeling far less than okay.

He narrowed his eyes. "Do you know who I am?"

"Know you?" She turned to face him. He stood so close she took a step back, hitting the door. "You were in the coffee shop."

"Yes. I've been wanting to talk to you for a long time." He smiled. Cool. Casual. But his eyes…something about them seemed hard. Something about his smile felt less than friendly.

Was she imagining it?

"Excuse me. Hate to interrupt." The voice came from behind the man. Someone else.

She peered past one of the skinny shoulders. Another man stood in the doorway to the stairwell, his tall, well-muscled frame filling the space. Everything about him—the expression on his face, the way he held his body, the look in his eyes—exuded calm and control. And even though she didn't know anything more about this man than she did the guy who'd followed her from the coffee shop, she let a relieved breath escape from her lungs and sagged back against the door. "No interruption. Really."

The man staring at her turned to face the interloper. "Who in the hell are you?"

"I'd like to ask you the same question."

"Too bad I asked it first."

He walked from the stairwell. His steps came slow and steady but Natalie could feel something coiled underneath. Power. Readiness. He stopped a few feet away. His eyes focused on the smaller man, hazel slits. "I'm a friend of Ms. Kendall's. You?"

The man closest to her looked away to the door. His shoulders seemed to grow even more slight. He shuffled away from her, one step, two. "I'm… This is a misunderstanding."

She wasn't sure what was misunderstood. He hadn't said or done anything. Not really. Looking at him, Natalie couldn't quite remember why she'd felt so threatened. He seemed anything but threatening now.

"I think we understand each other just fine," said the second man. He ran a hand over his cropped, brown hair. "Now if you don't mind, I'd like a word with Ms. Kendall. Alone."

The thin man nodded and made for the ramp Natalie had followed into the garage, shoulders hunched. He didn't look back.

As soon as he climbed out of sight, Natalie focused on the man in front of her. Of the two of them, he was definitely the strongest, physically the more threatening. He even knew her name, although she'd never seen him before. She was sure she hadn't. She'd remember. But despite the fact that she was alone and defenseless in the same position as she'd been with the other man moments ago, this time she felt inexplicably safe.

But, of course, taking her history with men into account, that was probably a bad sign. "So who are you? And how do you know my name?"

## Chapter Two

As soon as Gray stepped from the stairwell, he knew
this question would be coming. He also knew he didn't
have an answer for it. Not one Ms. Natalie Kendall
would like, anyway. If he wanted to follow his client's
directions, he was going to have to lie. Or at least tweak
the truth a little. He just hoped Natalie's brother was
ready to cover his tracks. "Grayson Scott. Call me
Gray."

She stared as if waiting for the rest.

"I work at your company."

A tiny crease dug between her eyebrows. "I'm sorry.
I don't remember ever having met you."

"I just talked to Mr. Kendall about the job today."

The crease didn't fade. Her mouth dipped in a frown
and she glanced off to the side, as if she knew what he
was saying wasn't exactly the truth and she was conjur-
ing a way to trip him up. "Which Mr. Kendall did you
talk to?"

"The CEO, Devin Kendall." At least that answer was
the truth. "He's your brother, correct?"

"Devin isn't looking to fill any vacancies. Not that
he told me about."

He gave a shrug. "Kendall isn't a tiny company. Do you usually know about all vacancies?"

"Usually, yes."

He held her gaze, hoping he appeared to have nothing to hide. That was the problem with off-the-cuff lies. It was impossible to make sure your cover story held water. And stacking one lie on top of another tended to multiply the potential for leaks.

"What division?" she asked.

Best to stick as close to the truth as he could. "Security."

"That's convenient."

He didn't react. Part of selling a lie was resisting the urge to explain.

She pushed strands of her straight, blond hair back over her shoulder. "I happen to know we just hired a bunch of extra security people over the past couple of months. We don't need more."

"You'll have to ask your brother about that." And he had to talk to Devin before she could.

"I will." She narrowed her eyes. "You're not a bodyguard of some kind, are you?"

He'd been hoping she wouldn't ask that precise question. The woman seemed to have pretty good lie radar. He sure hoped the acting skills he'd honed in his one-and-only grade school play performance would be enough to see him through.

He gave her an aw-shucks grin. "Nothing so glamorous, I'm afraid. I work with locks and alarm systems."

"Really?" She looked at him harder, if that was possible.

If she didn't blink soon, he was going to start to

sweat. "You don't like locks and alarm systems?" he tossed off, hoping a little levity would help his case.

"I thought that was Glenn Johnston's area."

He'd figured a company like Kendall would already have locks and alarms covered, so he was ready with a twist. "I have a meeting with Glenn tomorrow. Your brother said he'd set it up. He wants to update to the newest technology. That's where I come in."

She crooked one eyebrow. "And Glenn is going along with this idea?"

"I haven't met him yet, so I have no clue."

Her face seemed to relax, one corner of her lips turning up slightly with amusement. "Good luck with that meeting."

"Don't tell me, Glenn's a technophobe." He gave her what he hoped was a worried expression. Hell, he was worried. He seemed to have chosen just the wrong cover story. He hoped it wouldn't be too tough for Devin to back up.

"He's a little resistant to new things, that's all. As long as Devin paves the way for you, it should be fine." She nodded, her mood shifting from suspicious to encouraging.

"Thanks for the heads-up on Glenn Johnston. It helps to know I should tread softly." So far, so good. Now to angle the conversation toward the subject he really wanted to address. "In the meantime, who was that guy you were talking to?"

She glanced at the ramp leading out of the garage, as if half expecting him to be waiting in the shadows. "I don't know."

"You've never seen him before?"

"Not before tonight. He was in the coffee shop I just left." She held up a large to-go cup with the logo of a nearby coffee shop emblazoned on the side. "He followed me."

"Why?"

She shook her head, looking a little lost. "I have no idea."

She really seemed at a loss. He fought the urge to reach out and rub his hand up and down her arm. Somehow he doubted she'd see the move as supportive coming from a guy she'd just met. "Did he say anything to you?"

"Not much. He asked if I knew him."

"Knew him?"

She gave a little shrug. "From the coffee shop, I guess."

"And you're sure you've never seen him before tonight?"

"I don't remember him. But he might have been there before. It's the closest coffee shop. I go there all the time. I like their lattes." She held up her cup again as if showing him proof. "Thank you, by the way. He really didn't do anything, and I'm not sure I actually needed saving, but I appreciate it anyway."

"Not a problem. I am joining the security crew tomorrow. Might as well get an early start on the job. Just glad I didn't have to install an alarm right on the guy's nose." He feigned giving the air an awkward punch.

She laughed, the sound tinkling off the concrete around them, frothy and fun and yet something deeper underneath.

He'd been following her for a while now, but he'd

never been face-to-face like this and he'd never before heard her laugh. He'd like to hear more of it.

"Well, thank you. I really do appreciate you stepping in to help. There aren't a lot of Good Samaritans around these days." She started to angle her body away from him, suggesting it was time to go.

He nodded and smiled. Of course, he wasn't a Good Samaritan, although that was what he'd wanted her to believe. He was paid to stick his neck out. Even though this case hadn't required much stretching so far. "Let me see you to your car."

She flicked her eyes back to his, her expression carrying a hint of question but not the suspicion that had been there earlier. "That's not necessary."

"Yes, it is. I need to know you're safe. I couldn't live with myself if I just walked away and something happened to you."

She raised her chin as if she'd figured him out. "Because I'm the new boss's sister and an executive at Kendall?"

"No. I suppose that's a good reason, but it's not my primary one." Of course, technically protecting the boss's sister *was* his reason for being here, but the words felt good on his tongue.

She tilted her head to the side and arched her eyebrows as if waiting for him to come clean.

"Let's just say I'll be thinking about you all night. I don't want those thoughts to be laced with worry." It sounded like a line, and as soon as he'd said it he'd wanted it back. The ironic thing was it was one of the first honest things he'd said to her.

She smiled.

Despite the greenish flicker of the parking structure's fluorescent lights, he picked up a little more color in the apples of her cheeks. Encouraging. "So will you let me see you to your car?"

"I guess it wouldn't hurt." She looked down at the keys in her hand then returned her gaze to his. "But I'm having trouble with my keys. You're a Kendall employee. Security, even. Do you have yours?"

He could feel his grin from the inside out. "Testing me, huh?"

"Does that seem paranoid?"

"It seems smart." And luckily Devin had given him keys to the parking garage weeks ago. He pulled them out and made a show of unlocking the door. He held it open for her to pass through.

She shot him the kind of smile that had him thinking all sorts of things, none particularly protective. "Thank you." If he wasn't mistaken, there was a flirty lilt to her tone.

This job was getting a whole lot more interesting.

They walked side by side through the structure, the wide-open space feeling more intimate than it had a right to. He found himself thinking about leaning close, trying to detect a whisper of her scent over the odor of concrete and old exhaust. Of all the lies he'd told her tonight, the fact that he was attracted to her wasn't one. Ever since he'd started following her, he hadn't been able to help thinking of her—day and night—and not in a typical bodyguard sort of way. But none of those thoughts compared with being face-to-face.

Of course, he'd never intended to actually meet her. And now that he had, he found himself with a problem.

For weeks he'd kept an eye on her without her noticing he was there. But after tonight, he had the feeling she'd notice, no matter how good his surveillance skills were. If he wanted to continue to perform as her bodyguard without her knowledge, he had to find some kind of reason to hang around.

And it seemed one had just landed in his lap. He just had to play it right.

A cherry-red sports car sat at the far end of the structure. Natalie pointed her remote at the car and the driver's door opened with a chirp. Hand on the door handle, she offered him a smile. "Thank you."

"Like I said, it's not a problem."

"Still, I appreciate your concern."

"Do you appreciate it enough…" He looked away. "No. Sorry. I think I'm flirting with overstepping my bounds."

"What were you going to say?" She looked straight at him with clear green eyes, as if she really wanted to know.

Just the response he was after. "You won't hold it against me?"

"After you saved me from the notorious coffee shop mugger? How could I?"

"Okay, I was just going to ask if you'd like to meet for lunch tomorrow."

Her smile grew to a full-fledged grin. "I think I could fit it in."

"OH, JOLIE, YOU'RE NOT going to wear *that,* are you?" Natalie tried to sound serious, but the look on Jolie's face made her bubbly good mood even better. She let loose with a smile, despite best intentions.

Jolie shot her a dry look. "It looks fabulous, doesn't it?"

Natalie skimmed her eyes over the one-shoulder peacock silk number. Jolie's red hair, creamy skin and green eyes looked unbelievable with the silk's rich color, and the dress itself looked like something straight off the red carpet. Natalie couldn't lie. Her friend and future sister-in-law looked breathtaking. "Devin is going to want to marry you on the spot."

Jolie laughed and held up a hand. "If he does, he's out of luck. You have to see Rachel's bridal gown."

Set to marry Natalie's notorious bachelor cop brother, Ash, Rachel was the bride-to-be. The reason she and Jolie were here. But Jolie had a rock on her finger that was twice as big as Rachel's and a wedding to Natalie's brother Devin to prepare for, as well. "I can't wait to see Rachel in her dress. I'm sure she looks gorgeous."

Jolie sashayed in front of the multiangle bridal shop mirror. "I want the whole wedding thing for myself, too. Including that white dress. For real, this time. No pretending."

Natalie nodded. As part of a plan to distract the media who had taken to following Devin's every move, Jolie and Devin had staged a fake engagement and pretended to plan their wedding. It had been tough on Jolie, who'd been in love with her boss for a long while. But in the end, she and Devin had both realized they wanted to be married.

For real.

On the other hand, Natalie only had bridesmaids'

dresses in her future, and as fabulous as this one was, it didn't compare to the white, fairy-tale gowns.

But maybe...

A shimmer warmed her chest as she thought of how wonderful Gray would look in a tuxedo, waiting for her at the altar. She let out a sigh and tried to tamp down the fantasy, tough since she'd had her wedding planned out since she was about seven. It was definitely too soon for marriage plans, but at least she had a lunch date to look forward to.

"What are you so happy about?" Jolie stared at Natalie via her reflection.

"It's a great dress."

Jolie shot her a no-nonsense look. "That's not a dress smile. I know you. That's a man smile."

Natalie couldn't help but laugh.

"I knew it." Jolie turned away from the mirror and faced Natalie directly. "So spill. I just saw you at the office and your mood wasn't *this* fabulous. What happened?"

Natalie was far more excited than she should be to tell Jolie the story of how she met Gray.

Jolie reacted in all the right ways. She gasped at the image of Natalie being followed from the coffee shop. Her eyes widened when Natalie described the man emerging from the stairwell. And she let out a relieved breath at Gray's well-timed rescue.

Natalie paused for dramatic effect. "And my rescuer? He asked me out."

Jolie's lips flattened into a line.

Not the response Natalie was after. "I thought you'd be happy for me."

Jolie glanced away.

"What is it? You said yourself that I needed to meet different men. And this one is…wow."

"I wasn't thinking of some guy who suddenly appears in a parking garage."

"He works at Kendall."

Jolie's frown grew deeper. "How do you know that?"

"He said Devin hired him to be part of the security department, and he had a key to the garage."

"Devin hired…" Jolie pulled in a long breath and shook her head. "Going out with him doesn't seem like a very good idea."

"You're not warning me about workplace romances, are you? You, of all people?" She never would have expected this kind of response from Jolie, who had just gotten engaged to Natalie's brother Devin…who also happened to be her boss.

"It just doesn't feel right, that's all. You don't know anything about him."

"I know he's nice and good-looking and he saved me from a guy who was a little bit creepy and wore really bad shoes."

Jolie normally would have laughed at a comment like that, but she didn't even crack a smile.

"I don't believe this. I thought you'd be happy for me."

"I just think you should be careful."

"Careful?"

"You have to admit, you've picked some losers."

"But Gray isn't like those other guys." Natalie couldn't even count the ways he was different.

"How do you know that?"

How *did* she know? "I don't know. I just do."

Once again, Jolie gave her head a slow shake. "He could be something totally different than what you think. You might really start to like him only to have him turn around and leave."

*Like all those other guys…*

Jolie hadn't said it, but she might as well have.

Natalie wanted to protest, but at the moment, the words were totally out of reach. If she was honest with herself, she had to admit Jolie was probably right. Her friend knew what kind of men she'd dated. She'd heard the horror stories, even witnessed some of Natalie's epic fails.

She tried her best to give Jolie a smile and plucked a gorgeous midnight-blue silk dress with a dramatic draped neckline from the rack. "You're right. He can't be as good as he seems."

Jolie tilted her head and offered an apologetic smile. "I'm sorry, Nat. I know you thought I'd be happy for you. I just don't want to see you hurt again."

She couldn't blame Jolie. "I know. I've done a good job of picking jerks over the years, haven't I?"

"It's not only that. You know, things have so been… crazy. Call me paranoid, but I don't want any of that to rub off on you."

She understood where her future sister-in-law's worry was coming from. The Kendall family had faced enough danger in the past two months to make anyone a bit wary, even someone as plucky as Jolie. She and Devin had been through a lot and so had Ash and Rachel.

She gave Jolie a smile. "You don't have to worry about me."

"But I do."

"Well, stop it. I know things have been weird, but no one is going to want anything from me."

Jolie didn't look convinced.

"Really. Ash is a cop, Rachel a crime scene investigator and Devin is CEO of the company. Fair or not, they're going to make enemies. And with everything we believed about the past blowing up, they've had a lot to deal with. But no one is going to target someone like me. I'm not part of the investigation. I was only six years old when…you know, they died." She paused to take a breath. She didn't normally talk about her parents' twenty-year-old murders, not even to Jolie, and it took a second for her to compose herself and go on. "I have no power outside of the public relations department at Kendall Communications. I'm a threat to no one."

"I'm not so sure."

"I am. The biggest thing I have to fear is giving my heart to another man who'll stomp on it and throw it away." And in worrying about that, Jolie was right.

"Natalie?" Her future sister-in-law's voice was steeped in concern. "I didn't mean—"

"It's okay. I know I don't have the most reliable taste when it comes to men. But at least I do know my dresses, and this one that Rachel picked out for me is divine." She turned the hanger of the midnight-blue dress in her hand and the skirt flowed with the movement as if dancing on air.

Jolie tilted her head to the side and studied Natalie. From the look on her face, she wasn't falling for the dress distraction. "You're not going on the lunch date, are you?"

She didn't want to say the word, but she knew she had to. "No, of course not. That would be stupid."

"I'm glad. The whole situation feels weird to me. Especially now, with all that's been going on. I don't think you should risk seeing a guy who conveniently shows up out of the blue like that."

"I didn't say I wasn't going to see him again."

The warning was back in Jolie's eyes.

"I don't have his phone number, okay? I have to see him to tell him I'm not going to lunch."

"Natalie…"

"Don't worry. I'll just find him at the office tomorrow. Nothing bad will happen to me." She started for one of the tiny dressing stalls off the mirrored salon. "How about I try on this gorgeous dress, and we'll go see if we can find Rachel? I want to see that gown."

She closed the door behind her and leaned back against it just in time to hide the stupid tears brimming in her eyes.

# *Chapter Three*

The barista raised a brow, the silver hoop skewering her flesh glinting in the coffee shop's warm lighting. "Why're you asking about Wade? He's harmless."

Gray didn't know about that. As soon as he'd left Natalie in the parking garage, he'd walked over to the coffee shop to get some information about the man who'd been following her. "Do you know his last name?"

She switched on the milk steamer and for a moment Gray couldn't make out a single word over the loud whirring and slurping sound of the machine.

Finally she set his cappuccino on the counter. "Will that be all?"

"Wade's last name?"

She rolled her eyes. "I said I didn't remember it. I'm not a damn directory."

"He followed a woman from this shop tonight. I want to determine if this could be a problem."

"Oh, her. Yeah, I saw that. He's been watching her for a couple weeks now. Every time they're in here together. Coffee shops are the new pickup spots, you know."

"You think he's trying to ask her out?"

She tossed him a shrug. "She often comes in after

work, and he's here. Like he's waiting for her but can't get up the nerve to say hello. Like I said, he's harmless."

She might be right. He'd seemed nervous in the parking ramp earlier tonight, but there wasn't anything overtly threatening about him. Still he had to wonder about a guy who would follow a woman through the deserted downtown streets at night. If he wasn't trying to intimidate her, then he must be the most insensitive and clueless man on the planet. And that was saying something.

The bleat of his cell phone interrupted his next thought. He looked down at the display. Devin Kendall. Gray glanced up at the barista. "Thanks." He grabbed his cappuccino and held the phone to his ear. "Yes?"

"Jolie just called." The CEO's voice sounded curt and authoritative, as always. "They're getting ready to leave the bridal shop."

"Okay. I'm on my way back." He was about to end the call when Devin spoke again.

"What did you find out about the creep you said was following my sister tonight?"

He'd filled Devin in as soon as he'd seen Natalie safely inside the bridal shop. "A first name. Wade. Not much else. He could be just some aspiring Romeo."

"In Natalie's case, that's reason to worry."

Gray was curious about the statement, especially since he'd like to cast himself as that Romeo, but he resisted the urge to ask for the story behind the comment. Everything he knew about Devin Kendall suggested he was an overprotective big brother. Gray doubted he'd be eager to share stories about his sister's love life, especially with a hired bodyguard. "Don't worry, I have it under control. I'm heading back to the bridal shop now."

"Good. Don't let her see you this time."

"I think I've figured out a way to deal with that problem."

"Does this have something to do with wanting me to say I've hired you on as the new alarm system wunderkind on Kendall's security team?"

"That's part of it." Gray had decided to tell Devin all of his plan when he'd talked to him the first time. Now he wasn't sure he wanted to mention the rest in light of Devin's comments about Natalie and Romeos. At least not yet.

"Fine. Whatever your plan is, just make sure it works. I don't want to have to explain why I hired a bodyguard behind her back. She would be less than understanding." Devin hung up.

Gray stuffed his phone in his pocket. He had a short hike back to his car. He'd better hurry.

"I thought that was you."

He recognized her voice immediately. How could he not? Her words the day of her husband's funeral echoed in the back of his mind every night when he closed his eyes and every morning when he opened them. "Sherry." He turned around.

Her eyes glinted hard like shards of black glass and on her finger sparkled the ring she'd gotten from Jimbo, the man he always thought of as his brother. "You have a lot of nerve, coming back to St. Louis, Grayson."

He didn't know what to say to that. She was probably right. But as out of place as he now felt here, he didn't feel comfortable anywhere else, either. He couldn't spend his life running away. "It's my home, Sherry. Just like it's yours."

"And Jimbo's."

He nodded, his chest aching at the bitter edge in her voice. "Yes. And Jimbo's," he said in a quiet voice.

She blinked as if fighting tears and shook her short, dark hair. "I hear you got yourself a job as a bodyguard. What a laugh. Does your client know that you aren't the type to lay down his life for anyone?"

He stood straight as if taking a drill sergeant's abuse and met her eyes full on. "You're wrong."

"Wrong? No. If I was wrong, Jimbo would be here right now instead of at Jefferson Barracks National Cemetery. I wish I was wrong about you. I wish it every day."

The pain aching in her voice stole his breath. "I miss him, too, Sherry."

"Yeah, right."

He opened his mouth to protest, then shut it without speaking. Whatever he said wouldn't change how Sherry felt about him, what she thought she knew. He wasn't sure how she'd found him, but he could tell it wasn't an accident. She'd come looking for him. And she looked prepared to take a pound of flesh.

He blew out a breath, and it condensed into a cloud in the cold air. Truth was, he couldn't blame her. Whatever cruel words she wanted to hurl, he deserved them. He'd said worse to the reflection in his mirror. The bottom line was that one of the best men Gray had ever known had died and Gray hadn't. And if Jimbo's wife couldn't forgive him for that fact, she wasn't alone.

Gray couldn't forgive himself, either. "I'm so sorry, Sherry, but I have to go."

"Don't want to face the truth?"

He shook his head. He felt for Sherry. And he missed Jimbo, his friend, his brother. If he could change things, he would. But right now, the best thing he could do was steer clear and focus on his job. He had to get back to the bridal shop before Natalie left. He couldn't change the past, but he could shape the future. His future. His redemption.

And it all started with keeping Natalie Kendall safe.

NATALIE WAS RELIEVED when she finally pulled her car through the gate surrounding the Kendall Estate, the iron scrollwork closing securely behind her. It used to be that her aunt and uncle often didn't bother to close the gate. They just left it open, the quiet upscale neighborhood giving them little reason to worry about security. But with all the trouble the family had been having, that practice had changed.

She looked up at the traditional gray stone mansion and let out a long, relieved breath. Maybe it was the strange run-in with the guy who'd followed her from the coffee shop, or maybe it was Jolie's mistrust of Gray, but she could have sworn a car had followed her home from the bridal shop.

She let her car idle in the driveway and eyed the street through the tall fence. The street was quiet. No headlights. No car creeping past, slowing down to see where she'd turned. Nothing.

Maybe she was losing her mind.

She shifted her sports car into gear and continued

past the main house where her aunt and uncle lived. She'd grown up in the Kendall mansion, and living inside its walls still made her feel like a child. That was why, after she'd returned from college, she'd moved into the guest cottage in the rear of the estate. It was easier to deal with the memories if she wasn't living them every day.

Of course, all that had happened the past two months had brought those memories out, front and center. And even her little house among the gardens couldn't hide her from them.

She followed the winding drive past the pool house and rose garden and cove of evergreens until she reached her cottage, nestled among tall oaks. On the verge of shedding their leaves, the trees reached twisted limbs into the night sky. A scene that reminded Natalie far too much of Halloween horrors.

Or much worse, the real kind.

She parked in her little garage and let herself into the house. She loved her cottage. With only two bedrooms, one she'd transformed into an art studio, the place was cozy, warm on nights like these, and safe. At least it always had felt that way.

Now every part of her life felt uneasy.

She switched on the light and stepped into the kitchen. The window over the sink stared at her like an unblinking eye. She pulled the blinds, crossed her arms over her chest and tried to rub warmth through the jacket sleeves.

She was being ridiculous, freaking herself out this way. And over nothing. Sleep. That's what she needed. A good night's sleep and the morning light would make the world look much different. Tomorrow she would be able to put everything back into perspective. The man who'd followed her...Gray...Jolie's nerves...she just needed sleep.

She passed through the dinette and the living area, turned down the hall to the bedrooms and shivered, despite herself. A draft seemed to be moving in this part of the little house. She switched on the hall light. The flow of air seemed to be coming from her studio. Strange. And the door stood open.

A door she always kept locked.

Her heartbeat launched into double time. She reached out a hand and pushed the door open farther. Curling her arm around the doorjamb, she felt for the light switch and flicked it on.

At first she wasn't sure what she was seeing. Shreds of canvas hung from her work easel. Red paint pooled on the floor. The glow of the moon sparkled on shattered glass.

A gasp caught in her throat, and she turned to run.

## Chapter Four

"Here you go, dear." Angela Kendall pushed a mug of tea into Natalie's hands, plopped down on the kitchen chair next to her and studied her niece with concerned brown eyes. "It will calm you, make you feel better."

Natalie wrapped both palms around the hot mug, grateful to have something to hold on to that would help to steady her shaking hands. The scent of chamomile wafted toward her. The tea her aunt pulled out to soothe any trauma Natalie faced, from her love life woes to the nightmares she'd had since she was six.

Natalie hated chamomile tea.

Aunt Angela leaned toward her, the kitchen light glinting off the few strands of gray that threaded her brown hair. "Is the tea all right, honey?"

"It's great." Natalie gave her aunt what she hoped was a grateful smile and dutifully lifted the tea to her lips. She took a sip of the dreadful brew and then returned the cup to the table. "Thank you."

Angela gave her a smile and ran her hand over Natalie's arm in a comforting caress. When Natalie had burst into the main house in a panic after finding the broken window and slashed paintings in her cottage, her aunt had been wearing her bright pink bathrobe and match-

ing pajamas, ready for bed. Somewhere between soothing Natalie, alerting Uncle Craig and brewing tea, she'd
changed into an orange sweater and jeans, combed her
hair smooth and dashed on a bit of mascara and tinted
lip balm.

The woman was nothing short of amazing.

Natalie was lucky to have her, back when she was six
and her aunt and uncle had taken in orphaned Natalie
and her three older brothers as their own and now. But
as much as she appreciated her aunt's nurturing, this
much coddling made Natalie feel as if she was once
again a weak, traumatized little girl.

Uncle Craig walked back into the kitchen before Aunt
Angela had a chance to urge Natalie to take another sip.
"Ash is bringing a couple of patrol officers with him."

So now the whole St. Louis Police Department was
going to get involved? Natalie supposed it made sense,
but she still felt like hiding her face. "I'm sorry for all
this."

"Sorry? Why should you be sorry?" Uncle Craig's
eyes flashed blue fire. "You didn't break into your own
cottage and vandalize it. The person who did this, that's
who should be sorry."

"That's right, dear," Aunt Angela chimed in. "How
long before Ash gets here?"

"He was getting into the car when I hung up."

The grandfather clock down the hall chimed loud
and slow.

Natalie glanced around the kitchen. The room was
immaculate, as usual. Beautiful cabinets, gleaming
countertops, and just the right decorating touches. Yet
nothing was stuffy or showy. She didn't remember

much about the house when her parents lived here, but since her aunt and uncle had moved in to take care of Natalie and her brothers, the house had felt like Angela. Warm, well cared for, welcoming.

She choked down another sip of tea for her aunt's sake. She hated being so needy, so clingy. She wanted to feel strong for once in her life, confident that she could stand on her own feet. That she could love as an equal and have that love returned. She wanted to forget that night twenty years ago. That night that chewed at the back of her mind.

Before she knew it, Ash was striding into the kitchen. He wore jeans and a simple shirt. A leather jacket spanned his broad shoulders and muscular chest. With his light brown hair, glinting green eyes and confident swagger, it was no wonder he had been known as the Casanova of the St. Louis PD. That is, until he fell hard for Rachel and their unborn child and realized all he really wanted was to settle down.

He immediately crossed to Natalie. "You okay?"

The concern in his voice made her throat feel thick. She managed a nod.

"Uncle Craig said someone broke into the cottage?"

"That's right," Craig answered.

Natalie forced her voice to function and filled her brother in on how she'd sensed the draft and found her studio door open and the window shattered.

"Did you notice if anything was missing?" he asked when she'd finished.

"I don't know. I ran out." She had. Like a scared little girl.

"You did the right thing. There's always a chance the

intruder could have still been there. When the squad car gets here, I'll go out and take a look around."

Her throat closed. The paintings. She hadn't even thought about the fact that her brother and his fellow officers would need to investigate. And when they did, they'd see the shreds of her canvases littering the floor.

Would Ash realize what the images were? Was she ready for him to see what she'd been painting?

"Is that okay?" He narrowed his green eyes.

She forced a nod.

"What's wrong?"

The disadvantage of having a cop for a brother. He could sense when she wasn't being totally up front. "Nothing. I'm just a little shaken."

"You can stay here tonight, honey. In fact, you can move back in. We'd love to have you. You know that."

She gave her aunt her best attempt at a smile. Her aunt and uncle were the only parents she'd ever really known. Sure she had images of her mother and father. But she'd only been six when they died. And the images she had of them were all mixed up with memories of the Christmas morning she'd awakened, excited about seeing what Santa brought her, and instead had discovered her parents' murdered bodies.

"A squad car just pulled into the drive. Oh, here comes Devin, too."

Natalie almost groaned. With her aunt and uncle, Ash and Devin all hovering over her, all she was missing was her third brother, Thad. Of course, she was sure he'd be here, too, if he wasn't on assignment as a photojournalist in some remote locale. He probably hadn't even heard about all that had happened in St. Louis the past couple of months. They'd tried to reach him to tell him their parents' murderer had been exonerated, but hadn't been able to find him. Devin had left a message with a woman at the news network, but they hadn't heard a word since.

Another concern to add to the rest.

"We'll handle this. You don't worry." Ash gave her a quick hug and headed for the door.

To her studio…

"Ash, wait. Can I talk to you?" She had to prepare him for what he would find.

He turned around and paused, as if he expected her to start talking right there in front of her aunt and uncle.

"In the study?" She tried not to notice the slightly hurt expression from her aunt.

Ash motioned for her to lead the way. Once he shut the door behind them, he turned to her with a spill-it-all look he'd mastered long before he'd become a cop.

Natalie's throat felt dry as sawdust. "The paintings in my studio…I just wanted to warn you…" She tried to swallow.

"Your nightmares?"

She nodded.

"I should have known they'd come back after all that's happened the past two months. You should have told me."

"It's not so bad. Not as long as I paint them, to get them out of my head." She hadn't told him to elicit his concern. God knew, she had plenty of that. "The paintings were slashed. I wasn't in the house long, but I didn't notice anything else damaged."

"Just those paintings…"

"Do you think it means anything?"

"Maybe. Maybe not. I'll take a look around."

He hadn't answered her question, but that was as good as an answer with Ash. If he could have told her this had nothing to do with their parents' murders, he would have.

"Don't worry. You're safe now. Go upstairs. I'm sure Aunt Angela has your old room ready for you. Get some sleep and we'll get to the bottom of this. It will be all over before you know it, and the situation will be back to normal."

She pressed her lips together. Not a smile but as close as she could get. Even though she knew he was right, that she was safe, she couldn't help feeling this mess wasn't over.

No, she suspected it was just beginning.

"So NEEDLESS TO SAY, I didn't sleep much."

Gray leaned his elbows on the too-small café table and tried his best to seem shocked by Natalie's story. Of course, he'd followed her to the cottage from the bridal shop last night just as he followed her home every night. He'd been just about to go home himself and get some sleep when he'd seen her bolt from her cottage and dash to the main house where her aunt and uncle lived. It hadn't taken long for Devin to call him on his cell and demand answers Gray didn't have. Minutes after that, Natalie's cop brother, Ash, had squealed into the drive, eventually followed by a squad car and Devin himself.

It had been a long night for all of them.

"I'm sorry for laying this on you."

"What do you mean? I had to drag it out of you." He

had. And he felt bad about it. But since he knew the events of the night before, he was afraid he'd slip up unless he convinced her to tell him herself. This way, he didn't have to keep as many details straight. And he had a seemingly legitimate reason to worry about her and insist he stay close.

The waitress swooped in on their table, deposited the check and two cups of coffee and removed the remnants of their lunch, panang chicken for her, pad see ew for him. It had been a stellar lunch, great Thai food and even better company. The time had gone far too fast. Gray could see making lunch with Natalie a daily ritual. The only thing that could make it better would be not having to worry about keeping his cover story intact. "Did you stay the night at your parents' house?"

"Aunt and uncle. Although they raised us. Especially me."

Of course, he already knew her family history, and he felt guilty at once for causing her pain, especially in service of his subterfuge. "That's right. Your parents... they've been in the news lately. I'm sorry."

She waved his apology away, but a sadness touched her eyes that suggested she couldn't so easily dismiss the memories of her parents' murders.

Not surprising. Who could?

She sipped her coffee, then leaned back in her chair, playing with a spoon still on the table. "You know, it's funny."

"Funny?"

She shrugged a shoulder as if trying to convince herself as well as him that what she was about to say was no big deal. "Funny that I've never felt comfortable talking about this."

"I'm sorry." Another dose of guilt. "I didn't mean to make you uncomfortable. We can talk about something else."

"No, that's the funny part."

He shook his head. "I'm not following."

"I don't feel uncomfortable. Not when I'm talking to you. Is that weird?"

"I don't know if it's weird. I think it's kind of nice." He reached across the table and took her hand before he thought to stop himself.

She accepted his touch, curling her fingers around his. "Me, too. My family likes to hover. Sometimes they act as if I'm six years old all over again."

Six was a young age to lose one's parents. He gave her hand a squeeze he hoped she'd read as understanding and not hovering. "It probably helps that I didn't know you when you were six. You don't seem to need hovering now."

A smile curved over her lips and sparkled into her eyes.

Suddenly *hovering* was at the bottom of his list. Tasting those lips, watching her eyes sparkle with passion when he kissed her...he took a sip of black coffee and focused on a colorful painting on the wall behind her. "Did the police find anything last night?"

"A mess." She shook her head. "My brother Ash is a detective. He, Devin and a couple other officers were out there half the night, but..."

"Nothing?"

"I can't figure it out. Why would someone want to

destroy my paintings? I mean, these aren't great works
of art. I don't show them or sell them or anything. It's
just my pastime, you know?"

He knew more than she could guess. And one of the
things he knew was she was more than a hobby artist.
She might head up Kendall's PR department now, but
she'd been a serious artist in college. When it came to
looking for someone who would want to shred her paintings, maybe that was a place to start. "You've never had
offers to show your work? Never had art lovers looking
to buy?"

She tilted her head to the side. "A few. But that's
when I was doing more commercial stuff. These paintings were just for me."

"Just for you, huh? So you don't show them to anyone?"

"No. No one would be interested anyway."

"I have trouble believing you haven't had interest."

"One dealer who liked some of my previous work
has asked. But I told him no."

Interesting. "Who was that?"

"It's not important. I'm not going to show them to
him, let alone sell them."

He would have to find out who this dealer was,
although he wasn't sure how to go about that at the
moment. He sensed if he badgered her about a name,
she'd get suspicious. He didn't want to ruin the easy
rapport that had bloomed between them. But there was
another thing he was curious about. "So I can talk you
into letting me have a peek?"

She looked at him out of the corner of her eyes.
"What, are you a secret art collector?"

"No. But I have a certain interest in the artist. I've heard looking at an artist's work is the best way to get to know her." He knew it sounded like he was playing her, but he wasn't. Not really. The truth was, he really was interested in seeing Natalie's paintings. He was interested in learning everything about her. At least everything he hadn't already seen by following her around for the past month or so.

Maybe that was his fascination. Nothing had happened in the past weeks. Natalie shopping. Natalie going to and from work. Maybe his thirst for a bit more adventure than this was fueling his need to get closer to her. Or maybe he'd spent so much time watching her, he was developing a bit of a crush. Either way, this was the most alive he'd allowed himself to feel in a long time. "What do you say? Will you show me?"

"That's a pretty intimate request for a first date."

"Did I cross a line?"

She gave him a little smile. "No harm in asking."

"I could think of a more intimate request." He didn't even hope she would grant him what was in his imagination right now, but he didn't try to hide the interest in his voice.

"Can you? And what would that be?" She looked at him straight on, a mischievous glint in her green eyes.

He almost shook his head. "Man, I love a woman who ups the ante."

She arched her brows. "Well?"

He was tempted to tell her exactly where his thoughts were leading, but he sensed that might be pushing things too far. He couldn't afford to come on too strong and risk scaring her off.

Or even worse, she might take him up on the offer. He could just imagine what her brother's reaction to that would be. "No harm in asking."

She laughed, the sound drawing him in as it had in the parking garage. If this was a real date, he'd lean over and kiss her. He could imagine how she'd taste. Sweet and light and spiced with Thai curry and a touch of coffee.

Instead of giving in to the urge, he grabbed the check folder off the table. "I would like you to let me buy."

"That's your intimate request?"

"Not intimate enough?"

She canted her head to the side. "I have an expense account here. And no, letting you buy lunch is not all that intimate."

"Sorry to disappoint." He slipped cash into the folder and handed it to a passing server. Then he looked into Natalie's cool, green eyes. "Okay, if you want something more intimate, may I escort you home after work tonight?"

"To see my paintings?"

"To make sure you get there safe and no one is waiting inside."

"Really?"

"After last night? Yeah, really. I'm worried about you."

"You hardly know me."

"True. But what I know, I really like. I want you to stay safe so I can get to know more."

She picked up her coffee cup and gave him a smile over the rim, as if he'd said precisely the right thing.

THE ENTIRE WALK BACK to Kendall Communications, Natalie mentally pinched herself. Since the moment she'd opened her studio door and found the room in shambles, she'd felt so violated, so vulnerable, she didn't think she'd ever feel strong and happy again. All night she'd been convinced someone was watching her from the darkness outside, even though the estate had been swarming with police. She could have sworn someone was trailing behind her on this morning's commute to work. She'd even felt the hair on the back of her neck rise while she was waiting for the parking ramp's garage door to open. So how was it possible that she felt so carefree and radiant after a simple chat over lunch?

Love was an incredible thing.

She turned away from Gray for a moment and smiled to herself. She wasn't in love, of course. She knew she was getting ahead of herself. Way ahead. But it was nice just to entertain the fantasy for a moment. To have found someone who made her feel giddy and warm and safe and sexy all at once. To have a future before her filled with love and family and happiness like Devin and Ash did. To plan her own wedding and know her husband would be there to share coffee with her in the evening and hold her warm and safe all night.

An old dream. Maybe an impossible one. But a good one all the same.

Jolie's warning flitted through her mind. She'd promised her friend she would call off today's lunch with Gray. But when it came down to telling him she had to cancel, she'd changed her mind. She was glad she had, despite having now lied to her best friend. Sure, Jolie was probably right. Sure, Natalie didn't really know

Gray. Sure, her fantasies could come crashing down at any moment. But at least the dream would last over the lunch hour. After last night's trauma, she needed to hold on to this great feeling as long as she could. "So, we've talked a lot about me during lunch. Tell me about yourself."

Gray chuckled. "Believe me, you're a lot more interesting."

"I can't help liking that you think so, but beyond the trauma of last night, I'm afraid my life is pretty dull."

"There is nothing about you that's dull."

She let out a laugh. "You flatter," she said dryly.

He shot her a smile.

They reached the end of the block, and Gray held out his hand, preventing her from stepping into the street without him checking it out first. Natalie had to admit that if one of her brothers had made that move, she probably would have felt he was hovering. From Gray, it made her feel nothing but special. "I have to admit, compared to having my cottage broken into, dull is looking pretty appealing."

"I'm with you there. I'm just relieved you weren't hurt."

Footsteps shuffled behind them. Natalie resisted the urge to spin around and look. She shouldn't have brought up last night's break-in. Just a single mention and she was back to hearing things and feeling threats where none existed. She was walking down a public street, for crying out loud. Not only that, but anyone would be a fool to mess with the strapping man beside her, at least in a violent sort of way. Now, in a sexual way…

"What's so funny?"

Oh, God, she'd been grinning at her own joke. "Nothing."

"You sure about that? It looked a lot more interesting than nothing. And not dull at all."

She let out a giggle despite herself. She sounded like a teen with a crush. Hell, she felt like one, too. And she had to admit, it was kind of divine.

"Beautiful," Gray said under his breath.

Now it was her turn to be confused. She shot him a look. "What's beautiful?"

"The sound of your laugh. I like it. I want to hear more of it."

She laughed again. "You're just being sweet."

He gave her a playful wink. "On you? Maybe a little."

She wanted to hold on to his words. To run them through her mind and focus on the warm feeling spreading through her chest.

Man, she wished she'd met Gray years ago. Or at least a couple of months ago, back when her life felt more normal. This lunch hour would be perfect if not for the anxiety humming along her nerves like the buzz of a mosquito she couldn't swat.

She could still sense the person behind her, still there, still walking too close. Turning her head to the side, she caught a reflection in a store window. A powder-blue sweatshirt, large and slumpy enough to land whoever was wrapped in it a spot on *What Not to Wear*.

Natalie shook her head and directed her attention to the busy intersection ahead. The chrome exterior of the Kendall building rose over the surrounding cityscape, nearly blinding in the bright sun. Only one more block and her lunch with Gray would be over. There must be something wrong with her. A riveting man by her side dishing out compliments, and all she could focus on was paranoia and some woman's bad fashion choices.

They reached the end of the block and stopped at the crosswalk.

"What is it?" Gray glanced around.

She shook her head. "It's nothing."

He gave her a relaxed smile, scanning the cityscape. "You sure?"

His muscles were tense, alert, but Natalie sensed a strange calm coming from him that belied her jumpy nerves. "Yeah, I'm sure. I'm just being paranoid."

"In light of what happened to you last night, I don't think you can call it paranoia."

"That's nice of you to say."

"I mean it. You feel scared, whether you think it's real or not, you just let me know. Okay? I'm here for you."

A flutter lodged under her rib cage. He really was too good to be true. Something she'd have to keep in mind. She gave him a smile. "Thanks."

"Being here for you is not a problem. Trust me." He looked straight into her eyes.

A flush of heat started to pool in her cheeks. The mix of brown and green of his irises mesmerized her. The sincerity in his expression made her ache to step into his arms. She looked at the cars streaming past, not wanting him to see her melt. The curb under her toes felt like a cliff, one step and she'd be head over heels. And despite the fact that she didn't know Gray well, despite Jolie's warnings, despite all the disappointments she'd weathered in the past, Natalie was tempted to look back into his eyes and let herself fall.

Something hit her hard in the back and shoved her forward, into the street. She hit the pavement hard, the force jarring her knees and shuddering up through the heels of her hands.

All around her tires screeched and cars swerved.

# Chapter Five

Gray didn't think, he didn't breathe, he just moved. He dashed into the street. Reaching Natalie, he grabbed her by the waist and lifted.

Drivers hit the brakes. Cars and trucks swerved as if skating on ice.

Gray backpedaled, half pulling, half carrying Natalie with him. His heel hit the curb and he fell backward onto the sidewalk. He hit the concrete on his back, rounding his spine and rolling up to his shoulders to absorb the impact and prevent his skull from hitting the hard surface. Natalie landed on his stomach, knocking the breath from his lungs.

For a second, he just held her, just struggled to breathe. He couldn't begin to process what had happened. One second they were talking, the next Natalie was flying into the street, traffic bearing down.

"Oh…oh…"

He could feel the sounds she made more than he could hear them. He loosened his grip and struggled to a sit. "Are you all right?"

Her skin was pale, her green eyes wide with shock. She stared at him, mouth open, but no words came.

"Natalie?"

"You saved me."

"It's my job."

"What?"

He shook his head. He needed to think before he talked. After following her for weeks, he hadn't really believed she was in danger. He'd allowed himself to grow complacent, paying more attention to how Natalie looked and what she was wearing than his surroundings. He was lucky he'd been walking so close beside her. If he'd still been merely watching her from a distance, she'd now be lying battered and bloody on the pavement. "I said I'd watch out for you. I meant it."

She let out a little puff of air.

Lips parted like that, adrenaline blasting through his body, he had a nearly overwhelming urge to kiss her.

Talk about inappropriate. "Let's get you off the street."

She looked around her, as if just remembering where she was, what had just happened. "She pushed me."

"Pushed you?" That would explain a lot. He looked around. An older couple strolled arm in arm about a half block away. Three executive types argued with waving arms as they stepped out of a nearby restaurant. A handful of pedestrians were scattered on the opposite side of the street. No one was anywhere near them, certainly not close enough to give Natalie a shove. "Who did it?"

"A woman. She was following right behind us. It had to be her."

"A light blue sweatshirt?"

Natalie nodded. "I saw her reflection in the store window."

"Did you recognize her?"

"I didn't see her face. Only the baggy sweatshirt. I didn't really get much of a look at her at all."

"Me, either." Some bodyguard he was. All these weeks of no activity had lulled him. He'd been so distracted by Natalie's laugh, by flirting with her, by his own damn fantasies that he hadn't paid blue-sweatshirt woman much attention at all. It had been his job to notice any threats to Natalie, and she'd gotten as good a look as he had.

His arms were still around Natalie, and he could feel her body begin to shake.

"Come on." He could beat himself up for his self-centeredness later. Right now, he wanted Natalie behind friendly walls. Preferably concrete ones.

Hurrying beside him, Natalie fished in her bag and pulled out her BlackBerry. "I'll call Ash."

"What are you going to tell him?"

"I don't know. She could walk up to me right now, and I wouldn't recognize her." She started to move the handheld back toward her purse.

"No, make the call. Please. Even if we can't tell him what she looked like, he needs to know what's going on." Gray would also have to fill Devin in on the situation. He doubted either brother would be surprised at the attack. They'd been worried about it, bracing for it. It had been him who was caught flat-footed.

Natalie finished leaving a message on Ash's voice mail by the time they reached the front entrance of Kendall Communications and ducked inside. A little late for lunch hour, the building felt still. The airy atrium smelled of delicious food and floor wax. Only a few diners remained in the café, probably shoppers enjoying a quiet afternoon in the public restaurant. He glanced up at the twenty-foot trees overhead. The place felt like a quiet garden cove, not the busy building it was, most employees in their offices organizing for their afternoon schedules, he supposed. They made it through the lobby and to the elevator bank. Almost the moment they arrived, a door opened.

The elevator car was empty. At least that worked out in their favor. He preferred alone, especially since he didn't know where any danger might be coming from. He ushered her inside and took what seemed like his first deep breath since he'd seen her flying into the street.

Soft music drifted in the air. Natalie hit the button that would take them to her sixteenth-floor office and looked up at him. Her face was still pale, but she had pulled herself together remarkably well for a civilian untrained in dealing with life-and-death stress. "It's amazing how you handled that."

"Amazing? Not really." She held out her scraped palms. Her fingers trembled visibly.

He reached out his own hands and gently folded hers in his. "I'm sorry I didn't notice that woman. I should have."

"For crying out loud, Gray. It's not your fault. You have nothing to be sorry about."

He did, but he couldn't see what good belaboring his apology would do. "I'm just so glad you're okay."

"I'm only okay because of you." She slipped her hands from his. But instead of stepping away from him, she moved closer. She looped her arms around his shoulders. She looked up at him, lips slightly parted.

As she had out on the sidewalk and yet…different. Not desperation and fear this time, but desire.

Close calls stoked the libido, he knew that. Danger. Sex. In circumstances like this, one twisted into the other. But although reason niggled somewhere in the back of his mind, he didn't want to listen. He'd spent a lot of time reading those lips all the times he'd watched over her when she didn't know he was there. He wanted to taste them.

He dipped his head and fitted his mouth over hers.

She tasted like exotic spices. But underneath there was something sweeter, warmer, a flavor that was purely Natalie Kendall. He wanted more.

He knew he shouldn't do it, but he pulled her close against his chest and delved deeper into the kiss.

A sound cut through the elevator music. The chime announcing they'd reached their floor. The whoosh of the door opening.

"Natalie."

Gray recognized the voice. He forced himself to release Natalie and end the kiss.

Then he turned to face Devin Kendall.

NATALIE HAD HAD A BAD DAY. Two bad days, really. Having her home violated last night seemed like child's play compared to being almost run over by cars today. She was shaking. Her knees and hands ached. And her beautiful new trousers were smudged with dirt and dust and one of the knees looked tattered. Now her only joy was being taken away from her by her big, overprotective brother.

She was less than happy. She was downright annoyed. "Hello, Devin."

"Ash called." Devin peered down at her, projecting his best stern, big brother look. Almost as tall as Gray, everyone always said he resembled their father almost exactly. But as stern as Devin came off sometimes, and as mad as she was at him now, Natalie always felt how much he cared for her. So much he came close to smothering her at times.

Times like right now. "So you know what happened. I hope Ash also told you that Gray pulled me out of the street. He saved me."

Devin didn't spare Gray a glance. He motioned to the inside of the elevator. "Is that was *this* is about?"

Natalie raised her chin. She was not in the mood for this. "If you must know, I was the one who kissed Gray."

Devin shifted his shoes on the floor. He finally pulled those sharp, blue eyes off Natalie and focused on Gray. "I need to talk to you."

Natalie resisted the urge to physically step between the men. Devin wouldn't dare fire Gray over this. At least she hoped not. But she was pretty sure he was set on embarrassing her. "You'd better not be planning to lecture Gray about kissing me," she warned. "It's none of your business, Devin."

"I need to talk to him about security matters. Alarms and such," Devin said in a flat voice.

Right. She opened her mouth to speak.

"I'll be right there, Mr. Kendall," Gray said before she could get out another word. "As soon as I see Natalie to her office. After what happened out on the street, I don't want to take any chances."

Natalie's heart gave a little hop. Devin wasn't her dad, and she was no teenage girl, but Gray's respect for Devin, yet polite defiance for her sake, thrilled her far more than it should.

If she wasn't so stressed over what had happened last night and on the street, and if Devin wasn't glaring at them right now, she'd be tempted to try for another kiss.

And she'd make it a doozy.

BY THE TIME HE WALKED Natalie to her office, took the elevator to the twenty-fourth floor and made the trek to the executive office suite, Gray was ready for whatever the CEO had to throw at him.

At least he hoped he was.

The door had barely shut when the first words erupted from Devin Kendall's mouth. "What the hell do you think you were doing?"

Gray stepped over to the leather chairs in front of Devin's impressive desk and lowered himself into one. He might send other employees quivering with that commanding tone, but he'd have to try harder with Gray. Nothing could beat the drill sergeant he'd had in basic training. That guy could shout paint off walls and fur off puppies.

Devin stood up and pushed back his desk chair. He gave Gray a quiet glare, eyes like blue lasers. "Kissing my sister is not part of your job description."

Gray gave a nonchalant nod. Couldn't argue with that.

"Jolie told me about your lunch plans today. What kind of game are you playing here?"

"No game."

"Really? That doesn't jibe with what Jolie said."

Jolie, Devin's fiancée. One of the women Natalie met at the bridal shop last night. Natalie must have told her about their lunch plans. He'd love to know what else Natalie might have said.

"I hired you to be Natalie's bodyguard, not some kind of boyfriend. I want you to stay away from her."

"And how am I going to justify watching her? She's seen me now. Talked to me. That's going to make it a lot tougher to keep her from noticing that I'm following her. If we're dating, I have a built-in excuse to be near her. I can more effectively protect her." He eyed Devin. "It's the only story I could come up with that would allow me to stay near her without her suspecting the truth. Of course, that wouldn't be a problem if you'd just tell her you've hired a bodyguard."

"No."

"Why not? She doesn't need you to coddle her like this. She's a grown woman, not a little girl. Tell her the truth."

The CEO shook his head and paced across his office. "You don't know Natalie. She won't cooperate. Even after what's happened these past two days, she'll still maintain she doesn't need a bodyguard. She'll think I'm being overprotective." He rolled his eyes as he passed Gray's chair.

"Aren't you?"

Devin spun around.

Gray held up a hand. "I don't mean hiring a body-guard is overprotective. Obviously something is going on here. But you should tell her. She'll deal with it."

Devin blew out a hard breath of air and shook his head. "I see she's told you how controlling I am."

"Not controlling. Overprotective. And it's not just you. She says she gets the same treatment from her brother Ash. And Thad, when he's back in the States."

"Did she tell you why?"

"No." But he found himself really wanting to know. "Care to fill me in?"

Devin shook his head and resumed pacing. "She just had a hard time when she was a girl, that's all."

He assumed Devin was referring to The Christmas Eve Murders. Gray had been only a teenager when it happened, but he remembered the stories about Joseph and Marie Kendall's deaths. It had shocked the community. St. Louis was a pretty big city. It saw its share of murders, but rarely were the victims part of the wealthy elite. And rarely did violence come to upscale neighborhoods like Hortense Place. The tragedy had been all over the news, and the recent developments in the case had consumed the media, as well. "Natalie was awfully young when your parents died."

"She was."

Seconds ticked by. Apparently Devin wasn't going to say more. Unlike his blustering first approach, the CEO seemed to draw into himself, as if he was watching Gray, carefully considering his next move.

Gray had the distinct feeling he'd underestimated Devin Kendall.

Finally the CEO spoke. "So what do you want? Besides my blessing to date my sister?" he asked in a tone that suggested a glacier would cover St. Louis before that would happen.

"I want you to either tell her I'm her bodyguard, or let me come up with my own cover story. Lucky for you, the second option is already under way."

"Lucky for me. Right."

Gray probably shouldn't say any more. Devin could fire him any moment and hire another bodyguard, one Natalie wouldn't recognize. But despite that risk, Gray knew he had to speak. Sometime in the past two days, the job had stopped being the important thing for him. Sometime Natalie had taken the number one spot. "For the record, I think she should know the truth. It would make things easier on all of us."

Devin paced to the window and stared out at the city below. The sun streamed in through the window, turning the rich brown of his hair to milk chocolate. His shoulders hunched, holding so much tension it was visible. He unbuttoned his jacket and stuffed his hands in the pockets of his expensive slacks. "This family has been through too much. Not just over the past couple of months, but the past twenty years. It's my job to make sure nothing else happens, that no one else gets hurt."

It seemed as if they'd already been over that ground. "I understand that."

Devin let out a heavy breath. "You'd better make sure Natalie doesn't fall in love with you. She's had far too much pain and sadness in her life. I don't want to be responsible for another bastard breaking her heart."

# Chapter Six

After the traffic incident, several days passed without anything notable happening. The bruises on Natalie's knees and hands turned from angry red to purple to an ugly yellow. A glitch with a local bakery had left Rachel scrambling to find a new baker to make her wedding cake. Natalie had the nightmare nearly every night and had used the early-morning hours to restock her collection of paintings she'd never show. But other than the creepy feeling that someone was watching her now and then, nothing bad or dangerous or even that unusual happened.

Gray hadn't even kissed her.

She couldn't see Devin scaring him off. Not the way Gray had refused to back down when her brother had interrupted them in the elevator. So she'd chalked up the step backward to her usual mistake of moving a little fast.

At least he still seemed interested.

He'd eaten lunch with her every day at the café in the Kendall building atrium and had insisted on following her to work in the morning and home at night. He'd even volunteered to make a run to the coffee shop tonight when she told him she needed to work late.

There was still hope.

That wasn't the case with the investigation into who had pushed her into the street. Ash had found nothing. No one who remembered a woman in a powder-blue sweatshirt. No one who noticed the vicious shove. No one who could tell them anything.

At least nothing like that had happened again.

Knuckles wrapped on the open door. Gray poked his head inside. "How's the work coming?"

"I'm craving my drug of choice."

He stepped into the room, two cups from her favorite coffee shop in his fists. "Caffeine, it is. Double shot, low-fat latte." He crossed the room and handed her one of the cups.

The rich scent of espresso perked up her senses. She brought it to her lips and took a long, creamy sip. "Ahh, you're my savior."

"You're staying awfully late."

"I need to get caught up. Rachel needs my help with some wedding details, but the work doesn't wait, you know?"

"Not unless you tell it to wait. You need to do that sometimes, you know. You don't want people to start calling you a workaholic." He gave her a smile and took a sip out of his own cup.

"Me? A workaholic? Nah, that would be my brother." At least it used to be Devin. Since he had asked Jolie to marry him, he'd mellowed and become a little more well-rounded. Jolie had a good influence on him.

He smiled and plopped down in one of the chairs facing her desk. "You can't like hanging out here this late at night. Everyone else has gone home."

It was true. Even Devin had left. "I'm a little nervous. But there's no reason. Being from security, you of all people can see I'm pretty safe here." Of course, the parking ramp would be empty and dark. And even though Devin had ordered increased security and she'd be driving instead of walking, the streets downtown were pretty vacant this time of night. She took another soothing gulp.

"But?"

Funny that she just met him, and yet he seemed to read her mind. She shook her head. "It's not logical."

"Fear often isn't. But that doesn't make it not real."

Where did this guy come from? He couldn't be this perceptive, could he? Could an actual man be this in tune with what she was thinking? Know just what to say and how to say it so she didn't feel like a wimp? She shook her head.

"What now?"

"You're too good to be true."

He looked away, as if expecting someone at the door. No one was there.

Natalie bit the inside of her lower lip. Leave it to her to go too far, say too much. Just like kissing him the day he'd saved her from traffic. Whenever she found a decent man, the one or two in existence, she had a habit of falling too hard, too fast. She couldn't help it. She wished she could skip the games, just get that ring on her finger and know he was always going to be there.

But men never saw it that way. They seemed to want the chase, the hunt. If she gave herself to them too fast, they no longer wanted her.

And that's when they would leave. "I'll be fine."

He unfolded himself from the chair and straightened to his full height. "I'll let you finish what you have to do. I'll be right outside the office catching up on some of my own stuff. Whenever you want to leave, I'm ready."

"You know, your security job doesn't require you to follow the executives home."

"This has nothing to do with the job. Don't you know that yet?" He gave her a smile that made her bones feel soft. "Unless you want me to install an alarm system at your place while I'm there."

She let out a laugh. It felt good. Normal. And she had to admit, she was glad he was willing to stay until she was finished with this project. She had been dreading the trip home without his reassuring headlights shining behind her more than she wanted to admit. "Can you give me about two hours?"

He didn't hesitate. "No problem."

She still felt guilty. Two hours was a long time to sit around and wait. She was probably pushing it. "You sure you don't mind?"

He held her gaze, his hazel eyes clear and sincere. "I'm sure. And the next time you ask, I'll still be sure."

Warmth spread over her skin. Her knees felt a little wobbly. Crazy. Flushing. Weak knees. She was turning into a cliché. The next thing she knew, she'd be picking out a song for their wedding and he'd be running for the hills.

"I'll meet you at the elevator in exactly two hours."

He gave her a nod, not breaking eye contact for a second. "Two hours it is."

He took his coffee out into the hall and closed the door behind him.

By the time she'd gotten herself composed, almost ten minutes had passed, and she had to work as fast as she could to accomplish all she needed to by the two-hour deadline she'd set.

He was waiting for her at the elevator as promised. She'd never known a guy this considerate, let alone dated one, if one lunch and one kiss and a lot of following her in his car could be considered dating. Here she'd just met him, and yet he made her feel so cared for, so safe, she wanted him to put a ring on her finger right now, recite the vows and be done with it.

God, she was pitiful. Give her a double shot, low-fat latte, and she'll promise her life. Maybe Jolie was right, in a way. But instead of it being Gray who couldn't be trusted, it was Natalie herself.

She took a gulp of coffee and willed the caffeine to clear her mind and bring her back to reality. Unless she wanted to chase him off, she'd better watch it.

She behaved like a perfect lady, yet as they rode down to the parking garage, got in their cars and he followed her through the dark streets to Hortense Place, all she could think of was how hard she could fall for this guy. How much she wanted to kiss him again.

And how much she wanted more than that.

She turned into the long driveway and passed through the gate. The grounds were quiet, only a single light gleaming from the mansion's first floor. She wound past the pool house and through the gardens. She pulled up in front of the little garage. Lights flicked on. For a second, her heart jolted, then she remembered the motion sensing lights her uncle had promised to have installed.

She hit the button on her remote, and the garage door rose. But instead of driving inside, she pushed open the door and stepped out into the drive.

She had to be out of her mind, doing this. But she couldn't resist. This tension between her and Gray either had to lead to another kiss, or she had to put the friend label on him and make sure it stuck. This not knowing if there was something between them was driving her crazy.

A tremor seized low in her belly. She forced her feet to carry her to his car.

When she arrived, he already had the door open and was uncurling his body from behind the wheel. "Is something wrong?"

"Ahh, no."

"Then what is it? The garage door not working or something."

"No. I was just wondering…" She swallowed into a parched throat. She couldn't go on. She had no idea what to say.

"You're going to show me your paintings?"

The request caught her off guard. She'd totally forgotten he wanted to see her paintings. Paintings she hadn't purposely shown anyone except Ash the night of the break-in. Paintings which would not make him interested in her, but likely have the opposite effect.

To her horror, she found herself nodding.

"Great." Gray reached into his car and shut off the ignition. He slammed the door and turned to look at her.

Her paintings. A quiver started in her chest and moved through her whole body. Could she really show Gray something that personal? Something that raw?

What had she gotten herself into?

NATALIE STARED AT HIM as if shell-shocked.

He narrowed his eyes on her. He'd tossed out the idea of seeing her paintings because he wanted a look at them. Obviously that was not what Natalie had in mind. He reached out and laid a hand on her arm. "Are you okay?"

"Um, yeah. Come on in." She waved an arm, motioning for him to follow her into the garage.

He didn't budge. "You don't really want to show me your paintings, do you?"

She chewed on her bottom lip. Her fingers flexed at her sides, her fists opening and closing.

Obviously her paintings were very personal. He felt guilty for pushing. "I understand."

She met his eyes, as if looking for something.

He gave her what he hoped was an understanding smile. Natalie might not be considered a classic beauty by some people, but he found her more attractive than any movie star he'd ever seen. There was something about her that riveted him. She had such a joy for life, yet underneath he sensed a sadness he wanted to soothe. Standing here right now, it was all he could do to keep from kissing her. No, not just that. He wanted to make love to her and know everything about her. He wanted to hold her and make her his.

"No, it's okay. I'll show you."

"You sure?"

She nodded. "I want to." She led him into the little house.

The cottage was light and airy inside, just as he expected. Hardwood floors stretched through the kitchen and dinette. Light marble countertops and bright splashes of color here and there looked cheery, yet soft. The living area featured neutral carpet, a fireplace and a light leather couch that looked comfortable enough to melt into. Natalie turned into a hallway. She passed a bathroom and stopped at what looked like a bedroom door.

"This is it?"

She glanced back at him. Pushing the door open, she stepped back. "This is it."

He stepped onto the smooth tile floor, Natalie right behind him. The space was a good size for what was originally a bedroom, but it was jammed with half a dozen easels, four of which had partially shredded canvases propped on them. Other painting supplies, including more canvas, filled a series of shelves and other storage stretching along two walls. "Looks like you have a nice setup here."

"My aunt and uncle insisted. I don't think they really wanted me to move out of the big house. But since I did, they wanted the guest cottage to have everything I needed."

"Nice." He crossed the room to get a better look at the easels. Natalie followed, her heels clicking on the floor. He scanned each canvas, piecing together shreds where he had to, hyperaware of her watching him.

All the paintings had a similar theme. Shadows. The dark figure of a man. And on each, pools of red that looked like blood. Some of the images were at a distance. Some close-up. But whatever the perspective, all had an ominous feel. A shiver clawed at the back of Gray's neck.

"You don't like them."

He shook his head. "It's not that. They're just so dark. I didn't expect that from you."

"I told you they aren't exactly commercial. I paint my nightmares."

Those had to be some awful dreams. He focused on what appeared to be blood spatters covering a shadowy close-up of a man's face. "Nightmares about what?"

She shifted her shoes on the tile. "Just nightmares. I paint them to get them out of my head. I try not to dwell on them."

In other words, she didn't want to tell him. He couldn't blame her. They hadn't known each other that long, at least she hadn't known him. He'd been watching her so closely the past weeks, he had the sense that he knew her. Obviously what he knew only scratched the surface. "Do you only paint nightmares?"

"I don't have a lot of time to paint now that I'm working so much at Kendall Communications. But I used to paint flowers in the shade garden and frost on the evergreens." She gestured to the panel of windows peering out into dark gardens. "Those subjects were a lot more commercial. I sold quite a few paintings back then."

From the corner of his eye, he spotted something shifting in the shadows outside. Bigger than an animal, too substantial for a swaying tree branch.

"Do you want to stay a little while? I have wine. We could build a fire."

He focused on the spot where he'd seen movement. Too late. The gardens and the cove of evergreens beyond stood perfectly still. Beyond that, it was too dark to see.

"Or not. It's kind of late, and I'm sure you are busy tomorrow."

"No." He grasped her hand. Truth was, he'd love to spend some time with her all cozy in this cottage of hers. He'd been thinking about it all week. Dreaming about it. He must have taken five extra showers in the past few days, all of them cold. "I think it's a great—"

There it was again.

Gray didn't want to pull his eyes from Natalie's. Not now. Not when he knew she'd read it the wrong way the first time. But there was no helping it. He could swear something was moving out there.

He turned away from her and looked out the window. He'd only gotten the slightest glimpse, but he could swear the darkness shifted. Moved.

There it was again.

His gut tightened. Devin hadn't mentioned anything about the police staking out Natalie's cabin. That left only one likely explanation. Someone was out there. Watching. Waiting for him to leave. Biding his time until Natalie was alone. Vulnerable.

He'd never let it happen.

Even though the lights were somewhat dim inside Natalie's studio, they were still bright enough to give him more reflection than night vision through the glass. He needed to get out there, find out who was watching. "I really have to go."

"Oh. Okay."

He recognized the hurt in her voice. No doubt she thought he was rejecting her. A misperception that would make him laugh if the situation wasn't so serious. "I'll see you tomorrow?"

"Of course. We work in the same building."

"I'll meet you here. We can drive in together."

She narrowed her eyes, as if trying to figure out what was behind the offer. "That's not necessary."

"I want to."

"You don't want to stay tonight, but you want to drive all the way up here just so you can follow my car?"

Little did she know he didn't plan to go anywhere tonight. "I would like to stay. I just…can't."

She nodded, a resigned look on her face. "I'll see you at work."

He wanted to explain. Not tell her the truth. He'd promised Devin he wouldn't do that. But the idea of her believing he didn't want her…

She walked him to the door. Standing to the side, she crossed her arms over her chest.

"I'll be here tomorrow morning." Without waiting for another protest, he opened the door and stepped into the night. She shut it behind him, and he could hear her slide the dead bolt into place.

He walked to his car and slid behind the wheel, before turning back to check on the house. The foyer light clicked off.

Natalie giving up on him.

He should ease out of the drive, park on a side street and return on foot to surprise whoever was hiding in the gardens. With Natalie as bait, he could stalk the stalker, get the drop on him.

Instead he pulled out his cell phone and called up a number.

"Yes?" Devin Kendall answered in a clipped voice.

"Grayson Scott. Do the cops have someone outside Natalie's?"

"They said they couldn't. Not enough manpower, and she hasn't been attacked. The best they would do was take a drive by every hour or two."

That's what he'd suspected. If the Kendalls weren't loaded and brother Ash wasn't a cop himself, Gray doubted the locals would have been able to do that much in light of recent budget cuts.

So it wasn't a cop. That made his choices clear. "Thanks."

"What's going on?"

"I think someone might be watching Natalie's house."

"Gray, you'd better—"

"Natalie's safety is my only priority. She'll be fine, I guarantee. But you might want to ask that cop to stop by five minutes ago. And tell your aunt and uncle to lock their doors." He disconnected the call. Setting the ring to mute, he returned it to his pocket, pulled out his Glock and climbed from the car.

He kept close to the evergreen trees rimming the garden. It was cold again tonight, unseasonably cold for November in St. Louis. His breath fogged in the air. With each step, he could feel the grass—stiff with frost—crunch slightly before giving beneath the sole of his shoe.

When he reached the area where he thought he'd spotted movement, he paused, willing his eyes to see in the tree-filtered moonlight. Sure enough. The frost-touched grass bowed, flattened to the ground.

The prints were smaller than his, but considering he

wore a size twelve, that wasn't saying much. He traced their path, circling the garden's edge, flanking the house. Reaching an expanse of bare earth, he stopped to study a print on the edge.

And noticed something shining in the moonlight.

Nails. The four-inch spikes littered the mulch under a set of windows. What the hell?

He pulled out his phone.

Devin answered on the first ring. "Yeah?"

"Has Natalie had any carpentry work done recently?"

"No, why?"

He filled Devin in on what he'd found. "In light of everything that's happened, I'd like to get Natalie out of here until your brother and the cops can check out what's going on."

"Good idea."

"Your aunt and uncle, too."

"Leave them to me. I'm on my way right now. Ash is, too." He cut off the call.

Gray circled the cottage and headed straight to the main entrance. Natalie's safety had to be his priority. As much as he wanted to catch this guy, that wasn't why he was here. Luckily Devin saw things his way and didn't hesitate to respond.

He made it back to the front door in seconds and hit the bell. A few more seconds and the soft footfalls of bare feet sounded on the other side.

Natalie pulled the door open and stared at him from under lowered eyebrows. Her long blond hair was pulled back from her face. Her bathrobe dipped in a deep V between her breasts and cinched tight around her narrow waist. "I thought—"

"Come with me."

"What?"

He took a breath. The damn footprint and nails had him so shaken, he'd forgotten she didn't know he was here to protect her. "Screw my early morning."

Her eyebrows shot upward.

"You showed me your place. I want to show you mine."

## Chapter Seven

Natalie didn't know what she expected Gray's apartment to look like, but it sure wasn't this. She scanned the Spartan room. White walls stretched from corner to corner, unbroken except by windows. The beige carpet seemed brand-new, and she doubted the stove had ever been used. "Did you just move in?"

"I suppose it looks pretty empty to you."

Empty, yes. But not the clichéd bachelor kind of empty. Except for a jacket draped on a kitchen chair and two pairs of shoes tossed carelessly to the side of the door, the place looked cleaner than her house.

And it was far from being a hovel. One look out the window and the sparkling lights of the city made one forget there was no art on the walls. And though little more than a leather couch broke up the living space, it was a piece anyone would be proud to own. Gray seemed to have good taste and money. "You don't spend much time at home?"

"No, not much."

She knew she was prying, but she couldn't help it. She liked Gray. A lot. He'd seen her paintings, and now she wanted to know everything about him, even though he seemed about as eager to share as she had been.

She could just imagine what Jolie would say about that.

Pushing her friend's concerned warnings to the back of her mind, Natalie stepped to the window and peered outside. Jolie was probably right to worry and not just about Natalie's growing crush on a man she barely knew.

Something had been going on at the mansion tonight, something no one seemed to want to tell her about. She noticed Ash's car in the drive on their way out, and she could swear they passed Devin just a few blocks into the drive to Gray's. She called Ash on the cell, but while he'd admitted he was talking to Aunt Angela and Uncle Craig, he'd revealed little else. She had to wonder if they'd learned something.

Maybe something about whoever murdered their parents all those years ago.

She could feel Gray move up behind her. For a second, she could imagine him putting his arms around her and pulling her back against his chest. Warm, safe, protected. The sensation was so vivid, she let out a sigh.

"What is it?"

"Nothing." She had the urge to tell him what she'd been imagining, then discarded the idea. She really liked Gray, and one of the things she ought to have learned about men by now was she couldn't lay too much on them too quickly.

"Sure? You seem worried."

Too much too quickly included trauma and craziness. Considering the amount of each that had entered her life since Gray and she met, she'd probably reached her quota. "Not worried. Just looking out at the view."

"Afraid of heights?"

"Maybe a little. Especially when I look up." She craned her neck to take in the taller building visible at the side of the window. "But it is a stunning view."

"For a lower floor, it's not too shabby. That's the reason I rented the place." His voice rumbled close to her ear, but he didn't touch her.

She fought the urge to lean back against him. She couldn't figure it out. When he'd left her house, she assumed he wasn't interested. But then he'd returned and asked her to come to his apartment. And seeing that he'd refused her when she'd asked him to stay at her house, she'd better let him take the lead this time. Play a little hard to get.

A good idea…in theory. Too bad she was terrible when it came to playing love games. It always seemed dishonest to her. Her aunt always said she wore her heart on her sleeve. It sure made it easy to break, but she'd never figured out how to do things differently.

No wonder she was still alone.

She wrapped her arms around her middle.

"Cold?"

She gave a shrug, not wanting to tell him where the need to hold herself had really come from. "A little, I guess."

"Just a second." He turned away from her and walked down the short hall that must have led to the bedrooms. When he returned, he was carrying a dark colored blanket. He draped it around her shoulders.

Not what she had in mind, but she gathered the blanket tight anyway. It was prickly, probably made of wool. The kind of blanket that could get wet and wouldn't lose its insulating properties. "Is this a military blanket?"

"Except for the comforter on the bed, it's all I have. Sorry."

"You were in the army?"

A muscle along his jaw flexed and he peered past her and out the window. "Navy."

"So you served on a ship?" Funny, she didn't see him as the sailor type. Not at all.

"I was in special forces."

A little shiver ran through her. "A SEAL?"

He gave his head an almost imperceptible nod.

She always thought of Navy SEALs as being brash, larger than life. But while Gray was strong and had a forceful aura about him, he seemed more quiet and self-reflective. He did have the sex appeal she'd expect, though. Plenty of that. "Did you like being a SEAL?"

"It was the best time of my life."

"Why aren't you still serving?"

The muscle along his jaw twitched and tightened. Again he looked out at the lights as if he didn't want her to see what was in his eyes. "I was injured."

"Oh, my God, what happened?"

"You heard about the USS *Cole?*"

Of course she had. It had happened a long time ago, and she hadn't been old enough to really pay attention to the details. "It was bombed, right?"

He nodded. "By a small group of terrorists in a raft. They weren't seen as a threat and got close enough to damage the ship."

She remembered. "And people died. Sailors on the ship."

"Yes." He took a deep breath, the inhalation rough

enough to be a shudder. "That wasn't the only attempt of that kind on a navy ship."

"Another ship was bombed?"

"No. Thank God, the terrorists weren't successful. At least we were able to keep that from happening."

"We? Meaning your SEAL team? You stopped a terrorist attack?" Maybe the news should have come as a surprise, but although she hadn't heard about any other ships being attacked, she wasn't surprised Gray had been able to thwart terrorists. After the way he'd scooped her out of busy traffic, she'd probably believe he was a superhero without too much difficulty. "That's amazing. You're amazing."

He shook his head. His brows hunkered low over his eyes. "No, I'm not amazing."

"I don't understand."

"The operation didn't go as planned."

"And that's how you got hurt." What was wrong with her? Why hadn't she put that together before? "What happened?"

He waited a long time before he spoke again. "We stopped the raft before it got close enough to damage the ship, but the ordnance was on a timer."

"It went off?"

He nodded.

"You're lucky you weren't killed."

That faraway look again. As if he was peering back at a past he didn't want to acknowledge, didn't want to remember. As if he felt somehow responsible.

She knew that look. She still saw it in the mirror some days. "Somebody *was* killed."

He didn't move. He didn't answer.

He didn't have to. She knew she was right. Even without knowing the details, she wanted to tell him it wasn't his fault. Maybe because she'd heard those words so many times when she was young. But words like that didn't do any good. At least she'd never believed them. Still didn't. "Who?"

"Best SEAL I ever knew. And a good friend. We grew up together right here in St. Louis."

"Oh, my God, I'm so sorry."

He turned his head to look at her for the first time since she'd asked about the blanket. "It should have been me."

"Oh, Gray, no." Natalie covered his lips with her fingertips. "You can't say that."

He didn't speak, but she could see by the sadness in his eyes that no matter what she thought about his statement, he wasn't about to change his mind.

That didn't mean she wasn't going to try. "I know how you feel, but you can't let yourself think that. You can't go there."

He didn't move. For a moment she wasn't sure if he was listening to her or had faded off once again to that faraway place.

She moved her hand from his mouth and smoothed it over his cheek, razor stubble prickling her fingers. She cradled his jaw beneath his ear. She didn't know what to say to make him listen, but she knew what she could do to show him how she felt. Rising onto her tiptoes, she covered his lips with hers.

Her kiss was tentative at first. Gentle. Sweet. She wanted more than anything for him to know she cared. That she wanted to take away his pain, even though she knew she never could. She kissed his upper lip, then his lower, each a whisper of a touch. She looked into his eyes.

He returned her gaze. Not faraway now, his eyes delved into hers. He brought his arms up her sides and around her waist. He pulled her body against the length of his and claimed her mouth.

This kiss was far from sweet, far from gentle. She'd never felt anything so urgent before, on the edge of control. She wanted to let loose. To taste him, feel him, have him for her own. She circled his neck with her arms and stretched tall to press the length of her body against him. Her senses melded together, the scent of his body, of his leather jacket, the cinnamon fragrance of the room. The scent of her own perfume. The roughness of stubble on his chin and solid muscle of his chest.

Before she realized what she was doing, she found the buttons of his shirt. She fought them open with shaking fingers. She pulled his shirttail from his pants and slipped her hands inside. Her fingers skimmed over smooth skin and hard muscle. She closed her eyes and just felt.

He hesitated, then drew back from the kiss. "We can't do this."

She opened her eyes and looked into his. "It's okay."

"I'm sure your brother wouldn't agree."

She smiled up at Gray and shook her head. "If you hadn't noticed before, my brothers are a little overprotective."

"They care about you."

"They do. But that doesn't mean they know what is best for me." Or even if they did, she didn't care. Right now all she could think about was how much she wanted Gray. She knew she was too impulsive, too eager to give her heart, too quick to throw herself over the cliff. But that didn't change anything. It was who she was. And no matter what Devin said and Jolie said and anyone else said, she knew Gray was different. She could feel it every moment they were together.

She unbuttoned her blouse and let the silk slide down her arms. She wasn't sure why she'd worn her black lace bra today. She'd thought of Gray when she'd put it on this morning. Fantasized about him seeing her in it, her breasts full, her nipples straining against the delicate fabric. The lace's light floral pattern concealed nothing, and as the blouse fell to the floor, she felt a thrill at being so exposed.

His gaze ran over her.

Her skin felt electric, as if he was touching her with his hands. Her nipples hardened and pressed against the lace. She wanted more than his eyes on her; she wanted to feel his rough palms, the warm wetness of his mouth. She wanted his heat pressed against her, wrapped around her, inside her.

She stepped toward him and reached for his hands. She placed his palms over the lace cups and molded them to her.

He smiled. "You are something."

She returned the smile, feeling emboldened by his tone of voice. "I hope you mean that in a good way."

"I mean it in a great way." He moved his palms against her. He lowered his head and took one nipple into his mouth. He caressed her and kissed her until she couldn't take it anymore. If she didn't have him now, she thought she might scream.

Pulling away from him, she slipped the bra's straps down her arms. She was taking a risk, but after making the leap of showing him her paintings, this felt easy. Natural. And the way he was looking at her made her feel she could do anything and Gray would be there for her anyway. She hadn't known him long, and yet she felt as if she knew him better than anyone she'd ever dated.

And she wanted to know him every way she could.

She arched her back and unhooked her bra, letting her breasts spill free. She threw the bra to the side then slipped off her trousers. Wearing only a thong, she climbed up on Gray's bed.

Moonlight streamed through the bank of windows and bathed her skin in its blue glow. She stretched out on the bed and turned to Gray, wanting to feel him beside her. He hadn't moved, not one muscle but his eyes. Those sexy eyes. They reached out to her, hunger plain on his face, and right then she felt like she was the sexiest and strongest and most secure woman on the planet.

GRAY COULD HARDLY BELIEVE he was there, watching Natalie climb on his bed, the moonlight caressing her body, her breasts. He shouldn't be doing this, shouldn't be taking advantage of her this way. She didn't know who he was, not really. Didn't know her brother had hired him as her bodyguard. She deserved to know.

But how could he walk away from a dream?

His fingers found his belt and unbuckled it. He

might regret this later, but now he couldn't think that far ahead. He wouldn't let himself.

He had just stripped his pants and was about to divest himself of his briefs when he noticed it. A spot of red. It skipped over the bed and skimmed Natalie's flat belly and centered right above her perfect left breast.

Realization clicked into place. What he was seeing. What it meant. His breath froze in his chest.

*Oh, God, no.*

He sprang onto the bed. He felt like he was moving too slow, too awkwardly. He grabbed Natalie's ankle, his fingers closing around her smooth skin, holding her tight. He yanked her toward him with all his strength.

Her mouth rounded into an O. A shocked cry escaped her lips. She slid over the comforter, away from the window, out from under that deadly red beam.

When she reached the edge of the bed, he bent down and scooped her into his arms. He had no time to lose. He shifted his weight, wanting to dash clear, knowing he could never move quickly enough.

The window exploded. Glass rained across the bed.

Natalie screamed.

Gray clamped her tight to his chest and ran.

# Chapter Eight

A second shot smashed through the glass and hit the bed. The next pinged off the floor a few feet away.

Adrenaline pounded through Gray's body, sharpening detail, making everything feel as if it was moving in slow motion.

Especially him.

He had to move faster. He had to reach cover. He had to ensure Natalie's safety.

He reached the master bath and dashed inside. His feet slapped cold tile. He slipped and went down to a knee. The force shuddered up his bad leg, but he hardly noticed.

"Natalie. Please say you're okay. You have to be okay." He brushed his fingers over the silk of her hair. His hand trembled.

"I'm okay. I'm okay." Her voice sounded as shaky as he felt, but it was the sweetest sound he'd ever heard.

"Thank God." He pulled in breath after shuddering breath. For someone who had seen combat, he felt like he'd just gotten out of basic. He was a shaking, out-of-control mess. They were out of the line of fire. His next step had to be getting control of himself.

He concentrated on slowing his breathing. He laid Natalie gently on the bathroom rug.

She sat cross-legged and braced herself with her hands. She was nearly naked, but she didn't move to cover herself. She simply stared at him with wild eyes. "What was that?"

He scanned her body, looking for injuries. "Are you hit?"

"Hit? You mean, shot? Someone was shooting at us?"

"Yes. Are you hurt?" The flesh that had been so sexy just moments before now seemed incredibly fragile to him, precious. He'd never forgive himself if she was hurt.

"I'm okay. How would somebody be shooting?"

He continued to look her over. He couldn't see any blood, but he needed to make sure. A lot of glass had been flying. As frightened as she was, she could be cut and not even notice.

"Oh, my God, you're hurt." Natalie pointed out a trail of blood on his arm, not much more than a scratch.

"It's nothing."

She pulled her legs up and huddled forward, as if she'd recovered from the shock enough to feel the need to cover her bare breasts. "Now what do we do? My phone is out in my bag. We need to call the police."

Gray thrust to his feet. He grabbed his robe from a hook near the shower and gave it to her. "Put this on."

Remaining seated, she pulled the robe over her body and tied it snug at the waist. She wrapped her arms across her chest as if cold.

He ran a hand down her arm. "Now you're going to stay here. I'll take care of this."

"The gunman could be still out there."

"I know. I'll be careful."

At first she looked like she might argue, then she dropped her gaze to the floor and gave a weak nod.

He hated to see her like this. When she was on his bed, she looked beautiful, powerful, brash. Now she seemed smaller, and the thought of that transformation being his fault dug deep.

He never should have brought her to his apartment, to his bed. He knew why he'd done it. It was obvious, after all. After her invitation back at her cottage, he'd known what she was thinking. And instead of checking her into a hotel and standing sentry outside her door, he'd brought her here so he could sleep with her.

He'd been self-centered and way out of line. And then what had he done? He hadn't bothered to take a glance at the building next door. He hadn't drawn the blinds. He'd stood there and admired how the moonlight showed off Natalie's breasts.

He really was as selfish as Sherry had said.

Patting her hand a final time, he forced himself to step away and slipped out of the bathroom. He moved quickly, his breathing regular and controlled, his heartbeat steady as spring rain. Now that he was alone and didn't have to worry about Natalie getting hit, he felt like he was back in his own skin. He'd spent years training for combat, and he was damn good at it.

Using furniture as cover, he went for the closet first. There he slipped on a pair of sweatpants and some sneakers, grabbed a weapon from his gun safe and jammed a loaded clip into place. If the sniper was still in the neighboring building, he'd be dead before he could squeeze off another round.

He went for his pants next and the cell phone strapped to his belt. Glass shards crunched under his rubber soles. Wind whistled through the shattered pane. He eyed the windows and followed the trajectory to the neighboring building. No figure in any of the possible windows. No movement. The guy had probably been smart enough to clear out. The gunshots had been loud. They would have been noticed. Likely the police were already on their way.

The faint sound of sirens screamed above the howling of wind through the window, as if answering his thought.

He shook the glass from his pants and retrieved his cell phone. Locating Natalie's clothing, he shook out glass. She couldn't wear them like this. He'd have to find something else for her to put on. Something that would broadcast to the world why he'd taken her back to his apartment and what they'd been doing when the bullets had started to fly. By the time this was over, he'd be lucky he had a job, but the thing he really regretted was never again seeing the confident gleam in Natalie's eyes that she'd had lying in the middle of his bed.

After this, he'd be lucky if she wanted to look at him at all.

NATALIE CROSSED HER ARMS over her chest and tried to pretend that every cop in the place couldn't see that she was braless under Gray's oversize T-shirt. She still felt as shaky and out of breath as when the glass had shattered over her head, but now she could add a touch of nausea to the mix. At least Devin hadn't commented when he saw her wearing Gray's things. Neither had Ash, a miracle in itself. But she knew it wasn't because they hadn't noticed.

Ash finished talking to an evidence tech and motioned Natalie into the hall. As soon as he closed the door, he wrapped her in a hug. "Thank God you're okay."

She pressed her head against his shoulder and willed herself not to cry. As much as she bemoaned her family's hovering, she always knew they cared about her. And that they would be there for her whenever she needed them.

And that was the best feeling in the world.

Ash ended the hug. He held her upper arms and studied her eyes. "Do you remember a guy named Timothy Walters?"

She knew the name. She searched her memory. "He used to work for Kendall, right?"

"He was in your department."

"I remember." Her stomach felt even more unstable at the memory. A clean-cut guy with a short temper and a habit of snapping at clients. "I had to fire him."

Ash nodded. "Seems he was upset about it, too. Upset enough to send you threatening letters to the office and your place."

"I never got any letters."

"Uncle Craig didn't want you to see them. Neither did Devin."

Now her uncle was throwing in with her brothers, too? She pulled in a deep breath. Not that she could say she would have welcomed the letters. Firing the man had been stressful enough. "So what does that mean? I fired him a couple of years ago."

"Yes, but I want to talk to him anyway. Sometimes the resentments build up only to explode much later. Our family has been in the news. Something like that could have set him off."

She nodded. It didn't make a lot of sense to her, but she had read stories in the paper and seen plenty of dramas on television where just such circumstances led to murderous sprees. But even though she knew it was possible, the thought that *she* would be in the middle of circumstances like that seemed unreal.

"There's another possible trigger, too," Ash continued. "I talked to his wife. She just split with him the day before your cottage was vandalized."

A shiver fanned up her spine. "So he split up with his wife, and he blames me in some strange way?"

"I don't know. We have an APB out on him. We'll find him, and we'll find the truth." He gave her another quick hug. "Don't worry."

She'd been nearly shot and might be the target of a sick mind holding resentments. What was to worry about?

She offered Ash her best confident smile. "I'll be fine."

The fact that Ash was on the case and making progress should make her feel better. But her hands still shook, and her knees still felt like they'd buckle at any moment. Even hovered over by her brothers and standing in an apartment crawling with cops, she didn't feel safe. "Where is Gray?"

"In the kitchen with Devin. I don't know if you want to go in there, though."

"Why not?"

"You know how Devin gets when it comes to protecting family."

Great, so her older brother hadn't said a word to her about being in Gray's bedroom when the shooting started, because he was saving it all for Gray. She eyed Ash. "Yeah, I know how he gets, as if you're any better."

Ash shrugged. "Devin gets first crack at him. I'm next. Gray is just lucky Thad isn't here. Then he'd have to explain himself three times."

"Ash, I don't need my brothers to be breathing down the neck of every guy I date. I can make my own decisions."

He gave her a raised-brow look that answered for him.

Arguing was no use. She turned away from Ash and started for the kitchen.

"Good luck, Natalie," Ash called after her.

Natalie stopped outside the arched entrance to the kitchen and listened for a second. It didn't take more than that for Devin's voice to reach her.

"I told you to take her somewhere safe, not take her to bed." Her oldest brother was in full-on protective mode, as Ash had warned. She hadn't heard him so angry in a long while.

"My building is security locked and has a doorman. It's the safest place I know," Gray said. "I didn't intend for the rest to happen."

Devin scoffed. "So while Ash and I were busy checking the cottage and mansion grounds, you thought you'd take advantage."

Buzzing rose in Natalie's ears. She'd been with Gray since they left the Kendall offices. When had he talked to Devin? Her breath caught in her throat. There had been those moments after she'd asked him to stay and before he'd invited her to his place. Had Gray spent that time calling her brother? Why on earth would he do that?

"It wasn't like that."

No, it wasn't. If anyone was taking advantage and pushing for sex, it had been her. And she didn't feel a bit sorry about it.

She'd wanted to make love with Gray. She'd more than wanted it; she'd done her best to make it happen. And despite the gunshots, she wanted it to happen again. She finally found a guy who was different. Who she really liked and who seemed to like her in return. Maybe enough for it to lead somewhere. And now her brother's overprotective bullying—

"Devin, it won't happen again."

A leaden weight settled into Natalie's stomach.

"You're damn right it's not going to happen again. Because as soon as I arrange for a replacement tomorrow, you're fired."

Natalie gasped out loud. She couldn't believe what she'd just heard. She whirled around the doorjamb and glared at her brother, her fists balled by her sides. "How dare you, Devin? You can't fire him. He deserves to have a private life, too. You might be able to lay down the rules at the office, but you can't dictate what employees do on their own time."

Devin's eyebrows pulled together.

Gray stepped toward Natalie before her brother had a chance to speak. "It's okay, Natalie. He's right. I never should have brought you here."

If she thought she felt nauseated before, she'd been wrong. She wrapped her arms around her stomach. She knew that tone of voice. The tone that led up to *it's not you, it's me.* Or *it's just not a good time in my life right now.* Or *the boss says I should back off and I don't like you enough to disagree.* "What are you saying?"

Gray looked at her, his lips half-open, but no words came out. Instead, it was Devin who spoke. "Grayson isn't on his own time, Natalie. This is his job, being with you, keeping you safe. I'm sorry I didn't tell you, but I knew you'd argue, say I was hovering. But after tonight, I think we can agree the steps I took were warranted."

Natalie couldn't breathe. She could see the pieces of the puzzle displayed in front of her, but her mind resisted shuffling them into place. Or maybe it was her heart.

She looked from her brother to Gray. "I don't understand."

Gray met her gaze, his expression a mix of regret and defeat. "I work for your brother, Natalie. But I'm not an alarm system expert. I'm your bodyguard."

GRAY WATCHED THE LOOK in Natalie's eyes go from confusion to betrayal.

"Why didn't you tell me? Did Ash know about this, too?"

"Natalie," Devin said, as he stepped toward his sister and took hold of her arm.

She ripped away from his grasp. "I don't want to talk to you, Devin. Ash, either. This doesn't even surprise me about the two of you."

Gray stepped toward her. Devin was far from his favorite person at the moment, and he should have been honest with Natalie at the first about hiring a body-guard. But even so, the last thing Gray wanted was for Natalie to blame her brother. All that would do is drive a wedge in the Kendall family and cause Natalie and her brothers more pain. "Natalie, there's a real danger out there. You can't deny it. Devin was only trying to keep you safe."

Natalie spun around and glared at him as if he'd just slapped her. "Devin, will you leave us?"

Devin didn't budge. "I think we should talk this out."

She spoke to her brother without sparing him a glance. "So you can say what? Someone is trying to kill me and you were protecting me. I get that. Someone just shot at me. I'm not trying to deny I'm in danger any longer. What I don't get is why you didn't tell me the truth."

"I did tell you I was worried for your life after all that happened to Ash and me since Rick Campbell was exonerated. You said I was overreacting. You said you didn't want a bodyguard hovering over you."

She still didn't look at her brother, her gaze riveted on Gray. "I did say that, and you should have listened to me. Or at least talked about it again after my cottage was vandalized and I was pushed into the street. But you didn't have to revisit the subject, did you? Because I already had a bodyguard."

In his peripheral vision, Gray could see Devin glance

from Natalie to him. He'd do anything to fix this rift, to say the magic words that would make this go away, to go back in time and tell her the truth that first night in the parking garage, anything. Obviously his options were much more limited. Still, he had to find some way for this to work out. For Natalie and her brothers and for him.

Natalie raised her chin and let out a shaky breath. "Now please leave us alone, Devin. I need to talk to Gray."

"Okay, okay. We can talk more later." Devin strode from the room and closed the door behind him.

For a long while, neither Gray nor Natalie spoke. Low voices filtered in from the room next door. The clock in the corner chimed the hour.

Gray's pulse thumped in his ear. After the shooting tonight, he'd expected Devin to fire him. He'd made peace with that. But he'd hoped Natalie would never have to know about his official role.

It wasn't the job. In the past days, he'd ceased to care about that. Now all he cared about was Natalie. About her relationship with her family. About keeping her safe. But it was more than that, too. And he couldn't deny some of his concern was selfish.

Natalie spoke first. "You lied to me."

What could he say? He had. Straight to her face. "I'm sorry."

"Why didn't you tell me you were my bodyguard? Why didn't you tell me in the parking garage that night?"

"Devin didn't want you to know."

"I know that. I'm asking about you. Why didn't you

tell me the truth? Why did you worm your way into my life and make me care about you?"

He'd made a mistake not coming clean with her from their first face-to-face meeting. He needed to come clean with her now. "You were never supposed to know I was following you. But when I saw that guy follow you into the garage, I thought there might be something to it. And by the time I caught up to him, he was already talking to you."

"What do you mean? How long ago did Devin hire you?"

"He called shortly after Campbell was exonerated for your parents' murders and the trouble began."

"You've been following me for weeks."

"Yes."

She opened her mouth, to ask something, to yell at him, to tell him she never wanted to see his face again—he didn't know. She closed it again without speaking.

"It was all about keeping you safe, Natalie."

She turned around. "Really? Was that what it was all about? Because I thought we liked each other. I thought we were dating. But then, stupid me, I also thought you were a Good Samaritan I happened to meet by chance." Her eyes glistened and her lashes spiked with tears. She tilted her head back as if to keep them from brimming over and running down her cheeks. "I am the worst judge of men ever."

"No, you're not. I lied to you. You couldn't have known—"

"That's the point. I never know. I always see what I want to see. With you, I saw someone different. Someone who cared about me. Someone who made me feel secure and strong and good about myself."

"I am those things. I want to be."

She shook her head and let out a bitter laugh. "You were paid to make me feel secure. I'll give you that. But the rest?"

"I do care about you, Natalie."

"Give me a break. If you really cared, you would have told me the truth about who you are. You wouldn't have been able to lie and then sleep with me."

She was right. He'd cared for her, but not enough to tell her the truth. Not enough to bring her to a hotel and sit outside her door. He'd brought her home because he'd wanted what had unfolded in his bedroom. And he'd been willing to keep up the lie in order to take it.

To take her.

At Jimbo's funeral, his wife had called him self-centered. No one had ever been more right. Even when he wasn't conscious of it, Gray made sure he got what he wanted. No matter who it hurt. No matter who died.

It was other people who were big enough to make sacrifices. Not him.

If he really wanted to make this easier on Natalie, it was about time he started. "You're right. About all of it. And I want you to know that as asinine as I've been these past couple of days, I do care about you."

She said nothing, and he wasn't surprised. He pushed on. "I will get out of your life, let you move on and find a man who deserves you. I promise I will. But—"

She pulled in a sharp breath.

For a second, he thought she might ask him to stay.

But again, she didn't speak. She just waited for him to continue.

"But I can't leave until Devin makes arrangements for another bodyguard to take my place."

"I don't want a bodyguard at all."

"Come on, Natalie. I know how you feel, but you can't deny that you're in danger."

"Maybe someone was trying to shoot you. It's your apartment. Maybe I wasn't the target at all."

"You don't really believe that."

She looked back out the window. Tears wound down her cheeks.

Gray wanted nothing more than to wipe them, but he knew she wouldn't accept his touch. He couldn't blame her.

"Tomorrow, when Devin finds a replacement, I'll leave you alone. You can forget you ever met me."

"I will," she said, but her voice lacked conviction.

He nodded. He hoped she could. Because, although he'd only known her up close and personal for a short while, he was certain it would be impossible for him to ever forget her.

*Chapter Nine*

Natalie stared at her face in the mirror behind the bakery's showcase. Her cheeks were pale, her eyes red and puffy, and despite an almost insane love of cake and frosting and all things wedding, she had no desire to sample any of the amazing creations lined up in front of Rachel, Jolie and her.

Rachel, on the other hand, looked absolutely gorgeous. Although her baby bump was only beginning to round, her face showed all the best signs of motherhood.

In a word, she was glowing.

Natalie had read somewhere that many brides weren't so lucky. Nasty side effects like acne, the redness of rosacea and dry skin were just as common as any kind of attractive glow in the cheeks of a pregnant woman. But not for Rachel. Her skin was creamy, her cheeks holding a delicate flush. Her dark brown hair, pulled back from her face in a half up, half down style, was thick and lustrous. And her hazel eyes glittered as she eyed the cakes. "I have to try the lemon poppy seed and the carrot cake, and I can't pass up something with that chocolate Bavarian crème filling."

The baker, a young energetic woman, smiled. "How

about white almond cake, chocolate Bavarian crème filling and whipped crème frosting?"

Jolie moaned and Rachel nodded as fast as her head would move. A second later, the enthusiasm on her face gave way to worry. "The last baker bailed on us without much notice. Our wedding is only a week away. You're sure you can make such a fancy cake so quickly?"

"Not a problem. And we'll guarantee that in writing. If we can't fulfill your wedding dreams, we'll find and pay for someone who will."

Rachel and Jolie exchanged pleased looks.

The baker directed their attention to another batch of little cupcake samples and rattled off possible fillings and frostings, each more decadent than the last. By the time they sat down at a small table with their cake samples, they'd added another half dozen to their tasting plates.

"You're awfully quiet, Natalie," Rachel said as they started to dig in. "Thinking about last night?"

How could she not? "I'm okay."

"Yeah, right," Jolie said. "You're so used to getting shot at that it doesn't even bother you anymore."

Rachel nodded. "You're forgetting who you're talking to, Natalie. All of us have been through some bad stuff lately. We know you're not all right. I don't think any of us are, even now."

Natalie scooped in a deep breath and let it out. "You're right, of course. But that doesn't mean I'm going to let it ruin your wedding preparations. We're sitting here with a table full of cake, for crying out loud."

"We can talk and taste at the same time." Rachel

picked up her fork and for a few seconds it was poised over a cupcake-size chocolate-fudge cake with a chocolate-mint filling and whipped cream frosting. "So I'll taste, and you talk."

Jolie picked up her own fork. "And don't forget to dish on Mr. Scott outside."

Natalie resisted the urge to glance out the window where Gray was sitting on a bench, waiting for her to finish cake sampling. Last night she'd been certain that she never wanted to see him again. Today, she was trying her best to stick to that.

Too bad her heart didn't want to cooperate.

She gave her future sisters-in-law a rundown of the shooting, leaving out the fact that she was lying on Gray's bed basically naked when bullets crashed through glass. Even so, when Jolie had asked where they were, Natalie had to admit to being in his bedroom, and judging from the looks they gave her, they didn't need more than that to form a picture in their minds.

"I thought you'd decided you weren't going to get involved with him." Jolie set her fork down and focused a look on Natalie that was more concern than anger.

"I know. I'm sorry I didn't tell you. It was just..." What could she say? How on earth could she possibly explain herself?

Jolie nodded, as if Natalie really didn't have to. "You really like him, don't you?"

Natalie shook her head, but that, too, was a lie. "You were right, Jolie. He wasn't what I thought. Devin hired him to be my bodyguard."

Neither Jolie nor Rachel looked surprised.

"You knew?"

"We weren't supposed to tell," Rachel admitted around a bite of white cake with Frangelico buttercream filling. A spot of frosting dotted her lip. "Ash and Devin thought you'd think they were hovering."

Of course that is what she would have thought. And as last night had proven, she would have been wrong. The danger was plenty real.

Natalie let out a sigh. She picked up a forkful of lemon poppy seed then set it back down without even tasting. "Am I really that difficult to handle?"

"Difficult to handle?" Jolie said, her voice rising with disbelief. "Of course not. You want to be independent, live your own life. That's understandable. And for the record, Devin and Ash *can* be a bit overprotective when it comes to you."

Natalie smiled at her friends. "Thad, too, if he were here. But I don't think it qualifies as overprotective if there is a real danger." The similarity of her words to what Gray had said days ago struck her. He'd been right. Devin and Ash had been right, too. It almost pained her to admit it, but there was no point in denying it now. Someone was after their whole family. She might as well face the facts.

"So what happens now?" Jolie asked.

Natalie could only wish she knew the answer to that question. "I suppose we'd all better be careful."

"That's a given, Natalie, and not what I was asking about." She nodded her head in Gray's direction. "It's obvious that you really like him."

Thickness filled her throat, and she couldn't bring herself to follow Jolie's nod. "Yeah. I do."

"But?"

"But Devin is hiring a new bodyguard for me today."

"Not if you tell him you want Gray," Rachel said.

"He lied about who he was."

Jolie laid her hand on Natalie's arm. "We've all been doing our share of lying, it seems. I'm sorry, Natalie. I was trying to keep you from getting hurt, and I did a lousy job of it. If I'd told you who Gray was from the beginning…"

Natalie held up a hand, cutting off her friend. "I'm sorry, too."

"Me, too," Rachel said. "And your brothers, well, they are who they are."

"They just wanted to protect me, too. I get it."

"So what are you going to do?" Jolie asked. "You know, I'll bet he never *wanted* to lie to you."

"Probably not." Last night, Gray's lie had felt like a major betrayal. But if Natalie was honest with herself, she had to admit Gray's failure to tell her he was a hired bodyguard wasn't what bothered her most.

Natalie took a bite of cake and forced herself to swallow. She was sure it was delicious, but she couldn't appreciate the flavors. She doubted anything would taste good to her today. She wasn't used to being shot at. She wasn't used to being in danger. And she wasn't used to wanting a guy despite knowing he'd been hired to hang out with her…and there was a good chance he would turn around and leave as soon as the job was over.

"So?" Rachel prompted. "What happens between you two now?"

It was a good question. And one for which Natalie wasn't likely to get a reliable answer until she was out of danger, and Gray was free to walk away.

GRAY WAS SURPRISED when Natalie emerged from the bakery without Rachel and Jolie. He held up a hand, signaling for her to stop at the door and wait for him. After making another visual sweep of the area to confirm it was clear, he joined her at the door. "What's the problem? Where are Jolie and Rachel?"

"They're going to stay and try more cake."

"And you?"

She held her hand against her stomach. "I've had enough. Can we leave?"

"Of course." He strode beside her. When they reached his car, he opened the passenger door for her, then circled to the driver's side and climbed in. He started the car and pulled into traffic before he asked where they were going.

"I'm not sure. It depends, I guess." She stared out the window, her arms crossed over her chest, her fingers fidgeting with the sleeves of the sporty leather jacket she often wore on her days off.

"What does it depend on?"

She didn't speak, but her fidgeting moved to her feet.

"I can tell you've got something to say. Go ahead."

"I want to bring this to an end."

She'd said something to that effect last night, but it managed to make Gray's chest ache all over again. "When Devin gets another bodyguard in place—"

"That's not what I mean."

He raised his brows and waited for her to continue.

"I want this whole thing over, this threat to my family."

He nodded, still not sure where she was going with

this. "I'm sure Ash and his fellow officers have a few new leads after last night."

"He does. And he's following up on those. But the St. Louis PD is like any other city police department these days, overworked and underfunded."

True enough. "So what do you have in mind?"

"I'm going to see what I can find out."

Now he hadn't seen *that* coming. "And how do you plan to do that?"

"I'm not sure yet. Talk to people? See if anyone noticed anything? I mean, this guy is after me. Maybe I'm the one in the best position to figure out who he is."

Gray wanted to tell her no, to shut her away and keep her safe from the world. "I might not have known you long, but I suspect you're going to do this whether I like it or not."

"Smart man."

"So if you're going to be skipping around town talking to people, I'm going to be there with you."

She nodded. "You are my bodyguard."

"And you're okay with that suddenly?"

"You mean, do I realize I'm in danger now? Yes. Am I still angry with you for lying to me? A bit. But…"

"But?" he prompted.

"But I called Devin and told him I don't want another bodyguard. That I only want you. You saved my life twice, and I trust you. At least as far as that goes."

And he would make damn sure her trust was warranted. "So where do we start?"

She shot him a slightly embarrassed smile. "I don't have a clue. I was hoping you would."

He couldn't help but chuckle. This woman was something else. Even when she wasn't quite forgiving him, she still made him feel as if every moment around her was a gift.

He took a deep breath and reined in those sentiments. He'd let himself get distracted before, started thinking of Natalie as his plaything rather than someone he had been hired to lay down his life if necessary to protect. He wasn't going to make that mistake again. He needed to be ready to take care of her, not focus on his own needs. Her life depended on it. "This started with your paintings being slashed. What if we start there, too?"

"Go on."

"You mentioned an art dealer who wanted to show your work, and you turned him down."

"Maxim Miles. But I can't imagine why he even wanted them, let alone why he would try to kill me. They aren't exactly commercial."

"Judging from what I saw, they were pretty amazing."

She shook her head, as if to say he had no idea how to evaluate art.

He supposed he didn't. "I know I'm not an expert, but those paintings were beautiful. Haunting."

"But why would he destroy them?"

"Maybe he didn't destroy them all. You said yourself that you weren't sure if they were all there."

"I said that to the police, not you."

He gave a shrug, not crazy about reminding her of the secret he'd kept.

"And my brothers passed it along to you."

He nodded. "What if he took some of them and vandalized the rest to hide what he'd taken? You said he sold work for you before, right?"

"He even bought a few of my paintings for himself."

This was seeming like more of a lead all the time. "And what tends to happen to the work of artists who…" He stopped himself. His theory wasn't bad, but he couldn't quite bring himself to lay out the rest of the scenario.

"Artists who die? Especially in a dramatic fashion when their family has been all over the news for months?" Apparently Natalie wasn't quite so squeamish.

"If that is his plan—"

"To kill me?"

"Or to make it look like someone is trying to kill you. All he needs is the publicity in order to inflate the price."

Natalie nodded for him to go on.

"If that is his plan, he's only taken his first step last night."

She frowned. "Unless…"

"What?"

"I keep thinking about that woman in the powder-blue sweatshirt. I never saw her face, you know. She was kind of big, and the sweatshirt was very shapeless."

"You're thinking it might have been a man?"

"It might have been Max. I really can't say."

"But pushing you into traffic didn't do the trick, so he escalated to shooting. Could be. And he would have seen you with me, so he might have followed me and staked out my place. Then he was already familiar with it when I took you there last night."

Awkward silence dropped like a curtain between them. Gray felt horrible about how last night had turned out. It never should have happened. He never should have let things go that far. But he'd apologized several times already, and he sensed another round was the last thing Natalie wanted. "If that scenario is even close, Max couldn't have sold the paintings yet."

Natalie turned to him, eyes sparking. "They have to be in the gallery somewhere. They'd probably be in his office."

"Can we get in there somehow?"

She pursed her lips. "Maybe."

"What do you have in mind?"

She laid out a rough plan for him. It wouldn't be easy to pull off, but it just might work.

Gray nodded his approval. "Who knows, maybe we'll have this mess all sorted out, and before you know it, you won't need a bodyguard anymore."

She pressed her lips into a line and nodded, but instead of the excitement and grit he'd seen a second ago, she looked strangely sad.

MAXIM MILES OWNED an art studio in the fashionable Central West End in Saint Louis. Natalie had always loved the neighborhood. Even now, looking up at the glittering green dome of the Cathedral Basilica of Saint Louis gave her a feeling of awe and excitement. Too bad the prospect of seeing Max Miles again did not.

They made their way through the neighborhood. Turning down the tree-lined street where Max's gallery was located, Natalie wished she could reach out and grab Gray's hand. That physical reassurance that he was there with her would help her jittery nerves. At least she liked to imagine so. Deep down she suspected she was fooling herself.

"Is this it?" Gray's steps slowed.

Natalie focused on the row of shops and upscale restaurants. Delicious scents drifted from a bistro on the corner. Two doors down, the familiar white wood columns rose into the sky and curled into carved swirls like decorations on a wedding cake. "Yes, this is it."

He held the door open for her.

She took a deep breath and stepped inside.

The interior of the gallery was also just how she remembered it. Muted colors made the walls, flooring and ceiling fade into the background. Sophisticated lighting enhanced paintings, photography and sculpture displayed throughout the rooms. The scent of jasmine and soft lilt of classical music made the space feel expensive and sexy at once.

She'd been so excited when Max had first accepted one of her paintings, a stylized vision of the Kendall Estate's shade garden in black, white and deep greens. She'd been over the moon when he'd given her her first real show. Now she wished she'd never met the man.

"Don't tell me." Max stepped from behind a sculpture of a nude made from swirls of silver metal. He was still thin. His hairpiece was still too dark and too full. His black suit, shirt and tie had the same easy elegance. And his face still held the same hard smile. "Isn't this a coincidence? After all this time, you finally have something for me."

"No, I don't," Natalie said. She tried not to enjoy his fallen expression too much.

"Then you are here to buy?" He glanced at Gray, as if it was no question that the man would be wielding the checkbook, even though he knew full well Natalie could buy her own art.

Gray nodded, as they'd agreed. "I'm here to buy some of Natalie's paintings, in fact."

Max's eyebrows shot toward his synthetic hairline. "You have the artist here, and yet you want to buy from me?"

"She won't sell anything she has. But she said you used to show her work and might have some now."

The excuse sounded unbelievable, contrived and for a second, Natalie thought the art dealer would call Gray on it.

Instead, Max shrugged. "I did show her work. I would still be showing her work if she would cooperate."

Gray shook his head. "Artists are so fickle and eccentric."

"Exactly."

Natalie could feel her cheeks starting to heat. She was pretty sure this was an act, and Gray didn't really feel that way about her. But she supposed it didn't matter. When they found out who was trying to kill her and she no longer needed a bodyguard, then she would know the truth. Then Gray would either walk away or not. "So what is it, Max? Do you have any of my paintings or not?"

"I believe I might."

Natalie peered up at Gray. "I can tell you if he is charging too much."

Max held up a hand. The glow from a recessed light

glinted off several gaudy rings. "Your job is to make the art, my dear. My job is to sell it. I will not haggle about price with you. Either I show him alone, or I do not show him anything."

Gray shot Natalie an apologetic glance, then he smiled at Max. "I don't need an advisor."

"Gray."

"We'll just be a few moments. Have a look around. See if there's something here you like." Gray looked back to Max. "Lead the way."

If Gray's placating tone had not been part of their plan, Natalie might just have to slap him. As it was, Max led him away to one of the back storage rooms. Before the door closed, she caught the sound of Max issuing orders to his assistant in the back, and then Natalie was alone.

When she'd dealt with Max, he'd had only one assistant working during the week and used part-time help for special events. She hoped that was still the case.

She pulled in a calming breath and took off in the direction of Max's personal office. Rounding an abstract sculpture made from hammered copper, heavy wire and stone, she slowed her steps. Once she turned down the hall that led to the office, she could no longer say she was checking out the pieces of art. Max would know she was snooping. She stopped at the mouth of the hall, listening for any movement.

Not hearing any sign of life, she stepped quickly down the hall and found Max's office door. The door was locked, as usual, with a keypad doorknob. She punched in the old code she remembered him using, a string of nines, and tried the door.

It held fast.

So Max had changed the digits in his code. That shouldn't surprise her. She punched in his birthdate.

Nothing. She tried his birthdate along with the date he'd opened the gallery.

No good. She was nearly out of options when she had an idea. She pulled out her iPhone. Checking to see which numbers corresponded to which letters on a standard telephone, she typed in *Miles*. It didn't budge. She typed in *money*.

The lever turned under her hand.

Figured. She slipped into the dim office and closed the door behind her.

Nearly as large as one of the small gallery show-rooms, Max's office held a large desk, a leather couch, a wide credenza and jumbles of boxes and stacks of paintings.

How would she find anything in this mess? She had no idea. But she didn't have time to sit around and reason it out.

She started with the closest pile of paintings. Each was stored in protective crates or other types of packing. She didn't have enough time to sort through all of these. By the time she was able to reveal even one painting, Gray and Max would be finished with their business and looking for her. There had to be a faster way.

She focused on breathing. In, two, three, four. Out, two, three, four. Her pulse throbbed in her ears, making it hard to hear any noises outside the room.

If Max had taken anything from her house, he wouldn't have had the paintings long. He also wouldn't want them to get tangled up with the other consignments. He'd hide them someplace special.

She threaded through the stacks of artwork and slipped behind his desk. Two cartons leaned up against the credenza, plenty big enough for each to hold one of her paintings.

Voices erupted outside the door.

Natalie tried to think, to breathe. Her pulse pounded in her ears. She couldn't hear if one of the voices belonged to Max or someone else, but it didn't really matter. There was no talking her way out of this one. Losing her way while looking for the restroom wasn't going to cover breaking into a locked and darkened office.

The door rattled as if someone was punching in the code.

She dropped to her hands and knees and shuffled closer to the desk. She forced her breathing to slow. She wasn't alone. She had to remember that. Gray was here, and he was armed. He wouldn't let Max hurt her.

The pressure in the room changed, and Natalie could tell whoever was at the door had opened it and was inside the room.

"I'll be with you in just a moment."

*Max.*

Footsteps shuffled toward her followed by the scrape of crates rubbing against one another.

"My time is valuable." Gray's voice boomed from the doorway. "You said this phone call would only take a minute."

Natalie let out the breath she hadn't been aware she was holding. Gray would get Max out of the office. He would give her time to look at the contents of the cartons. She just had to make sure Max didn't discover her before Gray could coax him back into the storeroom.

"You're a valuable customer, Mr. Scott. Let me find what I'm looking for. I think you'll be pleased."

"I'd better be, because this seems to be taking forever."

"Trust me, you will be. And since Natalie is here, she can verify them for you."

Verify them? He must be talking about her paintings. Natalie glanced at the cartons behind the desk. In the dim light filtering through the blinds, she could barely make out a scrawled name in the corner. She leaned closer, squinting.

"Ahh, yes. I remember where I tucked them."

She spied the name and her breath caught in her throat. *Demetrius Jones*. It had been a long time since she'd thought of him, but not long enough.

Footsteps rounded the desk, coming toward her.

She squeezed past the chair and slipped into the darkness under the desk. Keeping her breathing shallow, she willed Max not to hear the mad thump of her heart.

Max's Bruno Magli shoes gleamed even in the dim light. He stepped straight to the cartons Natalie had found, the ones Demetrius had sent him. He picked them up, straightened and paused.

She tried to shrink farther back under the desk. She couldn't tell how long he stood there, but it seemed like forever. Finally he stepped around the desk, left the office and closed the door behind him and Gray.

Natalie sagged against the desk. She'd thought for sure he'd see her, sense that she was there. But now that he hadn't, she had another problem. Not only had he taken the paintings, based on what he'd said to Gray, he was taking them out to the main gallery to show her.

*And she wasn't there.*

She rolled the chair back and scrambled out from under the desk. Bits of paper packing clung to her skirt, tights and boots. One look and Max would wonder why she'd been crawling on the floor. She brushed her clothing and legs. Fairly certain she was clean, she wound through the maze of crates scattering the floor. She reached the door and paused, hand on knob, to listen.

No sound came from the hall. Either Gray had convinced Max to go back to the storeroom, or they were now about to realize she was no longer in the main gallery.

She had to make up a cover story. And she had to hurry.

She pushed down on the lever and pulled open the door. Taking a deep breath, she stepped out into the hall.

"So there you are. What a surprise." Max's voice was as hard as his eyes.

# Chapter Ten

"What were you doing in my office?"

Natalie's heartbeat stuttered in her chest. She tried for words, but she couldn't grasp any that made sense. Her fallback, the bathroom excuse, obviously wouldn't fly. She looked past Max and focused on Gray at the end of the hall.

He gave her a tight smile, as if everything was under perfect control.

"No explanation? Then I can only assume you and your friend here are trying to rob me." Max reached for his phone. "I'm calling the police."

"Go ahead." Gray stepped toward Max. At well over six feet, Gray towered over him. "And when you do, ask for Natalie's brother, Detective Ash Kendall. I'm sure he'd like to know why you vandalized her studio, destroyed half a dozen paintings and stole a couple more."

Max's eyebrows shot toward his synthetic hairline. "What are you talking about?"

Natalie looked at Gray as well, waiting for the explanation.

"You broke into Natalie's house and vandalized some of her paintings and stole others. Don't bother denying it."

"Okay, I won't bother. But then I have nothing to say, because I wasn't there."

Gray picked up one of the cartons Max had taken from the office. He reached inside and pulled out a canvas.

Natalie could have sworn Max turned a shade paler. After all the times Max Miles had tried to bully her, she couldn't help feeling as if she was finally getting a little justice.

Gray turned the canvas around.

It was a painting of a dark figure in a shadowy room. A drapery floated in the background, white and tattered, and red pooled on the floor.

"Where did you get this?" Natalie demanded.

"Demetrius Jones brought it in yesterday. He said it was one of yours."

Natalie's face felt hot. She could feel Gray watching her, waiting for some kind of explanation. "Is there another in the other crate?"

Max nodded.

Gray pulled out his phone. "Don't bother making that call to the police, Miles. I'll make it for you."

"Wait." Natalie held up a hand.

Gray paused, questions in his eyes.

Natalie looked once again at the painting. The dark colors. The shadowy figure just like the one she'd painted so many times. The bright red of blood. "This painting isn't one of mine."

NATALIE'S STATEMENT didn't make sense. Gray shook his head and took another look at the painting. Then he returned his gaze to Natalie's face. "What do you mean, it isn't yours?"

"Just that. I didn't paint this."

Maxim Miles bit out a curse. "I should have known it. I never should have believed that crook."

"What crook would that be?" Gray asked.

"Demetrius Jones. He brought these in yesterday. Said he got them from Natalie. That he finally talked her into selling some of her newer work. I suspected he was trying to pull something over on me, as usual. Should have told him to get the hell out. Should have known from the beginning it wasn't on the up-and-up."

Gray got the idea Max was a regular expert when it came to things that weren't on the up-and-up. He turned away from Max and focused on Natalie. "You didn't paint this?"

She shook her head. "Demetri, he's an artist, too."

Max let out a bark of a laugh. "He's not *really* an artist, babe. Let's be honest. He's a wannabe who thought that by dating you he could steal a little of your talent. Or at least your connections. And I haven't been able to get rid of him since."

So he'd tried to become successful by using Natalie. Was that what these paintings were about, too? "Am I really the only one who has seen your newer paintings?" Gray asked.

"Except for Ash and the officers who were with him the night of the break-in, yes. You're the only one."

"Then if this is a copy that Demetri painted in order to pass it off as one of yours, when did he see the paintings?"

Natalie nodded. "The night he broke into my cottage and vandalized my studio."

As soon as they left The Miles Gallery, Gray turned to Natalie. "Do you know where Demetri lives?"

She nodded. "I got a look at the mailing label on one of those cartons. It's not too far away. You want to go have a talk?" She seemed less than enthusiastic about the idea.

"I think it might be enlightening," he admitted. "But if you'd rather not, we could just let Ash know and be done with it."

"No. I want to see his face when he tries to explain his way out of this one."

Gray could tell there was a significant history between Demetri and Natalie. And somewhere deep inside, he couldn't prevent a twinge of jealousy. He wanted to find the truth, but he had to admit he also wanted to size up this guy. Find out what Natalie saw in him.

"You want to tell me about him?"

"There's not much to tell." Natalie's cheeks shone pink. Combined with the way she was avoiding looking him in the eye, Gray doubted the bloom of color was solely due to the wind.

"Is what Miles said true?"

"What, that he was my boyfriend? That he took advantage of me?" She let out a long, shaky sigh. "Yeah, it's true. Demetri was never that interested in me. He wanted my connections. He wanted my family's money. He wanted me to teach him what I knew. And when I did, he left. It wasn't one of the best times in my life."

"I'm sorry."

She shrugged, as if her history with this guy meant nothing.

Gray didn't buy it. He'd seen the humiliation in her face and the hurt in her voice. The thought of some idiot hurting her made him want to turn his fists on that idiot. If anyone deserved a good man who would put her before his own selfish wants, it was Natalie. Why she had to be tangled up with a loser like this guy obviously was, he'd never know. "He shouldn't have used you like that."

"It could have been worse."

"How?"

"I could have actually been in love with him."

He felt those words like a kick to the gut. Hadn't Devin warned him about just such circumstances? At least when she'd found out he was her bodyguard, she hadn't been in love with him. At least he hadn't hurt her that much. "Do you think Demetri might resort to murder?"

"I doubt it."

"You don't sound sure."

"I'm not sure of anything anymore."

"Are you sure you feel up to talking to him?"

"I might not have had him figured out all those years ago, but he can't fool me now."

They walked in silence until Natalie stopped in front of a shop selling beeswax candles and other useless gifts. She gestured to a narrow staircase leading to the floor above the shop.

Demetri Jones lived in one of the tiniest apartments Gray had ever seen, unexpected since the tree-lined streets of the prestigious neighborhood itself were populated with stately homes and upscale shops and restaurants. Even more surprising was the fact that Demetri was not a small man. With the face and charm of a movie star and the muscle of a bodybuilder, he was almost as tall as Gray and his shoulders were nearly as wide.

At least they could be pretty sure he wasn't the person wearing the light blue sweatshirt who'd pushed Natalie into traffic.

He frowned at Gray, but when he spotted Natalie, he opened the door as wide as his smile. "Babe."

Gray hated him even more.

Natalie entered the apartment and stepped away from the big man's attempt at a hug. "We have something to talk to you about."

"Who's *we?*"

Gray pushed his way in behind Natalie. "We hear you've been copying Natalie's paintings and trying to sell them as hers."

Demetri didn't even blink. In fact, his smile got a little wider. "I'm just trying to make a living. You can't blame me."

Natalie plopped her hands on her hips. "Where did see my paintings, Demetri?"

"What do you mean, where'd I see your paintings. At your place, baby."

"I never showed them to you. Not my new work. I never showed that to anyone."

"You saw them at Natalie's house almost a week ago, didn't you?" Demetri might be almost as big as Gray, but that didn't mean much. Gray had taken men his size.

Even with his bad knee and other injuries from the incident in Yemen, he still had the strength.

His eyebrows pulled low and he looked at Gray as if he'd just spouted gibberish. "A week?"

Gray took a step forward. "You shredded most of them. And took a couple, too. Where are they, Demetri?"

"What are you talking about?"

"And there's more, too. You hired or at least convinced someone to push Natalie into the street. You've been lurking around outside her cottage at night. And last night you shot up my apartment."

Demetri shook his head. He shot Natalie a desperate look. "Who is this guy?"

Natalie ignored the question. "Explain, Demetri."

He threw out his hands, palms up. "Why would I do any of that?"

"You're copying her paintings. You want to increase their value."

He actually had the nerve to smile. "You got that part right. What can I say? The Christmas Eve Murders have been in the news. But the rest of what you were saying...I don't know anything about that stuff."

"Then when did you see my paintings? The newer ones? Like the ones you forged and tried to sell to Max."

"Oh, damn. You talked to Max? You didn't tell him those paintings I sent him aren't yours, did you?"

"Of course, I did. They aren't mine. They aren't even all that close to mine."

"Oh, great. Thanks a lot, Natalie. I needed that money. Now what am I supposed to do?"

Gray had enough. Of this guy's lies, of him calling

Natalie *babe* and most of all of the insensitive comments he let fall from his mouth.

Gray lunged forward. Bringing the flat of his forearm up under Demetri's chin, he pushed the big man back and pinned him against the hallway's wall. "Unless you want to start a little trouble, you need to answer. Where and when did you see those paintings?"

"Hey, slow down, man," he said in a strangled voice.

"When and where?" Gray repeated.

"Let up. Let up. I'll answer your damn questions."

Gray lowered his arm and took a step back.

Demetri's movie-star handsome face was flushed. He rubbed his throat with a hand. "I didn't see them a week ago. But I did get a glimpse back when Natalie and me were an item."

Beside him, Natalie shuffled her feet on the floor. She brushed her hair back from her eyes. "I never showed you my paintings."

"I didn't say you showed me."

Gray narrowed his eyes on the man. "How did you see them?"

Demetri gave him a half smile. "She ever tell you about her nightmares?"

Gray glanced at Natalie.

"So you haven't slept with her then, have you?" He shot Gray a taunting smile.

Gray had the urge to wipe it right off his face.

She looked to the floor and once again swiped her hand across her cheek. "Answer the question, Demetri."

"Oh, shouldn't I kiss and tell?"

The only thing keeping Gray from punching the guy

in the mouth was that he needed it to talk. "Answer the question."

"I snuck a peek. I was curious."

"In her house a few days ago, we know."

"No, after we'd had some great sex." Another grin. "I had to get a look. You can't blame me. I was in her bed plenty of times when she had those nightmares. And afterward, she didn't sleep. She just went into her studio and locked the door. When she came out in the morning, she always had paint on her fingers and clothes. Shades of black and gray and blood…bloodred. I was curious. So one day I peeked. Disturbing stuff."

Natalie avoided meeting Gray's eyes.

"So I need some cash, and I thought I might be able to find a gallery interested in stuff like that," Demetri drawled on. "But if I didn't, I figured I could always try some kind of house of horror. That's where that kind of art really belongs."

## Chapter Eleven

Gray didn't say anything for three blocks, and neither did Natalie. They walked through the streets, back in the direction of his car. The sun now hid behind hazy clouds, and the wind had turned cool. The scent of Italian herbs drifted from a gourmet pizza place, and Gray's stomach growled, despite the fact that he didn't feel hungry. He stole a glance at Natalie.

She stared straight ahead, her hair swirling around her cheeks. Tears glistened in her eyes and streaked paths down her cheeks.

Somehow he doubted it was all due to the wind. "Do you want to tell me about these nightmares?"

"Not really, no."

He knew she wanted him to back off. A gentleman probably would. But since that wasn't something he'd ever been accused of being, he pushed on. "Do they have something to do with your parents' murders?"

She shook her head, but Gray got the idea the gesture didn't necessarily mean her answer was no.

"Don't want to talk about it?"

"I'm sorry. I just can't."

"That's fair."

They returned to silence, completing another block.

The cloudy sky turned to rain, small drops pattering on their heads and darkening sidewalks and streets. The Cathedral Basilica of Saint Louis's dome towered in front of them, glistening almost as brightly in the rain as it had in the sun. The car wasn't far now, but Gray wasn't ready to bring Natalie home. He had a hunch she would hide out in her bedroom or studio and he would never find out about the paintings and nightmares. And maybe as a simple bodyguard he didn't need to know what was so troubling and painful to his client. But as a man, he wanted to help. "Let's step in out of the rain."

She opened her mouth to protest.

He kept talking. "I haven't seen the mosaics for a long time. It'll just take a minute. This shower looks like it will blow over pretty quickly."

She nodded, and they ducked inside.

The interior of the cathedral was as amazing as he remembered. Every inch of the place seemed to be covered with mosaics made from tiny tiles. It smelled like serenity and candle wax. Quiet seemed to echo from every corner, and except for a few people taking in the famous site, just as they were, the place felt quiet, safe, calm.

He led Natalie to a secluded hallway off the cathedral's nave. "I want you to know you can talk to me, Natalie. It seems like there are a lot of things you're keeping bottled up inside. It might help to let some of that out."

She didn't say anything, just kept moving through the hall, very slowly, taking in the artwork. Gray had nearly given up when she finally spoke. "I don't know, sometimes…"

"Sometimes what?" he prompted.

"Sometimes I wonder if the Kendalls aren't all just marked or something."

"Because of your parents?"

"And everything else that's happened since DNA tests showed Rick Campbell didn't kill them. I mean, we still don't know who really murdered them. He's still out there."

That had to be hard. So hard, Gray didn't know how any of the Kendalls dealt with it as well as they had. There was also another thought that had been bothering him. It started as an uneasy feeling, but it had grown as they'd talked to Max and then Demetri. "Do you think it might be the person who shot at you?"

She gave a hint of a shrug. "And pushed me into traffic? I don't know. I don't think it was Max or Demetri, though."

"Me, either. If Max had any of your real paintings, he would have shown them to me. Also, I can't see that guy ever destroying artwork. Not when he could sell it."

"I agree." She shrugged and wrapped her arms around herself, as if she was chilled from the rain.

He took off his jacket and draped it over her.

"Now you're going to be cold."

"I'll manage."

She stopped and looked up into his eyes. "It could be the same person, couldn't it? Someone who wants to silence our family so he will never be discovered."

Gray frowned. It was a theory, but he wasn't sure it added up. "I thought the people who were after your brothers were stopped."

"They were." She thought for a moment. "So I suppose that can't be the reason they were targeted."

An uneasy feeling tensed his shoulders and neck. "But you're thinking that might be the reason someone is trying to kill you?"

"It sounds silly, doesn't it?"

"It doesn't sound silly at all. It sounds like there's a lot you haven't told me."

Ignoring his prompt, she sighed and scuffed her shoes on the marble floor. "Sometimes I wonder if things will ever be normal again."

"So you don't have to have a bodyguard anymore?"

She looked away from him, but once again he caught a sense of sadness in her expression.

Strange. Knowing how upset she'd been at learning she had a bodyguard, he'd think the idea of him gone would cheer her. After all, last night at his apartment and this morning at the bakery, she'd made it perfectly clear that while she might need him in the short term, as soon as she didn't have someone shoving her into moving cars, taking potshots and running around outside her cottage at night, she would be all too happy to tell him goodbye. "Are you having a change of heart?"

"Over what?"

"You look so sad at the idea of not needing a bodyguard."

"It's not that."

He tried not to show his disappointment. "What is it then?"

"I wish none of this was happening. I wish you weren't my bodyguard. I wish you could be what I thought you were. Just a guy I like."

He nodded. "I wish that, too."

"But it's not possible, is it?"

He thought about how wrapped up in her he'd been when she was pushed into traffic, so wrapped up he hadn't gotten as much of a look at the person following as she had. He'd ignored that warning sign. Ignored it until the shots came crashing through his bedroom window, shots that had almost killed her. "To keep you safe, I have to make sacrifices."

"Sacrifices?"

"I have to pay more attention to everything around us. I'm afraid when I'm kissing you, that's all I can think about."

She gave him a sad smile. "I like that."

"Then why do I get the feeling that you don't believe me?"

"It's not you. I just don't have the best of track records when it comes to men. At least the ones I like."

After this afternoon, he could see why. "Maybe you shouldn't like them in the first place."

"You're talking about Demetri. Yeah, he's a jerk. I'm not sure what I was thinking dating him. No, not true. I wanted to believe he liked me. He didn't fool me as much as I fooled myself."

"I'm sure a lot of men like you, Natalie." Him included. No, him especially.

"Thanks. But that's not it, really. The problem is finding a man who will stick around. It seems like whenever I start to really like a guy, he pulls away."

"I'm not pulling away. I mean, not on purpose, not by choice."

"I know. But I end up alone either way." She gave a shrug, as if it was no big deal.

He didn't buy it. Not for a second. "For what it's worth, if I really was that regular guy who worked with alarm systems, I wouldn't pull away."

"So it's the job."

"Yes." But even as he said the word, he knew it wasn't true. It wasn't simply a matter of being her bodyguard. It was about who he was. What he had to prove. "And no."

She crooked a brow. "You said you blamed yourself for your buddy's death."

He nodded. She'd connected the dots almost as if she could read his mind. But he didn't want to talk about Jimbo. Just the memory of what had happened off the coast of Yemen still ached like an open wound. But he couldn't cut Natalie off. If he wanted her to open up to him, he had to be willing to open up to her. "At Jimbo's memorial service, his wife, Sherry, said something that really struck home."

"What?"

He swallowed, trying to rid himself of the thick feeling in his throat. It didn't do any good. Sherry had lashed out at him due to anger and grief, but that didn't make her words untrue. "She said I should have died instead of her husband. She said I only survived because I wasn't willing to make the kind of sacrifice Jimbo made."

"What a horrible thing to say."

"It's true." It hurt to say those words out loud, especially to Natalie, but there they were.

She shook her head. "It's not."

"You don't know me, Natalie. I grew up with everything. Money. Enough smarts to do well in school. Opportunities to do anything I wanted. I've never had to sacrifice for anything, not my entire life."

"So you grew up wealthy. So did I."

Now it was his turn for a head shake. "You're very different from me."

"How?"

"First, your father was a self-made man. He sacrificed a lot to build Kendall Communications."

"So did my uncle and my brother. But I didn't."

"I'm willing to bet you sacrificed time with your dad. I'll bet he was never home."

"No, I suppose he wasn't. My memory of my parents is a little foggy. I was only six when they died." She bit her bottom lip and blinked as if driving back tears. "But I sometimes wonder if they were very happy. I have shadowy memories, but I don't know if they're all that accurate. I asked my aunt, but she kind of avoided the whole topic."

"That's the other thing. You lost both your parents so young. I can't imagine a bigger sacrifice."

She turned her face to the side, but she couldn't hide her tears.

He felt for Natalie. He couldn't imagine losing his parents at age six. He couldn't imagine losing his parents at all. Right now they were in Italy, exploring Venice. But they would be back to celebrate Christmas. He could count on it. And that was an assurance Natalie would never have. "So you see, we're very different."

"But you jumped into heavy traffic to save me. And

you risked your life to get me out of the line of fire last night."

"It's my job."

She narrowed her eyes on him, as if she could see right through his defenses and into his heart. "Is that why you took the job? To prove you can sacrifice your life like your friend did?"

He'd asked himself that countless times. And each time, he came up with the same answer. "Probably."

"You know, even if you do manage to get yourself killed, it won't bring your friend back."

His chest felt hollow. "I know that. It also won't erase my failure in Yemen."

"But you didn't fail. You said you kept the ship from being bombed."

"I lost men."

"It isn't just about sacrifice then. You blame yourself for your friend's death."

He didn't know what to say. Of course he did. And he knew nothing he could ever do would change the fact that Jimbo was dead, when it should have been him.

"That's what my nightmares are about."

Her voice was quiet, almost a whisper, and at first he wasn't sure what she said. "The nightmares you painted?"

She nodded. "I could have stopped my parents' murders."

He studied her for a moment, not sure what to make of her statement. He'd heard of children blaming themselves for their parents' divorce. He supposed a child could feel as if she should have stopped a murder, too. But Natalie was no longer a child. Surely she could see that a little girl could never wield such power. "You were six years old."

"Someone came into my room that night. At first, I thought it was Santa. It was Christmas Eve, you know. Then when I saw he wasn't fat and didn't have a big beard, I figured it was my dad. When he worked late, he'd sometimes come in and check on me before he went to bed."

"But it wasn't your dad?"

"I don't think so. I think it was their murderer."

The man's face cloaked in shadow. The dark figure in her paintings. "How do you know it was the killer?"

"I don't, really. It's just a feeling." She stared at the tiles covering the walls and arching across the ceiling.

Gray had to wonder if she was looking at the mosaics at all, or if she only saw her memories. "You can't blame yourself for a hunch you're having twenty years after the fact."

Natalie glanced at him for a second and then looked away.

She wasn't going to let herself off the hook. At least not because of what he had to say. "What do you remember? What did the man do?"

"He was sitting on the edge of my bed when I woke up. He was watching me." She bit her bottom lip.

"Do you remember what he looked like? Any facial features? What he was wearing?"

She shook her head. "There was a light in the hall behind him. It was dim, but compared to the darkness in my room everything seemed black. I could only see his silhouette, just enough to know he wasn't Santa."

"So he sat on your bed. What else do you remember?"

She looked past Gray, as if back in her bedroom all those years ago. "I remember him touching my hair, very gently, as if I was the most precious thing in the world to him. And he smiled at me. I couldn't see his face, not really, but I could feel his smile. It felt like a nice smile."

"Did your dad usually do that kind of thing when he checked on you?"

She gave her head a little shake. "He never did. He would just peek in the doorway for a few seconds, then leave. But I always wanted him to sit on my bed, to check on me. I think that's why I believed it was my father. I *wanted* it to be him."

So far, he couldn't see a reason she was so certain it wasn't her father. The fact that he usually checked on her from a distance didn't mean he hadn't sat on her bed that night. There had to be more. "Did he say anything?"

"*Go back to sleep*. That's what he said."

"Did you recognize his voice?"

"That's just it. His voice wasn't my dad's." She focused on Gray, her eyes shining with unshed tears. "I should have screamed. Right then, I should have screamed as loud as I could. If I had, my parents would still be here."

Gray's throat ached. He wanted to say something, but he didn't know what. He wanted to wrap her in his arms and make everything better, but he knew that wasn't so simple. Instead, he said nothing, did nothing, just waited for her to continue if she chose.

She looked away from him, took a deep breath and swiped at her eyes with her fingertips.

The air in the basilica was still as that of a tomb, and for a long time there was no sound besides her ragged breathing. He could smell the fragrance of her hair, something slightly floral, sweet. He wondered if her skin smelled the same way. He wondered what she would do if he leaned in close and nuzzled her neck, if he took her in his arms. He wondered if he could help ease her pain, if anyone could.

Finally she turned back to look at him, shadows cupping her reddened eyes.

"It's okay," he said, his voice the slightest whisper.

She shook her head. "No. It will never be okay. I should have screamed, but I didn't make a sound. I just pretended it was my daddy who touched my hair, who looked at me like that. And early the next morning, I went into my parents' bedroom to see if they were ready to go down to the tree and see what Santa brought, and I found them. Dead."

## Chapter Twelve

The days running up to Ash and Rachel's wedding were uneventful, much to Natalie's relief. Gray moved into her cottage and slept on the sofa, and it was all she could do to keep herself from wandering out in the middle of the night to see what might happen.

Nearly every night she dreamed of lying naked on his bed, the moonlight illuminating his face as he watched her. Sometimes she touched herself in her dream, massaging her breasts and sliding her fingers between her legs. Sometimes she just lay there with splayed thighs and begged him to join her. But he never did. And every time, after she'd pleasured herself in front of him or grown exhausted from begging, every single time, he turned away from her, walked out and left her alone in the room.

She didn't need a psychology degree to figure out the meaning of that one.

She leaned close to the bathroom mirror and finished putting on her second coat of waterproof mascara. That day in the basilica, the way she'd poured out her heart to Gray, had changed things between them. But she suspected it was really her it had changed. She wanted Gray more each day. And while he did seem in tune with her and as wonderful as ever, there was a distance, too. A physical one, for sure. But also an emotional uncertainty. As if neither one of them knew what happened next and neither one was bold enough to take that step, even if they did.

She wasn't going to dwell on her impossible longings today. Nor her insecurities. Nor the threat to her life, the only reason Gray was still with her. Today was her brother's wedding, and she couldn't wait to get to the chapel they'd chosen for the ceremony and into that beautiful dress.

It was a day to celebrate love.

She found Gray waiting in the living room. Dressed in one of the most gorgeous tuxedos she'd ever seen, he looked like a movie star waiting to take a red-carpet stroll.

"You're wearing that?" she joked.

He turned a smile on her. It faded to confusion as he took in her jeans, blouse and cardigan. "Ready to go?" He glanced at his watch.

"Yup. How do I look?" She did a pirouette. She started laughing before she'd completed a three-sixty. "We're changing into our dresses at the chapel. That way they don't get wrinkled before the ceremony."

"I knew that." He gave a chuckle and stretched his arm out as if dramatically ushering her out the door. His tuxedo jacket opened with the gesture, revealing a crisp white shirt and a black holstered gun.

Natalie swallowed, her throat dry. She'd gotten used to Gray being armed, even gotten used to having a bodyguard. But somehow it was still a little sobering to see his weapon even under his festive, formal attire.

A reminder of reality.

The ride to the chapel didn't take long. As they parked outside and walked to the front steps, Natalie couldn't help thinking how lucky Ash and Rachel were to find such a lovely place in such a short time. The best wedding venues in St. Louis tended to book up a year in advance and often more. And this chapel, with its classic spire and picture-perfect front steps, was one of the most charming Natalie had ever seen.

A huge graveyard flanked the building and stretched several lots deep. But due to the many trees and amazing landscaping, it looked more like an expansive garden than a cemetery. It really was perfect. As bad as she felt for whoever the couple was who had to cancel their wedding, she was glad Ash and Rachel had the opportunity to slip into their place.

They climbed the steps and entered the front doors. Natalie led Gray through the narthex and into the nave. The first thing Natalie noticed was the beautiful yet simple stonework behind the altar. The second thing was the scent.

The flowers in the graveyard gardens outside were winding down for the winter, but the altar was blooming with breathtaking arrangements of roses and seasonal planters of chrysanthemums. Two tables behind the back pews held low boxes filled with boutonnieres and corsages ready for the family and wedding party to don when they arrived.

People were scattered throughout the chapel. A string quartet warmed up just to the right of the altar, playing scales and tuning their instruments. Aunt Angela bustled down the center aisle, adjusting pew bows. Uncle

Craig stood grimacing while the florist pinned a white rose to the lapel of his tux. A few of Ash's friends from the force stood joking in the corner and stashing bags of streamers, clattering cans and who-knew-what that Natalie assumed would soon festoon Ash's car.

"So where do you need to be?" Gray said, voice clipped and businesslike.

"The church office. Rachel and Jolie are probably already there."

"All right." He turned to lead the way.

Natalie grabbed his arm. "Wait."

He turned back to look at her.

Nearly as soon as his gaze touched hers, it darted off, circling the room, checking the perimeter. Under his tux jacket, his muscles felt hard as rock.

"You're so tense."

"This place might not be huge, but there are a lot of ingresses, egresses. I have a lot to check before the wedding starts."

"Okay. Of course, I don't want to keep you. But there's one more thing." She plucked a boutonniere from one of the boxes.

"Oh, I don't need a flower."

She pulled the pins from the tape-wrapped stems. "Actually, you do. You may be my bodyguard, but today you're also my date."

His eyes met hers, and he gave her a little smile. "Then by all means."

She didn't remember a time when she was so clumsy. After sticking her fingertips twice and Gray's chest once, she finally secured the rose.

"How does it look?"

She stepped back and took him in. The tux skimmed over his broad shoulders and muscular body like it had been tailored specifically for him, which it probably had. Add that to being a good-looking man anyway, and the complete picture put any image of red-carpet movie stars she'd ever seen to shame. She couldn't resist giving him a flirty smile. "It'll do."

He chuckled. "Probably the most I can hope for."

She tried to keep a tight rein on her own hopes. And her own tongue. "I'd better go. Where are you going to be?"

"For the ceremony? Up there." He nodded to the back of the church.

She traced his gaze up to the balcony overlooking the pews.

"Your brother also arranged for additional security at the entrances. You'll be safe."

She brought her focus back to him. She couldn't help it. Just like with her thoughts, her eyes kept returning, as if pulled by a magnet. "I never doubted it. Not with you here."

Gray looked away first. "Go ahead. I can't wait to see you walk down the aisle."

A shiver peppered her skin. The man, tux, the flowers, the music—it was all straight from her fantasies. Whatever disappointment she felt at him breaking eye contact first was wiped away by the thought of him there, watching her as she walked down the aisle.

Of course, in her fantasies, he wouldn't be standing on the back balcony. He'd be at the altar.

GRAY HAD TO ADMIT, he wasn't looking forward to the wedding, not that he'd ever confess that to Natalie or any of the other Kendalls. Not even under pain of torture.

He was happy for Ash and Rachel. But a crowded church and a set time were like neon-sign invitations to anyone who wanted to cause trouble. The only thing that made his job at all easier was the fact that a large percentage of the guests happened to be cops, and most of them happened to be armed.

He checked in with Ash and the additional security. Standing at the entrance, he greeted guests as they arrived, as if he was head usher. Three of Ash's fellow cops took it from there, seating the guests in the chapel while the string quartet played Mozart. As the time for the wedding approached, Gray left the door to the outside security and the ushers and took his place in the balcony.

One of the ushers seated Natalie's aunt and uncle, then the bride's mother, and then the minister, Ash, Devin and a couple of men Gray didn't know filed in and stood at the altar. Natalie had a third brother, but although a woman at the cable news network had promised by phone to give Thad the message he was needed at home, he had yet to show. Gray couldn't help thinking that was a bit odd, even for a world-traveling reporter like Thad, but the Kendall family had taken it in stride.

The music soared and the women started filing down the aisle.

Gray didn't recognize two of them. Of course, he knew Devin's redheaded fiancée. And then there was Natalie, her straight, blond hair shining against the deep blue of her dress.

He had to admit, her power over him was disturbing. The moment she walked in the room, his attention riveted to her, her smile, the way she moved, every detail. He wanted her to turn around and look for him. He wanted to always be the man she looked for.

He gripped the rail in front of him, steadying himself. He couldn't let himself get carried away like this. His obligation was to keep Natalie safe, not take her for his own.

He tore his eyes from her and swept the crowd. He had to focus on the people below, their behavior. Any detail could cue him to a threat. The rest he couldn't think about. He forced all of it into the background, the sound of the minister's voice, the music, the vows. But despite his best efforts, he still found his eyes lingering on Natalie.

When the minister finally pronounced Ash and Rachel as husband and wife, Gray felt exhausted. He watched the wedding party file out and then descended the steps.

He moved through the receiving line with all the other guests, shaking hands and smiling. When he reached Natalie, she took him into a polite hug and it was all he could do to keep from pulling her closer. Instead, he whispered, "good job," into the silk of her hair and moved on to shake Devin's hand. After wishing the newlyweds well, he took up position at the base of the church steps and scanned the assemblage.

Two security guards flanked the gathering crowd, the third still inside the church. The sun had started to dip behind the cityscape, and shadows stretched across the tombstones surrounding the church.

Gray eyed the happy couple, willing them to hurry it up. He hadn't liked the idea of a receiving line outdoors. But since the chapel was too small to accommodate one inside, he'd been overruled, and Ash had arranged for additional security instead. Now Gray just wanted this part of the tradition over and the Kendalls all safe in their cars, speeding toward the reception they'd planned for the evening. Maybe then he would let himself relax.

"Rose petals?" A little girl beamed up at Gray and pushed a small bag tied by a ribbon into his hand.

"Rose petals?" Gray echoed.

"To throw at the bride and groom. You know, instead of rice. Rice is bad for the birds."

"Thanks." He gave her a smile, and she scampered away to hand out more rose petals.

The receiving line broke up, and Natalie joined him at the bottom of the steps.

His smile grew. "Congratulations."

"For what?"

"For being the most beautiful bridesmaid."

"Gee thanks, but I'll bet Devin wouldn't agree."

Gray glanced at Natalie's older brother who stood arm in arm with Jolie. He could see the huge diamond on her finger from here. "She's beautiful, too. But I prefer blondes."

She smiled. "Thanks. But at a wedding, all eyes are on the bride." She looked back to her brother's new wife.

Ash and Rachel stood in the doorway of the church, poised to start down the steps to their car under a shower of rose petals.

"She's so lucky. Ash will always be there for her, and now they have a baby on the way." She drew in a shaky breath. Tears sparkled in her eyes, making them shine like emeralds. "And soon Jolie will be married to Devin, too."

"You're a romantic."

"I suppose so. I've always wanted someone just for me, you know? Someone to share things with. Someone to care for."

"Someone who will be there for you."

"Yes. Someone who will never leave."

He didn't want to tell her that love didn't mean people would never leave. He was no authority, anyway. Maybe some people did have that kind of bond. He didn't even know if he was capable. Or that someone like Natalie would even want to take a chance on him.

But he had to admit, spending all this time with Natalie, he was starting to understand the appeal. He almost had enough courage worked up to voice the thought when the first shot rang out.

# Chapter Thirteen

Natalie heard the pop of gunfire, but for a second, she couldn't get her body to react.

Screams erupted around her. Many of the guests ran, colliding into one another, some falling. Rachel dropped her bouquet and it thumped down the chapel steps. Groomsmen drew guns. Rose petals floated in the air.

Gray grabbed her by the elbow. "Natalie, move."

She stared at his face, a mask of calm. In his other hand, he held a gun.

Oh, God, this was really happening.

They'd prepared for it, planned for it. But to her, the possibility of someone shooting up her brother's wedding had never seemed real. More like a game of pretend her big brothers played as kids, with her too young to really contribute but valiantly trying to play along.

*Her family. Oh, God.*

At the top of the stairs, Ash pushed Rachel back inside the church. Natalie couldn't see where Jolie had gone or Devin or her aunt and uncle. A woman she didn't know grabbed the flower girl and raced for cover behind a hedge.

"Come on, Natalie." Gray half picked her up, half pushed her.

She forced her feet to move, willed her legs to carry her where Gray was leading.

In moments, the area around the church steps cleared. Guests continued to scream. Men barked orders. Car doors slammed and engines roared to life.

Gray pushed through the gate and pulled her into the graveyard. Still holding her elbow, his grip firm as a vise, he steered her down a cobblestone walk that flanked the church.

Natalie's pulse throbbed in her ears. Her heel sank into a space between the stones. She stumbled forward and Gray caught her.

The church's wood siding splintered a foot from her head.

Gray bit out a curse. He released her, and both of them fell to the ground.

Natalie hit the stone path. Pain slammed through her hands and knees. Her ankle turned and she felt her heel snap.

Another shot hit a nearby tree.

"Behind the tombstone. Now!" Gray crawled for the closest stone, still grasping Natalie's arm, pulling her with him.

She pointed her toe, letting her broken shoe slip off, leaving it behind. Wet grass squished under her knees. Her dress tangled around her legs. She couldn't breathe fast enough, couldn't scoop in enough oxygen to fill her hungry lungs.

They reached a patch of mud and kept crawling. A wide monument of red granite loomed ahead, spanning two or more graves. Gray pressed her up against the cold stone and covered her with his body.

She panted, trying to think, trying to breathe. The full impact of what had just happened slammed into her, making her dizzy. All the guests, some of them children. What kind of monster shot into a crowd filled with children?

"Is anyone hit? Did you see if anyone was shot?" She tried to raise her head, to look around, but she couldn't move.

Gray's chest was a solid wall behind her back. He splayed one hand on the crown of her head, preventing her from moving. "You have to keep your head down. Whoever this is, he's gunning for you, Natalie. Stay down."

Gray didn't understand. This wasn't just about her. Not this time. "He was shooting into the crowd."

"But after the crowd broke, he kept gunning for you. He knows where we crawled. He might still be watching us through his sights right now."

She moved her head in a nod. She realized that. Yes. Gray was right. She had to keep her head down. The bullet that splintered the chapel's siding was meant for her, as was the one that hit the tree. She could absorb that much. What she couldn't fathom was the fact that he'd shot into the crowd. That innocent people who couldn't possibly have anything to do with this man could have died. They could be lying on the pavement dying right now. "Did anyone get shot?" Her voice sounded strangled in her own ears.

"I didn't see anyone go down." His voice was gentler, though still commanding.

"But you don't know. I don't want anyone hurt because of me. I…"

"Listen, Natalie." He spoke into her ear, his breath warm against her cheek and neck. "I didn't see anyone get hit. But even if someone was, *you* can't do anything about it. You rush out there, and you're dead. That crowd was half made up of cops. They have the training to deal with this. They know how to handle situations like this better than you do. They'll make sure everyone's safe."

She knew he was right. "I just—"

"You just nothing. The shooter is tracking *you*. He's waiting to get an angle on *you*. If you go back to the front of the chapel, you'll be putting everyone else in danger."

A sob lodged thick in her throat. He was right. Of course, he was right. Ash and his fellow officers could handle the crowd. Anyone around her was in danger. Someone was trying to kill her. If she didn't want to truly accept that after the push into the street and the shooting at Gray's apartment, she had no choice but to accept it now.

Her heart was beating so hard, she felt dizzy and nauseous. She pulled in a shuddering breath and struggled to find some amount of calm. "What do we do next?"

"We find a way out of here."

"How?" She didn't know if panic had short-circuited her brain or what, but she couldn't seem to think. And she had no idea how they would ever get out of this.

"We wait."

"Wait?"

"He knows right where we're hiding. As soon as we move out from behind this tombstone, he'll get his shot."

So they were trapped? "Where is he?"

"As far as I can tell, he has to be somewhere in those buildings across the street. Probably an upper floor. The longer we make him wait, the better odds the police have of finding him."

Sirens screamed, the sound echoing through city streets.

"So he'll either wait and get caught or run."

She could feel Gray's nod. "That's his choice."

Everything he said made sense. At the same time, every nerve in her body was still screaming to run. She stayed still, trusting Gray.

More sirens joined the cacophony, the cavalry on its way.

"See? He can't afford to stay there much longer."

Relief trembled through Natalie's body.

Gray shuffled behind her. Before she could tell what he was doing, he draped his jacket over her bare arms and shoulders.

She realized tears were streaming down her face, but she didn't wipe them away. She just focused on the heat of Gray's body. The scent of him, so clean and masculine, wrapped around her like his embrace. "Thank you."

"For what?"

"Being here."

"I'll always be here when you need me."

As much as she longed to take his promise at face value, she knew she couldn't. He would be there while he was working as her bodyguard. But always?

"Tell you what…" He slipped his hand along her body, dug into the interior pocket of his tux jacket and pulled out his phone. Shifting so he sat slightly to the side of her, he tapped in a number and held it to his ear.

"Who are you calling?"

"Ash."

He held a one-sided conversation Natalie could only guess at, but by the time he cut off the call, she was feeling a little calmer. She waited for Gray to report what her brother had said.

"First, no one was hit."

Natalie shifted her hip against the tombstone and slumped against the cold granite. "Thank God."

"But they didn't find the shooter yet. They're still searching."

"So what do we do?"

"There's no way he's still set up in that building. By now, he's probably gone. He would have been seen. So I'm taking you out of here."

She braced her hands on the stone, ready to push herself up.

He held up a hand. "In a few seconds."

"What happens until then?"

He gestured for her to wait. Then before she realized what he was going to do, he stood up.

Natalie cried out. She caught his fingers and tried to pull him down.

He stood for a few long seconds, then crouched back beside her.

Anger swept over her, fluctuating from cold to hot. "What were you doing?"

"Testing the water."

"You were trying to draw his fire." She wanted to hit him, wanted to pound her fists against his chest. "Why did you do that?"

"To draw him out. I had to be sure he was gone, that he hadn't just changed positions before I let you move."

"You could have gotten killed."

He had the nerve to look her in the eye and nod. "Instead of you getting killed. It is my job, Natalie."

She shook her head. Her whole body trembled. She wanted to scream. She wanted to cry. "Getting killed is not your job."

"If it saves you, it is."

Tears filled her eyes, and she couldn't stop them. She didn't know if it was facing the fact that Gray could have died or that he was willing to lay down his life for her that hit her hardest. Unable to sort one feeling from another, she covered her face in her hands. Leaning against the headstone, she let the sobs sweep her away.

A LOW MIST SETTLED over the graveyard as twilight approached. Red-and-blue lights swirled outside the front of the chapel, and voices rumbled through the dim haze.

When Ash finally called with the go-ahead, Gray holstered his weapon and lifted Natalie into his arms. She circled his neck with her arms and held on, one foot dangling bare. She had stopped crying by then, but neither of them said a word.

She felt light in his arms, fragile. When he thought about how close she had come to getting hurt, not once but three times, it made him break out in a sweat. And after witnessing her fear and tears, it was obvious that the past couple of weeks had taken its toll.

He needed to take care of her, and the sooner he could get her someplace safe, the better.

Gray carried Natalie into the chapel where the Kendall family had gathered along with many of the other guests. They exchanged relieved hugs as officers took statements. Gray let her out of his sight only once, leaving her discussing plans with her aunt, uncle and brothers as he described his version of events to law enforcement.

As he returned to the nave to collect Natalie, Devin clapped him on the shoulder. "Thank you. I know I was hard on you before, but…"

Gray waved away the rest. He didn't need apologies. Not when everything Devin had ever criticized him for had been spot-on.

The moment he reentered the nave, Natalie's eyes locked on his. She looked tired, her makeup smudged from crying, her dress covered in mud. Nasty bruises marred her knees. She padded to him, feet bare. "Rachel and Ash are calling off the reception."

"Of course." He'd never considered them going ahead with the postwedding party. Not in light of what had taken place.

"We have all these rooms at the hotel. We were all going to stay there after the reception."

A hotel sounded like a good idea. But judging by the implications of Natalie's words and tone, she didn't agree. "And those plans have changed?"

"My aunt and uncle are going to stay. I don't know about my brothers. But I just want to go home. Do you think that would be a problem? Devin said he has arranged for two security guards to be posted at the estate grounds all night anyway, and Ash promised police would drive by often."

As much as he preferred the hotel idea, Gray found himself nodding. After all Natalie had been through, if she wanted to spend the night in her own bed, he was not going to deny her. "I think with three of us and police backup, you'll be the safest woman in St. Louis."

She gave him a smile.

"Do you want to go?"

"Please."

She fetched her street clothes from the church office, slipped on her sneakers and coat and said her goodbyes. Outside, two uniformed officers circled outside the cemetery fence, walking along the street where Gray's car was parked. After a few words with a lieutenant at the scene, confirming none of the guests had been seriously hurt, they were finally on their way.

Twice on the way back to the Kendall Estate, Gray noticed cars following. He turned off, taking circuitous routes. Both times, his paranoia was just that. Paranoia. By the time they wound through the gardens and spotted Natalie's house, he was pretty sure both of them were totally wrung out.

They entered the house. While she showered, he peeled off his now-ruined tuxedo and pulled on jeans and an old flannel shirt. He doubted there would be much sleep for him. What he'd told Natalie at the chapel had been true. He really didn't see any lone gunman making it past the two guards in the grounds and him. Hell, after today, the police would probably be looking over the place every ten minutes, as well. But it wasn't fear that threatened to keep him awake. It was concern for Natalie.

He'd never been good at dealing with emotions, but Natalie's crying jag in the cemetery had particularly scared him. Life-and-death stress like that was hard for special forces to take. For a civilian, it could be devastating.

He heated water and found the tea bags right where Natalie's aunt said they'd be. He'd just filled a cup and plopped in a tea bag when Natalie emerged.

She padded out of the bedroom hallway wrapped in a fluffy robe. Her hair was dry and pinned up on top of her head. Her cheeks were rosy, a nice contrast from the stark paleness of her skin earlier.

He carried the steaming cup from the kitchen and met her in the living room. "I have some tea for you."

She raised her brows. "Oh, please, tell me it's not chamomile."

"I hear it helps you sleep." The slightly dry grassy smell wafted toward him on the steam.

"You're worried about me having nightmares after today?"

He had to admit, it had crossed his mind.

She wrinkled her nose. "If I have to drink that stuff, I can guarantee nightmares."

"Don't like chamomile, eh?"

"I just don't have the nerve to break it to my aunt Angela." She crossed to bookshelves lining one wall and took a decanter down from one shelf. "How about scotch instead?"

He set the cup down. "Now you're talking."

She carried the booze to the kitchen, pulled out two

tumblers and poured two fingers in each. Then they sat on the couch and sipped their whiskey.

The heat of the alcohol seared Gray's throat and warmed his head. Slowly he felt the tension of the past two weeks unfurl from his muscles.

He couldn't afford to have more than one drink. Natalie was safe with the men outside, but he wasn't about to take any chances. Still, this was precisely what he needed. He hoped it was everything she needed, as well.

He eyed her, sitting a foot away on the couch, staring at the blank television screen. She'd been quiet since she'd poured their drinks and she had begun to worry her lower lip between her teeth.

"What are you thinking?" he said.

"Honestly?"

He nodded. He knew it could be dangerous to ask a woman that question, but he really wanted to know. And it was better she voice her concerns to him than dream about them tonight.

"I was just going over why you stood up in the grave-yard, why you risked your life like that."

"As I said, it's my job."

She shook her head, having none of it. "You say you regret your friend dying, that you feel you should have been able to save him."

The warmth in his bloodstream turned to cold and his head started to ache. When he'd asked, he'd been trying to help her. He didn't much like the spotlight to be turned on him.

Natalie watched him carefully and went on. "But that's only part of it. You wish it was you who died in

Yemen. You wish you had been killed instead of him, don't you?"

Did he? Of course, he did. Not that Natalie could understand. "You don't know—"

"Don't give me that. I could have saved my parents. One scream and they never would have died."

He nodded, remembering word for painful word each thing she'd told him days ago in the basilica. "But you were six years old. And you don't know that you could have saved them. If it was the killer who came into your room that night, he might have visited you after they were already dead."

She stared down at the tumbler in her hands. It took her a moment, but she finally looked back up into his eyes. "You couldn't have controlled your situation any more than I could. Could you?"

Could he? He didn't know. But he should have. "I should have seen the risk of the charges going off. I should have taken them myself."

"Why? Your friend was doing his job, same as you."

He shook his head. He didn't expect her to understand. "Jimbo, he had a wife."

"So that makes you worth less?"

He shook his head. She didn't understand. How could she? "I promised her I'd watch over him, that I'd bring him back to her. I always came through before. With everything in my life, I've always come through." His throat tightened. A weight bore down on his chest. "But not that day. That day, I failed."

"Have you talked to her? Since it happened?"

"Yes." He didn't want to think about the memorial service, let alone the other night outside the coffee shop.

Sherry's words were burned into his mind. He'd never forget them. Never forget the pain in her eyes. Never forget the look of betrayal and contempt.

"It didn't go well, I take it."

"You could say that."

"She blames you?" Natalie set her glass on the coffee table and folded her hands between her knees.

He wasn't sure how to explain it to her. None of it was simple. None of it was easy. "I've never had to sacrifice to get what I want, not like she and Jimbo did, even before his death."

"And that's why you think he's a better man?"

"He *was* a better man." Of that he had no doubt.

"Obviously, I didn't know him. But if you admire him that much, that says he was pretty special."

Gray nodded, and he took a sip of scotch. He didn't know what else to say. He didn't even know if his voice would function.

"I don't know Sherry, either. And I don't know what happened in Yemen. But for what it's worth, I think you're a very special man."

He shook his head and looked away. He couldn't say her statement didn't feel good. It felt better than good. But he wasn't sure he could bring himself to believe it.

She slipped her hands free and shifted closer to him. She raised her fingers to his jaw, stroking his cheek, and turned his head back to face her. "I'm not saying that to be nice. I mean it with all my heart."

Shivers fanned over his skin, starting at her fingertips and moving outward like ripples in a pond. He skimmed his knuckles down the silky blond length of her hair. He didn't know if he was ready to absorb the idea that she cared for him. He couldn't quite digest it. But the surge of feeling he had in answer was no surprise. "I appreciate the thought. Really. But no matter how special you think I am, it can't be half as special as you are."

Her lips parted. She tilted her face up to him.

He didn't know if he deserved it or believed it, all he knew was he couldn't stop himself. He brought his lips to hers.

She tasted sweet, and warmth moved through him just as it had when he'd first sipped the whiskey. He kissed her lightly, grazing her lips with his, teasing her with his tongue. Then he gathered her closer and delved deep.

She looped her arms around him. Her breasts pressed against his chest under the soft terry cloth. Her hair fell over his arms, soft as silk.

He breathed in the light floral scent of soap and something so much sweeter beneath. He skimmed his hand under her robe and touched smooth skin. The last time he'd touched her like this, he'd known it was wrong. That she didn't know the real him. That she wouldn't accept him if she'd known the truth.

Now every movement, every sensation, felt natural. As if he couldn't do anything else. As if he shouldn't even try.

She shrugged the robe from her shoulders. She was naked underneath, and in the back of his mind, he wondered if she'd hoped for this all along. Longed for it as much as he did.

He cupped her breasts in his hands and found her

nipples with his fingers. He massaged and kneaded, and suckled them with his mouth.

She arched her back, pushing into him, asking for more. A moan vibrated low in her chest, and he thought it was probably the sexiest thing he'd ever heard. When he returned his lips to hers, she clawed at his shirt, opening buttons, discarding it on the floor.

He held her skin to his and kissed her deep. He didn't know how long they kissed like that. Time seemed to blur. Thoughts seemed to fade until there was only her. Only them.

She lowered her hand to his waist and unbuttoned his jeans. The denim was tight, his erection stretching the fabric to its limit. She lowered the zipper.

He stood. This time he didn't bother to divest himself of the jeans first then the briefs. He pushed them all down his legs at once, eager to be naked, wanting to be as close to her as he could get.

He paused for a moment and just drank in the sight of her sitting on the couch naked and flushed. He'd seen her naked before, and still the beauty of her body, the perfect shape of her breasts, the trim V between those long, long legs…he was struck all over again.

She moved her own gaze over his chest, his belly and down to his cock. And when she smiled, he felt like a damn superhero.

He had no idea if he deserved this woman, but he wanted to. He wanted to make love to her at night and wake in the morning with her wrapped in his arms. He wanted to bask in her smile and make her the most important part of every day. He wanted her to be proud of him. He wanted to give her everything.

He knelt down on the carpet.

She leaned forward, and he claimed her mouth. He littered kisses down her neck and over her collarbone. He suckled her nipples and devoured her scent.

Nudging her knees apart, he slipped his body between them and fitted his mouth to her most intimate place.

She tasted fine and clean. He moved against her, thrust his tongue into her. And when her moans built until she cried out his name, he knew he had to hear more of that glorious sound.

Their night had only begun.

## *Chapter Fourteen*

When Natalie woke, she was sore. Muscles she hadn't even realized she had ached. And she knew she had Gray to thank.

He lay on his back next to her, one arm cupping her shoulder, the other cradling her to his chest. Last night, he'd made her feel things she never had before. Not just sexual pleasure, although there was plenty of that. But deeper satisfaction. He not only had a talent for protecting her, he made her feel strong all on her own.

She could stay in this bed, in his arms, all day and still not want to leave by nightfall. She nuzzled his neck, and his arms tightened around her.

"Umm, ready for more?" He peered at her through one open eye.

She giggled like a woman who was in love.

Her heart stilled. She couldn't keep a smile from spreading over her lips. A woman in love. That was what she was. As much as she hadn't wanted to admit it, deep down she'd known she was falling for Gray Scott for a long time. Maybe since they'd met. But it was only now she could let the thought fully bloom in her mind.

Last night, he'd made her feel so loved. So strong. So

secure with the world. She wanted that feeling forever. And she wanted this man in her bed for the rest of her life.

"What is that smile for?"

A jitter seated itself somewhere between her stomach and her chest. She wanted to tell him. She wanted to tell everyone she knew. She wanted to scream it to the world.

"Is it a secret?"

"I suppose." Not exactly as bold as she'd been feeling. But it was the best she could do. After she'd discovered Gray was her bodyguard, she'd planned to hold off on investing her feelings until she could see if he would leave when his job was over. Obviously after last night, his job was far from over. Also, after last night, she'd already invested her mind, heart and soul.

"Can I guess what it is?" His hazel eyes sparked green among brown, like trees sprouting in spring.

She propped herself up on one elbow. The sheet fell away from her body and exposed her bare breast.

His eyes flicked down her body. Raising his hand, he brushed her nipple with a finger until it was stiff with want.

A breath shuddered from her chest.

He grinned. "So, can I make a guess?"

She swallowed into a dry throat. In a perfect world, he would guess what she was feeling. He would swear he was falling in love with her, too. He would promise to never leave. "You can try."

He pressed his lips together and rolled them in toward his teeth. "You are thinking of what we did last night, and you're hoping I'll be up for more this morning."

She laughed. It wasn't that she wasn't thinking that. How could she not? But she was a little disappointed he hadn't professed his undying love all the same.

So much for her perfect world. Good thing this one was pretty close. "Care to try again?"

He sat up on his pillows and put his arms behind his head. His body stretched long and lean on the bed. The sheet slipped down, exposing his muscular arms, broad chest and six-pack abs.

She traced the line of his scars with her eyes, scars she'd kissed and licked last night, as if by her kiss, she could heal them. She could only hope that would be true, with time. And that he could heal hers, as well.

"Hmm." He hummed, the sound rumbling in his chest. "I got it. You want to try something totally different? Out in the garden? Swinging from a tree?"

She smiled and focused on his eyes. "Last night meant a lot to me, Gray." Her voice was barely a whisper, and she hadn't really said all she wanted to, but she still felt a jolt from exposing herself so much. A jolt, and then a surge of power.

He swallowed, his Adam's apple moving smoothly up and down. "It meant a lot to me, too, Natalie. More than you could ever know."

She leaned down and kissed him, her hair falling around them like a curtain, cutting them off from the world. They kissed for a long while. Finally Natalie sat up straight, the sheet slipping totally off her body.

Gray's gaze roamed over her breasts and down between her legs. Everywhere his eyes touched, she felt hot as fire. He circled one nipple with a finger, then trailed it down between her legs. "Is this what you had in mind?" He pushed back the sheet. He was ready for her, as hard as he had been last night.

She glanced away from him just long enough to get a glimpse of the clock. "We have to get ready for brunch."

His eyebrows shot upward. "Brunch?"

"Ash and Rachel are opening their gifts this morning."

He moved his hand between her thighs. "And we can't skip it? Or at least be a little late?"

She stifled a moan. "You still haven't guessed what I was thinking."

"Please say you weren't thinking of brunch."

She shook her head, his motions and the sensations they were causing making it difficult to speak.

"Okay, then you got me. What was it?"

"I was thinking that if we shower together, we might save a little time. And water."

His grin spread over his lips and sparkled in his eyes. "Oh, yes, I like how you think."

WATCHING NATALIE WALK buck naked to the bathroom, Gray had to smile. She was truly gorgeous, and so sexy, it made him hot all over again looking at her, not that he'd cooled yet.

Far from it.

But as hot as she was, he had to admit it was more than physical beauty with Natalie. She had a generous heart, a good soul. She made him feel stronger than he had with any other woman he'd ever known. Strong and good. Like he could do anything.

He had no earthly clue how he'd gotten so lucky. All the fortunate circumstances of his life—the affluent parents, his physical gifts, the purpose he'd found in the military—all of it paled in comparison to this woman and the fact that she cared for him.

From the bathroom, he could hear the water of the shower hiss to life.

He sat up and threw the covers back. He was ready for her still. He seemed to be ready all night. And if she'd have him, he was pretty sure he'd be ready for the rest of his life.

The doorbell chimed through the cottage.

Great. He levered himself up from the bed. So much for his hopes of joining Natalie in the shower. He strode to the living room, dug his robe out of his suitcase and threw it on. Then he strode to the front door and peered through the monitor window.

Natalie's brother Ash stood outside.

A small jolt of adrenaline spiked Gray's bloodstream. He opened the door. "I thought we were going to the hotel for brunch. And aren't you supposed to be starting your honeymoon?"

"Police work doesn't always wait for brunch. Or for honeymoons." Ash walked into the living room. He appeared to take in the surroundings casually, but Gray could see what he was doing. A once-over of the living room stalled at the couch, the couch on which no one had slept last night. He cocked his head as if listening for something, then turned back to Gray. "Natalie?"

"In the shower."

Again, he eyed Gray and the empty couch. "Sleep well?"

"Yes." Gray braced himself for the brotherly warning that was sure to follow.

But instead of launching into a protective diatribe à la Devin, Ash gave a businesslike nod. "We have pushed the brunch gift opening thing back to dinner. We have a lead."

"Something on the shooter?"

"Possibly."

"What is it?"

Ash stepped past Gray and into the room. "You might want to sit down."

Sit down? Gray shook his head. How did that make sense? Was he trying to protect his sister? Keep her from getting upset? "Natalie is in the shower. She can't hear us."

"I'm not concerned about Natalie." He shrugged. "Well, not any more concerned than usual. This morning, I'm concerned about you."

"Me?" Again he shook his head, as if rearranging the brains inside would help make sense of the detective's strange comments.

"They received this at the Kendall Communications office." He pulled out a sheet of paper and handed it to Gray.

The printout of an email. Gray skimmed the page. And as he took in the name of the sender, his gut ached as if he'd been punched.

The image of the person in the light blue sweatshirt flitted through his mind. The shooting at his apartment. The sniper at the wedding. He'd been wrong about all of it. So wrong. Natalie might have been the target, but only to get at him.

How could he have let this happen? How did he not see where the threat was coming from? How could he have been so deaf and blind?

He looked up at Ash. "Have you found her?"

"We're looking for her now."

"I can give you a list of people she knows."

Ash nodded. "That would be helpful."

He knew there was more that he had to do. More that he couldn't put off, no matter how much it hurt. "And tell Devin he needs to hire a replacement. Natalie must be protected, and I can't put her in danger anymore."

NATALIE TURNED OFF the shower and grabbed a towel from the bathroom rack. When she'd stepped under the warm spray, she'd been expecting Gray to join her. He never had. Finally now that her skin was starting to prune, she couldn't wait anymore. She needed to find out why.

She dried her body and wrapped the towel around her hair in a turban. Last night had been amazing, and to wake in Gray's arms this morning and hear him tell her last night had meant so much to him, as much as it had to her...that had been even better. There could be countless reasons he hadn't made it into the shower. A myriad of things might have come up. She needn't feel uneasy.

So why did she?

She paused at the door. It was still open a few inches, just as she'd left it when she'd jumped under the hot spray. She could detect no sounds from the master bedroom. Bracing herself, she pulled the bathroom door open wide. The bedroom was empty. Gray's clothes were gone from the floor. There was no sign of Gray ever having been there, except that the bed was made.

The tremor in her stomach had nothing to do with the fact that she hadn't had breakfast. She hurried into the closet, selected a pair of jeans and a sweater and pulled them on. She rushed back into the bathroom. After untwisting the towel, she ran a comb through her hair and left it to air-dry.

She had to find Gray.

She tried to push away the irrational fear beating at the back of her mind. He wouldn't just leave. He couldn't. Not after she'd opened her heart to him. Not after all they'd shared.

She rushed out to the living room.

Gray stood in the kitchen, a cup of coffee in his hand, staring out the window above the sink. He was wearing the same jeans he'd changed into last night, and a long-sleeved T-shirt stretched across his broad shoulders.

He hadn't left.

Natalie's knees felt shaky with relief. She pulled in a breath, trying to steady herself. She had no reason to fear. None at all. She needed to keep calm. She pushed a lilt into her tone. "Decided not to take a shower?"

He turned to face her. Lines etched his forehead and bracketed his mouth. He looked more serious and worried than Natalie had ever seen him. "Coffee?" He turned back to pour her a cup.

"What happened?" Natalie wasn't sure she wanted to know, but she forced the words out anyway. "Was someone hurt?"

"No one was hurt. It's not that." He crossed the kitchen and handed her the cup.

"Thank God." She wrapped her fingers around the warm ceramic mug and breathed in the rich scent. At least she didn't have to worry that yesterday's gunman had done something horrible to someone she loved. But as relieved as she was, she suspected she wasn't going to like whatever Gray had to say. And she had a feeling the warmth and belonging and joy she'd felt last night and this morning were at an end. "So tell me."

"Your brother Ash stopped by."

"Ash?" She could just imagine her brother finding Gray half-dressed, figuring out what had happened between her and Gray and making some kind of attempt to protect her heart. "Did he say something to you? About me? About us?"

"I think he knows I spent the night in your room last night, but no. That's not why he was here."

Her throat felt dry. She tried to swallow, but it was no use. "Then why?"

"They got a lead on the shooter."

"But that's fantastic." There had to be something he wasn't telling her, something he was hesitant to say. "Why is that not fantastic?"

"It is fantastic."

"You don't look like it is."

"It's not that this isn't a good development. I'm just…" He pulled out a piece of paper and offered it to her. "This was sent to Kendall Communications."

She took the sheet. It looked like a printout of an email. The paper rattled in her trembling hand. Scooping in a fortifying breath, she read.

Dear Kendall Communications,

I am writing to warn you about a man who is working for you. His name is Grayson Scott, and he is not only a liar, but a war criminal. He has proven selfish and dangerous in the past. He is also a murderer who brutally caused my husband's death.

If you don't fire Grayson Scott immediately, I will have no choice but to deal with him myself. And if any of you try to stop me or stand in the way, you will pay, too.

Natalie looked up from the paper and focused on Gray. The uneasy feeling she'd had when she'd first realized Gray wasn't joining her in the shower buzzed along every nerve. "Do they know who wrote it?"

"The police believe it's from Jimbo's wife. Jim Russel. The friend I told you about."

*The friend who had died in Yemen.*

She looked back down at the email and read it again, but she still couldn't make it turn out any differently than the first time. "It doesn't make a lot of sense."

"She blames me. She might want to hurt you to get back at me for Jimbo's death."

She'd gotten that much. The rest shuffled into place when she looked into Gray's eyes. "So the person who pushed me into traffic, the one who shot up your apartment, the sniper at Ash and Rachel's wedding, all those were her?"

"It looks like it, yes."

She could see where this was going. Gray was blaming himself. Just as he had blamed himself for his friend's death, he was now blaming himself for putting her and her family in danger. "She must be very troubled."

He pressed his lips into a bloodless line and said nothing.

She reached out and laid a hand on his arm. "You know this isn't your fault, either."

Circles dug under his eyes, not from lack of sleep but from stress. "You could have been killed, Natalie."

"But that's not because of you."

"Who is it because of?"

"Sherry. If she's really the one running around shooting at people, it's Sherry's fault. Sherry's actions. You're not responsible for the things she chooses to do."

He shook his head. "She hasn't been stable since Jimbo died. She's had emotional problems. A nervous breakdown. I don't know what else."

She wasn't getting through to him. That was obvious. He'd stacked up years of guilt and self-blame and an annoying habit of taking responsibility for everything and everybody. She had to find some way to get him to listen. She had last night. Maybe she could break through his walls again. "You told me I couldn't blame myself for not screaming the night my parents died."

"We've been over that, Natalie. It isn't the same." He pulled his arm away from her touch and paced the length of the living room floor. "Here your brother hired me to be your bodyguard, and yet you would have been far safer if he'd never called. By just being here, being around you, I've put you in danger."

She shook her head. She wanted to touch him, hold

him. She needed to make him see. "But you couldn't have known that."

"I should have. I saw Sherry."

"When?"

"That night we first met, I went back to the coffee shop to ask the barista about your admirer. Sherry was waiting for me outside. She threatened to make me regret breaking my promise and letting her husband sacrifice his life for me. She must have followed me, saw I was protecting you."

"That was the night my house was broken into and vandalized."

He nodded. "That was the night it all started. I was following you for weeks before that. There was no sign of any danger. That's because Sherry didn't know about your connection to me until then. I brought the danger down on you that night."

She clawed her wet hair back from her face. She had to convince him to listen, but how? She was so frustrated, she could hardly breathe. "I'm getting the feeling I could repeat that it wasn't your fault for the rest of my life, and you would never believe it."

He crossed to the bay window overlooking the cottage's front gardens.

She followed him, stopping about ten feet behind. They were quite a pair, weren't they? Both crippled. Both unable to see beyond the prisons they'd built for themselves, constructed from their own guilt and blame. "I get it. I know how you feel. And I've done the same thing with my parents' murders. But I'll make you a promise. If you at least try to let this go, I'll do the same."

He turned away from the window, grabbed his jacket from the back of the couch and put it on.

Natalie watched him, no clue what to say or do. For the first time, she noticed the couch where, except for last night, Gray had been camping out since his apartment had been shot up and he'd confessed he was her bodyguard. The pillows were neatly arranged. The blankets he'd been using were nowhere to be seen.

And the small suitcase he'd brought from his apartment was gone. "Where are you going?"

"To the police station. Ash and the rest of the P.D. are out trying to find Sherry right now. I want to be there in case they're successful."

"I'll get my coat and bag."

"No, Natalie. You need to stay here. I've asked Devin to hire another bodyguard. He just arrived."

"What?"

He motioned out the front window at a hefty hulk of a man striding up to the cottage. "If I'm Sherry's target, I need to stay away from you. That's the only way you'll be safe."

Natalie felt sick. After last night, she hadn't seen this coming. She'd really thought what she'd found with Gray was different. Maybe even permanent. Obviously it was all wishful thinking. "You're leaving."

"I'm sorry."

She could cry, she could plead with him not to go, she could grab him and kiss him and attempt to seduce him into staying. But it was no use. She felt bone tired, like she could curl up and sleep for weeks.

If he wanted to leave, he would. Nothing she could say or do would change it. "I'm sorry, too."

# *Chapter Fifteen*

The police station seemed busy for a Sunday, not that Gray visited regularly enough to know. When the officer manning the entrance ushered him into a tiny, vacant room holding a table and two chairs bolted to the floor, Gray was more relieved to be by himself than unnerved by the camera peering down at him from the corner. The room smelled like body odor mixed with some kind of minty aftershave, but at least it was quiet enough to think.

Not that he relished more time to dwell on what he'd done to Natalie.

He'd hurt her when he'd left. Hurt her so badly, he doubted she would ever be able to forgive him, even when this was over. The look of abandonment in her eyes would haunt him forever. But he couldn't change it. He'd only wanted to do his job, to keep her safe. He couldn't let his feelings for her and his selfish need to be near her interfere with her safety. He had come close enough to making that mistake already.

The sound of knuckles rapping wood came from the door behind him. As he looked up, the door swung wide and Ash stepped into the room.

Gray shot up from his chair. "Well? Did you find her?"

"Yes." Ash's face looked drawn.

A bad feeling worked its way up Gray's spine and pinched at the back of his neck. He couldn't help fearing the worst. "Is she alive?"

"Yes."

He let out the breath he'd been holding. He just wished Ash would come out with it instead of making him ask for every crumb of information. "Is she here?"

Ash raked a hand through his hair. "She's not the one trying to kill Natalie."

No, she hadn't been trying to kill Natalie. He knew that already. If anything, she had intended to hurt Natalie to get at him. But he knew what was more likely to be her endgame. "She was trying to kill me."

Ash shook his head. "No. She has a lot of resentment aimed at you. That's obvious from her email to Kendall Communications. But Sherry Russel wasn't the shooter. Not at your apartment and not at the wedding."

Gray shook his head. When Ash had showed him the email from Sherry, it had all added up. It had all made sense. He couldn't quite wrap his mind around what Ash was trying to tell him now. "Why do you think that?"

"Don't think it. Know. We found her at a mental health hospital. She's been there since the night you ran into her, the night she sent the email, the night Natalie's cottage was vandalized."

"That's not possible."

"The hospital records back it up. She's been in and out since her husband's death. She had her third nervous breakdown that night."

"Triggered by seeing me."

Ash tilted his head in acknowledgment. "Seems like it. But whatever the cause, she wasn't trying to kill Natalie. Or you. She was in the hospital during the shootings. It couldn't have been her."

Gray's head spun. He wanted to tell Ash he was wrong, but he clearly couldn't argue with hospital records.

Ash shifted his feet on the floor. "I'm sorry I dragged you into this. If I hadn't needed some background in order to find her, I wouldn't have come to you until we determined whether she was a viable suspect."

Gray waved away the apology. It hadn't been Ash's fault. It had been his own. And now that the first thing he'd done when the going had gotten tough was the one thing Natalie had feared all along, he wasn't sure where to turn.

He swallowed into a dry throat. "Do you have any other leads? Any ideas about who the shooter really is?"

"Afraid not. We followed up on what you and Natalie discovered about Demetrius Jones. He has solid alibis for the shootings, as well. But I still think you two might have been on the right track with those suspicions. The shredded paintings might very well be the detail that breaks this case."

Gray hadn't known Natalie's brother long, but the police detective had always seemed confident, maybe even to the point of being cocky. He didn't seem that way now. Something was bothering Ash, something a lot deeper than running low on leads. And Gray had a feeling he could guess what he was getting at. "You think the attacks on Natalie might be related to your parents' murders?"

Ash flinched, ever so slightly, but he didn't deny that was where his thoughts were leading.

"You're looking for…who?" He thought about what Natalie had told him had happened that night. "The real murderer?"

Again, Ash didn't answer. Not directly. "We're looking for someone older. Someone who might suspect the paintings mean Natalie is able to identify him."

"Someone who might have also committed The Christmas Eve Murders," Gray supplied, and Ash didn't correct him.

NATALIE LEANED CLOSE to the mirror. She was still trembling, making it difficult to sweep mascara on her lashes without stabbing herself in the eye. Not that an accident like that could make her eyes any more sore than they already were from crying.

She'd spent the morning trying to pull herself together. Finally she'd decided it was silly to knock around the cottage alone when she could simply show up at the hotel a little early and spend time with her family. If she could just lose herself in gift opening and wedding celebration, she wouldn't have to think about Gray leaving her.

Another surge of tears blurred her vision. How she could produce more, she didn't know. She abandoned the idea of mascara and walked to the living room.

Her bodyguard, a perfectly nice man named Chet, was watching a cable news channel on television. As she entered the room, he looked up. "Ready to go?"

She nodded and hoped she didn't look half the total mess she felt. "Whenever you are."

He pushed up from the couch. Tall and lean with plenty of muscle, Chet was the type of man Natalie was sure countless women swooned over. She half wished she could be one of them. It would be so much easier to fill the void Gray had left in her heart. Unfortunately she suspected no man would be able to do that for a long, long time. If ever.

He pulled on a dark blue jacket and held up a hand. "Let me bring the car around. I'll come back in and get you."

"You really think that's necessary? No one is really after me, as it turns out. All of this was about hurting someone else."

"My orders are to provide protection. You need to let me do my job."

She let out a sigh. Maybe she really was that hard to deal with. Obviously Devin thought so, otherwise he wouldn't have hired Gray to protect her on the sly. Now she was harassing poor Chet, when all he wanted was to do his job. "I'm sorry. It's been a tough weekend. I'll try not to take it out on you."

Chet gave her a smile that would melt most women's hearts. "Not a problem. Understandable. In this line of work, I usually see people when they aren't at their best. Now you wait. I'll come back in when I have the car ready and am sure the coast is clear."

She answered his smile the best she could. "Thanks, Chet."

He opened the front door. On the step outside, he paused. "Flip the dead bolt when I leave."

Natalie forced her eyes not to roll. Chet was doing his job and doing it well. He likely didn't know they'd already caught the shooter and now that Gray had walked out, Sherry no longer had reason to try to kill her. "Will do, Chet."

When the door closed behind him, Natalie did as he'd asked, locking the place up tight. Then, making herself pass by the couch where Gray had slept, without looking at it she wandered into the kitchen.

She took a few sips of cold coffee and cleaned up the countertops. When she'd finished, Chet still hadn't returned. She checked her watch. There was no way it would have taken him this long to get her car. She peered out the front bay window. The wind was still tossing trees and swirling dried leaves through the garden in mini tornadoes. Dark clouds scuttled across the blue sky, gathering in number. Her gaze rested on something dark between gold and white chrysanthemums and bushes of purple aster.

She shifted to one side of the window, trying to get a better look.

Natalie's heart stuttered.

The dark color was the deep blue of a jacket. And wearing that jacket, was a man. Chet. Facedown in the garden and not moving.

# *Chapter Sixteen*

Gray loaded the heavy file box into the trunk of his car and climbed behind the wheel. He closed the door, grateful to get out of the wind. The weather's dark bluster seemed to reflect the turmoil inside him. He longed to go back to Natalie's house, to beg her to forgive him, to promise he'd never leave her again. But he couldn't put her through that. Not when leaving her might possibly have been the best gift he could have given her.

He never should have mixed his personal feelings with his duty. He should have learned that lesson in Yemen. All SEALs watch each other's backs, but Natalie was right last night when she said by promising Sherry that he would be Jimbo's protector, he'd upset the balance. He'd become Jimbo's protector instead of his fellow soldier. And as a result, he'd failed everyone involved.

And now he'd done the same thing with Natalie. This morning, protecting her had meant walking away, loving her had meant staying. He'd been torn between the two, and as a result, he hadn't succeeded in accomplishing either.

At least now she had a bodyguard who had his head in the right place.

He slipped his key in the ignition and started the car. He knew what he had to do. He might not be on the Kendall payroll any longer, but that didn't mean he was going to give up protecting Natalie. And he was going to start by finding the bastard who was trying to kill her.

He'd start with the old case file Ash had let him copy. He'd hole up in his apartment and go through each interview, each report. He wasn't as good an investigator as a detective like Ash; he knew that. But maybe looking at the case with fresh eyes would help.

It certainly couldn't hurt.

He leaned forward, ready to shift the car into gear, and then paused. An uneasy feeling pinched the back of his neck. He rolled one shoulder then the other, but it did no good.

He fished in his jacket and pulled out his cell phone. He couldn't drop in on Natalie and check on her just to leave again. Not unless he wanted to prove Sherry was right about his selfishness and disregard for others. That's why, before he'd left, he'd gotten her new bodyguard's cell phone number.

He punched in the digits and held the device to his ear. Five rings later, he was switched to voice mail.

Damn.

He punched in the number again and got the same result. This time, he waited for the tone. "Chet, this is Gray Scott. I just wanted to check with you. Make sure everything's going okay and Natalie is safe. Call me back as soon as you get this. Please call. Right away." He left his number, even though Chet's phone should have a record of it, then cut the call.

He shifted into Drive and pulled out into traffic. Shoulders tight, he willed the phone to ring, for Chet to respond to his message, but the call never came. He'd driven about a mile in the direction of his apartment, when he finally gave in and turned around.

Chet Lawson might not be answering for a myriad of reasons. But that didn't mean Gray could leave a message and go on with his business. Above all, he had to know Natalie was okay.

To him, it was the only thing that mattered.

NATALIE'S HANDS SHOOK so badly, she dropped her cell phone. She picked it up off the carpet and managed to hit the numbers 911. She held it to her ear, a silent prayer racing through her mind.

Nothing.

No ringing, no dial tone, nothing—only static and the sound of her pulse drumming in her ears. She stared at the little screen. *No service.*

It couldn't be a coincidence. Someone was blocking the signal. They had to be.

Sherry?

She glanced out the window again, focusing on Chet's still form, then skimming the garden's bushes and wind-tossed trees.

She couldn't see anyone outside, but that didn't mean Sherry wasn't there. Natalie thought about yesterday, the bullet slamming into the church, just missing her head.

Was that what happened to Chet? Had he been shot? And if she stepped outside, if she made a run for it, what would stop her from being gunned down?

She moved away from the window. If Gray were here, that was the first thing he'd tell her. Stay away from windows. A thought shuddered into her mind.

If Gray were here, would he be the one lying out in the garden?

A strangled sound whimpered deep in her throat. She couldn't think that way. She had to make a plan. And in order to do that, she had to calm down.

She forced herself to breathe. In and out. In and out. She hadn't heard shots fired. She'd heard banging and other wind sounds, but no shots. Unless the sound had been suppressed in some way.

She didn't know what to do, but she didn't want to stay here and wait to die. Maybe she could risk running for it. Maybe she could get away. She didn't have to walk out the front door.

She grew up on this estate. She knew every inch of these gardens. Maybe she could go out the side door, cut through the shade and rose gardens and make it to the mansion to call for help before Sherry knew she was gone.

She grabbed her jacket. If her heart beat any harder, it would burst through her rib cage. She moved through the dinette and reached the side door. The thin, white curtain stretched over the glass inset from top to bottom, letting in light but obscuring the view. She hooked the fabric with a trembling finger and did her best to peer through the space. She could see nothing but bushes and trees tossing in the wind. The frying-pan size leaves of a hosta lily rocked back and forth like a small child soothing itself to sleep.

Here goes nothing.

She released the curtain and grabbed the doorknob. One, two, three. She scooped in a deep breath, twisted the knob and yanked.

The door didn't budge.

She yanked again. No movement.

Something crashed toward the back of the house.

A scream started to fill her throat. She choked it back along with a breath…a scent. She'd been an artist too long not to know that smell anywhere.

Paint thinner. And something else.

*Smoke.*

She pulled at the door, throwing her full weight behind the yank. No good.

"Oh, my God. Oh, my God."

It was only a smell, but it gained strength fast. She had to get out of here. She pushed away from the blocked door. Reaching the living room, she froze.

What should she do?

Sherry could still be in the front. Waiting.

As if confirming her fears, a loud crash hit the front door. Not gunfire, something heavy thrown against the house.

Then she heard the crackle. Smoke drifted through the crack under the door.

The front of her house was on fire.

She turned in the direction of the bedrooms. The smoke was building right in front of her eyes, starting as a slight haze then getting thicker, denser with each step she took.

The fire alarm in the bedroom hall shrieked to life. A few seconds later, the living room unit joined in.

She couldn't get out the front door or the side, and

if someone was in front of her house, running into the garage wouldn't get her very far, either.

The back of the house was her best bet. She could escape through the windows and disappear into the thick gardens and cove of evergreen trees.

The smoke grew thicker, building impossibly fast. She reached out a hand and dragged her fingertips along the wall to guide her way. By the time she reached her studio, her eyes stung and tears soaked her cheeks.

She twisted the knob and gave the door a shove. It flew open. A hot whoosh hit her full in the face. She threw her arms up, trying to shield her eyes.

Instead of finding a way out, she'd walked right into another raging fire.

Blinking her eyes, she tried to look for the window, for a way out. Instead, all she saw were the bright flames and curling canvases as the remaining paintings of her memories burned.

GRAY TURNED DOWN THE tree-lined street leading to the Kendall mansion and Natalie's cottage, pressing down harder on the accelerator. Something was wrong; he could feel it. Why had he wasted valuable time questioning his instincts? Why had it taken him so long to decide to check on Natalie?

He swung the wheel, shooting for the driveway of the Kendall Estate. His tires screeched. The back end fishtailed, nearly hitting the curb. By some miracle, he made the turn. He gunned the engine again, swerving down the narrow twisty road winding through the gardens.

The security guards who had been posted on the

property last night were gone today. When Gray had left, he hadn't thought that would be a problem. He'd thought that as long as he wasn't around, Natalie wasn't in danger. But that was before Ash had learned Sherry couldn't be the shooter. Now he wished those guards were here. Now he wouldn't feel comfortable unless he had an army.

The gray stone mansion peered down at him, three stories high. He drove past. No one was home, the entire family still at the hotel getting ready for their dinner and gift opening celebration. Gray prayed that was where Natalie had gone, as well. That his inability to reach Chet was due to overloaded downtown cell phone usage. But he suspected it wasn't that simple.

He continued past the pool house and followed the curving drive into the Kendall Estate's twenty acres of gardens.

A sharp pop split the air. Cracks spiderwebbed across his windshield.

His heart slammed in his chest. He'd been right. There was something wrong. Very wrong. He bit out a curse and kept driving. He couldn't see the cottage. Not yet. He had two more bends to navigate.

He swerved around the first. Borderline too fast. A second shot hit, jarring through the car. The end swung wide. The sickening crunch of metal and the shattering of glass filled his ears and rattled through his brain. He jerked forward against his seat belt, then slammed back against the seat. The car slid to a stop against the broad trunk of an old oak.

He pulled in breath after breath. He was okay. He could still move. At least nothing had hit the front end.

At least the air bag hadn't gone off and trapped him in the car for precious seconds.

He unhitched his seat belt and drew his weapon. The side of the car closest to the cover of trees and other vegetation bent inward toward him. He reached across and tried to open it anyway, but it wouldn't budge.

He'd have to take the hard way.

He grasped the driver's door latch. Drawing in a deep breath as if ready to plunge under water, he pulled. At the same time, he put his weight behind the push.

The door swung open and he went straight to the ground. Holding his pistol in front of him, he crawled on his belly.

Another shot exploded near him. A bullet pinged off the pavement a foot away.

He kept moving the way he'd been trained. He had no choice. Stop and he was dead.

He made it to the other side of the car and dived into a cluster of bushes.

Branches scratched at his face and hands. Damn. Roses. Their thorns ripped into the leather of his jacket.

He tuned out the needlelike pricks and squinted in the wind. Judging from the trajectory of the gunfire, the shooter was somewhere between the mansion and Natalie's cottage, probably on the roof of the pool house.

He pulled out his cell phone. Since he hadn't realized his hunch was correct until turning onto the road leading to the estate, he hadn't tried to reach anyone other than Chet and Natalie. Now he wished he'd called 911 right away.

He punched in the three digits. No signal.

Damn. Whoever this shooter was, he was serious

enough to have used a mobile cell phone jammer to interfere with reception. Unfortunately that meant Chet and Natalie could still be in the cottage and the jammer was preventing calls from going out and coming in.

He slipped the phone back into his pocket, wiped his sweaty right palm on his pants, then adjusted his grip on his gun. What he wouldn't give for an assault rifle about now. A 9mm Glock was nothing against the hardware this guy had. Probably the rifle he'd used to fire on the wedding and Gray's apartment.

He scanned the area, looking for areas of vegetation he could use for cover. A scent reached him, the unmistakable smell of smoke riding on the wind.

No, no, no, no.

He squinted through the gardens in the direction of the cottage. From here he could only see one corner of the little house peeking through the trees. But along the tiny snatch of roofline was a white haze.

The cottage was on fire.

He detached himself from the rosebush. Keeping low, he half ran, half crawled through the gardens. He had to reach the cottage. It didn't take much imagination to guess the gunman's plan. Jam the phone signal and smoke Natalie and Chet into the open. Shoot them when they tried to escape the fire.

He prayed he wasn't too late to stop that from happening.

He moved into a grove of evergreen trees. Here the cover was thick enough for him to risk rising to his feet. He moved into a sprint. Wind howled through the trees, the branches' sway camouflaging his dash. Reaching the edge of the trees, he hunkered down behind a hedge that bordered the patch of yard and swooping lines of garden and cobblestone patio that flanked the cottage.

He could see the smoke clearly now. Flames rose from the main entrance and licked outside the front door. Other wisps of gray seemed to be issuing from a broken pane on the side of the structure before swirling away in a squall. If he was judging the inside floor plan correctly, that set of windows belonged to the studio.

A sound came from behind him. He wasn't sure how he noticed it above the wind or why it stood out in his mind. But he'd been trained to react to threats, to depend on instinct and muscle memory.

He spun around, hands up.

A man lunged toward him, a small branch in his hands. Only about a foot and a half long and an inch in diameter, the stick didn't look like much, but Gray knew in the right hands, even a small, simple weapon like that could be deadly.

The man struck Gray across the stomach in a vicious circular motion. At the same time, he shifted his weight, putting the full force of it behind the blow.

Gray grunted, the breath whooshing from his lungs. His chin jutted forward in an involuntary movement. He brought his hands up, trying to block what he knew would come next.

Still gripping with both hands, the man jabbed upward with the end of the stick, trying to drive it into Gray's neck, trying to kill him.

Gray brought his arm around, blocking the blow. The stick's point raked the side of his hand, drawing blood.

The man recovered quickly, trying to smash Gray across the face with the end of the stick.

Pain ripped across Gray's cheekbone. He staggered back, struggling to stay on his feet.

The attacker tried for a second blow, this time going for Gray's throat. Another shot aiming to render him unconscious or dead.

Gray was ready this time. He grabbed the stick. Twisting it with his right hand, he brought his left elbow hard into the guy's temple.

The blow jarred through his arm. Still gripping the stick, he struck again, then brought his knee up.

The man angled his body to the side, blocking the attack. He released the stick and came at Gray with an uppercut to the jaw.

The strike clanged through Gray's head. He counterstruck wildly, missing the target.

The attacker landed another bash to the side of his head.

Who was this guy? He was too young to be the murderer of Natalie's parents. He was too trained to be a civilian. The only thing clear was that he was well versed in hand-to-hand combat. Gray had to end this before the guy ended him.

Gray seized the man's left arm with his right hand. Digging his fingers into the canvas jacket, he pulled downward. At the same time, he brought his right hand up, striking him under the chin with the heel of his hand. He gave a backward kick with his rigid left leg, throwing the guy to the ground.

He landed on his side, gasping for breath.

Twisting his arm behind his back, Gray flipped him to his stomach and pinned him facedown in the evergreen needles and mulch. "Who are you?"

The guy sputtered and said nothing. He turned his head to the side, breathing heavily.

Gray stared at him. That face. He'd seen that face before. Not in real life, though. In a photograph. "You're Natalie's brother."

Again, the man remained silent.

"You're the news reporter. The third oldest. The one who's been overseas." Gray searched his memory for the name. "Thad, isn't it?"

"What the hell's going on here?"

Gray wished he could answer that one. He was still trying to put it together, and with his head still ringing from Thad's blows, thinking wasn't the easiest of tasks. He wiped the side of his face. His fingers came back coated with blood. "Man, where did you learn to fight like that?"

"Let me up."

Gray wasn't sure that was a good idea. Not until he and Thad reached an understanding. "That wasn't you shooting, was it?"

"It was you."

"No. I am Natalie's...I *was* Natalie's bodyguard."

"You're Gray."

He squinted down at the man. From everything Natalie said, the family had never gotten a hold of her third brother. The most they'd been able to do was leave a message. He wasn't sure how that added up to Thad knowing his name, but for now he'd just have to chalk it up to being part of a lot of things that weren't adding up about Thad. "Yes, I'm Gray Scott."

"Let me up, Gray, or I'll go back to trying to kill you."

Gray released his arm and took his weight off Thad's back. He held out a hand to help Natalie's brother to his feet.

Thad ignored the offer. He brushed evergreen needles and other debris from his face and clothing. "Where's Natalie?"

"I don't know. Dear God, she could be in the house." His own words sounded hollow and hopeless in his ears. "I have to get in there. I have to find her and get her out."

Thad narrowed his eyes, and Gray got the feeling he was being sized up. "You special forces?"

"Former SEAL."

"Sweet."

"You?"

"Reporter."

"Bull. No reporter fights like that."

Thad looked him straight in the eye. "I'm a foreign correspondent. I know how to defend myself."

Gray still didn't quite buy it, but they had no time to argue details. It would be tough to save Natalie and take down a gunman armed with an assault rifle all on his own. But with two of them, maybe they could be successful.

*They had to be successful.*

He scanned Thad's sides, looking for the bulge of a holster. "Are you armed?"

"If I was armed, do you think I'd attack you with nothing but a twig?"

Good point. "Here." Gray pulled the Glock from his holster and handed it butt first to Thad.

"You have another?"

"No." He wished he did.

"Sure you don't want it?"

"You'll need it more."

Thad took the weapon, inspecting it as if he knew what he was doing. "How many in the clip?"

"Fifteen." There were clips that held more rounds, but they made a weapon heavy, awkward. Now Gray wished he'd accepted that trade-off. It would be nice to have twice as many bullets to work with. "Can you draw his fire? Give me a chance to get inside the house? Maybe give the neighbors enough reason to worry and call the cops?"

Thad nodded. "I'll do you one better. You save my sister, and I'll make sure the bastard comes nowhere near you."

Thad was a good fighter, but even so, Gray had his doubts. And if Thad was hurt in this, or killed…Gray shook his head. "I can't let you do that."

"What do you mean, let me? I thought we were working together in this. I don't need you to protect me. I need you to save my sister."

He was right. Gray hadn't trusted Jimbo to do his job. Instead he'd tried to watch out for him, take care of him. As if he was the only one responsible. The only one who could do his duty and everyone else's.

He'd gone to the opposite extreme with Natalie. As soon as it seemed there was a conflict, he'd abandoned her altogether and left her with another bodyguard. As if he had to be responsible for everything or nothing, everyone or no one. As if that was the choice before him.

He focused on Thad. "You sure you can handle this?"

Natalie's brother stared back. He didn't look that much like his sister. He more closely resembled his brothers Devin and Ash. But similar features or no, he had that same Kendall determination Gray had witnessed shining in Natalie's eyes. "I can handle this," he said. "Trust me."

Gray nodded. He would. He did.

"Save my little sister. Do what it takes."

"I'll lay down my life for her," Gray whispered into the wind, but Thad was already gone.

## Chapter Seventeen

Gray gave Thad a couple of seconds head start before he made his move. From here, he could hear the smoke alarms wail from inside the house. Gunfire erupted from the area near the swimming pool. Reports cracked out over the whistle of the wind, the flat pop of the pistol and the deeper, rounder timbre of the rifle.

Now.

Gray scooped in a deep breath and ran. As he emerged from cover, he half expected to hear bullets breaking the sound barrier around him, half expected to feel lead plowing into his back. He shoved the feelings aside. He had to concentrate on the mission. He had to focus on saving Natalie. And to do that, he first had to get into the cottage.

He raced across the area of lawn and vaulted low bushes and tall clusters of flowers. He came down on the patio, shoes skidding on cobblestone. Regaining his balance, he covered the rest of the distance to the side door that led into the dinette. He turned the doorknob and pushed.

It didn't budge.

He studied the frame. Long nails, like the spikes he'd found in the back of the cottage a week ago, had been driven through the wood and into the door itself. The shooter had nailed the door shut, and he'd obviously been planning this assault for some time.

Gray thought about the cottage's other entrances. He could try the front door, but he'd be exposing himself to the gunman once again, and judging from the burning pile on the front stoop, he might not be able to get in even if the door itself wasn't compromised.

He glanced along the side of the cottage. The bedroom windows were a possible entrance point, but they weren't very wide. He'd be lucky if he could squeeze his shoulders through. Same with the studio window, which was pouring smoke.

His gaze landed on a heavy wrought-iron planter at the corner of the patio. He made a step in the planter's direction.

The crack of a shot split the air. A round hit the cobblestone in front of him.

He fell back into the cover of the house.

Two pops came from deep in the gardens. Thad returning fire, drawing the shooter's attention.

Heart pounding in his ears, Gray kept low this time. Crouching forward, he ran for the planter, grabbed it at either edge and lifted. It was heavier than it looked. Although harder to lift, that should make it even more effective for his purposes.

He made it back behind the corner of the house before another shot was fired. Resting for only a second, he pulled in a deep breath and heaved the planter through the patio door's window.

Glass shattered and scattered in tiny, rounded pebbles over the patio. The scream of the smoke alarms burst out along with a haze of smoke. He grabbed the sheer curtain stretched tight over the opening and gave a yank. The light fabric ripped from its rod and flapped to the ground.

Gray scooped in one last clean breath and stepped through the opening, angling his body to slide through.

Once inside, he lowered himself to hands and knees. Smoke rose, and if he had any hopes of finding breathable air, he needed to stay as close to the floor as possible. He could only hope Natalie was doing the same.

If she was still alive.

He pushed the possibility of anything else from his mind. He wasn't even certain she was still in the house. But he needed to focus on searching every inch. He'd meant what he promised Thad. If Natalie was here, he'd find her.

Or he'd die trying.

He crawled through the dinette. Smoke burned his eyes and caused tears to run down his cheeks. He could still see, but he wasn't sure how long that would last. He needed to hurry.

He swept the kitchen with his gaze then moved on to the living area. No sign of Natalie there, either. He made for the hall leading to the other rooms. As he moved into the narrow space, the fumes grew thicker. He blinked back their sting and kept moving.

The lack of windows in the hallway combined with the thicker smoke made seeing anything difficult, if not impossible. He couldn't keep his eyes open. Even when he did, the area was so dim and gray, he had a hard time making out his hand when he held it in front of his face.

He reached out his left hand and dragged his fingertips along the wall to keep his bearings. With each scoot forward, he swung his right leg out to scrape across the floor, feeling for Natalie where he could no longer see. He coughed with every other breath, the fumes hot and foul.

He heard the sound of flame up ahead, snapping and crackling in a low background roar. If Natalie was in this part of the house, he had to find her now. Most people who died in a fire perished from the smoke. He had to hurry.

Sweat trickled down his back and neck. He shucked his jacket then kept moving. The hall had never seemed long, but navigating it blind while crawling in this awkward way seemed to take forever. The door to the studio had to be here somewhere.

Light glowed from his right, slightly orange in the gray haze. The studio. Natalie's paintings. Judging from the broken pane he'd noticed outside, whoever had done this likely tossed a Molotov cocktail through the window as well as the front door, aiming to burn the paintings and trap Natalie inside.

He swept his right foot wide, dragging his toe along the baseboard. The wall gave way to the indentation of the studio's doorway. His foot ran into something soft and solid.

*Natalie.*

He found her with his hands. He skimmed his fingers over her face. Her body was warm, but with the heat in the hallway, he wasn't sure that meant anything. He found her throat and felt for a pulse. The beat thrummed steadily against his fingertips.

She was alive. *Thank God, she was alive*.

Now he had to get her out of there so she'd stay that way.

He rolled to his side and draped her arm over his shoulder. Grabbing her wrist, he heaved her onto his back and caught her leg with his other hand.

He could feel her cough, her diaphragm moving in a spasm. She gripped his hand.

"I'm here, babe. I've got you."

"Trying to get out." She coughed several times and muttered more words he couldn't understand, ending with "…to the bedroom."

"Okay, to the bedroom. We're going to get out of this mess."

"No, the window. No, jammed." She seemed disoriented, but he understood the gist of what she was trying to say.

Probably nailed shut the way the patio door had been. He felt for the wall, trying to recalibrate his sense of direction. "Okay. I have another way out. Leave it to me. You just hold on as tight as you can."

"You hold on, too."

"You bet I will, Nat. No matter what happens, I'll never let you go."

She clung to him as he crawled along the wall. He made it out of the hall in much less time than it had taken going in, now that he didn't have to search. His knees were sore from crawling, his head ached to high heaven and his lungs felt like glowing, red cigarette ash. He hoped the fumes of the paints weren't toxic. He had no idea how long the studio had been aflame or how that might affect Natalie.

He pushed those worries to the back of his mind and kept moving. If he didn't get them out of here, he needn't concern himself with anything else.

He made it into the living room and took a turn into the dinette. The hardwood floor made his knees ache even more. Natalie gripped his hand, still coughing. Now that they were away from the fire, he could hear the rasp of each of her breaths.

They reached the patio door. Fresh air streamed through the hole. Glass crunched under his knees. Uncomfortable, but since it was tempered, it wasn't sharp. "I'm going to stand up, Nat. Hold tight."

She squeezed his hand.

He climbed to his feet. Stepping through the hole he'd bashed in the door, he angled Natalie to the side so they could both fit through.

Now he had to pray Thad had been able to what he'd promised.

He lowered Natalie to the patio, snug in the lee of the cottage. The shooter could have changed positions while he'd been in the burning structure. He had no way of knowing. He just hoped by keeping low, they could avoid being spotted.

Natalie doubled forward in a coughing spasm.

He stroked her hair and blinked his eyes, letting his tears cleanse away the smoke. Now that he could begin to see a little more in the light and fresh air, he noticed a rosy cast to her skin. The wind whipped around them, cooling his sweat-soaked shirt and chilling his skin, but Natalie's color didn't fade.

God, no.

He knew what that color meant, why she'd been on

the floor, why she'd been disoriented. Why he had a splitting headache and nausea from the short time he'd been inside.

Carbon monoxide.

Her cells were filled with it. So filled they couldn't accept oxygen. If he didn't get her medical help, she would die.

He slipped one arm under her legs, one under her back. "I'm going to take you to the hos—"

He felt the bullet hit before he heard the report.

The force of the impact shoved him forward onto Natalie. Cold sliced through his chest and spread through his body. He gasped for breath, but as hard as he strained, it wouldn't seem to come. "Nat?"

Footsteps crunched through the fall garden, slowly coming toward them.

Gray forced himself up, bracing himself into a sitting position with his hands. Still struggling to breathe, he looked down at the blood covering Natalie.

*His blood. God, let it be his blood alone.*

Pain breaking through some of the frigid cold claiming his body, he twisted to look at the shooter.

The man held his assault rifle in front of him, finger on the trigger. Brows low and mouth in a tight smile, he looked at Gray with hard eyes.

Eyes that Gray recognized. "You."

Gray should have thought of him. Maybe he should have known, but he hadn't. Whoever this guy was, he wanted to kill Natalie. He wanted to finish what he'd intended ever since that night he'd followed her from the coffee shop.

He raised the rifle to his shoulder. "Get out of the way," he said.

Gray threw his body over Natalie's. The bullet would go through both of them. He couldn't stop it. But he couldn't just give up. He had to do anything, everything, *something* to save her life.

A shot exploded in his ears.

# Chapter Eighteen

Gray never thought he'd wake up. But when he opened his eyes, Thad was pulling him up from Natalie and pushing his jacket against the wound in his chest. "Where is he?"

Thad glanced at something on the ground, something Gray couldn't see. "Dead."

Gray grabbed the jacket from Thad and propped himself into a hunched forward sitting position. The past few moments shuffled through his mind. The rifle pointing at Natalie. Covering her with his body. The shot ringing in his ears. "You were the one who fired?"

Thad nodded. He knelt down beside Natalie.

Sirens screamed from somewhere in the distance. "You found a way to call out?"

"Must have been the neighbors. Is Natalie…"

"The blood is mine. But she's in rough shape. Carbon monoxide."

Thad nodded at Gray's chest. "Looks like you're in rough shape, too."

He glanced down at himself. Blood already soaked Thad's jacket. Breathing was becoming difficult. He felt dizzy. Weak. "Only because you kicked the hell out of me earlier."

Thad gave a strained laugh.

Gray tried to laugh along, but it ended up in a series of choking coughs that felt like they were ripping his body apart.

When the coughs subsided, he glanced back at Thad. "The shooter. I recognized him."

"Who was he?"

"Name is Wade. All I know. Could be fake." He shook his head, wishing he'd realized the Romeo wannabe was really a dangerous threat from the first.

"Why was he trying to kill Natalie?"

"I have no clue."

Police cars streamed into the driveway, an ambulance behind.

Gray leaned heavily forward on his hands and struggled for breath. Then everything went black.

WHEN NATALIE WOKE IN THE hospital, her throat was more sore than it had ever been in her life, including all the times she'd had strep throat as a kid. A heart monitor beeped at her bedside. A plastic tube snaked under her nose and looped behind her ears. A medicinal smell hung in the air.

"Welcome back."

She looked in the direction of the voice and focused on a face. A face she hadn't seen for a long time. Her heart gave a little hop. "Thad," she whispered in a croaking voice.

He smiled. His blue eyes twinkled. "Am I glad to see you. You just missed Aunt Angela."

"You're home." She probably sounded stupid, stating

the obvious like that. But she could hardly believe it. It was so good to see him.

"I have been back in St. Louis for a few days now."

"A few days?" She didn't understand.

"You're in the ICU. You've been here for three days, recovering from carbon monoxide poisoning. You were on a respirator, so they kept you knocked out."

She shook her head. She didn't remember how she'd gotten here. She had no idea she'd been asleep that long.

Thad narrowed his eyes on her. "How much do you remember?"

She searched the images in her mind, the feelings. "I remember Ash and Rachel's wedding. The shooting. And the night after…" She pressed her lips together, keeping the events of that night to herself. But as soon as she recalled making love with Gray, the rest came back, too. Gray leaving her. And Chet, lying motionless in the garden. "My bodyguard, is he okay?"

"You mean Gray?"

She shook her head. "Gray? Was Gray hurt?"

Thad nodded. Holding her hand carefully so as not to disturb the IV needle in her hand, he propped one hip on the edge of her bed. "You remember the fire?"

She nodded.

"The cottage. The man who was trying to kill you started it on fire."

Shock vibrated through her. She remembered bits. The smell of smoke. The choking panic. The darkness and confusion.

"The firefighters put it out. But there was a lot of smoke damage. Gray Scott, he was the one who rescued you. He was shot in the chest."

Her breath hitched.

"It's okay," Thad said. "He's going to be all right."

She let out a shuddering breath. "And Chet?"

"He was killed. He was dead before Gray or I got there. I'm sorry."

She lay still for a long time, her brother holding her hand, gently rubbing her fingers. So much had happened she wasn't sure if she could ever get it all straight in her head. "And the man who shot Gray and Chet?"

He was quiet for a long while. Finally he said, "I took him out."

"You? How?"

Thad explained what happened, blow by blow. When he was finished, Natalie was able to connect some pieces in her mind, although most parts were still foggy. But out of all the traumatic things that had taken place, the hardest thing for her to believe was that the normal-looking guy with bad shoes was the person who'd been trying to kill her all along.

Still, she couldn't ignore it. Judging from all Thad told her, the evidence was conclusive. His fingerprints matched the ones Ash had lifted from inside the cottage after her paintings had been shredded. The over-size powder-blue sweatshirt worn by the person who'd pushed her into traffic was recovered from his apartment. And the rifle he'd used to shoot Chet and Gray matched the slugs found in Gray's apartment and outside the wedding chapel.

Natalie's head whirled. It seemed like it should all add up. It seemed like it should make sense. But try as she might, she couldn't grasp any of it. "Who *is* this Wade guy? Why would he want to kill me?"

"We don't know that yet. But believe me, all of us are working on it. Ash even postponed his honeymoon."

She knew Thad, Ash and Devin wouldn't rest until they found out the truth. She would help, too, if she could, as soon as she was well enough. "You said Gray was shot, but he's okay." Just saying the words, just thinking about Gray being hurt, made her start to tremble.

Thad nodded. "He's going to be fine. I just popped in to see him about an hour ago. He's right here in the hospital. They moved him out of ICU a couple of days ago, so I guess you could say, he's doing better than you are. When you get strong enough, I'll take you to see him."

Shivers spread over her skin. "No, that's okay."

Thad's eyebrows arched toward his closely cropped dark brown hair. "He saved your life. In fact, when Wade was about to shoot you, Gray threw himself over you. As if he thought he could shield you from the bullet."

Tears filled her eyes. The hospital whites and beiges swam in front of her, mixing until she could see nothing but a bland wash.

"You care for him, don't you?"

She didn't say anything. She couldn't.

"You love him."

A rumble of voices sounded in the hall outside. Natalie wiped her eyes just as the curtain whooshed back and Devin and Ash stepped into her ICU cubicle.

After a flurry of exclamations about her being awake and a bunch of gentle hugs, Devin focused on Thad. "Natalie loves who?" he asked.

Thad looked up at their oldest brother. "Gray Scott."

Devin frowned.

Natalie shook her head. "I don't want to talk about this."

Natalie glowered at her traitorous brother. Of course, she never could have expected Thad would stay silent on the matter of her love life, or lack thereof. All three of her brothers tended to gang up when it came to protecting her.

"Maybe we should drag him in here," said Ash. "Make him do right by our little sister."

Devin nodded. "Got any handcuffs on you?"

"Stop it, guys." Natalie had meant to throw the words at them in a joking fashion. Instead they came out on a wave of tears.

All three of her brothers stared at her with expressions of horror on their faces.

Devin hovered over her first. "I'm sorry, Natalie. Don't cry. We didn't mean to joke. You know I wasn't happy with Scott taking advantage of you in the first place. But if you love him, he should damn well be here for you. And we'll make sure he is. Better yet, we'll make sure that when he comes to visit you, he brings a diamond ring with him."

Ash nodded, joined by Thad.

Natalie closed her eyes. She knew they loved her. She knew they meant well. But they didn't understand. "Don't you dare say one word to Gray. Understand?"

She looked at her brothers in turn, waiting for each to nod, before she went on. "I don't want a man to ask me to marry him because my big brothers bully him into doing it."

She wiped her eyes with the hand not hooked up to the IV. "I'll admit it. Most of my life, I've dreamed of getting married, of having my own family, of having a man who would never leave me. But I can see how misguided that is now. How it led to me grabbing for whatever male attention I could get, just so I could get a ring, just so I wouldn't be alone."

Her throat closed. She held up a hand to keep her brothers from interrupting until she could regain her composure. "I used to want to get married for marriage's sake, I guess. Because I thought it would give me something I didn't have. But my priorities have changed. I don't want that anymore."

Thad squeezed her hand and gave her an understanding smile. "We only want the best for you, Natalie. You know that."

Her other two brothers nodded their agreement.

"I know. And the best for me is a man who wants to be with me. A man whom I don't have to worry will leave me, because he loves me so much, he doesn't want to be anywhere else." The short time she'd known Gray had taught her that. And after all she'd felt with him—even though it hadn't lasted—she wasn't going to settle for anything less from here on out. "If he loves me enough, he'll come to me. If he doesn't, he's not the one."

All her brothers beamed at her. Devin was the first to speak. "I'm so glad to hear you say that, Natalie. You deserve the best. And I hope you really do believe it, because the three of us, we always have."

GRAY'S CHEST HURT LIKE hell as he slowly climbed from his car and hobbled up to the three-story gray stone mansion, and he doubted the fact that his heart was beating faster than a damn rabbit's helped the issue. He had no idea if Natalie would agree to see him. He wouldn't blame her if she didn't. But whatever the case, he wasn't leaving until he'd had his chance to speak.

He pushed the button to the right of the grand front door. Chimes echoed through the entry hall. Before long, footsteps clicked on the marble floor inside. The door opened and Natalie's uncle Craig peered out.

"Hello, Mr. Kendall. I'm here to see Natalie." He felt as nervous as a teenager, even though his body ached like an old man's.

Craig Kendall frowned. At first, Gray thought the man would brush him off, order him to get lost. Instead, he pulled the door wide and let Gray step inside.

"Wait here," he said, and walked from the foyer.

Gray fumbled with the box in his pocket. He let his gaze skim up the split staircase, one branch leading to the east wing, one to the west. It had been almost two weeks since he and Natalie had gone off in their opposite directions. At first he had no hope of them ever coming back together. Then he knew he had to do something, that he could never go on if he didn't try to fix what he'd broken.

Now he was here to give it his all.

Natalie stepped into the foyer. Dressed in jeans and a sweatshirt, she had her hair pulled into a ponytail. She eyed him, a little wary, but boldly met him in the center of the wide marble floor. "It's good to see you."

He hoped she really meant that. "You look good. How are you feeling?"

"Pretty good. More like myself every day. And you?"

She glanced down at his chest. She couldn't see the bandages still wrapping his torso, but judging by the look on her face, she had picked up the fact that he was still less than one hundred percent.

"I'm okay. Healing."

She nodded.

He hated the fact that they were so stiff with one another, so awkward. He wanted the teasing flirtiness back, a tone that had always bloomed so naturally between them. "I miss you."

She pressed her lips together and nodded, as if she was unable to speak.

He wanted to pull her into his arms, to kiss her until all the hurts between them went away. But he realized she wasn't ready for that. He didn't know if she'd be ready for him to touch her ever again. "I'm so sorry for leaving you that day."

She nodded again.

His chest ached, but not from the gunshot wound. That pain would fade in the weeks and months ahead. He had no idea if the wounds between them could ever heal. All he knew was that he needed to tell her everything that was in his heart. That was all he could do. "I realize I screwed up. In trying to take responsibility for everything, I didn't own the one thing I needed to. The one thing that is most important. I love you, Natalie."

A slip of a whimper sounded deep in her throat.

"Duty and responsibility and doing the right thing— it doesn't mean anything to me without you in my life. I can't go through a second of the day without thinking of you. I can't sleep at night without dreaming of all the ways I screwed up. I don't know if you can forgive me or even if you want to, but I love you, Natalie Kendall. And I can't go one more day without telling you that."

She stepped toward him. "I love you, too, Gray."

His breath caught in his throat. Her words were all he wanted, all he needed.

He took her in his arms and brought his lips down to hers. Her kiss was the sweetest thing he'd ever tasted. And when he looked back into her eyes, his own vision was misty with tears. "In the fire, I promised I'd never leave you, that I'd never let you go. I meant it, Natalie. I realize I can't control the world. That I can't take care of everyone. That it isn't even my duty to try. But I want to take care of you, if you'll have me."

She nodded. A little smile touched her lips. "How about if we try taking care of each other?"

No wonder he loved her so. "Yes. That sounds right. We take care of each other for the rest of our lives."

He grabbed a deep breath and lowered himself to one knee. His bad knee was stiff and both were still bruised, but he didn't care. He'd gone through worse in combat; the least he could do was sacrifice a little comfort for love.

He reached into his pocket and pulled out the velvet box. Opening it, he held it up in one hand for Natalie to see, clutching her hand in the other. "Natalie Kendall, will you marry me?"

She pressed her lips together and frowned down at him. "Did my brothers put you up to this?"

He tilted his head. Not exactly the response he'd expected. "Your brothers? Are you kidding?"

A laugh bubbled from her lips.

He still didn't get it. Maybe she was making a joke.

"They'd probably be more eager to break my kneecaps than see me propose."

She knelt down beside him on the cold marble floor. Tears filled her eyes, making her green irises sparkle like they were made of emeralds. "Yes, Gray. I'll marry you."

He took her face in his hands and kissed her lips, her cheeks, her cute little nose. Her tears tasted salty on his tongue. Her skin smelled like heaven.

They slid down until they were both sitting on the floor in the big, formal foyer, holding each other. And Gray knew from that moment on, he would never, ever let her go.

## Epilogue

Thanksgiving at the Kendall mansion had always been something spectacular. Turkey and stuffing, cranberries and pumpkin pie. The works. They ate like gluttons, then watched the St. Louis Rams take on the Dallas Cowboys. Then after the game, they ate some more.

Natalie had been so proud to have Gray sitting at the long, festive table beside her. He held her hand under the tablecloth, twirling her ring around and around her finger. And that night, even though neither of them was yet in the best health, he stayed with her in her newly refurbished cottage.

The next day was set aside for one of Natalie's favorite holiday treats. Trimming the tree. After Thad and Ash cut a gorgeous fir, the whole family gathered in the mansion's large living room.

Aunt Angela and Jolie opened boxes of ornaments while Devin and Uncle Craig strung the lights. Rachel passed out plates of leftover wedding cake to anyone who would have some. And the rest of them waited their turn to hang their favorite ornaments, some of which they'd had since they were children.

When they were stuffed with white almond cake with chocolate mousse filling and buttercream frosting,

Gray pulled Natalie off to a quiet corner. "I know this is bad timing, but I need to talk to you about something I noticed. Something that's been bothering me for a while."

In the past, a comment like that would have sent Natalie's heart racing. She would have been certain he was going to tell her he was unhappy, announce there was nothing left for him to do but leave. But this time, she was certain none of those nightmares would play themselves out. She felt totally at ease. Totally sure of the man beside her. Concerned only that something might be causing him unease. "What is it?"

He dipped a hand into his pocket, pulled out a photograph and handed it to her.

She looked down at the picture. It was the face of the man at the coffee shop, the murderer who'd killed poor Chet and tried to kill both of them. Her heart gave a little shudder.

She glanced back up at Gray. "What about him?"

"The day of the fire, I noticed something. I kept telling myself it's not important, that it's really nothing, but I can't let it go."

"I don't understand. What?"

"Does he look familiar to you?"

She looked back at the picture. It had been taken by the police, after the man was dead. The whole idea of looking at a dead body this way was pretty creepy. The fact that the last time he'd been alive he'd tried to kill them made it even worse.

"What do you think?" Gray prompted.

"There is something that's bothered me, too." Now that Gray had brought it up, she could no longer deny the niggle at the back of her mind whenever she'd thought of the mysterious Wade. She'd been haunted by his features, too, seen his face in her dreams, and she still had no clue why. "I can't help thinking that maybe I should know him. He looks kind of familiar to me."

Gray frowned. "He looks like you."

"What?"

"Without the brown eyes. Not as pretty, obviously. Don't take this the wrong way, Natalie, but Wade, whoever he was, looks more like you than your own brothers do."

She looked back down at the picture and pressed her hands between her knees to keep them from trembling. "You really think so? What does that mean?"

"Maybe nothing." Gray slipped an arm around her and held her close. "But I think we should find out."

She didn't want to think too hard about what finding out could mean. Not until she had to. "You're thinking about a DNA test?"

"Rachel could take a swab from the inside of your cheek right now. If the crime lab is too backed up, we could take it to a private lab, have the test expedited. Maybe it will tell us who he really is. And if he's related to you, maybe that will explain why he tried to kill you."

She felt a chill work up her spine. Arm still tight around her, Gray rubbed her shoulder with his fingers.

She looked into his eyes and nodded. "I want to know the truth. And whatever it is, I know I can take it. I can handle anything with you and my family by my side."

He brought his lips to hers and gave her a gentle kiss. "And I'm never leaving."

She couldn't help but smile. "I know."

* * * * *

**He had fantasized about what they could have had**...

A lopsided snowman in the front yard. No, this would have never been his home. Ever since his parents had been murdered in their beds on Christmas Eve, Thad had never had a home, or at least he'd never let any place feel like one.

But Thad needed an angel now. As much as he needed to leave Caroline alone, he needed even more to see her face.

She wasn't the one who opened the door at his knock, though.

At first it looked as though it had swung open of its own volition, until Thad adjusted his line of vision way down to the little boy who stood in the doorway. With his dark brown hair and blue eyes, the kid was a miniature version of Thad.

*Caroline had had his son.*

First published in Great Britain 2012
by Mills & Boon, an imprint of Harlequin (UK) Limited,
Eton House, 18-24 Paradise Road, Richmond, Surrey TW9 1SR

Special thanks and acknowledgement to Lisa Childs for her contribution to the SITUATION: CHRISTMAS series.

© Harlequin Books S.A 2011

ISBN: 978 0 263 89583 4
ebook ISBN: 978 1 408 97754 5

46-1212

# DADDY BOMBSHELL

BY
LISA CHILDS

Bestselling, award-winning author **Lisa Childs** writes paranormal and contemporary romance for Mills & Boon. She lives on thirty acres in west Michigan with her husband, two daughters, a talkative Siamese and a long-haired Chihuahua who thinks she's a Rottweiler. Lisa loves hearing from readers, who can contact her through her website, www.lisachilds.com, or snail mail address, PO Box 139, Marne, MI 49435, USA.

To Melissa Jeglinski for being a wonderful, supportive friend as well as an amazing agent!

# Chapter One

His finger twitched and, as if by reflex alone, he squeezed the trigger. The gun vibrated in his hand as the bullet propelled down the barrel. He didn't miss.

*He never did....*

The body dropped facedown onto the flagstones of the patio. Blood saturated clothing and pooled on the patio beneath the body.

Thad Kendall closed the distance between them and hunched down, feeling for a pulse. Nothing flickered beneath the skin, which was already growing cold despite the heat of the fire that was burning down the cottage on the other side of the patio.

Who the hell was this person who had set fire to the cottage and killed the man near the front of the cottage—not to mention fired all those shots that Thad had barely dodged?

He drew in a deep breath of acrid smoke. Then he reached out and rolled the body over so he could see the face. His sister's distinctive green eyes, wide with shock, stared up at him.

"No!" Thad awoke with the shout and jerked upright in bed! He had already kicked off the covers, and a fine sheen of sweat covered his chest and back. The perspiration chilled him nearly as much as the dream had.

But it wasn't just a dream; it was a memory of the shooting that had happened a week ago.

A knock rapped softly against his door, but before he could clear his throat to respond, it creaked open. "You okay?" a feminine voice gently asked.

He grabbed up a T-shirt from beside the bed and dragged it over his head. "Yeah, yeah…"

Just as she hadn't hesitated before opening the door, she didn't hesitate before crossing the room and sitting on his bed. "You were yelling," she said. "Did you have a bad dream?"

Thad stared into his sister's wide green eyes, which were full of concern and—thank God—life. He hadn't shot her that night, and the man he had shot hadn't really had her eyes. His had been a flat brown color, but something about the size and shape of them—as well as the man's other features—had reminded Thad so much of Natalie that the image had haunted him ever since he'd turned the body over.

"The worst…"

She shuddered. "I know what that's like."

He snaked an arm around her shoulders. "Yes, you do."

Twenty years ago, Natalie had found their parents dead in their beds on Christmas morning, and even though she later hadn't remembered finding their bodies, nightmares had plagued her ever since their brutal murders. A man had been arrested, convicted and sentenced to two life terms, but just recently DNA evidence had proved that man's innocence.

So the real killer was still out there.

It couldn't have been the man Thad had shot. He hadn't been much older than Thad's thirty-one, so he would have been just a kid himself two decades ago. That was about all they knew for certain about the dead guy—his approximate age and that his first name had maybe been Wade.

Even though *Wade* hadn't been old enough to be the Christmas Eve Killer, as the media had dubbed their parents' murderer, Thad still wanted to learn more about the man he'd killed. Like why he'd been stalking and trying to kill Natalie....

"You used to come into my room and comfort me," she remembered with a wistful sigh.

"And now you're comforting me." He grinned at the irony.

She leaned her head on his shoulder, her blond hair tickling his cheek. He and his oldest brother, Devin, were dark haired and blue eyed like their father had been, while his brother Ash and Natalie had their mother's green eyes. Natalie had her straight blond hair, too.

But her sensitive heart was hers alone. "It's my fault you're having nightmares."

"No, it's not," he denied. She couldn't have guessed what he'd realized—he had been the first to notice the resemblance between her and her stalker.

"Yes, it is, because you had to shoot that man to save me and Gray." She lifted her head and stared up into his face. "I can't imagine how horrible that must have been for you, killing a man. That's why you're having nightmares, Thad."

If killing a man gave him nightmares, then he

wouldn't have been able to sleep for the past several years.

"Maybe you need to talk to someone," she suggested, "so that you can sleep. I bet Gray could help you." Love radiated from her at the mention of her fiancé. "He was a Navy SEAL, you know."

"I know." That was why their brother Devin had hired Grayson Scott to protect her when Natalie had first mentioned her stalker to Devin's fiancée, Jolie Carson.

"Or if you're not comfortable talking to Gray, you could talk to Ash." Ash, the second oldest of the Kendall orphans, was also former military and a detective with the St. Louis Police Department.

The oldest, Devin, had joined their uncle, who had become their guardian after their parents' murders, in running their father's communications business. Natalie, the baby at twenty-six, worked for Kendall Communications, too, as a graphic artist in the PR department. Thad was the only Kendall who had left St. Louis and hadn't come back except for very rare visits to check on his family.

Even now he wasn't back for good. Once his parents' murderer was finally brought to justice, he would leave again.

"Natalie." He squeezed her shoulders. "I don't need to talk to anyone about the shooting." But he needed to talk to someone. The DNA results had to be back by now. But instead of thinking about the crime-scene tech who was now his sister-in-law, another woman came to mind. Hell, that woman had never really left his mind once during the four years since he had seen her last.

"If you don't want to talk to anyone about the shooting, you're not going to want to leave the estate," she said with a glance toward the window. Sunlight streamed through the partially open blinds.

"Those damn reporters camped out yet?"

She giggled. "You say that like you're not one of them."

He wasn't. But only a very few people knew that. Everyone else believed he was really just an award-winning photojournalist for a cable network. "Well, I'd rather be doing the interviewing," he clarified, "than being interviewed."

"Wouldn't we all," she murmured.

Growing up a Kendall in St. Louis had been like growing up royalty. The media had recorded their lives, snapping pictures at school dances and proms and their high school graduations. And that coverage always intensified this time of year, around the anniversary of their parents' murders. Since the discovery that their killer had never been caught, the media had gone crazy trying to get the siblings' reactions. And in Thad's case, his story about the shooting his first night back in St. Louis.

"Is that why you're here and not at Gray's?" he asked. "You're hiding out?"

Her face flushed with embarrassment. "Hey, we're not married yet."

"Hasn't stopped the two of you from being joined at the hip," he teased, amused that her big brother's knowing that she stayed at her fiancé's would fluster her so much.

"Well, he's my bodyguard," she reminded him. "He's supposed to be with me 24/7."

He chuckled. "Somehow I don't think he considers that a duty of his job. He loves you."

She emitted a happy sigh. "Isn't it wonderful? Devin, Ash and I all found love—true love."

"Yeah, wonderful," he murmured sarcastically.

She pinched his arm. "You're such a cynic. I can't wait until you fall in love, brother dear. You're going to fall the hardest of all of us."

He already had. But that was just one more thing his family didn't know about him. Hell, until he'd left her *he* hadn't even known how hard he'd fallen for her. By the time he'd realized the extent of his feelings, he had been a world away from her and in too deep to get out.

Hell, he hadn't even been able to come back when his family needed him most. By the time he'd finally escaped the life that hardly anyone knew he lived, he'd almost been too late. Natalie had nearly died in the fire her stalker had set to her cottage, and her fiancé had nearly been shot to death trying to save her from that fire. The stalker had ambushed Gray as he'd carried Natalie from her burning cottage.

Thad had absolutely no regrets over killing her stalker. In the same situation, he would not have done anything differently—except for making sure he'd had the kill shot before Gray had taken a bullet for his sister. But his future brother-in-law was fine now, fully recovered. Thad was the one everyone kept looking at like he was going to fall apart. Because none of them knew about his work for the U.S. Department of State, they thought the shooting was bothering him.

What was really bothering him was the fact that his parents' murderer had never paid for his horrific crimes. Thad wanted justice.

But that wasn't all he wanted.

CAROLINE EMERSON CROOKED her neck to cradle the cordless phone between her ear and her shoulder while she folded laundry. Her best friend was given to marathon telephone calls even though they'd just seen each other that morning at church and saw each other every weekday at the elementary school where they both taught.

"You still haven't heard from him?" Tammy asked.

A hard knot tightened in Caroline's stomach, but she forced a smile into her voice. "No."

"But he's been back in St. Louis more than a week now."

And what a week it had been. His handsome face had been all over the news.

Caroline reminded her overly romantic friend, "He's been a little busy."

For once he had been making news instead of reporting it: *World famous photojournalist who spent years in war-torn countries finds most danger at home, forced to kill to protect his family.*

"I was sure he would call you," Tammy said, her voice heavy with disappointment.

"I was sure he wouldn't." But even though her head had been sensibly convinced that he wouldn't, her stupid heart had held out hope, so she was disappointed, too.

"I set the two of you up four years ago because I knew you were perfect for each other." Because Tammy had found the love of her life, she was convinced that everyone else could find the happiness she had with her husband. She didn't realize how fortunate she had been to find Steve Stehouwer—the sweet man was one in a million.

For the magical month that Thad had been home in St. Louis, Caroline had believed Tammy's matchmaking successful. But she'd had years since then that had proved how wrong her friend had been. Thad Kendall had not been perfect for her at all. But he had given her one perfect...

"He has been busy." Tammy rallied her eternal optimism. "So you should call him."

Caroline choked on her own saliva and the nerves that rushed over her. "No."

"You should have called him right after you found out you were—"

"I couldn't reach him then," Caroline interrupted, "and I doubt I'd be able to reach him now."

"I could see if Steve has a contact at the station who could get a message to him." Steve and Thad had taken a journalism class together in college; that was how Tammy had met and then proceeded to introduce Thad to Caroline.

But Steve was an anchor at a local station whereas Thad traveled the world. He'd only been home a month when they'd been going out. Between assignments, he'd explained. Somehow she hadn't thought he was talking about just photojournalism jobs.

The ever-romantic Tammy had believed he would fall in love with Caroline and stay home. And maybe, for a little while, she had let herself believe that, too.

Or at least hope. But those hopes had been dashed forever when he'd left.

As far as Caroline knew, this was the first time he had been home in nearly four years. And in all that time, he hadn't called, hadn't sent her a letter or even a text message. He had obviously forgotten all about her.

BEFORE COMING HERE, Thad had driven all around St. Louis, over the Poplar Street Bridge and under the shadow of the infamous six-hundred-thirty-story-tall Gateway Arch. Sentimentality hadn't inspired his impromptu tour of the city he hadn't seen in years, though.

He had driven all over Greater St. Louis to lose whatever reporters and whoever else might have been following him. So he was certain that his was the only car that turned onto *her* street.

Four years ago she'd lived in an apartment building, close to the elementary school where she taught second grade. She still worked at the same school, but she had moved out of the apartment into a subdivision with cul-de-sacs and a mixture of newer ranch homes and well-maintained older brick Cape Cods. Thad glanced down at the paper on which he'd scribbled her house number, but before he could locate her address, his cell rang.

The distinctive ring belonged to his boss—his *real* boss—not the executive at the network everyone else believed to be his real boss. He answered with a succinct "Kendall."

"We have a problem."

He mentally cursed. "Michaels still hasn't been found?" He shouldn't have left—not with a man missing. But if he hadn't come back when he had…he shuddered to think what would have happened to Natalie and Gray that night.

"He's been found," Agent Anya Smith replied.

His gut tightened with dread. "Not alive?"

"No. And before he died, he'd been tortured. We have no idea what he might have revealed to his captors before his death." That was what she considered the problem.

Thad considered the problem the senseless murder of a good man. "Len Michaels wouldn't have given them any information."

"He had a wife and kids he wanted to get home to," Anya warned. "He would have revealed anything if he thought it might get him back with his family."

Grief and regret tore a ragged sigh from Thad. "His wife lost her husband, his children their father," he reminded his boss.

"He should have gotten out before now," Anya said. "Being a family man made him a liability…to the rest of us."

"I don't really believe—"

She obviously didn't care what he thought, as she interrupted him to warn, "He might have given you up, Kendall."

He hadn't worked with Michaels that often. The agent had acted as a translator, and Thad's fluency with languages was too well-known for him to warrant a translator. But their last assignment had taken him to an unfamiliar territory, and so he and Michaels had worked together.

Then Anya had passed on Devin's message to Thad that he was needed back home, and he'd had to leave.

Michaels had disappeared shortly after. Guilt twisted Thad's guts. If he hadn't left, maybe Michaels would have made it home to his wife and kids.

"If he did give me up, I'm not sure that I'd blame him," he murmured.

"Kendall, don't beat yourself up about this," his supervisor advised. "I authorized your leaving. I sent in another operative...." Her voice cracked with regret, but then she cleared her throat.

"That operative obviously wasn't as good as I am," he said without conceit. It was simple fact that he'd never lost another operative or a contact.

"You're one of the best," she agreed. "You need to wrap up whatever's going on in St. Louis and get back in the field."

"Soon," he vowed.

His parents' killer had gone free for too long; justice could wait no longer.

"I need you back out there. I don't have to worry about you," she said. "You're not a liability."

"No, you don't have to worry about me," he agreed. He had no wife. No kids.

But he might have...had he not left Caroline. She was the marrying kind; he never should have called her after that first disastrous double date with her friends. But she was so damn beautiful. And it wasn't because of her summer-sky-blue eyes or her silky dark blond hair; it was the kind of beauty that radiated from the inside out. And he'd wanted to see her again and again.

And now, nearly four years after he had left her, he'd wanted to see her again. He clicked off with his boss and then looked up at her house. He didn't need to check the address—he instinctively knew it was hers.

The brick Cape Cod had a giant wreath on its oak front door. The house sat behind a white picket fence, garlands strung from each snow-topped picket. At night, lights would probably twinkle against the evergreen branches. Lights were also wrapped around the pine tree in the yard and hung like icicles from the eaves.

All the decorations had his stomach churning with his revulsion for Christmas. Caroline loved it, which was just another thing they hadn't had in common, another reason they could have never made a long-term relationship work.

He had often wondered, over the years, if he should have left her. He had fantasized over what they could have had if he'd stayed instead....

A lopsided snowman in the front yard. No, this would have never been his home. Ever since his parents had been murdered in their beds on Christmas Eve, Thad had not had a home, or at least he'd never let any place feel like one.

And Caroline was all about home and hearth. Smoke puffed out of the top of the brick chimney—her house even had a fireplace. She probably had two-point-two children by now and a loving, devoted husband who worked a boring nine-to-five job so that he could be home every night to help her with dinner and the kids' baths.

Thad respected that she had her own life now, and that was why he hadn't given in to his temptation to mine his St. Louis sources for information about her.

He'd hoped she had the life she had always wanted and deserved. He needed to just drive away and leave her alone. But instead he shut off his car and stepped out onto the snow-dusted street. Since getting Devin's message, he'd been in hell. How could his parents' killer be free?

But there'd been more, so much more that had happened to his family. His brother Ash had nearly lost his fiancée and their unborn child. Uncle Craig had nearly been framed for his own brother's and sister-in-law's murders. And Natalie, sweet Natalie, had been stalked and terrorized. His family had been through hell.

So Thad needed an angel. As much as he needed to leave her alone, he needed even more to see her face.

She wasn't the one who opened the door at his knock, though. At first it looked as though it had swung open of its own volition, until Thad adjusted his line of vision way down to the little boy who stood in the doorway. With his dark brown hair and blue eyes, the kid was a miniature version of Thad.

*Caroline had had his son.*

## *Chapter Two*

"Good luck," Tammy whispered through the open driver's window after Caroline had buckled Mark into his booster seat in the back.

"Thank you," Caroline replied. For the good-luck wishes and for picking up her son, so that the little boy wouldn't overhear the explosion that was certain to come from Thad Kendall.

Despite the cold wind that drove icy snowflakes into her face and chin-length hair, Caroline stood outside, watching Tammy's minivan drive away. And avoiding Thad.

But he deserved an explanation, which he'd already agreed to wait for until Tammy picked up Mark, so they could talk in private. She drew in a deep breath, the cold air burning her lungs, and turned back to the house. Through the big picture window, she could see Thad pacing the length of her living room—giving a wide berth around the Christmas tree as if it were a vicious dog that might attack if he got too close.

She pulled open the front door and stepped into the room with him. Warmth from the crackling fire immediately melted the snowflakes from her hair and skin so that they ran down her face like tears. Her fingers trembled as she brushed away the moisture. Despite the warmth of the room, she kept her coat on, wrapped tight around her as if she still needed the protection.

Thad didn't stop pacing. She remembered how he had never stopped moving. How had he ever managed to hold still long enough to take the poignant photos of war and tragedy that had earned him such accolades in his nearly decadelong career?

"So are you going to try to lie to me?" he asked. His voice, colder even than the winter wind, chilled her to the bone.

"Lie to you?" she repeated, the question echoing hollowly off the coffered ceiling.

"Play me for a fool, deny that that little boy is my son," he said, heat in his voice now as his blue eyes burned with anger.

Still, she shivered. "Mark is definitely your son."

"Then why did you keep that from me?" he demanded to know with an intensity that might have had Caroline taking a step back if righteous indignation wasn't pumping through her veins right now.

Except for on the news and in newspapers, she hadn't seen him in nearly four years. Her anger ignited and she lashed out, "How was I supposed to tell you? When you called me? When you wrote me? Oh, yeah, you didn't do any of those things!"

He shoved his hand through his hair, tousling the dark brown strands. "We agreed that a clean break would be easier."

"I agreed." As she'd fought back her tears and silently called herself all kinds of a fool for falling for him when he'd been clear right from the start that he had to leave again. Why hadn't she listened to him instead of Tammy and her own stupid heart? "But the clean break was your idea, so I figured you wanted nothing to do with me anymore."

"Caroline…" He reached out but pulled his hand back before touching her face. "I never led you on. I was straight with you up front."

And that was why she should have never gone out with him. But the attraction between them had been so strong—as strong as it was now, her skin tingling even though he hadn't touched her—that she hadn't been able to resist. And she really had hoped that her friend was right, that if he fell in love with her, he would stay.

But he hadn't….

"I know you had to leave," she said, and she suspected she even knew why—because it was too hard for him to stay in the city where his parents had been so brutally murdered. "But I didn't know where you were."

"You could have given a message to my brothers Devin or Ash or to my uncle Craig," he said. "They would have made sure I got it."

She laughed, but with bitterness not amusement. "I don't know your brothers or your uncle. I never met your family," she reminded him, feeling now as she had then, as if she had been some dirty secret of his. Had dating an elementary school teacher been so far beneath the status of one of the illustrious Kendalls of St. Louis that he'd been embarrassed to introduce her to his family?

"But you know who they are and how to reach them," he stubbornly persisted.

Of course she knew; everyone in St. Louis and most of the United States knew who every one of the Kendalls was.

"But your family doesn't know who *I* am," she retorted. "What reason would they have to believe that I was really carrying your child and not just trying to make a claim on the Kendall fortune?"

According to local gossip, several other women had tried to get their hands on some Kendall money albeit through his brothers and not Thad.

"My brothers or uncle would have told me that you'd come to see them—"

"When?" she interrupted. "Are you in regular contact with them? Have you even come home in the past four years?" She waited, almost hoping he hadn't so she wouldn't be disappointed that he hadn't contacted her earlier.

"I would have gotten word," he insisted, a muscle twitching along his tightly clenched jaw.

"And what would you have done?" she wondered. "Would you have come back home? Would you have given up your nomad lifestyle for diaper duty and two-a.m. feedings?"

"You did that all alone?" He glanced around the living room as if he were looking for her support system.

Her parents had moved to Arizona years ago, coming back to St. Louis for only a few weeks every summer. Except for her friends, she had no one.

She nodded in response, but she didn't want his sympathy or his guilt. "And I loved every minute of it. Mark was the easiest baby and now he's the sweetest little boy."

"I guess I will have to take your word for what kind of baby he was since I've missed out on those years," he said.

He had stopped his restless pacing and stood now in front of the portrait wall of her living room, staring wistfully at all the pictures of their son. In addition to the studio portraits she'd had taken every few months, she'd framed collages of snapshots, too. She'd recorded every special moment in his life, and hers, because she'd been there. Thad hadn't. Maybe he wouldn't have been even if he'd known. But she'd robbed him of that choice.

Now the guilt was hers. She should have tried to talk to his family so that one of them might have gotten word to him. It hadn't been fair of her to just assume that he wouldn't have wanted any involvement in his son's life just because he hadn't wanted any involvement in hers.

"But I don't intend to miss out on anything else, Caroline," Thad said, his voice low and deep as if he were issuing a threat. "I am going to be part of his life."

"For how long?" she asked. "Just long enough to break his heart when you leave again?" Just like he had broken hers.

THAD'S HEAD POUNDED, tension throbbing at his temples and at the base of his skull. Maybe it was the chemicals in his new sister-in-law's crime lab at the St. Louis Police Department that had caused the headache.

But the fumes weren't toxic or Rachel wouldn't have been working still, not in her condition. The petite brunette was very pregnant, her belly protruding through the sides of the white lab coat.

What had Caroline looked like when she was pregnant? She was taller than Rachel with more generous curves. Had she hidden her pregnancy for a while? Being a single mom might have caused her problems at the elementary school where she worked.

He hadn't asked about that. He'd been too stunned and angry to do more than yell at her. And he hadn't talked to his son at all. Knowing how close he'd been to losing his temper, he had let her call her friend to pick up the boy. Instead of talking to him while they waited, Thad had just stared at the kid and had probably scared him.

Had he scared Caroline, too? After he'd demanded a relationship with his son, she had asked him to leave, saying that she needed time to think. That had been a couple of days ago.

All he'd been doing was thinking.

"Hey, little bro!" Devin snapped his fingers in Thad's face. "You called this meeting. Down here." The CEO of Kendall Communications glanced around the sterile lab and shuddered. "What's going on?"

"I don't care," Ash murmured as he pressed a kiss against the nape of Rachel's neck, which her high ponytail left exposed. "He gave me an excuse to see my gorgeous wife."

"Get a room," Thad grumbled.

"You're just jealous," Ash teased. But he was also right.

Thad was jealous that he'd missed out on seeing Caroline like Rachel was now, glowing and beautiful in her pregnancy…with his son.

The door to the lab opened again. "I'm here," a deep voice murmured as former navy SEAL Grayson Scott joined them. "And if my fiancée asks, I was out bonding with my brothers-in-law-to-be."

"How are we bonding?" Devin asked with a grin. His eyes gleamed with curiosity and mischief. "Drinking? Working out?"

Color flushed Gray's face, and he grumbled his reply. "We're Christmas shopping."

Rachel laughed. "Now you're going to have to actually go shopping, so that you weren't really lying to Natalie."

The thought of Christmas shopping, of the music and the crowds and all the goddamn cheer, had Thad's stomach churning.

"It's better that she doesn't know why we're all together," Thad pointed out. "There is no point in upsetting Natalie until we know the truth."

Rachel nodded and was suddenly all business. "The FBI lab results came back." She stared at Thad, her hazel eyes narrowed with suspicion. "I don't know how you got the results rushed, but the DNA report is back already. It confirms my findings."

Thad hadn't needed a DNA test to prove that he was Mark's father. The little boy was him twenty-eight years ago.

"So was I right?"

Rachel studied him again. "I don't know how you knew…."

He shrugged. "I didn't know for sure. But the eyes…" He shuddered even now, thinking of how looking into the dead man's eyes had been like looking into his sister's. Only the color had been different. "So Natalie is only our half sister?"

"According to the DNA tests you all took in comparison to Natalie's samples that you had taken while she was in the hospital, and the dead man's samples I took from the morgue—" Rachel's ponytail bobbed as she nodded "—her stalker was her half brother."

"So she had a different father from all of you?" Gray asked, looking somewhat ill.

"That's the most likely scenario," Devin said with a weary sigh of resignation, as if this was merely confirmation of something he had already suspected.

He'd been older than the rest of them, sixteen, when their parents had been murdered. He remembered them best. Or perhaps, *worst*.

"We need to tell her," Gray said. After dragging in a deep breath, he added, "*I* need to tell her."

"No," Thad said with a head shake that only intensified the throbbing pain. "I'll tell her."

Gray's jaw clenched. "Any particular reason you want to be the one to tell her?"

Over the years, Thad, Devin and Ash had given Natalie's boyfriends a tough time because none of them had ever been good enough for her. Until now. Grayson Scott was a good man, but that hadn't stopped them all from being a little rough on him in the beginning. He'd had to prove to them, as well as Natalie, how much he loved her. Taking a bullet to save her life had pretty much sealed the deal for all of them.

"I'm the one who killed him," Thad offered in explanation. "I'm the reason she'll never get to know this guy."

"He didn't want to get to know her," Gray reminded him. "He wanted to kill her."

"Why?" Devin asked. "Knowing now that they're related, it makes even less sense that he was stalking her."

"Did you find out anything else from his DNA?" Ash asked his wife. "Like who the hell he is?"

She shook her head. "We already ran his prints. While they matched the ones from the break-in at my apartment, he wasn't in the system."

"So he is the guy who tried to get the DNA results from our parents' crime scene?" Devin asked. "He's the one who tried to destroy the evidence that cleared Rick Campbell?"

The petty thief had been in the wrong place at the wrong time and had done twenty years' time for someone else's crime. He never got the chance to enjoy freedom again. He'd been killed to cover up the corruption that had rushed his conviction in order to clear a high-profile case and advance a career.

Ash gave a grim nod in response to his older brother's question. Rachel had been hurt during the break-in; it was how he had learned she was pregnant since they'd broken up months earlier.

"We need to find out this guy's identity," Gray said. "I'm not even sure Wade is his real first name. It's just what he told the girl at the coffee shop Natalie goes to."

"Did you get any leads from the photograph that was released to the media?" Devin asked Ash.

Ash shook his head. "The new chief wouldn't let us release the morgue photo, and that surveillance photo from the ATM camera outside the coffee shop is too grainy for anyone to make a positive identification."

Devin turned to Thad. "Why don't you leak a better photo?"

"The chief will know where the photo came from," Rachel warned them.

"We don't need to know who this guy was," Thad said, which elicited gasps from his family.

Gray's neck snapped back in indignation. "What the hell—he tried to kill Natalie—"

"He's dead now. He's no longer a threat," Thad pointed out. "He was about my age. He couldn't have been our parents' killer."

"Our parents' killer might not be out there anymore," Ash remarked. "He could be locked up or dead. But *this guy,* Natalie's half brother, is the one who attacked Rachel to try to destroy the DNA evidence from our parents' murder—"

"Why did he do it? He couldn't have been their killer," he repeated, "so he must have been trying to protect someone."

Gray sucked in a breath. "Maybe that's why he tried to kill Natalie."

"Because she did see something that night our parents were murdered," Ash said. "Maybe the killer…"

"We don't need to know who this Wade guy was," Thad repeated, "although finding that out will help us learn what we really need to know—who his father is."

"And if he was locked up or dead, his son wouldn't have gone to the extent he had to protect him," Ash reasoned. He wrapped his arms around Rachel, as if he needed to protect her even inside the lab in the basement of the St. Louis Police Department.

Gray swore beneath his breath. "So even though that son of a bitch is dead, there's still a threat out there?"

Thad shrugged. "I don't know for sure. Rachel, we'll need you to run the DNA from the old crime scene and compare it to the stalker's DNA."

Her brow furrowed. "I don't have access to any of the original evidence anymore," she said, patting her belly. "Not even the results. I've been taken off the case because no one with any connection to a Kendall is being allowed near the case files or the evidence."

"They don't trust that we really want justice," Ash said.

"Can you talk to someone with access and have them run it?" Thad persisted.

She shook her head. "The stalker was too young to be considered a viable suspect in the old murders. They won't look at him for any connection."

"That's why the Kendalls should be running the investigation," Thad said. It was why they were going to damn well run their own.

A short while later, when Thad walked through the parking garage to his car, he knew that there was definitely a threat. He felt someone's gaze boring into his back. It could have been reporters, but he doubted it. If they'd made it past the police department parking garage attendant, then they would have been rushing him with cameras and questions. They wouldn't have just watched him.

But then why would the killer watch him? He hadn't

witnessed anything the night his parents died. He'd done nothing to save them. But he had saved lives in his real job. He'd also taken lives. Maybe Michaels had given him up. He reached beneath his jacket, but his holster was locked up, with his gun, inside his glove box. He wouldn't have gotten it past the security scanners in the police department unless he'd had Ash clear it for him. And his brother would have had too many questions about Thad having a license for a concealed weapon.

Now, as the hairs on the nape of his neck lifted with foreboding, Thad wished he'd answered those questions, so that he was armed. Keeping close to vehicles for cover, he visually scanned the garage, looking for whoever was staring at him with such intensity. Yes, there was definitely a threat still out there, and it was focused wholly on Thad.

*ONE KILLER ALWAYS RECOGNIZES another...*

Thad Kendall couldn't see him through the tinted windows of his SUV, but still Ed ducked down when the man turned toward his vehicle. How could anyone be fooled by Kendall's *cover?*

He was so much more than a bored rich kid or a globe-trotting reporter. Sure, maybe it was because of where he'd reported stories that he moved as he did— as if he had a target on his back. But when he'd felt Ed watching him, he had reached for a gun whereas a reporter's instinct would have been to grab a microphone or a camera instead. Not a weapon.

Kendall was also a damn good shot…when he was armed. But he had no gun now. No protection at all.

And he was so close. All Ed would have to do was start the engine, stomp on the gas and run him down. Ed shook with anticipation—not withdrawal. He didn't need a drink. He needed vengeance. He could almost imagine the satisfying crunch of the man's bones beneath the tires of his SUV.

It would hurt Kendall. But not enough....

The son of a bitch wouldn't feel as much pain as he had caused. So killing him wouldn't be satisfying at all—not until Thad Kendall had suffered. All Ed had to do was watch and figure out what would cause Thad the most pain.

# Chapter Three

This time Caroline opened the door to his knock. And no one was surprised, like when Mark had let Thad into their house. Then she had been on the phone with Tammy when the doorbell rang, so her son had beaten her to the door and totally disregarded the rule of not opening it unless he knew who was at it.

This time she'd known Thad was coming because she had invited him. But still her heart started beating faster at the sight of him. Fluffy snowflakes melted in his dark hair and clung to his high cheekbones and strong jaw. She stepped back to let him inside, but he hesitated, glancing over his shoulder.

She followed his gaze to the street. Was he waiting for someone? A lawyer? That was why she'd called him—because she hadn't wanted to force him to fight for his parental rights. With the full resources of the Kendall money and power, he couldn't lose.

But she could potentially lose her son. Her salary barely stretched to cover her mortgage, Mark's day care and their living expenses. She couldn't afford a lawyer, too.

Thad finally stepped inside and closed the door,

shutting out the snow and the cold and whoever he might have been looking for.

"Is Mark here?" he asked, glancing around the inside of the house like he had the outside.

Was that a habit he'd picked up from traveling to war-torn countries? He'd probably had to learn to be vigilant in order to stay alive. A lot of reporters hadn't made it back from the places Thad had been.

Caroline drew in a shaky breath. "Mark is upstairs."

"So you're not worried about him hearing us fight?" he asked with a glance toward the open stairwell.

"I'm not going to fight you."

"What does that mean?" he asked. His eyes, which were the same sapphire-blue of his son's, widened in surprise. "You're going to let me see him?"

Her stomach tightened with nerves, but she couldn't deny her son the chance to get to know his father. Given Thad's lifestyle, this could possibly be the only chance the boy would ever get. Too bad he would probably be too young to remember him. "If that's what you really want…"

"He's my son. Of course I want to see him," he replied, as if offended by her suggestion. "I've already missed so much."

"And you'll miss even more when you leave again."

He ducked his chin as if she'd taken a swing at him. But he didn't deny that he would leave. "I have a job to do."

"You don't have to leave St. Louis to be a reporter," she pointed out. "You could get a job at any station or paper in the city."

"Not *reporting* the story," he said. "In St. Louis, I would *be* the story."

"Because of the shooting."

Everyone else had been so surprised that Thad Kendall had killed a man. Everyone but Caroline. Beneath his charm and devastating grin, there was a ruthlessness that she had glimpsed the day he'd left her without even a backward glance.

He had a single-minded intensity about his job that seemed to be about more than achieving success or fame. She suspected there was much more to Thad Kendall than anyone realized.

And he was her son's father. She swallowed a sigh.

"You're not looking at me like everyone else has been," he said. He was actually the one looking at her, his gaze intent on her face.

"How's that?" She had barely let herself look at him at all, as she was determined to not let her foolish heart rule her head once again. She would not fall for Thad Kendall, no matter how damn handsome he was.

"All my family," he said, "even members of the press keep looking at me like I'm going to fall apart because I pulled the trigger and killed a man."

"I think you've had to do a lot harder things than that in your life," she admitted.

He jerked his head in a grim nod. Then he stepped closer and skimmed his fingers along her jaw. "Leaving you was one of the hardest."

She sucked in a breath as her traitorous heart slammed against her ribs. "Don't." She moved back so that his hand fell away from her face. "Just don't..."

"It's true."

"You left and never looked back," she reminded him. "I'm not looking back, either. I'm looking ahead to when you leave again and I have to explain to Mark."

"I'll explain to Mark that it's my job to go to other countries."

"Will you want to make a clean break with him, too?" She'd worried about that for the past few sleepless nights since her son had opened the door to his father. Mark had had so many questions about the stranger who'd come to their house, and he had deserved to know the truth.

"No. I'll stay in contact with him," he promised as he stepped closer again. His voice dropped to an intimate murmur. "And with you…"

His lips curved into that devastating grin. He was arrogant—he couldn't look like he did and not realize how women wanted him. And he was a Kendall, used to getting what he wanted, and apparently since he was back in St. Louis, he wanted her.

With an effort she steadied her racing pulse and shook her head. "I don't want a relationship with you."

His grin faded. "Caroline…"

"Truthfully, I don't want you to have a relationship with Mark," she said, keeping her voice low so that her son wouldn't overhear. "I'm afraid you're going to break his heart like you did mine."

He groaned. "I never meant to hurt you."

"I know," she admitted. "And you won't mean to hurt him, either. But you will."

"So what do you want me to do?" he asked. "Pretend that I never saw him? That I don't know I have a son? Do you want me to just walk away?"

That was the problem. She didn't want him to walk away. Ever. But he would. "It's what you do best."

"Damn it! You're not being fair!"

"No. I'm not," she readily agreed. But she needed to keep reminding herself that she couldn't fall for him again. She wouldn't be able to help heal her son's broken heart if she was dealing with her own.

"I didn't know how much I hurt you," he said. "I'm sorry."

She shook her head, refusing his apology. "I'm over you," she said, trying to convince them both of that. "And I intend to *stay* over you."

"If you're so over me, why haven't you moved on?" he challenged her. "Why aren't you married or involved with someone else?"

"How—how do you know that I'm not involved with someone?" she asked.

"Since finding out about Mark, I checked with some of my sources...."

Damn Tammy. "I'm focused on my son right now," she said, "not dating."

"I can't believe men haven't been beating down your door to take you out," he said.

She laughed at the outrageous compliment, refusing to be charmed again. Mark was three and a half, but she had fifteen pounds of baby weight to lose yet. Maybe twenty.

"You're beautiful," he said. "Even more beautiful now than you were four years ago."

Her stomach muscles tightened with desire, but she shook her head. "I am smarter now than I was four years ago. I'm not going to fall for your patented Kendall charm."

"Patented?"

"Already at three, Mark has it. He can wrap me completely around his little finger." Just like Thad used to be able to do.

"You're not immune to me," he said, his voice husky and his eyes bright with desire. "And I can prove it to you."

When she opened her mouth to ask him how, his lips were there covering hers. His tongue delved deep, stroking over hers, stroking her passion from flickering flame to full conflagration. He'd wrapped his arms around her, too, so that she couldn't step back. But she didn't want to get away; she wanted to get closer. His chest pressed against hers, his heart beating the same frantic rhythm as hers.

"Hey!" exclaimed a little voice, full of curiosity. "What are you doing to my mommy?"

They broke apart as guiltily as teenagers caught necking on the couch. Caroline would have laughed at the shock on Thad's flushed face if she hadn't felt more like crying. She didn't know what was bringing her closer to tears—the kiss or the fact that her son had interrupted it.

THAD'S SKIN BURNED, his fingers numb from the cold as he rolled a snowball across Caroline's front yard. He'd brought no gloves with him and Caroline's were too small. But when Mark had asked him to build another snowman to go with the lopsided one already in their front yard, Thad had been unable to refuse no matter how many excuses he'd had to do just that.

She was right. The kid had the Kendall charm but with Caroline's innate kindness and generosity.

"I can roll it," Mark said, putting his mittened hands over Thad's. "You're cold."

Maybe his skin was cold, but the rest of him was still on fire from kissing Caroline. If Mark hadn't interrupted them...

Caroline probably would have pulled away. She was over him. He'd kissed her to prove her wrong, but instead he'd proved to himself that he wasn't over her. Not even close.

He wanted more than a kiss, but she wanted nothing from him but for him to not hurt their son. He stared at the tiny, mittened hands clasping his, and his heart twisted in his chest.

"Just a li'l bigger," the boy directed. When the snowball grew to the size of a beach ball, he stopped and tried to lift it.

Thad lifted it instead, setting it atop the other two balls they'd formed into the base of the snowman. The lopsided snowman was actually a snow lady, and he and Mark had already made a snow boy. "There. It's done."

Mark shook his head. "We gotta make his face." He reached in his pocket for the things that Caroline had given him after she'd bundled him into a snowsuit, boots, mittens, scarf and hat.

She was a great mom, just as he'd known she would be. That was another reason he'd forced himself to leave her four years ago. She'd deserved more than he was capable of giving. Because of his real job, he'd never intended to be a husband or a father. He hadn't wanted to leave a family behind like Len Michaels had.

But he had left behind a son…without ever realizing he'd become a father.

"Here," Mark said, shoving a carrot into Thad's cold hand. "You're gonna have to put it on 'cuz I'm not big enough."

Thad handed back the carrot and then, his hands shaking slightly, he slid them around his son and lifted him onto his shoulders. "You're big enough now."

A giggle slipped from Mark's lips. "I'm too big now." He wrapped one arm around Thad's neck and leaned forward to reach their snowman. His tongue sticking out between his lips in concentration, he carefully arranged the carrot and a collection of colored stones to make the snowman's face, which he must have been comparing to Thad's because he kept looking back and forth between them.

"Mommy says these rocks are the same color as my eyes," he remarked. He turned toward Thad. "They're the same color as yours, too."

"You look like me when I was a little boy," Thad said.

After discovering he had a son, he'd found some of the old photo albums his aunt Angela kept in the library, and he'd flipped through the pictures of himself and his family. He hadn't looked through the albums in years because he hadn't wanted to see old pictures of his parents. Surprisingly there hadn't been as many in the albums as he'd thought there would have been. The photos had mostly been of just him and his brothers and some of Natalie.

He lifted Mark from his shoulders and then crouched down to the boy's level. "Do you know why you look like me?"

The child gave a solemn nod. "'Cuz you're my dad."

Thad sucked in a breath of surprise. "You know?" Kissing Caroline had distracted him so much that he hadn't known whether the boy actually knew who he was yet or not. Mark hadn't said anything to Thad but to wonder what he'd been doing to his mother and then to ask him to make a snowman with him.

"When I came home from Aunt Tammy and Uncle Steve's, Mommy told me who you are," he said, as if it had been no big deal for his father to finally show up after three years.

"Do you have any questions for me?" Thad said. He had a million for Mark. He wanted to learn everything about the little boy, everything that he had missed.

Mark shook his head, though, and returned his attention to the cluster of snowmen. "Look!" he exclaimed with pride. "There's a snow mommy and a snow kid and now a snow daddy."

"Wow," Thad said, trying to sound suitably impressed. This meant a lot to his son.

"We have a snow family," Mark said with a bright smile of satisfaction, as if a family was something he'd wanted for a while.

Thad stood back to admire the family, but then the sound of an idling engine drew his gaze to the street beyond the picket fence. Had the white SUV followed him again?

He suspected it had been in the parking garage the day before when he'd felt someone watching him. Then he'd thought he glimpsed it near the estate, as well. But he'd made sure he wasn't followed here, taking a circuitous route again.

And really he was probably overreacting. There were a million white SUVs. He hadn't noted the plate, so he couldn't be certain if the one he'd seen near the estate was the same one or even the same make and year as the one from the parking garage.

But he couldn't shake the uneasiness he'd felt in the parking garage, the sense of foreboding that someone was watching him with an intense hatred. He glanced toward the house and confirmed that he was being watched.

Caroline stood at the living-room window, staring intently at him. He doubted she was reliving that kiss as he had and wishing they hadn't been interrupted. He suspected instead that she was watching to make sure that he hadn't already screwed up with Mark.

She was right to worry about his parenting skills. The only parenting he'd ever really known had been when Uncle Craig and Aunt Angela became his and his brothers' and sister's guardians. But that had been a long time ago.

Where he'd been the past several years had had nothing to do with family and everything to do with survival. His own and all those he'd been able to save. He had to go back to finish his assignment and make sure Michaels's killers were brought to justice. But what kind of father could he be to Mark if he wasn't even around?

Something struck the back of his head and exploded in shards of ice that ran down his neck and inside his collar. Thad whirled around so quickly that Mark shrieked and ran from him. He'd stayed alive for years in the most dangerous places in the world but had taken one in the head from his own kid.

He grabbed up a handful of snow and gave chase.

CAROLINE GIGGLED, echoing her son's laughter that she could hear even through the double panes of glass. He'd nailed his father with that snowball. Thad threw a couple at him, careful to miss wide while stepping squarely in front of the ones that Mark threw back at him.

He had no hat, no gloves, not even a scarf, but he didn't seem to care about the cold. The only thing he seemed preoccupied with was the street, as he kept glancing back at it.

Was he expecting someone or was it just a habit for him to constantly survey his surroundings? He hadn't seen that snowball coming.

Just like she hadn't seen his kiss coming. Or maybe she had but she'd wanted it too much to push him away. If Mark hadn't interrupted them, she wouldn't have stopped Thad. Being back in his arms, kissing him, had felt too good—too right. She touched her lips, which tingled yet from the contact with his. She could taste him, too, from when he'd slid his tongue between her lips deep into her mouth.

But she'd meant what she'd told him. Not about being over him—that had been a lie that he'd easily disproved. But about not wanting a relationship with him.

He was her son's father, and that was all he would

ever be to her. Not her lover. Not her boyfriend. Not even her friend.

Because she couldn't trust him. But she wouldn't have been able to beat him, either, if she'd fought to keep him away from Mark. Now, seeing them chase each other around the yard, she was glad that she hadn't tried. She'd worked hard the past three years to be both mother and father to her son, but the little boy needed more than she had been able to give him.

He needed Thad.

And, as Thad grinned and laughed, she began to wonder if Thad didn't need Mark, too. Enough to stay?

But then he glanced to the street again, his body tensing as if he'd identified a threat. To himself or to their son?

She knew when he left St. Louis that Thad put himself in danger. But she hadn't realized until now that he could be in danger in St. Louis, as well. He had killed his sister's stalker, but maybe in doing so, he had picked up his own. Or he had brought danger back with him from one of those war-torn countries?

She'd already had her doubts, but now she was certain that Thad Kendall was more than just a photojournalist.

Whatever else he was, he was also a father now. Would he put their son in the danger that he had constantly put himself in?

# Chapter Four

Thad paced his brother's office at Kendall Communications. This was all Devin had ever wanted, to be CEO and take over the running of their father's company.

Uncle Craig might have been technically in charge ever since Joseph Kendall's murder, but the business had grown even more after Devin had joined the company. The stock each of the Kendall siblings had inherited had definitely increased in value due to Devin's initiatives.

Over the years, throughout his travels, Thad had come up with some ideas he'd love to see the company explore. While it may have been just a cover, he had become an expert on communications, some less legal than others.

Devin opened his office door but didn't see Thad yet as he continued his conversation with the red-haired secretary who was also his fiancée. "I didn't give you a chance to give me my messages," he murmured to her as he wiped her lipstick from his mouth. "Did Turner call back?"

"No," she replied. "According to his staff, he hasn't been in the office at all this week and not much in the past few months. Not since his wife died. Maybe he is ready to retire and sell the company."

Turner Connections LLC? Excitement coursed through Thad at the thought of Kendall Communications acquiring the company, which had a good number of defense contracts.

Devin snorted. "He's younger than Uncle Craig. I doubt he's ready to retire."

Jolie sighed. "So you're going to be one of those guys who never knows when to quit…."

"I thought that's what you liked about me…." He leaned forward and kissed her again.

Thad cleared his throat to make them finally aware of his presence.

Jolie pulled free of Devin's arms, her face flaming nearly as red as her hair. "I forgot to tell you Thad was waiting for you."

"Probably because the two of you were too busy making out to remember I was back here," Thad teased.

Jolie's ringing phone drew her back to the outer office. With only a wave at Thad, she closed the door, leaving him and Devin alone together. Her fiancé stared after her for a moment, as if he'd not been ready to let her go. Natalie was right that each of his siblings had found true love.

"I'm surprised you manage to get any work done around here."

"We don't have a choice." Devin pushed his hand through his hair as he made his way around his desk and dropped into the chair behind it. "It's been pretty crazy around here since September."

That was when Rick Campbell, the man behind

bars for their parents' murders, had been cleared of the crime. It hadn't been long before authorities had been looking at a new prime suspect, though.

"I can't believe that damn D.A. tried to blame Uncle Craig." Thad wished he'd been home then; he would have skewered the man in the media. Instead, his family had been smeared. One of the first things he'd noticed on his return was how much his aunt and uncle had aged since he'd been gone. He suspected most of that had happened since September.

"He's a son of a bitch," Devin bitterly murmured. "But clearing Uncle Craig hasn't ended the media circus."

"Some good things came out of the coverage," Thad reminded his older brother.

To protect Jolie's reputation and the company image, Devin had proposed a fake engagement with his secretary. But that engagement had quickly become real when his stubborn brother had finally realized the depths of his feelings for the amazing woman who'd been his friend and right hand for years.

"It would be nice if the press would give us a break for a while," Devin said, "especially with Christmas coming."

"The media coverage has always been bad around Christmastime," Thad reminded him. "And it's even worse this year."

Devin groaned. "It was going to be bad enough, given the twenty-year anniversary, but then with everything else that's happened, the reporters have been relentless."

Which was why Thad had told no one about Mark

and Caroline. He didn't want them being pulled into the media circus that was life as a Kendall. It might make Caroline change her mind about allowing Thad time with the boy, and it would no doubt frighten the child. Sure, his family wouldn't let anything slip to reporters, but they would want to meet his son and that meeting would not go unnoticed by the press.

Thad glanced at his watch; he had a meeting to go to. He couldn't believe he'd agreed to what he had. But then Mark had asked and he doubted he'd be able to deny the kid anything. It was a wonder that Caroline hadn't spoiled the little charmer rotten. But he was a great kid. And kids loved Christmas. At least kids whose parents hadn't been murdered on the holiday.

"Will you actually be here this Christmas?" Devin asked.

Thad shrugged. "Depends on when we catch our parents' killer. Finally finding the real murderer is the only way to stop the media frenzy." His body tensed with anger. "And get justice."

"Is that why you came to my office?" Devin asked. "Have you found out something new?"

"*I* did," Thad said, "when we found out that Natalie is only our half sister. But *you* didn't seem very surprised by the news." News that they hadn't shared with anyone who hadn't been at the meeting at Rachel's lab. Thad had to tell Natalie first, but not only did he dread doing that, he'd also been too busy with Mark and Caroline.

Devin leaned back in his chair and rubbed his hand over his face. He had always looked the most like their father but never more so than now. Despite the happiness he'd found with his fiancée, he looked tired and tense, as if he'd been working too hard. At the family company or at keeping family secrets?

"What do you know about that night?" Thad wondered.

"I wasn't even home," Devin reminded him, his voice gruff with guilt. "I'd snuck out."

"You were sixteen," Thad said. "You wanted to hang out with your friends like other sixteen-year-olds. None of what happened was your fault. You couldn't have prevented their deaths if you'd been home."

Knowing Devin, he probably would have gotten himself killed, as well, if he'd even heard anything at all. The master bedroom was in an entirely separate wing of the house from where the kids' bedrooms were, accessed by separate stairwells.

"We'll never know that for certain," Devin pointed out. "But Jolie's helped me deal with it so that I could finally let the past go."

Thad wouldn't be able to do that until the killer had finally been brought to justice, and he wasn't sure that even that would be enough for him. But he wouldn't know until the killer was caught. "What do you know about the past that made Natalie's paternity no surprise to you?"

Devin sighed wearily. "You're not going to let this go. Damn reporter…"

Thad grinned. "That's what I am."

His brother fixed him with a steady gaze as if trying to determine if Thad told him the truth. "Is that all you are?"

Nerves tightened his stomach, but he forced a laugh.

"You're not getting out of this." Nor was he getting the truth from Thad. At least not the whole truth. For the most part, he was a real photojournalist, reporting real stories for a real news station, but that was only a small part of what he was.

"I'm not an eleven-year-old kid, Devin. You don't need to protect me anymore. Tell me everything you know about our parents. It's the only way we're going to catch their real killer."

Devin hesitated as if determined to protect their memory.

"I don't remember that much about them," Thad said with regret and guilt. He had been eleven when they'd died; he should have had more memories of them.

What would Mark have when Thad left? At three, would he remember his father at all if, like Michaels, Thad didn't make it out of his next assignment?

"I even looked through old photo albums the other day," he said, but that had been to compare how much his son looked like he had at that age, "and they were hardly in them."

"They weren't around much," Devin admitted. "Dad was here all the time, building this company. He was so ambitious." He surveyed the office with pride in their father's accomplishments.

He needed to take pride in what he'd accomplished, too. But there was something else he'd left out. "What about Mom?" Thad asked.

"You must remember how beautiful she was?"

Thad shrugged. "I don't know if it's my memory, though, or all the news reports that have been done about her over the years. They talk about her like she was a movie star or a princess."

"She was the perfect trophy wife for a rich and powerful man like our father," Devin said. "But she craved attention and always had to be the center of it."

Thad stilled his usual restless pacing and focused on his brother. "What are you saying?"

"I'm saying that they weren't happy."

Thad remembered yelling. Screaming. Slamming doors. And he winced, realizing now what had been happening. "You were the oldest. You knew what was really going on with them."

Devin nodded. "*Affairs.* While Dad was working so hard building this company, Mom was sleeping around."

"With who?" His gut churned at the prospect that there was more than one. Finding Natalie's biological father might not be as easy as Thad had hoped.

"I don't know." Devin shrugged. "I didn't really want to know." He sighed. "Hell, I don't think our father wanted to know, either. They fought about her going out all the time, but I don't think he realized she'd actually taken it as far as she had—to a hotel one of my friends worked at. Or maybe Dad was just too proud to admit it."

"We need to find out who these men were," Thad said, although the thought of delving into their mother's affairs made him nauseous. There had been no mention of her affairs in the police report. The detectives had figured the murders were the result of a botched burglary and hadn't looked any further for motives or suspects than the man who'd spent twenty years in prison for crimes he hadn't committed.

"Do you remember the name of the hotel?"

Devin named one renowned for its discretion. "That was twenty years ago. You aren't going to find out anything now."

"I'll try." But he didn't like his chances, either.

"That's your theory here?" Devin said. "That Natalie's real dad murdered our parents?"

"Why else would his son try to destroy the evidence that cleared Rick Campbell of the crimes?" he asked. "It's a lead. About the only one we have right now."

"You've been scarce lately," Devin remarked. "Have you been chasing down leads?"

No. He'd been chasing down a squealing little boy who'd thrown snowballs at him. And kissing a woman he'd had no business kissing. After he'd forced that kiss on her, he'd been lucky she hadn't thrown him out. Instead, she'd been accommodating about Thad spending time with their son. But usually she made herself scarce, going grocery shopping or Christmas shopping while he and Mark hung out.

He would spend tonight with both of them, as if they were a real family. But that they could never be, not just because of Thad's real job but because of his real past.

HE WASN'T GOING TO SHOW. Caroline had known it the minute Mark had asked his father to meet them at the mall this Friday night to see Santa. Thad Kendall had been hunkered down, deeply embedded, in war zones. He had nearly been blown up and had almost been abducted, if there was any truth to news reports about him. But Mark asking him to visit Santa Claus was the first time Caroline had ever seen a flicker of panic in his blue eyes.

He hated Christmas. She understood why. And if she didn't have a son who loved it, she would have been more sensitive to Thad's predicament. But she hadn't made an excuse to get him off the hook with Mark. She'd waited for him to come up with his own excuse.

Instead, he'd agreed, with a grim determination, as if he really intended to show up. And maybe he would. Maybe he hadn't lied to their son.

Mark, hanging tight to her hand, glanced around the crowded mall. At his height, there was no way he could see beyond the crush of bodies in the shopping mob scene.

"Where is—" his voice grew soft with wonder "—my daddy?"

The words clutched at Caroline's heart. Daddy. Mark hadn't ever asked very many questions about his father before, probably because he'd seemed to lose interest when she'd said that the man lived in another country and he wouldn't be able to meet him. And Mark hadn't ever acted as if he'd missed having a dad. But now that he knew Thad was his father, his *daddy* was all he ever talked about.

Wishing she could still be enough for him, she crouched down to her son's level. "He's really busy, honey."

Thad hadn't specifically told her, probably because she avoided conversations with him, but she suspected that he was personally trying to find his parents' murderer.

"Something might have come up that he had to deal with," she added. A lead that he was compelled to chase down, as he had chased down so many others in his career.

"But he said he'd meet us here," Mark reminded her, his bottom lip sticking out in a slight pout. Her son never pouted; he was too sweet-natured for petulance. But, as she knew too well, Thad had a way of making a person want more than they ever had before.

"And he might come yet," Caroline said, even though she doubted Thad would show. "But the line for Santa keeps getting longer, so we better get in it before we're so far back we don't get to see him tonight."

The mall stayed open later during the holiday season, but to accommodate the entire line, it would probably have to stay open all night.

"But we're s'pose to meet my daddy by the merry-go-round."

The carousel spun around behind them, Christmas lights twinkling from it and Christmas music blaring out of its speakers. The line for Santa started near it and stretched to the North Pole at the other end of the mall.

"He'll see us," Caroline promised. It wasn't as if the line actually appeared to be moving. The Friday-night crowd of teenagers and shoppers was so thick that people were barely able to move at all. Despite the heat from the crush of bodies, Caroline shivered as an uneasy sensation overcame her.

Maybe she'd picked up Thad's unsettling habit, because she glanced around, trying to figure out what had precipitated her shudder of foreboding. Was someone watching her and Mark?

She didn't notice anyone paying her and her son any particular attention. The other mothers and parents were struggling with their impatient children. The teenagers were more interested in each other, pawing at each other's pockets or holding hands. And the shoppers were focused on trying to make their way through the crowd in order to track down the next items on their lists.

Apparently, she had just picked up Thad's paranoia. At least he had a reason to be paranoid after all those years he'd spent in war zones. The most exciting thing that had ever happened in her life was *Thad*.

Maybe that was why it had been so hard for her to get over him. So hard that, with a flash of guilt, she acknowledged that she didn't really want him to show up at the mall. The less she saw of Thad's handsome face and rock-hard muscular body, the less she had to fight the attraction to him that had only grown more powerful in his four-year absence from her life.

She was so not over him.

Mark tugged at her hand, bringing her attention back to the only man she really needed in her life: her little man. "Your phone's ringing."

The jingle bells music playing from the carousel had an echo inside her purse from her Christmas ringtone. She fumbled inside for her cell and pulled it out. The number on the ID screen was unfamiliar. Maybe Thad?

"Hello?"

She could hear no voice on the other end.

"Hello? Is anyone there?"

Static or something emanated from the phone, but the music and crowd noise drowned it out.

"I can't hear you," she said, then tugged on Mark's hand to pull him from the line. "We need to go some-place quieter, so I can hear who's on the phone," she told her son.

"I don't wanna lose my place for Santa," he said, though just a minute ago he hadn't wanted to even get in line without Thad.

"But this could be your daddy." If only she could hear....

"I'll stay right here," Mark promised.

More static emanated from the cell as someone tried to talk to her.

"Hold, please," she implored the caller. "Let me get someplace quieter."

She tugged again on her son's hand, but he resisted her efforts to move him. "Please, Mommy. I wanna see Santa."

She glanced at the line, which was hardly moving except that it was much longer now, circling around behind them. With a sigh, she let go of his hand. "Stay right there," she ordered him. "I'll just step back until I can hear."

But the music from the carousel was so loud that she had to step back a few paces before she could hear any-thing beyond jingle bells. She kept her gaze on Mark, though, where he stood between a mom holding a tod-dler and a trio of probably ten-year-olds. He looked so small. She waved at him, and he waved back.

"Hello?" she said into the phone again.

But now there was no sound, static or otherwise.

"Thad, is that you?"

The line clicked off.

She held out the phone, so that she could call back the number and find out if it had been Thad calling. Mark was going to be so disappointed if he didn't show up. Before she clicked the redial button, she glanced back toward the line for Santa.

Her pulse quickened as she didn't immediately see Mark. Had the line moved? She saw the mom with the toddler and the trio of ten-year-olds standing where they'd been. But Mark was no longer between them. Her heart slammed against her ribs as fear overtook her. Pushing people aside, she ran toward the line.

"Where did the little boy go?" she asked the woman with the toddler.

The lady glanced down as if just realizing that he was gone. "He's not with you?"

Tears stinging her eyes, Caroline shook her head. She grabbed the shoulder of one of the older kids. "Did you see my son?"

The kid stared up at her.

"The little boy who was standing behind you in line," she clarified.

The kid glanced back and shrugged. "I didn't notice him."

She turned to his friends. "Did either of you see where he went?"

Both kids stared at her like she was crazy and then finally shook their heads.

*Where had he gone?*

Fear choking her, she could barely manage to whisper his name. "Mark…" Then she gathered her courage and yelled, "Mark!"

The music from the carousel drowned out her voice.

"Mark!" She pushed through the crowd, frantically searching for him.

Had Thad shown up and taken off with him somewhere? Even though she would be furious with him, she hoped to God that was the case. The Christmas mob was so large that she struggled to push through, let alone find a security guard. She needed to find the information desk. She needed to get help finding her son.

"Mark!" Strong arms grasped her shoulders and spun her around.

"Caroline, what's wrong?"

Relief shuddered through her at the sight of Thad's handsome face, his blue eyes full of concern. "Thank God you're here."

She glanced down, but no little boy stood happily at his daddy's side.

"I'm sorry I'm late," he said.

Panic chased away her momentarily relief. "Where is he?"

"Who?" Thad looked around her, and then his brow furrowed as he realized exactly who was missing.

"Mark," she said, her voice breaking on a sob.

The color drained from his handsome face. "He's not with you...."

"No," she admitted, her voice rising with hysteria "He's gone."

She had spent those sleepless nights worrying about allowing Thad a relationship with their son. She'd been concerned that he would fail as a parent and hurt her sweet baby boy.

But she was the one who'd failed as a parent; she was the one who'd lost their son.

"He's gone…."

His father hadn't taken him.

So who had?

*Chapter Five*

"I thought it was you on the phone, but I couldn't hear," Caroline said, her voice shaking with fear. "So I backed away from the noise of the carousel. But I kept my eyes on him."

She stared at Thad with eyes that were wide and wet with terror. "I could see him at all times. I only glanced down at the phone for a second. And then he was just…" A sob slipped out of her lips. "Gone."

Thad wrapped his arm around her, holding her close to his side as she relayed the information to him and the security guards he had summoned to search the mall for the missing child.

"We'll find him," he assured her.

Thad had convinced the head of security to lockdown the mall so that no one could leave. Mobs had formed at the doors, protesting the imprisonment. He only hoped it wasn't too late.

"How long ago did you lose sight of him?" he asked. Long enough that someone could have taken their son outside already?

Despite the watch on her wrist, Caroline grabbed

her phone from her purse. "Just minutes after the time this call came in."

Thad took the phone from her and noted the time. Because of the throng of shoppers, he had struggled to get through the mall at more than a snail's pace. That was why it had taken him so long to find Caroline— that and his reluctance to even step inside a mall full of Christmas decorations and music.

Guilt and anger at himself gripped him. If only he hadn't acted like such a fool.

His emotions must have shown on his face, because Caroline reassured him now. "We'll find him."

"Whose number is this?" he asked.

She shook her head. "I don't know. I couldn't hear who was talking. I thought it was you, calling to say you weren't going to make it."

He nodded. She'd already said that she hadn't thought he was going to come. When he had promised Mark that he would, he had seen the doubt on her beautiful face. She had thought then that he was lying to their son.

"Was Mark upset that I wasn't here?" he asked, worried that the boy had thrown a tantrum because Thad had been late.

"No."

Now he suspected she was lying.

"He was really anxious that he might not get to see Santa. That's why he didn't want to move out of line when I got the call." Tears streaked down her face. "I never took my eyes off him but for that one second...."

A second was all it took for a bomb to destroy an

entire village. He had seen it too many times, but he couldn't share that horror with Caroline.

"Has the St. Louis Police Department been called?" Thad asked the head security guard. He was in his fifties with a buzz cut and ex-military demeanor. Despite the fact that the boy might have just wandered off, the man had still sent his guards off with urgency to look everywhere for Mark. "My brother is Detective Ash Kendall—"

"You're Thad Kendall, the reporter," the head guard, Ron Thurston, interrupted. "I've seen you on the news." He probably wasn't talking about Thad's special reports on ZNN but rather the local reports about the shooting and the Christmas Eve Murders.

"Do you think the police need to be called?" Caroline asked, her face turning stark white as horror widened her tear-reddened eyes. "Do you think someone has kidnapped him?"

"We need to find him as soon as possible," Thad explained.

She blinked as if to dry her eyes and stared hard at him. "You didn't answer my question."

"I can't," he admitted, frustration eating at him. "I don't know."

"It's a possibility," the guard remarked, "given who you are."

"Has the entire building been searched?" Thad asked.

He needed to do it himself. He couldn't trust these guards to have conducted a thorough search. The ones under Ron were just kids, probably high-schoolers with no guns or badges or any real authority. He couldn't even trust his brother.

He reached for Ron's shoulder to guide him away from Caroline so that he wouldn't mention anything else about ransom within her hearing. "Show me where the public can't access—"

Caroline clutched his arm, holding him back from heading off with the guard. "Where are you going?"

"I'm going to look for him," he said. "You stay here, where you were supposed to meet me." By the carousel, where he would have found them had he showed up when they'd planned.

Caroline nodded. "I'll wait for him…and *you*…here." Before she released him, she squeezed his arm hard. "Find our son."

"I will," he promised.

Leaving her wrenched his heart. She turned toward the carousel, and her shoulders shook with sobs. He had managed no more than a few steps away from her when he heard a voice call out.

"Mommy, don't cry…."

He turned back in time to see Caroline drop to her knees and throw her arms around their son. When he hurried over to them, Mark glanced up from his mother's shoulder. "You're here now, Daddy."

It was the first time his son had called him…anything to his face. Like Caroline, Thad felt like crying, too.

"Where were you?" Thad asked. "Were you looking for me?"

Had he caused this whole nightmare?

Mark shook his head. "I was waiting to see Santa but someone grabbed my hand."

Alarm kicked Thad's heart rate into overdrive. "Who grabbed you?"

Mark shrugged his thin shoulders. "I dunno. I didn't really see him. He was very tall, and the mall was so crowded that people were jammed in all around us."

And the boy was too short to see much above anyone's waist.

"But you know it was a man?"

"His hand was big," Mark replied, "like yours."

Thad settled his hand, which was shaking, onto the little boy's head. "Did he hurt you?"

Caroline gasped as she realized what Thad was really asking their son. She pulled back from the little boy and studied his face. "Are you all right?"

"I'm good."

"Is he okay?" the head security guard asked, concern in his voice.

With a glance, Thad deferred to Caroline. She knew their son best.

She nodded.

"So we can open the doors?" the guard asked Thad, deferring to him.

He hesitated because he wanted to pull every man into a lineup for his son to pick out his almost-abductor. "You really didn't see his face?" he asked the boy.

"No. He was wearing those kind of light-colored pants." He glanced at Thad's khakis. "Like yours." And probably half the other guys in the mall.

The guard must have come to the same conclusion because he said, "He's okay. Probably someone just accidently grabbed the wrong kid. This place is a zoo tonight, and if we don't open those doors soon, we may have a riot."

Thad sighed. He had no right to hold the entire mall hostage, and if he wasn't a Kendall, the guard would probably have not even agreed to the lockdown in the first place.

"Yeah, go ahead." He reached out his hand and shook Ron's. "And thank you for your fast response."

"I have five grandkids," the guard said with a grin. "I would have been going crazy, too, if one of them went missing." He headed off, his radio at his mouth.

Despite the crowded mall, the three of them were suddenly very alone and very quiet as all the nerves gave way to relief and shock.

Mark glanced from his mother's face to Thad's, and then his bottom lip began to tremble as he realized the extent of their concern. "Am I in trouble?"

"No," Thad assured his son. "You didn't do anything wrong."

"You weren't supposed to leave the line," Caroline corrected them both. "Why did you let the man pull you away?"

The little boy's face flushed with bright color. "I thought the man was—" he turned back to Thad "—you."

"I wouldn't take you anywhere without telling your mother first," he said.

"I pulled away," Mark said, "when I saw it wasn't you."

"You saw his face?" He glanced in the direction in

which the guard had walked off, thinking about calling him back to keep the doors locked.

"No," Mark said. "But he was wearing gloves." He touched Thad's bare and cold-chapped hands. "And you always forget to wear your gloves."

A giggle slipped from Caroline's lips at the boy's precocious observation.

"How did you get away from him?" Thad asked, his guts too tense to find any amusement in the situation. He wasn't as convinced as the guard that someone had just grabbed the wrong kid.

Mark shrugged. "I pulled loose. But it's so crowded I couldn't see anything. I couldn't find you, Mommy." His breath hitched, and his lip trembled more. "I kept looking, but it was so busy."

Caroline wrapped her arms tight around the little boy. "You found me. You're safe now," she assured him and herself.

"How did you find us?" Thad asked, wondering if the man who'd grabbed him had led him back to the carousel. Then it might have been just an honest mistake.

"I heard the merry-go-round and kept coming to where it got louder."

Damn. Now Thad was going to have to start liking Christmas music again. It had led their son back to them.

His hand shaking harder, he barely managed to gently pat the boy's head. "You're so smart."

Mark blinked up at him, as if the compliment alone had brought him to tears. He flashed back to his father complimenting him once, on a story he'd written in el-

ementary school. Because his father was always so busy
and distracted with business, the fact that he'd read
the paper had been compliment enough, but then he'd
told Thad that he'd done a good job. Effusive praise it
wasn't, but Thad had been moved to tears, too.

He vowed then that he would be a better father.
He would praise his son so much that a compliment
wouldn't overwhelm the boy. And he would never again
disappoint him as he almost had tonight. If the man
who'd grabbed him had really intended to kidnap him,
Thad might have lost him.

And if he lost Mark, he would lose Caroline, too. She
loved their son so much. Like she had, Thad dropped to
his knees and wrapped his arms around them both—
holding them close to his madly pounding heart.

THE LITTLE BOY SLEPT peacefully, his lips curved into a
sweet smile as if he dreamed only happy dreams. Caroline wouldn't sleep at all tonight. She wouldn't dare
to even close her eyes for fear of reliving those night-
marish moments when Mark had been missing. Images
of what could have happened kept flitting through her
mind even with her eyes wide-open, though.

As she turned down the brightness of the lamp next
to his bed, she studied the picture propped up against
the fire-engine base of the lamp. That was what had
brought the smile to her little boy's face.

His dream.

The picture wasn't just of him sitting on Santa's
lap but of Caroline and Thad kneeling next to him as
he told the costumed mall worker what he wanted for
Christmas. In order to make the night less traumatic

for Mark, they'd let him talk to Santa. And the other people, knowing that the boy had gone missing for a while, had let them cut in line. So the little boy had gotten his picture with Santa—the picture he wanted to be a reality.

A family.

While tonight had had a happy ending, Mark's dream wouldn't. It would never be realized...at least not with Thad. After one lingering gaze at her son, she left the room and headed down the stairs to where Thad waited in the living room.

He had shut off the lamps, so that the only light came from the fire flickering in the hearth. But he hadn't dimmed the lights to seduce her. He didn't even turn toward her. His entire focus was on the street outside the window in front of which he stood.

"You don't believe it was an accident tonight," she said, "that some dad or grandpa grabbed the wrong kid in the crowd."

"I have no reason to think that isn't exactly what happened," he replied, and he finally turned away from the window.

She walked up to it now, but she could only see her own reflection in the glass. Dark circles rimmed her eyes; they were the only color in her pale face.

"What does that mean?" she wondered. "That you don't see anyone out there? That no one's made any threats?"

He nodded. "Both."

"But you're a Kendall," she said, remembering the security guard's awe at the realization. "And that puts anyone close to you in danger."

He tensed. "How's that?"

"Your family has a lot of money," Caroline said, as if he needed the reminder. Maybe he did. He had been gone a long time, maybe long enough to forget that the Kendalls were St. Louis royalty. "Someone could think that kidnapping your son for ransom is a way to get some of that money."

He chuckled. "My family has a lot of money. I don't." Then his brow furrowed. "I have stock, though. And with what Uncle Craig and Devin have done with the company over the years…"

"You're worth a lot of money," she said. That had never mattered to him, though, and it had certainly never mattered to her. Their relationship might have stood a better chance at surviving had he had no money.

"But no one even knows I have a son," he said.

Caroline sucked in a breath at the pain that jabbed her over his offhand admission. He had told no one about Mark? Was he ashamed of his son or of his son's mother?

"There's just so much going on right now," he said. "There's something else I have to tell my sister." He uttered a ragged sigh. "And it's such a media circus around the estate. I don't want to bring you and Mark into that craziness."

She nodded as if she understood. But she really had no idea what he was going through. She had no clue what it was like to be one of the infamous Kendalls who had grown up under the shadow of such tragedy.

"It doesn't matter that you haven't told anybody," she said, even though it did matter. To her. "All anyone would have to do is see the two of you together to know that Mark is your son."

He pushed his hand through his hair almost as if he was grabbing at the strands. "That's why the mall was such a bad idea for so many reasons."

"You don't want anyone knowing you have a son," she realized. It wasn't just for all the reasons he'd mentioned, either. There were reasons he hadn't mentioned, secrets he was keeping.

"Caroline—"

"Who are you?" she asked. "Really?"

He threw her words back at her. "You're the one who said my being a Kendall puts him at risk."

"But that's not why you've put him at risk," she said. "It's because of whatever you really are." She'd always sensed there was so much more to Thad Kendall, that there was a darkness and ruthlessness that came from more than reporting stories.

"You keep saying that…and it makes no sense." He shrugged as if brushing off her concerns. "You know who I am."

She shook her head. "No. Even when we were together, I knew you were holding back from me, that there was more to you than anyone else knew."

"I never held back with *you*," he said, his voice low and husky. He moved close behind her so that his chest pressed tight against her back.

Her skin tingled as his breath teased her neck before his lips touched it. "I wouldn't be holding back now if you weren't making me."

"Nobody stops Thad Kendall from doing what he

wants," she remarked bitterly, reminding herself that he'd had no problem leaving her last time.

But he must have taken her words as a challenge or an invitation because he turned her toward him and closed his arms around her. Now they were pressed chest to breasts. His chest was hard and muscular, and her breasts were full and sensitive and rising and falling with her now labored breathing.

He groaned, and his eyes dilated, the pupils swallowing the sapphire-blue. The attraction between them was even stronger than it had been four years ago.

Passion zipped through her veins, but she couldn't give in to it. She couldn't give in to him. "Thad…"

He took her open lips as an invitation, too, settling his mouth firmly onto hers. His lips moved over hers, and then his tongue slid between, tangling with hers, teasing her.

A moan tore from her throat as need coursed through her. She had never desired any man the way she wanted Thad. But wanting Thad was pointless when she would never be able to keep him. She wriggled free of his arms.

"I don't want you," she said.

"Do you really want me to prove you're lying again?" he challenged as he made a move to pull her back into his arms.

She stumbled back, out of his reach. "I don't want you unless I can have *all* of you," she said. "Unless you'll tell me the secrets that I know you're keeping from me and probably from everyone else who cares about you."

"Caroline, you don't know what you're talking—"

"I know that you're not just a photojournalist," she said, trusting her instincts. As a single mother, she had learned to trust them. Tonight they'd failed her because she never should have taken that call. "And I just hope like hell that whatever you really are hasn't put our son in danger."

ED TOUCHED THE COPY he had bought of the boy's picture with Santa. It sat on the passenger's seat beside him. He had his answer now…about what mattered most to Thad Kendall. After days of following the guy, which hadn't been easy since Kendall was an expert defensive driver, he'd figured out what no one else had about the infamous photojournalist.

The nomadic bachelor had a family. But he wouldn't have them for much longer.

His hand shaking, Ed touched the boy's face. "I almost had you tonight."

First he had distracted the woman with the call. Because she was one of those teachers who always wanted to be available to her students and their parents, it had been easy enough to get her cell number off the website of the elementary school where she taught and to which Ed had followed her one morning. It had even been easy to grab the boy's hand and lead him away from the line.

But when the kid had pulled free, Ed hadn't pursued him. There had been too many people around, which at first he'd thought would work in his favor so no one would notice him. But there had also been security guards around, and Kendall had had the foresight to order the exits locked down.

Ed wouldn't have escaped with the boy. So he had let him go.

Then he had watched them all play happy family with Santa. Now, after personally witnessing how much the kid meant to Kendall, Ed was more determined than ever.

Lights of a passing car shone through his windshield, so he hunched down in his seat. He wasn't parked where Kendall could see him, but this was the kind of neighborhood where strange cars were noticed and reported.

He couldn't be discovered yet. All these years had passed, and everyone who'd mattered to Ed had passed. But it wouldn't be over until everyone who mattered to Thad Kendall was gone, too.

He reached across the leather console and skimmed his finger over the boy's picture. "Next time you won't get away."

# Chapter Six

Thad hadn't slept at all the night before and not just because he'd spent the night sitting in his car keeping watch over Caroline's house but because her words had haunted him.

*"And I just hope like hell that whatever you really are hasn't put our son in danger."*

He needed to know if she was right to be concerned. He glanced around the St. Louis Police Department's interrogation room, hoping the cement block walls and thick mirror made this a secure place for the call he'd had to place.

"Are you sure my cover hasn't been blown?" he asked his boss.

"There's been no chatter about it," Anya said. "But they could have a code word for you, something we haven't cracked yet."

"Crack it!" he snapped, his nerves frayed from lack of sleep and the horror of those long moments his son had been missing.

"It's not that easy, and you know it," she replied with strained patience.

"Yeah, I know...."

"Has something happened?" she asked. "Has there been an attempt on your life?"

"No." But if Mark had been abducted, there would have been. If the fear of losing the boy hadn't killed Thad, Caroline would have managed the deed with her bare hands. And he wouldn't have blamed her.

"But you have cause for concern?" she asked, ever the professional. The woman never lost her cool.

Usually, neither did Thad. "I have concern."

"I know why you went home," she reminded him. "Your parents' murderer is still out there. Is that the reason for your concern?"

"It's the reason I needed out of my last assignment," he said. "But if my leaving got Michaels killed..."

"You couldn't have saved him."

"We'll never know for sure," he stubbornly maintained just as he had when she'd tried to absolve him of his guilt during their last conversation.

"I'll let you know when we break the code," she said, and then clicked off.

Thad sighed as he pocketed his phone.

"What will you never know for sure?" Ash asked from the open door to the interrogation room.

Lack of sleep must have dulled his reflexes, because he hadn't even heard the door open. He shrugged but answered honestly, "Work stuff."

"Isn't knowing for sure part of your job?" Ash asked. "All that digging until you get to the truth? You're kind of famous for it."

Thad narrowed his eyes in suspicion. "You're complimenting me?" Like their father, it wasn't something his older brothers had ever really done. They'd been more likely to beat the crap out of him and each other.

They had only ever been careful with Natalie because she'd always seemed so fragile. As adults, and after what she'd been through, they all knew better now. She wasn't easily broken. But still Thad stalled over telling her the truth of her paternity, wanting to protect her as he and his brothers always had.

Ash shrugged his massive shoulders. "Just stating a fact. You're good at getting to the truth."

Not so much at telling it, though. "It's my job."

"I'm glad you're back," Ash admitted. "We've all been working on this, but we need fresh eyes. We need *your* eyes." He glanced at the boxes of tapes Thad had set on the table next to the bracket where a suspect's handcuffs were clipped. "What's all this? Did you find another lead?"

"I don't know," he admitted. He would hate to think that last night had anything to do with his parents' murders. Or worse, with his dual career, as Caroline had accused. "But I need to have someone look at a few hours of this security footage. We need to find out who might have grabbed a three-year-old kid last night at the mall."

"There was no report of a kidnapping!" Ash exclaimed with all the horror of a man about to become a father himself. Then he nodded in sudden realization. "But I did hear about some kind of security issue at the mall. The exit doors were momentarily locked down, so no one could leave until the situation had been resolved."

"The kid got away from whoever grabbed him. He's not hurt." He hadn't even been all that shaken up until he'd noticed how scared his mother and father had been. Mark was one tough little guy. He was definitely a Kendall. Pride warmed Thad's heart along with the love that swelled it whenever he thought of his son.

"What happened?" Ash asked. "And how the hell do you know about it? I didn't think you were working for your network here. I thought you were just going to focus on family right now."

*For once.*

Ash didn't say it, but Thad heard the unsaid accusation that clearly glittered with a brief flash of resentment in his green eyes. Ash had left home for a while, for the service, but he'd come right back to St. Louis after his term was up. He hadn't kept going back overseas like Thad.

"I was focusing on family," Thad insisted.

"At the mall?" Ash scoffed. "You hate the mall. I saw your face when Gray was kidding about Christmas shopping a few days ago. You've never gotten over your aversion to Christmas. So what the hell were you doing at the mall *this* time of year?"

Thad drew in a deep breath and then admitted, "Going with my son to see Santa."

"Son?" Ash's voice rose with shock. "You have a son?"

He nodded. "His name is Mark. He's three years old."

"And you're just telling me about him now?" Hurt dimmed the anger in Ash's eyes. "Does anyone else know you have a son?"

"Until a few days ago, I didn't know myself," he said.

"But he's three years old...." Ash nodded as if he'd

done some math in his head. "And you've been gone longer than that. Are you sure he's yours?"

Thad hadn't asked to use the interrogation room just to make his call in privacy. He clicked the remote and turned on the TV in the corner. The security footage in the DVD was paused on his son's face. "You tell me what you think."

"Damn." Ash grinned. "He's you all over again. Cute little shit."

"Smart, too," Thad said.

Ash whistled. "Wow. You're already talking like a proud papa. Who's the mama? I don't even remember you dating anyone when you were home last. But you weren't around much. You were working on some special assignment at the local station."

"Her name is Caroline Emerson," he said. "She's an elementary school teacher."

Ash laughed. "Okay. I get why you didn't mention her."

"Why?" he asked. Caroline might have thought him a snob for not introducing her, but his own brother should know him better.

"Aunt Angela would've been planning your wedding if she'd met her."

His brother did know him better, and they both knew their aunt too well. "Yeah, she would have been ordering flowers and booking St. Luke's."

"Sounds like she should have been," Ash pointed out. "So you didn't know she was pregnant when you left?"

"She didn't even know yet," he said. Had Caroline known, she would have told him. He believed that she would have tried to contact him, too, had she not feared his family would think her a gold digger. She should have tried to get word to him after their son had been born, but he couldn't blame her if she'd wanted to protect the little boy from the fishbowl life of a Kendall.

"Would it have made a difference?" Ash wondered, staring at the boy on the TV. "Would you have stayed home?"

Remembering the importance of the mission he'd left to carry out, he shook his head. But he would have returned as soon as he'd been able to make sure both Caroline and Mark were okay.

"What about now?" his older brother asked. "Will you leave now?"

Subject to an intensity that had him squirming and unable to lie, Thad suddenly had insight into how Detective Kendall conducted an interrogation. "Once our parents' killer is caught I will go back to my job."

"Why does your job have to be over there?" Ash wondered. "Why can't it be here?"

"Local news has no interest for me," he said. Because it had nothing to do with his real job.

"What about your son and his mother? What's your interest in them?" The detective continued his interrogation.

"Right now I just want to make sure they're safe," Thad said, getting irritated with his brother and probably with his own inability to answer Ash's questions.

"So protectiveness only?" Ash persisted.

"Stop interrogating me," Thad snapped. "I need to know if someone tried to grab my son. And if so, I need your help to protect him and his mother!"

Ash squeezed his shoulder with reassurance. "He's my nephew. I'll help you look out for him. He's a Kendall."

Actually, he wasn't. Caroline had given the boy her last name. But Thad wanted Emerson changed to Kendall, as soon as he knew for certain that he wasn't putting them in danger.

CAROLINE'S HAND SHOOK as she held the telephone. It was the cordless house phone. Thad had taken her cell the night before, so that his detective brother could try to track down the person who had called her while she and Mark had been at the mall.

"Thank you for taking Mark tonight," she told Tammy. "I was freaking him out with being so nervous and overprotective." She hadn't dared to leave the house despite Saturday being their usual errand day. She hadn't gone anywhere, and she hadn't even let Mark play in the yard. "Is he okay?"

"Yes," her best friend assured her, "he and Steven Jr. and Steven Sr. are playing video games and having a great time."

Steven Jr. was three years older than Mark, and until her son had met his own father, he'd idolized the older boy and his dad. Now he had his own daddy. And he had asked about him the moment he'd awakened.

"Of course, you're probably freaking out even more that you're not here to watch over him yourself," Tammy commiserated. "You must have been so scared last night."

"Yes." But not just last night; she couldn't shake off her fear. "I just wish I knew if he's really safe, though."

She hadn't been able to sleep last night; she'd sat beside his bed, watching over him.

"We're staying home with the burglar alarm on. Steve and I won't let anything happen to him," Tammy assured her.

"I know." Caroline expelled a shuddery breath of relief. "I trust you." More than she trusted her own ability to keep him safe given how she had nearly lost him the night before.

"What about Thad?" Tammy asked. "Do you trust him?"

"Not as far as I can throw him." She couldn't trust him when she was convinced that he wasn't being honest with her.

"But he stepped up last night," her romantic friend reminded her. "He was there for you."

And he was here now, pulling his car into her driveway.

"Tammy, there's no chance of anything more between me and Thad," she cautioned her friend and her own foolish heart, which sped up its beat as soon as he stepped from his car.

All long legs and lean hips in slim-fitting jeans, he was so damn sexy. The wind played with his dark hair, tousling it and sprinkling it with snowflakes. He lifted a gloveless hand, as Mark had noticed, and pushed his hair back from his forehead. Then moments later he was ringing her doorbell; it echoed throughout the living room.

"Who's there?" Tammy asked.

"I have to go...."

"Don't open that door," Tammy advised her, "until you make sure it's safe."

She and Thad alone in the house damn well weren't safe, but she wanted to hear whatever he'd learned today. "It's okay."

"It's Thad," Tammy said with a triumphant giggle. "Have fun!"

Shaking her head at her friend's hopeless romanticism, Caroline opened the door.

"Did I do something wrong already?" he asked, noting her head shake. "Or is that still?"

"You tell me." Despite the warning bells ringing inside her head, Caroline stepped back to let him inside and closed the door behind him.

"Where's the little man?"

"At my friend Tammy's."

He tensed. "Is that a good idea?"

"Given how well I watched him at the mall, it's a great idea," she said, berating herself. "Tammy's never lost one of her children."

In addition to Steven Jr., she had a three-year-old daughter, Bethany. The little girl adored Mark, but he only tolerated her. Now. Tammy swore that someday they would get married.

Thad cupped her shoulders and squeezed them. "Stop beating yourself up about last night," he admonished. "You didn't do anything wrong."

"I never should have taken that call."

"You wouldn't have if I'd showed up when I was supposed to," he said, shouldering the blame himself. "And you really just glanced down for a second. I saw it on the security tape."

Fear quickened her pulse. "Did you see who grabbed him?"

He shook his head. "It was such a crowd. We couldn't even find Mark on any of the security footage except by the carousel."

"We?"

"My brother helped me go through the tapes." He sighed. "He knows about you and Mark, which means—" he glanced at his wrist watch "—that by now my whole family probably knows."

"Shouldn't you have told them yourself?" she asked, hurt that he wouldn't have chosen to make such an announcement personally.

"I would have," he said. "But I'm sure Ash didn't trust me to do it, so he spilled."

"You should go to them," she urged, worried about his family's reaction. The Kendalls weren't the type to have children out of wedlock. If Thad hadn't introduced her before because he'd thought his family wouldn't consider her worthy of a Kendall, they would probably hate her now. "Explain that you didn't know, that I didn't tell you…"

"You seem in an awful hurry to get rid of me." His blue eyes narrowed. "Are you worried about being alone with me?"

She forced a yawn despite the adrenaline coursing through her at his nearness. His hands still cupped her shoulders, kneading her flesh. "I didn't sleep last night. I was going to head up to bed soon."

"Don't let me stop you." He caught her hand and tugged her toward the stairs.

"Thad, this is a bad idea." But even she heard how

halfhearted her protest was. And she followed him up the stairs to the room he must have instinctively known was hers.

"I just want to hold you," he said, and now he tugged her toward the queen sleigh bed that was still neatly made because she hadn't even slept in it. "I'm tired, too. I couldn't sleep last night and then I spent hours going over that mall footage today, trying to convince myself that our son is safe."

"He's safe tonight," she assured him. She was the one in danger now, of falling for the man who'd already broken her heart.

While he had had no warning and no training, he was proving to be a good dad, patient and loving. And with her, he was attentive and reassuring and protective.

And so damn sexy.

She was tired, though, too tired to fight feelings for him that had never gone away even when he had.

"Let me make sure you're safe," he said. "Let me stay with you."

She shook her head. "Your staying puts me in more danger than your leaving."

"I'll just hold you," Thad said.

Was that really all he wanted? Because she wanted— she *needed*—more.

He let go of her hands to pull back the comforter and the soft flannel sheets. "I just want to hold you in my arms tonight."

And that was the problem. Caroline wanted to spend every night in his arms. But Thad would never give her forever.

Whatever he really was—and it wasn't just a reporter—had a tighter hold on his heart than she and their son ever would. But if whatever he was put Mark in danger, then his heart would get broken, too. He would never forgive himself for causing their son harm.

And neither would Caroline....

# *Chapter Seven*

Just as he'd promised, Thad had held Caroline in his arms all night. She had slept peacefully. But, like the night before, he had been unable to close his eyes. He hadn't wanted to take his gaze from her beautiful face. And his body had been too tense and achy with desire for him to relax enough to sleep.

He could have seduced her with kisses and caresses. Even though four years had passed, he remembered in vivid detail exactly what drove her crazy. A kiss on the back of her neck. A caress on the side of her breast, his thumb teasing ever closer toward the tight nipple.

And because he had been so tempted to seduce her, he hadn't. He didn't want to coerce her into making love with him. She would regret it and resent him.

He had already given her reason enough to resent him. So he'd forced himself to leave her first thing in the morning, before she awakened, before he gave in to temptation. But as he pulled into the nearly full driveway at the Kendall estate, he wished he'd stayed with Caroline instead.

With a groan he shut off his car, stepped out and headed into the three-story mansion. Someone must have been watching for his car because they all met him in the entryway, as if they were throwing him a surprise party. He wasn't particularly surprised, though. Over the years he had developed the intuition to detect an ambush.

"Thanks a lot," he told Ash, who grinned unrepentantly.

Natalie smacked Thad's shoulder. "I can't believe you didn't tell us you have a son."

"Someone didn't give me the chance." He glared at his older brother.

"You're not really great about using your chances to disclose information," Gray remarked with a sideways glance at his fiancée.

Thad needed to talk to Natalie—she deserved to know the truth about her parentage. But he understood it would hurt her, and she'd already been hurt enough.

"Well, I've been a little busy finding out that I'm a father," he said in an effort to excuse himself.

"Are you sure?" Uncle Craig asked as he led the group back to the family room with its cathedral ceiling and French doors that opened onto the brick patio. Sometime over the past four years, or maybe just the past four months since it was revealed that his brother's killer was still out there, Craig Kendall had aged. His hair was completely silver now. "Did you have a DNA test done yet?"

Thad reached for his wallet and the picture Caroline had given him after Mark's brief disappearance. But before he could pull it out, Ash produced a printout of the surveillance photo.

Probably dressed for church, in a brightly patterned,

stylish suit, Aunt Angela hurried after him, her heels clicking against the wood floor. She grabbed for the grainy picture but then took Thad's proffered colored snapshot, too. "Oh, my…"

Tears glittered in her warm brown eyes as she focused on Mark's little face. Thad grinned at her emotional reaction. "So, what do you think, Auntie, do I need a DNA test?"

Aunt Angela lifted her gaze from the pictures to Thad. "He looks just like you when you were that age." She smiled. "Now I know why you took the old photo albums out of the library."

Natalie leaned over their petite aunt's shoulder to see the pictures. "Oh, he's *so* cute. I don't remember Thad ever being that cute."

"Hey!" he protested.

"What's his name?" Rachel asked as Aunt Angela passed the pictures to her. She sat in the chair Ash had helped her into given her swollen belly.

"Mark."

"His mother must be beautiful," Natalie said, "for him to be so cute."

"She is," Thad said. So beautiful that he ached for her.

Devin wound his arm around Jolie's waist. "You'll make beautiful babies then, my love."

Aunt Angela patted Rachel's belly. "Our family is growing," she said with a mother's pride. And, truth be told, she'd been much more maternal to them than their biological mother had ever been.

"When do we get to meet your son?" Uncle Craig asked. His blue eyes held some skepticism yet. Despite how much Mark looked like him, his uncle wasn't entirely convinced of his paternity.

"He's at St. Luke's church right now with his mother." That was the church that Aunt Angela had occasionally convinced them all to attend.

"You should have gone along," Ash teased him. "You could use some saving."

If he only knew....

There was no saving him from what he had to do now. "Hey, Nat, I need a few minutes alone with you."

Her forehead creased, but she nodded her agreement.

As they left the family room, he overheard Devin asking Aunt Angela to add the owner of Turner Connections to the Christmas guest list. But their generous aunt, who lived by the motto of the more the merrier, declined, "It should be just family."

"This'll be his first Christmas without his wife," Devin pointed out.

"You're not doing business on the holidays," she scolded. "Family only."

Would Natalie feel as if she was still family once he revealed her true paternity?

She followed him up the stairs that led to the wing with their bedrooms. He had his own suite for his use whenever he was in town, which hadn't been often over the past several years.

"I was in your room last time because you were crying out," she mused. "Why do I think I'm going to be the one crying now?"

Because she was damn smart; she always had been.

"This isn't easy to tell you...."

"And everyone else already knows," she surmised.

"They've all been calling and checking on me, waiting for you to break whatever news you must have decided you needed to be the one to break to me." She chuckled at her own joke. "But I guess that's kind of your area though, *breaking news*."

He just hoped it wouldn't break her, but then he reminded himself she wasn't that fragile little girl anymore who'd discovered their parents' dead bodies. "This isn't going to change anything."

She groaned. "God, this is bad."

"Nat—"

"When someone says this isn't going to change anything, you know it's going to change *everything*." She grabbed his hands and held on tight. "Just tell me, Thad. I can handle it."

All her life, he and his brothers had tried to protect her because they'd never forgiven themselves that she'd been the one to find their murdered parents. But when he'd come back just in time to shoot her stalker, he'd finally realized that his little sister had grown into one tough young woman.

He dragged in a breath of air and then told her, "That guy I shot—"

"You found out who he was?" she asked hopefully.

He shook his head. "Well, we don't know his name."

"I thought it was Wade…something…"

"We don't know his last name yet." Or if his first name was even really Wade.

"But you do know something about him," she surmised. *Damn smart…*

He nodded. "He's your brother."

She laughed. "Yeah, right. Like I don't have enough big brothers…"

"He's your half brother, Natalie. Something about him looked familiar to me—"

"You thought he looked like me!" She shuddered.

He squeezed her hands back as she held his yet. "So I had his DNA run. They put it against what we had of yours from the hospital. And Ash and Devin and I gave samples of ours."

She gulped in a breath, as if fighting down hysteria. But her voice was steady when she said, "So he's just my brother. Not yours or Ash or Devin's."

"Yes."

She nodded. Despite how tough she was acting, tears began to streak down her face as she put it all together. "So Daddy wasn't really my dad."

"I'm sorry," he said. "So sorry…and if I'd known he was your brother…"

"You still would have had to kill him," she said, "or he would have killed me and Gray. You did the right thing."

"If there's anything I can do…"

The door creaked open behind him, as if someone had been listening outside it. Gray walked in and crossed the room to his fiancée, pulling her into his arms. "I've got this," he assured Thad.

She clung to him as if using his strength to shore up her own. As separate people they were strong, as a couple they were invincible. Thad, who had vowed to always remain single, envied the strength of their union.

As he backed toward the door to give them privacy,

Natalie lifted her head from Gray's shoulder. "You can do something for me," she told him.

"Anything, Nat."

"Find out who my father was." From the grim look on her beautiful face, she wasn't looking for a tearful reunion.

Like Thad, she was looking for a killer.

CAROLINE SLIPPED INTO the back row of church. She was late. She must not have set her alarm before she'd fallen asleep in Thad's arms. Wanting him as she did, she didn't know how she'd managed to sleep. Just sleep.

Thad Kendall had kept his word. He had only held her, his strong arms wrapped tight around her the entire night. She'd enforced her no-sex rule so that she wouldn't fall for him again. But because he'd abided by that rule when they both knew he could have seduced her at any time, she was in even more danger of falling for him than if they'd made love all night.

God, she was such a fool. She and Mark attended church every Sunday, and usually she prayed for peace and food for starving children. Today she intended to pray for wisdom. She needed it to remind her of all the reasons she shouldn't be in love with Thad Kendall.

But then her son wriggled out from between Tammy and Steve Stehouwer and ran down the aisle toward her. And she remembered the most important reason she loved Thad—he had given her their son. No matter how much he'd hurt her when he'd left last time and how much he would hurt her when he left again, he had given her the greatest treasure of her life.

"Mommy!" Mark squealed as he squeezed into the row next to her.

Caroline lifted him in her arms and hugged him close. "Shh…"

But instead of looking at them with disapproval, the people around them were chuckling or smiling. Her son always won the heart of everyone with whom he came in contact; he was that sweet and lovable.

She pressed a kiss to his forehead and then his cheek and then his chin. He giggled and wriggled down to stand beside her.

His hand slid into hers. "I missed you, Mommy."

"I missed you, too." The words brought back those horrible moments that he'd disappeared at the mall. What if he'd been gone longer? Or worse yet, what if he'd never been found?

Panic clutched her heart in a tight grip. And she forgot all about praying for wisdom. She prayed for her son to stay safe. As she prayed, goose bumps lifted on her skin. Someone had opened the door and let in a blast of winter air.

But the cold wasn't what caused the goose bumps; it was that eerie sense of foreboding that had chills chasing up and down her spine.

She'd had the same sensation at the mall. Like she had then, she looked around for someone watching her. Several people were still smiling at Mark and her. She smiled back despite the tension gnawing at her. But she kept looking around until she encountered an unsmiling face.

The older man's mouth was drawn tight, almost into a frown of disapproval, as he stared at her. She didn't know his name, but with his silver hair and intense gaze, he looked familiar to her.

Had she seen him in church before? Or had she seen him that night at the mall?

She leaned down to whisper to Mark. "Honey, do you remember—"

"Shh, Mommy, you gotta be quiet in church," he remembered. *Now.*

"But this is important, honey," she continued. "I need to know if you—"

But when she looked up, the man was gone. Had he taken off because she'd seen him and he was worried that Mark might have identified him as the man who'd grabbed him at the mall?

And if he was the same man, then Mark had not been grabbed by accident.

Someone was after her son.

MAYBE ED SHOULD HAVE taken down the dated wallpaper in the kitchen, but Emily had put it up when they'd gotten married. This was the first house they had ever lived in as man and wife. They hadn't lived there long, but sweet, sentimental Emily had never let him sell the house when they'd moved into a bigger and nicer one.

He had rented out the little bungalow over the years with the stipulation that no one touch the wallpaper.

The last person who'd lived there had respected that, but he was gone now. So Ed was using the house again. And he had finally papered over Emily's teapot wallpaper—with pictures of Thad Kendall.

The man was young, only thirty-one, but he had been all over the world—more than once. There were photos of him in every country as long as it was the scene of civil unrest or all-out war.

The photojournalist thrived on danger. He'd come out of some of the most dangerous places in the world alive. So killing him wouldn't have been easy. Or even all that satisfying....

There were recent photos of him, too, cut from local newspapers. Every day they ran a story about Thad Kendall being forced to kill to save his sister.

Forced to kill?

Ed doubted that it had been a hardship for the man. And he certainly didn't appear, in any of the photos, to be struggling with guilt or regret. A true killer, he wasn't suffering over what he'd done.

Not like Ed had suffered. Not like he was suffering now, shaking with the need for a drink. But he couldn't dull his pain with alcohol because it also dulled his wits. And he needed his wits about him to deal with Thad Kendall.

Thad needed to suffer, and Ed needed to make certain that he did. It was only too bad that to make Kendall suffer, the woman and the boy would have to suffer, too.

Ed had added pictures of them to his collection of Thad. The woman working at school and shopping at the store and attending church. The boy playing at day care and shopping with his mom at the store, her hand always on his, and her holding him in church. And in the center of the collage was their picture with Santa, their family photo.

But like Ed's, their family would not be together much longer.

# *Chapter Eight*

NERVES TIGHTENED THAD'S stomach, and he felt like a kid again, caught doing something wrong and waiting for his punishment. Since the age of eleven, Thad had received his hugs, encouragement and affection from Aunt Angela. Those were things he'd rarely had when his parents had been alive.

And he'd received his punishment from Uncle Craig. Having to go to his office at Kendall Communications was tantamount to being sent to the principal's office. But he had never had any doubt that his uncle cared, that he loved him, and that was why he punished—to make him a better man.

Thad wished that he could be the kind of father to Mark that Uncle Craig had been to him. But how was he going to do that from half a world away? Unlike Thad's father, Uncle Craig had always put raising the kids before the business, and it hadn't suffered any.

But running a communication company and doing what Thad did when he was *reporting* a story were two entirely different things. Uncle Craig had never put them in any danger because of what he did. But when the man arrested for their parents' murders had been cleared, Thad had wondered if their father had done something that had motivated the killings. He had been ruthless about getting ahead in business, just as ruthless as Thad was when getting the information he needed.

The door creaked open, startling Thad into whirling toward the entrance. Uncle Craig chuckled at his uneasiness. "Take you back?"

"Getting called to your office?" Thad sighed. "Oh, yeah…"

"You didn't have to come here as often as your brothers did," Uncle Craig said.

Thad grinned. "That's because I was the better brother."

Uncle Craig laughed harder. "You were probably the worst. You were just better at not getting caught."

The truth of his former guardian's statement elicited a laugh from Thad, too. That ability of which Uncle Craig spoke had gotten him out of trouble in his youth and had saved his life over the past several years.

"You got caught this time, though," Uncle Craig mused.

Thad tensed. Had his uncle discovered the truth about him?

"When I disappeared yesterday morning, it was because I stopped by St. Luke's," Uncle Craig admitted.

"You saw Mark and Caroline?"

Uncle Craig nodded. "He is definitely your son."

Maybe that wasn't a good thing…for Mark. Maybe that was what had caused the incident at the mall, if in fact someone had tried to grab him. Even Ash wasn't sure since they hadn't been able to see anything sinister on the security footage.

Uncle Craig settled behind his mahogany desk and pulled out the middle drawer where he'd always kept his checkbook. Over the years Thad had come to this office for money more than he had for punishments. "How much does she want from you?" he asked.

"What?"

"For support. She's been raising this boy alone for three years," Uncle Craig reminded him. "She must want some compensation for all the expenses she covered on her own."

Thad shook his head. "Man, she was right...."

"About what?"

"The money," he replied.

Uncle Craig flipped open his checkbook as if getting ready to write down a figure.

Thad continued, "She said that was what you'd all think she wanted if she tried contacting any of you. It's why she didn't try to get a message to me when she realized she was pregnant."

Now he regretted getting angry with her when he'd discovered he had a son. Having not introduced her to his family when they'd dated, he'd left her in an untenable position.

Uncle Craig leaned back in his chair, his blue eyes narrowed in suspicion. "So she doesn't want money?"

They had never discussed it, which had Thad flinching with guilt. He'd grown up never having to think about a mortgage or a car loan or student loans, so he'd forgotten that most people didn't have that same luxury.

He should have offered her money. For the past three years she'd supported their son all by herself, and for the great job she'd done raising him, she deserved the whole Kendall fortune. But she had never asked for any money from him.

He shook his head in response to Uncle Craig's question.

"Then what does she want?"

Thad expelled a ragged sigh. "For me to not hurt Mark." Or her again.

Instead of defending or supporting him, Uncle Craig looked more worried than he had about the money. "Will you?"

Thinking of those horrible moments when the boy had disappeared, and of that white SUV Thad kept glimpsing in his rearview mirror, he shrugged. "I don't know."

"Being a father is a huge responsibility," the oldest Kendall said. "One I wish I'd taken more seriously when my son was little. I kept thinking we had all the time in the world."

His and Aunt Angela's only child had been just a few years older than Mark was now, six, when he died in a car accident.

"But we both know no one has as much time as they think they have," Uncle Craig continued, "to spend with the people they love."

"What happened to Connor was a horrible, horrible accident," Thad said. One for which he suspected his aunt and uncle had blamed themselves for many years.

"As a parent, it's our responsibility to keep our children safe," Uncle Craig said, confirming Thad's suspicion and eliciting his own guilt.

If he had put Mark in danger...

"The boy's mother—"

"Caroline Emerson," Thad said, because she was so much more than just the mother of his child. He had loved her even before she'd given him a son.

"Caroline seemed especially nervous and protective, even in church," Uncle Craig remarked. "When she caught me watching them, she seemed truly frightened. I left quickly so I wouldn't upset her."

"Ash found out about Mark because of an incident at the mall. Didn't he tell you about it?" When he'd spilled Thad's secret...

Uncle Craig nodded his silver-haired head. "Yes. But he wasn't concerned about it. He wrote it off as the holiday crush and crowds at the mall."

Thad wished he could write it off as easily. But doubt and fear gnawed at him.

"But then Ash isn't a father quite yet," Uncle Craig continued, "so he doesn't have a parent's instincts. Caroline does, and she seems quite concerned about her son's safety."

"Our son," Thad automatically corrected him.

"What do your instincts say?" Uncle Craig asked.

Thad pushed a slightly shaking hand through his hair. "My instincts are overdeveloped," he admitted. "Because of the places I've been the past several years, I see danger everywhere."

"If you didn't, you wouldn't have survived," Uncle Craig said, his blue eyes bright with emotion. "And if you go back again, you may not."

He was used to his aunt begging him not to leave whenever he came home. But his uncle had always seemed to understand that it was something he needed to do.

"The first three years of that little boy's life, he didn't have a father," Uncle Craig reminded him. "Do you want him to grow up without one?"

"I just want him to grow up," Thad said, "safe and happy."

"So you do think he's in danger?"

Thad sighed. "I learned long ago that it doesn't matter where you are—a war-torn country or asleep in your own bed—you can be in danger."

"That's something you shouldn't have had to learn as young as you did," Uncle Craig said.

It was something Thad intended to do his damnedest to make sure Mark didn't learn for a long time.

WHEN SHE HAD AGREED to let Thad see Mark whenever he wanted, she hadn't considered how much he would want to. And how much that would make her want him.

He leaned over the bed and kissed Mark's forehead. "Good night, little buddy."

"Good night, Daddy," Mark murmured sleepily, his eyes already closed.

Caroline wished she could close her eyes and blot out the image of Thad Kendall as a loving father. It would have been better had he been unattached and uninvolved; then Mark wouldn't miss him so much when he left.

And neither would she.

He joined her in the hall, pulling the door almost closed behind him. "I'll never get used to that."

"What?" she asked.

"Him calling me Daddy." He touched his chest, as if the word physically affected his heart.

Maybe it did. Caroline's heart was reacting, too. It beat faster at the sight of Thad in a black T-shirt that was molded to his muscular chest.

"Looks like you got wetter during his bath than he did," she remarked.

He chuckled. "Yeah, sorry about that. I'll clean up the bathroom."

She shook her head. "I already did when you were reading him his bedtime story."

A muscle twitched along his cheek. "A Christmas story…"

"Sorry," she said with a gentle smile. "Like most little kids, Mark loves Christmas." Because nothing bad had happened on any of his Christmases. Her heart ached for the pain Thad had suffered at such a young age.

"That's good," Thad said. "I'm glad. And I'll make an effort to get over my aversion to it…for him."

"Finding your parents' killer would help you with that," she mused. "Are you any closer?"

He shook his head. "No. And that was the gift I really wanted to give my family this Christmas. Justice and closure."

"You'll do it," she said with absolute certainty. Thad Kendall was the kind of man who always succeeded in his goals. Too bad one of his goals was to remain single. "And you know you don't have to spend as much time around here as you do, if you'd rather be focusing on your investigation."

"Actually, I'd like to spend more time with Mark," he said. "I'd be happy to watch him during the day while you're at work."

"You want me to pull him out of day care?" She studied his handsome face through narrowed eyes, suspecting he had a reason other than just wanting to spend more time with his son.

He nodded. "I missed three years of his life. I'd like to get to know my son."

"I'll be off on my break in a few more days," she said. Because of the holiday falling on the weekend, she had only a half day off the Friday before Christmas Eve, but she didn't have to return until after New Year's Day.

"But it's crazy for you to have to pay for day care when I'm available to watch him," Thad persisted. The check he'd forced on her earlier weakened his argument. He insisted on paying for day care and all Mark's expenses.

Hell, he'd wanted to pay off her mortgage and her car, too. But she'd never wanted his money. What she wanted was much harder to attain: his heart.

"Watch him or guard him?" she asked.

Now she wondered about all the time he'd been spending with them since that night at the mall. In the past week and a half, he'd been over every day the minute she picked up Mark from day care. "You really think he's in danger?"

"Nothing's happened."

She nodded, clinging to the faint reassurance. "And you said that man at church was your uncle."

"Sorry about that."

"He wanted to see his great-nephew," she said. He had undoubtedly also wanted to check her out. He probably wondered what the heck Thad had ever seen in her. She wasn't a svelte socialite like Thad's mother had been; she was a real woman with real curves and damn proud of it.

"I need to bring you and Mark to Sunday dinner and have you meet the whole family," he said.

She heard the reluctance in his deep voice. "Need to—not *want* to."

He shrugged. "They can be overwhelming. Meeting all these new relatives at once might be a bit much for Mark."

She was touched that he had considered their son's feelings. "I think he'll like having a lot of family."

Thad chuckled. "They're all dying to meet him. Aunt Angela's been bugging me to get his Christmas list."

"He told Santa what he wanted for Christmas was family," she reminded him. "Sounds like he'll get it." With aunts and uncles, but not the family he really wanted—Mommy, Daddy and Mark.

"What do you want for Christmas?" she asked. "Besides your parents' killer brought to justice?"

He stepped closer, backing her against the wall. "You. I want you, Caroline."

He pressed his hips against hers, leaving her no doubt how much he wanted her. And he covered her mouth with his, parting her lips for the hot invasion of his tongue.

Her pulse quickened with desire. She wanted him, too. So much....

He lifted his head and implored her, his voice gruff with passion, "Let me stay tonight...."

To make love with her—or to protect her and Mark? He touched her then—with his intense gaze and with his hands, sliding them down the sides of her breasts. His wet shirt had dampened hers, so that her hardened nipples were visible through the thin cotton. He groaned. "Caroline."

She wanted him to touch her there. She wanted him to touch her everywhere. She slid her arms around his shoulders and tangled her fingers in his soft hair, pulling his head down for another kiss.

"Be mine tonight," he urged her.

She was already his; she had been his for years. But he only wanted a night. She wanted forever. While she knew, intimately, how good making love with him was, she wanted more.

She forced herself to push him back. "You need to leave."

EVEN THE COLD NIGHT AIR blowing through his open coat to his still-damp T-shirt didn't cool Thad's desire. He wanted Caroline even more than he had four years ago, and four years ago he'd wanted her more than he had any other woman.

She was so beautiful and smart. And it was because she was smart that she refused to let him any closer. He didn't blame her, not after he'd hurt her before. Leaving her last time had been the hardest thing he'd ever done. To leave her and Mark this time…

Pain clutched his heart at just the thought. Then pain nipped his hand when he gripped the door handle. Blood streaked from his fingers, glass embedded in his skin.

In the glow of the streetlamp, his own reflection radiated back from the shattered window of his driver's door. The windshield was also broken. Hell, every damn window had been broken.

He ducked down, in case whoever had damaged the vehicle was still around, and he noted that all his tires were flat, the sidewalls slashed. While he'd been inside the house with Caroline and Mark, someone had been just outside, vandalizing his vehicle with such malice.

And maybe that person was still outside or, worse yet, trying to get inside the house. Out of reflex he reached beneath his jacket, but his gun wasn't there. That first night back, when he'd shot Natalie's stalker— her half brother—he'd had to use Gray's gun because he never tried to bring one through airport security. In other countries, he got his weapons through secret contacts. Fortunately, he had a couple contacts in St. Louis, too, but because he hadn't wanted to alarm Caroline, he'd left the gun in the glove box.

Of his vandalized car…

Keeping low, he dragged open the door and reached inside. Glass littered the dash and the seats. He got cut again as he fumbled for the glove box. His gun glinted in the darkness.

Maybe the vandal hadn't been inside his car. Or maybe he hadn't needed Thad's gun because he was already armed. With his free hand, Thad reached for his cell. He punched in a number and gave an address.

"Get here as fast as you can."

He had no intention of waiting for his backup, though, not when Caroline and Mark could be in danger. His gun clenched tight in his bleeding hand, he headed toward the house fully prepared to kill again. He would do anything to protect his family.

# Chapter Nine

Caroline shivered with nerves and cold. If he hadn't flashed his badge, she wouldn't have let the man inside—not at this hour. He wasn't wearing a uniform or a suit but jeans and a wrinkled shirt that looked like he'd picked it up off the floor.

It was actually the name on the badge that had compelled her to unlock the door and let him inside: Detective Ash Kendall.

Cold air had rushed in with him. But what he'd told her had chilled her far more. "Thad's missing?"

"He called me—gave me your address and told me to get here right away," Ash said. "But he's gone."

"He just drove off?"

Ash shook his head. His hair wasn't as dark a brown as Thad's, and his eyes were green instead of blue, yet, from their guarded intensity, they were unmistakably brothers. "Not in *his* car."

"Why?" she asked. "Did something happen to it?"

Ash hesitated a moment as if deliberating how much to tell her. Then he admitted, "The tires have been slashed and all the windows broken."

"While it was sitting in my driveway?" she asked,

horrified that someone dangerous had been that close to her home.

"He'd parked a ways down the street," Ash said. "But the car was under a light. Whoever did this was really bold."

Or really crazy.

"Where would Thad have gone?"

"I have a couple patrols looking for him," he said. "I'm sure he'll turn up. You know Thad…."

Did she? Sometimes she believed she knew him better than his own family did. But at times like now, when he disappeared, she wasn't sure anyone knew Thad—even Thad.

"But what if the person who did that to his car took him?" she asked.

"More likely Thad's trying to track down the vandal himself," Ash said. "And it was probably just a vandal. We've had reports in this area of malicious mischief— stolen or destroyed Christmas decorations, that kind of thing."

She glanced out the big picture window and shivered. "Someone knocked down all our snowmen… Mark's snow family."

From what she could see in the dim light falling from the picture window into the front yard, the snowmen hadn't been just knocked down but crushed. Even the snow boy. Mark would be devastated when he noticed that the snow family he'd built with his daddy was gone.

Ash let out a breath of relief. "Yeah, it's probably kids then, getting antsy for Christmas break."

"But to break windows and slash tires…" To Caroline, that felt more personal than a random act of vandalism.

"You're a teacher, right?" Ash asked.

She nodded. "Elementary school. None of my kids would do something like this."

"Well, kids don't stay that sweet and innocent nowadays," he warned her. "They egg each other on to bigger risks and greater violence."

"I know some high school teachers whose houses have been egged and mailboxes knocked down," she admitted.

"Depending on where they teach, some have reported their cars stolen and themselves physically assaulted," he shared. "Even kids can be quite dangerous."

Caroline shuddered. "And Thad's out there by himself."

"We both know Thad's been in more dangerous places than a St. Louis suburb," Ash reminded her, "and he's come out without a scratch."

"I can't say the same now," a deep voice grumbled as Thad pushed open the door and stepped inside the living room. Blood dripped from a gash on his hand.

"Are you all right?" Caroline asked, her pulse tripping with fear.

His lips curved into a grim smile. "It's just a scratch."

"Looks like it might need stitches," Ash observed as he inspected the wound. "I wondered where all that blood had come from." He'd obviously been worried although he'd kept that information from Caroline.

She grabbed one of the Christmas stockings hanging from the fireplace and gently wrapped it around Thad's hand.

He groaned as he inspected the knitted reindeer-patterned stocking. "Yeah, that'll make it feel better."

"You need to stop the bleeding," she said, peeling back the stocking to look at the wound. "There could still be glass in the cut. You need to go to the emergency room and get this taken care of." She turned to his brother. "Why don't you take him?"

"No!" Thad said, his voice nearly a shout.

Ash shook his head. "She's right. It looks bad."

"I don't need to go," Thad said with a pointed stare at his older brother.

The detective nodded with sudden understanding of their nonverbal exchange. "Caroline could take you, and I could stay here."

"No," she said, rejecting the idea. "I don't want Mark to wake up with a stranger."

"He's his uncle," Thad said.

"Who he's never met," she reminded him. "He's a stranger, and after the incident at the mall, I put the fear of God in Mark about strangers. There's no way I could leave him alone with one."

Thad sighed. "You're right."

"So I'll take you then?" Ash asked tentatively.

With a grimace, Thad tied the Christmas stocking around his hand. "I don't need to go. It'll be fine."

Ash glanced out the window. "I need to go. Looks like the department tow truck is here."

"Department tow truck?" Thad asked.

"Yeah, we'll bring your car in," the SLPD detective

said, "and see if we can find any fingerprints or any-thing on it."

"But you said it was probably just kids," Caroline reminded him. The brothers' intensity unnerved her; something was going on.

Ash nodded. "More than likely, since they took out the snow *family,* too."

Thad glanced out the front window at the dese-crated snowmen he'd made with his son, and a muscle twitched along his tightly clenched jaw. "I'll go out to the tow truck with you," Thad said.

Caroline stepped closer, worried about more than his hand now. "But you're hurt—"

"I'll see that he takes care of it," Ash promised. "And it was nice to finally meet you. I'd like to meet your son—" his throat moved as he swallowed "—my nephew, too."

"Sunday dinner," Thad said. "She and Mark are going to come to Sunday dinner."

"But Sunday's…"

Christmas. Thad hadn't realized, nor had he obvi-ously intended to invite her home for Christmas. She'd actually forgotten, too.

"We'll see you Sunday then," Ash continued with excitement. "It'll be great to have a little one around to open up presents. It just might make Christmas special again."

Thad said nothing, neither taking back nor con-firming his invitation. He just opened the door for his brother and then followed him out. The door had barely shut behind them when she heard them raise their voices in an argument.

From the look on Thad's face, she doubted that she and Mark would be showing up on Sunday. She also doubted that Christmas would ever be special again for the Kendalls.

"WHAT THE HELL is the matter with you?" Ash yelled. "Why'd you go running after some malicious vandals unarmed?" He grabbed at Thad, patting the bulge under his jacket. "You're not unarmed. What the hell are you?"

"Prepared," he lied.

He hadn't been prepared at all, so it was good that he hadn't actually found anything more frightening than a half-frozen raccoon in the little alley behind Caroline's house. He hadn't even noticed that Mark's snow family had been destroyed. As he stared at the trampled mounds of snow on her front yard, his gut clenched with regret and anger. That bothered him more than the damage to his car.

Whoever had done all this had been so damn close to the house.

If only he'd looked out the window and caught him. But instead he'd been giving Mark a bath and then trying to seduce Caroline into bed.

"Where and how did you get a gun?" Ash persisted.

"I'm not entirely without connections in this town," he reminded his older brother.

Ash shuddered. "You don't need the kind of connections that'll hook you up with a gun," he said. "You need to focus on your connections in that house—that woman and your son."

"That's why I needed the gun," Thad admitted. "To protect them."

Ash's green eyes narrowed with suspicion. "What makes you so damn certain that they need protecting?"

He gestured at his damaged car and what had once been Mark's snow family. "This…"

"It could have been vandals, like I told her," Ash said. "The suburbs have been getting hit hard this holiday."

"And Mark nearly getting abducted at the mall?"

"Could have been the mistake the security guards thought it—"

"Why didn't whoever grabbed him bring him back to his mother then?" Thad said. "I thought you, out of everyone, wouldn't be so damn naive and trusting anymore."

Ash grabbed Thad's jacket, his face tight with concern and impatience. "And why the hell are you so damn untrusting? Has there been a threat against you?" He glanced back at the house, where Caroline watched them through the front window. "Against them?"

Thad shook his head. "But my gut's telling me they're in danger."

Ash sighed. "I'd put a car out front, but I need more than your windows shattered and your tires slashed to warrant around-the-clock protection. The best I can do is step up patrols in the neighborhood. I'll send a car past every hour or so."

Ignoring the pain in his wounded hand, Thad grabbed Ash's shoulders and squeezed. "Thanks. It'll help until I can convince Caroline to move her and Mark on to the estate with me."

"You think the estate is safe?" Ash asked.

Given everything that had happened there, in the distant past and not so distant past when Natalie and Gray had nearly died at the cottage on the grounds, Thad couldn't claim that it was. "I just want them with me."

"And she won't let you stay here?" His brother gestured at the brick Cape Cod.

"She doesn't trust me," Thad admitted.

"So she's as smart as she is beautiful," Ash remarked with a grin.

"Hey!"

"I don't trust you, either, little brother," Ash admitted. "I think you've been keeping bigger secrets than her and your son from us."

Just then Thad's cell rang, with the distinctive tone that indicated it was his boss, his *real* boss, calling. "I've gotta take this," he said, stepping back as the tow driver approached Ash.

While his brother was busy with the department employee, he walked farther down the block to get out of Ash's hearing, and Caroline's if she came out of the house. "Kendall," he answered the call.

"I got a message that you needed to speak to me immediately," Anya said.

He had called her after he'd called Ash.

"What's wrong?" she asked.

"I think Michaels gave me up," he said. "I think the wrong people have found out who I really am."

"Has there been an attempt on your life?" she asked, her voice full of concern.

"No." He glanced down at his hand. "But something

happened—someone's trying to send me a message."
And he had received it loud and clear. He and his family
were not safe in St. Louis.

"What happened?" she asked.

When he told her, she made no reply. "I know it
doesn't sound serious, but I'd like some protection."

"You would?" she asked, her voice sharp with surprise.

"Not for me," he admitted. "I discovered something
recently." Something that had changed everything for
him.

"Your parents' killer?" she asked. "That's good.
Then you can come back in now. I've been holding an
assignment that requires your special skills."

"To finish the assignment with Michaels and find
his killer?" He had always assumed that would be his
next job.

She made a noise like a pen clicking or gun cock-
ing. One never knew with Anya. "That assignment is
no longer a priority."

"A man died—"

"I need you for something more important. When
will you be ready to return?"

"I haven't found my parents' killer yet," he said. But
maybe, if he hadn't been compromised, the killer had
found him. "I found out that I have a son."

"You're a father?" she asked, shock clear in the sharp
crack of her voice.

"Yes. He's three years old, and someone tried to grab
him from the mall a couple weeks ago. And tonight
vandalism happened outside his house. I think some-

one's threatening my son." And his mother. "To get to me."

A sigh of heavy disappointment rattled the phone. "If you were compromised, no one would know that you had a son," she pointed out. "This has nothing to do with what you do for your country."

"So you won't help me protect my family?" After all the years he had cared nothing of his own safety, putting his life on the line, to protect others?

"I can't misappropriate manpower when there's been no obvious threat," she told him, clicking off the call as if she cared to hear nothing else he had to say.

And given that he had revealed himself to be as much a liability as Michaels, maybe she didn't care anymore.

He glanced up to find his brother watching him, his eyes narrowed with suspicion. Detective Kendall hadn't considered the damage here tonight a threat, either. Maybe it wasn't obvious to him or to Agent Anya Smith, but it was obvious to Thad that his family had been threatened.

SLASHING THE TIRES, breaking the windows, destroying the snow *family*—Ed had done it all in a fit of fury. Even now, hours later, his heart pounded erratically over the risk he'd taken.

He could have been caught, and then it all would have been over before he'd had a chance to mete out the punishment that Thad Kendall deserved.

But he'd had to wait too long to dole out that punishment. And while he bided his time—the most opportune time—to grab the boy, Thad Kendall got to play happy family.

But he had caught a glimpse of Thad's face tonight, when the man had discovered the damage to his car, and Kendall hadn't been happy. He'd been scared, not for himself but for them. He knew for certain that they were in danger now.

Sure, it would make him even more vigilant, more determined than ever to protect them. But then, when he failed, and Ed would see to it that he failed miserably, it would hurt him even more. Because there was no worse feeling than failing those you loved....

## *Chapter Ten*

"Are you okay?" Tammy asked, tapping her knuckles against Caroline's open classroom door. The children had gone down to lunch. Usually Caroline would have been with Tammy in the teacher's lounge by now, eating her own lunch.

She nodded, but her head pounded with the movement. She hadn't managed to get much sleep the night before, even after Thad and his brother had left her house. And every time she'd glanced out her window, she'd noticed a St. Louis Police Department patrol car driving past. Instead of the police presence reassuring her, it had made her more uneasy.

"I'm not sure," she replied honestly.

"Things not going well with Thad?" Tammy asked, her voice soft with sympathy.

"He's great with Mark," she admitted. "So patient and sweet."

"You sound surprised. Or disappointed?"

Caroline leaned back in her chair and sighed. "Maybe both."

Tammy chuckled. "I understand."

"How can you when I don't?" Caroline wondered.

"After we had kids and I saw what a great father Steve is, I fell deeper in love with him, deeper than I'd thought it possible to love anyone," Tammy shared.

"I can't love Thad," Caroline insisted.

"Why not?"

"Besides the whole leaving thing," Caroline said, "there's also the fact that I don't trust him. He's keeping something from me and his family, something important." Something that might have put their son in danger.

"Like another wife and kid?" Tammy asked.

She shook her head. "Something dangerous."

"Sure, he puts himself in danger when he goes to those countries to report on war," Tammy allowed. "But he's home now. What danger could he be in?"

Caroline flashed back to his car with the shattered windows and slashed tires. And Mark's poor, crushed snow family. Her little boy had been devastated when he'd seen the snowmen gone that morning. She'd promised him that Thad would come back and help him rebuild them even bigger.

But was it wise for Thad to be around his son if he was in danger? Maybe he hadn't brought the danger back with him from whatever war-torn country he'd been in last. Maybe the danger had been waiting for Thad to come home all along.

"His parents were murdered here," she reminded Tammy.

"The Christmas Eve Murders, everyone knows that," Tammy replied with a shudder of revulsion. She much preferred romance to reality. "That happened twenty years ago."

"But the man they'd thought had killed the parents wasn't the real killer."

Tammy nodded. "I know. My husband works for the news, remember?"

"I'm sorry—"

"You're scared," her friend observed, "about more than just falling for Thad Kendall all over again, too."

"Yes, I am. That killer—the real killer—is still out there, you know." And had he been out there the night before in her front yard, destroying the snowman family her son had made with his father?

Tammy shook her head. "No, you don't know that. Twenty years have passed. He could have died."

"But what if he didn't?"

Her friend shrugged off her concerns. "If I got away with murder, I would have gotten the hell out of town."

"But now, with the other man cleared, he didn't get away with it."

"Even more reason to stay far, far away from St. Louis," Tammy said. "Criminals very rarely return to the scenes of their crimes."

Caroline blew out a breath of relief. "You're right."

"So are you going to come eat now?" Tammy asked. "I brought salads for today, so we can pig out tomorrow when everyone brings something for our Christmas lunch."

Caroline's stomach growled, more at the mention of the Christmas lunch than the salad. But before she could stand up, her cell rang. She opened her bottom drawer, pulled out her purse and then her phone.

"It's the day care," she said. "I have to take this."

"I hope Mark's all right," Tammy said.

"I'm sure he is." This was probably about Thad. Had he shown up and tried to take Mark out despite her telling him not to?

"Have them give Bethany a hug from Mommy for me," Tammy said, referring to her daughter, who was in the same day care. Then she headed out the door, off to her salad.

"Hello," she said. "This is Caroline Emerson."

"Hi, Caroline," the day care director said.

"Is Mark all right?"

"Yes, yes, all the children are all right. But I felt I needed to call and let you know…"

Caroline's heart rate quickened with the nerves in the director's voice. "What?"

"There was a man hanging around earlier. He never approached the center or the children," the director assured her, "but he was standing around outside as if he was watching the place."

"Was he about thirty?" Caroline asked. "Good-looking with brown hair and blue eyes?"

The director chuckled. "No, it wasn't Mark's father."

"You know who Mark's father is?"

"Thad Kendall," the director said then sputtered, "but he didn't tell us that. He came by earlier with his brother, Detective Ash Kendall, and Mark called him Daddy."

"Thanks for letting me know that he came by," Caroline said.

And he'd brought Ash, too?

"He asked that we call him or his brother if we saw anything suspicious around the day care," the woman continued. "If he hadn't stopped by today and said that very thing, we might not have thought anything of that man standing outside. This is a busy area after all, so it's not unusual that someone stand outside the coffee shop across the street waiting for someone."

So Thad's suspicious nature had unsettled them, too.

"That's why I'm not certain we should even call them about the man," the director continued. "We may just be overreacting. He was an older gentleman and very well dressed. I'm sure he was just waiting to meet someone."

"No," Caroline said. "You should call them about it. Actually, just call Detective Kendall. He'll know whether it's anything to worry about."

Or just his brother's paranoia.

Why was Thad so certain that their son was in danger?

What the hell was he keeping from her?

HE WAS LOSING HIS MIND. Ash had told him as much, and so had Caroline. He had panicked when she and Mark hadn't been home after work. She hadn't appreciated his calling while she and their son were at her friend's house baking cookies for the Christmas parties at both her school and Mark's day care.

Needless to say, she hadn't invited him to join them despite her friend, in the background, shouting out an invitation. He smiled at Tammy Stehouwer's obvious matchmaking. The woman had been right, though, that he and Caroline would hit it off. They had four years ago.

And if Caroline would give him a chance, they would again. But she wasn't about to give him a chance, not until he was ready to tell her everything. No one deserved the burden of knowing everything about his life, about the things he'd seen and done. But he wasn't at liberty to reveal the things he'd seen and done or even what he really was. He would lose his job for certain and maybe even his life, given that the people he'd spied on were usually prone to vengeance.

But Caroline, being Caroline with her big heart and her maternal instincts, had assured him that she and Mark were safe. They were spending the night at Tammy's, and Steve Stehouwer had already turned on the security system.

Thad would have to trust that they were safe for the night. So, ready to give in to the need for the sleep he'd been denying his body, he climbed the stairs to his and his siblings' wing of the house. His was the only occupied suite at the moment. Ash and Devin had their own places, and Natalie had officially moved in with Gray. Guilt and regret tugged at him.

Did she not feel as if she belonged on the Kendall estate since she wasn't biologically a Kendall? Or did she just need the comfort and protection of her fiancé now? Thad would call her in the morning to make certain she was all right. She had acted so tough when he'd told her the truth. But maybe she'd only been acting.

Yawning, he reached the door to his suite and pushed it open, using his bandaged hand. Despite his protests, Ash had taken him to the emergency room last night and had his wound flushed out. He'd forgone the stitches and could probably lose the bandage when he showered. It hadn't been as bad as Caroline and Ash had worried it was.

He'd been hurt far worse than that before. And probably would again if he ignored his instincts. They were niggling at him now. His door hadn't been shut tight.

But maybe Aunt Angela had had someone clean the room today, which would have been kind of pointless when he'd actually spent so little time in it. Ever since the incident at the mall, he'd spent most nights in his car outside Caroline's house.

Maybe that was why his windows had been smashed, so that he couldn't spend the night protecting them. His guts tightened with fear and anger; someone was definitely after his son.

He stepped forward and in the semidarkness of the room, tripped over something on the floor. Whoever had cleaned up had done a half-assed job. He cursed and fumbled along the wall for the light switch. The lamp came on, but it wasn't sitting on the bedside table. Instead, it lay on the floor, its shade bent and the base cracked.

It wasn't the only thing broken in the room. Like his window, the mirror above the dresser was smashed, all the toiletries swept to the floor. And the photo albums that he'd borrowed from the library were strewn across the floor, the pictures torn or crumpled with the same rage that someone had destroyed his car and Mark's snow family.

Someone had been inside his room. Inside the house, just like they had the night his parents had been murdered. Natalie was gone. But Uncle Craig and Aunt Angela would be home.

He reached for the gun that he'd tucked into the waistband of his jeans. And, with his weapon drawn, he stalked around his own house as if he were in another country checking for insurgents.

His wing was empty. The first floor was deserted, too. So he headed up the stairs to the other wing of the house, where Aunt Angela and Uncle Craig used the master suite that had once been his parents'…until they had been murdered there.

The house looked nothing like it had before their deaths. As if to erase their memories of that horrible time, Aunt Angela had redecorated the whole house. While it was elegant, it was also as warm and vibrant as the woman herself.

His heart thudded in his throat as he approached the French doors to the bedroom where his parents' bodies had been found.

Where they'd been murdered.

His gun clutched tight in his bandaged hand, he pushed open the doors. And a scream rent the air.

Aunt Angela pressed her hand against her heart, which was dangerous as she held a pair of scissors. She'd been wrapping presents on the bed. "What are you doing?"

With a sigh of relief, Thad lowered the barrel of his gun. "Are you all right?"

She nodded. "Except for the ten years you scared off my life."

He glanced around the bedroom. "Where's Uncle Craig?"

"At work yet," she replied, hurt dimming some of the usual warmth of her brown eyes. "He's been working a lot lately." She focused on the gun again. "What are you doing with that? What happened to your hand?"

"I'm okay," he assured her.

"What's going on?"

"Someone's been in the house," he said. Pitching his voice low, he added, "They could still be here." He grabbed his phone, but instead of punching in Ash's number, he dialed 911. He needed the closest available unit for backup.

After dropping the scissors atop the unwound roll of paper, Aunt Angela reached out for his hand, hers shaking. "Stay with me."

"Of course." After pushing aside the wrapping stuff, he settled beside her on the bed. It wasn't the same bed where his parents had been murdered but it brought back those same horrific memories.

She squeezed his hand. "I'm sorry."

"What are you sorry about?" he wondered. His aunt had never done anything wrong.

"I thought it was all over for you—that the man who'd gone to prison was the killer. I thought we were all safe here." She shivered. "But I was wrong. He's back, isn't he?"

He'd thought the threat might have come from someone from his other life, from another country—but not now.

"Yeah, he's back."

And he was proving to them that he could still get inside the house as easily as he had the night he had killed Joseph and Marie Kendall.

He shivered, too.

"How do you know *he* was here?" she asked, trembling as she glanced around her room as if remembering that it had once been a crime scene.

"He was in my suite," Thad said. "I'm surprised and very glad that you didn't hear him." If Aunt Angela had heard anything and gone to investigate… Thad blocked out the images of everything that could have happened to her. "He really tossed the place."

"I left this morning after the cleaning staff had been here, and then I was gone all afternoon," she said. "Christmas shopping. I just got back a little while ago."

"Maybe he waited until after you'd left to break in." Maybe he hadn't wanted to hurt Angela Kendall. Thad glanced around his aunt's room again, which was untouched, as was the rest of the house. Maybe he was the only Kendall this guy wanted to hurt.

He remembered the pictures then. "I should have put those albums back right after I looked through them." Because now they were destroyed.

"We can figure out a way to replace pictures," she assured him. "We can't replace family."

"You did," he said, so grateful that she hadn't been harmed and so grateful for what she'd done for him and his siblings. "You were a better mother to us than she ever was."

"Thad," she gasped at his pronouncement. "You shouldn't say that."

"The truth?" He wrapped his arm around her. "It is the truth. You were always there for us, like she never was."

"Your mother was so beautiful," Aunt Angela murmured wistfully. "And your father was so driven. She needed attention."

"And when she didn't get it from him, where did she get it?" If anyone knew, it was Aunt Angela. While she and his mother hadn't had much in common, they had been family, if not friends.

She shook her head. "I can't speak ill of her."

"Because she's dead?" He'd never understood that. Since the person was already dead, what did it matter if anyone spoke ill of them?

"Because she was your mother," she said, "and you should have only good memories of her."

"She was pretty and she always smelled nice," Thad said. "That's what I remember about her. You're the one who came to all our sports events and school plays and pageants. You're the one who made us dinner every night and baked us cookies."

Tears streaked from her eyes, which she squeezed shut. "Oh, you were always the charmer, Thad Kendall."

"I realize that you're trying to protect me from the truth about my mother," he said, loving her for her sensitivity, "but I need the truth so that I can protect this family from a killer."

She sighed wistfully. "Your mother was so beautiful and charming. You get your charm from her. I used to think she might have been just a flirt…."

Thad shook his head. "A friend of Devin's worked at a hotel where she used to meet some guy. Or guys."

"Your mother flirted a lot," she said, "especially at the company functions we attended before your uncle and I moved to California." After their son had died in that tragic auto accident, Craig had sold his half of Kendall Communications to his older brother, who he'd known would have never let him have any real control of the company.

"So you think the guy—or guys—may have actually worked for Dad?"

"Marie liked to be flattered," Angela said. "And no one is as good at flattering someone as a salesman."

"So Mom liked the salesmen at Kendall Communications?"

Aunt Angela nodded. "Yes. At every company function, they fought for her attention, jumping around like puppies and bringing her drinks. But I don't know what ones it might have gone beyond flirting with."

"Ones?"

She drew in a deep breath and finally uttered a few names, which Thad had her jot down on a piece of her floral stationery. "They were the good-looking ones," she said as she passed him the paper. "The ones she actually seemed interested in, too."

"Did any of them have a son named Wade?"

She shrugged. "Twenty years was a long time ago."

Sometimes. And sometimes, as the anniversary of their murders approached, it seemed like just hours ago. He could remember the crime-scene techs and detectives all descended on his house, like they probably would be soon.

"I don't remember their kids' names," she said. "I barely remembered their names—just thought of one when your brother Devin mentioned him a few days ago."

"Devin mentioned him?"

She shrugged. "Something about business…"

So maybe some of them still worked for Kendall Communications. "I'll call Devin and have him check company records. They would have had their kids listed as dependents on tax and insurance documents."

He would have him check not just sons named Wade but any in the approximate age bracket. Thad reached for his phone again, but as he did, the bedroom doors burst open, and he was the one staring down the barrel of a gun.

This time his brother's.

Aunt Angela gasped and touched her heart again. "You boys…"

"I heard the call come over the radio," Ash said. "What the hell's going on now?"

"Check out my rooms," Thad ordered him. "They were vandalized like my car."

Ash looked from him to Aunt Angela, who'd gone deathly pale. "Are you both okay?"

Thad nodded and assured him, "I'll stay with Auntie."

"I'm fine," she said shakily as Ash rushed off to search the rest of the house.

Thad could have told him he'd already done that, but he figured a detective wouldn't trust a reporter to have done a thorough job. Even an armed reporter.

"We'll just stay here until Uncle Craig gets home." He was sure that Ash would call him, too, if he hadn't already.

"I'm sorry," she said, laying her head on his shoulder. "I should have told you about your mother earlier."

"You were trying to protect us," Thad said. "I understand that."

She patted his hand. "You do, now that you have your own son. I lost mine…." Her breath audibly caught. "But then I got all of you. And you became my children. I would do anything to protect you, like you will Mark."

"I will," he agreed.

But what he'd realized when he'd found the damage in his room was that the best way for him to protect Mark was to let him go.

# Chapter Eleven

The beeping of a breaking news bulletin drew Caroline's attention to the television in the teacher's lounge. She stepped away from the buffet table of goodies where everyone had congregated and walked over to the TV, which flashed an image of the infamous Kendall estate behind the female anchor.

"Police were called to the Kendall mansion last night, just days before the twenty-year anniversary of the Christmas Eve Murders of Joseph and Marie Kendall."

Tammy gasped and grasped Caroline's arm in silent support. "Steve took off this week and next so he could spend the holidays with me and the kids, so I didn't know about this yet."

Otherwise she knew her friend would have warned her. Why hadn't Thad warned her? Or at least called to assure her that he was all right? Because they weren't the happy family Mark—and she—wanted them to be.

Caroline shook off her flash of pain and focused on the anchor's report.

"The Kendall family would not make an official statement to the police, but an inside source confirms that acclaimed photojournalist Thad Kendall called 911 to report a break-in at the estate."

The woman smiled at the mention of Thad but then pulled her face back into a serious mask. "Could it be that the killer, who authorities just learned in the last few months is free, has returned to the scene of his crime?"

Tammy reached up and shut off the television. "That's ridiculous," she said. "There have been a lot of break-ins lately. There always is around Christmastime but given the poor economy, there are even more this year."

Caroline nodded, but she felt sick, the sweets she'd eaten rising up in her throat. Ignoring the party, she rushed out into the quiet hallway. The children had already been dismissed at noon to begin their Christmas break.

"He's okay," Tammy said as she followed her out. "They would have said had anyone been hurt."

Caroline nodded again. "I know."

But she wasn't worried about just Thad. She hurried into her classroom, dug her cell out of her purse and punched in the number for the day care.

"This is Caroline Emerson," she said. "Is Mark all right?"

The young assistant, who had picked up, laughed. "He's having a great time. We're playing games and eating the cookies you and Mrs. Stehouwer brought this morning."

Regret tugged at Caroline but she said, "I'm going to pick him up in just a few minutes."

Tammy had followed her into her classroom. "Let

Steve do it," she said. "He already picked up Steve Jr. from his half day of school, and he's picking up Bethany from day care in just a few minutes."

"But I can—"

"You have company," Tammy said, stepping back to allow Thad into the room. In jeans and a leather jacket, he was as sexy as ever.

Caroline clenched her hand around her phone, so that she wouldn't throw it down and run to wrap her arms around his neck. What if he'd been injured or worse during the break-in?

"Okay." She focused on her call. "Uh, Mr. Stehouwer will be picking up Mark today along with his daughter."

That was good. Mark would be safe with Steve.

She was the one in danger now...because Thad didn't look like the man who had built a snow family with their son and who had held her throughout the night. He looked as cold and distant as the man who'd walked away from her without a backward glance four years ago.

"I'll call Steve and let him know he's picking up Mark, too. We'll be happy to watch him until you come to pick him up," Tammy generously offered as she pulled shut the door to the classroom, leaving Caroline alone with Thad. If she'd been hoping to play matchmaker again, she was going to be disappointed.

But not nearly as disappointed as Caroline was sure she was going to be. She dropped into the chair behind her desk. "Why are you here?" she asked. "Has something happened...something *else?*"

"You heard about the break-in," he surmised.

"You should have called me." Heat rushed to her face. "For Mark's sake," she hastened to explain. "If he's in danger…"

IF THEIR SON WAS IN DANGER, it was because of Thad, so the best way to keep him and Caroline safe was to keep his distance from them.

"This was a bad idea," Thad said, forcing out the words. He couldn't look at her, so he gazed around her classroom instead. The walls served as sunshine-yellow backdrops for the kids' colorful artwork and starred papers.

"What was?" she asked, as if bracing herself for the worst.

"My trying to be a father." He swallowed hard, choking on the lies. "You were right that I'm not cut out for it."

She sucked in a breath of surprise, but she didn't argue with him. He had hoped she would argue, that she would tell him he was better at being a dad than he had thought he could be.

He had been so worried that he would have already done or said something to screw up his relationship with Mark and make the little boy hate him. But he was pretty sure his son loved him as much as Thad loved Mark. And it was because Thad loved him so much that he had to back away.

But if he told Caroline the truth, she might argue with him. She might think, as his brother had and she had earlier, that he was just overreacting and being paranoid. She might convince him to stay in his son's life instead of his convincing her that it was best he stay away from Mark.

The sad thing was that she seemed to need no convincing. Caroline said nothing, just stared up at him with dry eyes. It was as if she'd cried herself out over him four years ago and didn't intend to waste any more tears on him.

He didn't blame her. "I should have just stayed away from him and you," he said. "I'll be leaving soon anyways."

"You will?" she asked, her voice barely above a whisper.

He jerked his head in a sharp nod.

"You found your parents' killer?"

"Not yet," he admitted. "But we're pretty sure we're closing in on him now."

Yesterday he had only glanced over the names his aunt had written down, thinking that he wouldn't have recognized any of them since he'd just been a kid when his parents died. But when he'd studied the list more closely, one name had jumped out at him.

Ed Turner.

When he'd questioned Aunt Angela about him, she'd been unable to say for certain that his mother had had an affair with the man. But she'd admitted that the two had always looked at each other a certain way, as if they'd seen more of each other. A lot more of each other.

"So you know who their killer is?"

He sighed. "We don't have any proof yet." Of the affair or anything else. Hell, they hadn't even been able to find Turner yet. Devin had been trying to track down the man for months in order to extend an offer for his company.

And it was the man's disappearance that worried Thad. A lot of what he'd learned about Ed Turner worried him, and had made him Thad's prime suspect even though his brothers weren't as convinced of the man's guilt.

"Are the police looking at him as a suspect, too?" she asked.

A respected businessman whose company held several defense contracts for communications equipment? He would be their last suspect. But Thad's gut told him otherwise.

"We'll find the evidence with or without the police department's help." He would get Turner's DNA himself, court order or subpoena be damned. He just had to find Turner, in order to keep everyone Thad cared about safe.

"So as soon as whoever this guy is has been arrested, you'll be leaving?"

He nodded. "You've known that all along."

She surprised him with a laugh. "Wow. Here's déjà vu for you."

"We have had this conversation before." And it was almost as hard this time as it had been last time. But this time he was leaving for her sake and Mark's. To protect them.

She sighed. "And I knew we'd be having it again."

"That's why you didn't want me getting close to you," he said. "You were right about that. I shouldn't have tried to get close to Mark, either. Hopefully he's not too attached to me that he'll miss me when I'm gone."

"You haven't been around that long," she said, as if implying that Mark would forget about him.

Pain clutched Thad's heart. Would his son forget all about him? At three, he was young enough to do that. But Thad wasn't going to stay away forever, just until the threat against his son was gone.

But given the way Thad lived, would the threat against him ever really be gone?

"This is for the best," he said, trying to convince himself. "I'm not father material. You and Mark will be better off."

"With you halfway across the world? With you putting your life in danger?"

"It's what I do."

She nodded, and her eyes shimmered with tears. "We will be better off if you leave now," she agreed. "Because you're going to leave eventually anyways. For good, when you get killed because you put yourself in the middle of someone else's war."

*Someone else's war.*

Was that what he'd been fighting, someone else's war, when he should have been fighting his own here at home? Of course no one had known then that the wrong man had been convicted of his parents' murders.

"What I do is important," he defended himself.

She nodded. "And if you didn't do it, someone else would. It doesn't have to be you. But you'd rather go off alone to those countries and let someone else raise your son."

She hadn't married in the past four years, but Thad

wasn't arrogant enough to believe that was because she'd been in love with him. She'd just been totally focused on raising their son. But when Mark got older, she would find someone. That nine-to-five guy she deserved.

Pain clutched his heart. "Caroline…"

She shook her head. "It's fine. I didn't expect anything from you. Unfortunately, Mark did. But I'll tell him…" She sucked in a shaky breath. "You don't have to see him again." She stood, as if prepared to show him out the door. "And I don't have to see you again, either."

He turned for the door, walking slowly in case she changed her mind and tried to stop him. But he would never know if she would have because her cell phone rang. He opened the door, ready to leave her just as he had planned.

But she cried out, "No!"

His heart leaped against his ribs, and he whirled back around to her. "What's happened?"

Her face had paled, and she trembled uncontrollably, the cell phone dropping from her hand onto her desk. "A man with a gun stormed the day care."

*Oh, God. God, no…*

He fought down the fear. "Was anyone hurt?"

"Tammy's husband," she whispered. "Steve tried to stop the man, and he was shot."

"And Mark?" What had happened to their sweet little boy?

Her eyes widened with horror and filled with tears. "The man took him."

BLOOD SPATTERED THE little boy's face, and red streaks trailed down his cheeks with tears. His hand shaking slightly, Ed wiped a damp washcloth across the kid's skin and washed away the blood.

It wasn't the boy's blood. He hadn't been hurt. Yet.

"It's not real?" the kid asked, his bottom lip trembling.

"It's fake," Ed lied. "That man wasn't really hurt. We were just playing a game. Like cops and robbers, you know."

The little boy's breath shuddered out in a ragged sigh of relief. "Mommy doesn't let me play cops and robbins. She says it's too vi'lin." He shivered. "And it was a really scary game."

"Sometimes adults play scary games," Ed said. And then, inevitably, someone got hurt. Too bad that this time it would be this little boy.

"So you know Bethany's daddy?"

Even though he had only recognized Steve Stehouwer because he was the anchor on the local news, Ed nodded. The man shouldn't have tried to play hero, and he wouldn't have gotten shot. But there were always innocent casualties in war. And when Thad Kendall had killed his son, he had declared war on Ed Turner. Kendall wasn't the only one who'd spent years dodging bullets and roadside bombs in foreign countries. After he'd left his cushy sales job at Kendall Communications, Turner had launched his own company specializing in defense communications. In order to meet the needs of his clients, he'd walked in their shoes. He'd lived as a spy. That was why he had immediately recognized Thad Kendall for what he really was.

A killer.

Ed led the little boy out of the dated pink-and-lime-green bathroom into the kitchen. He didn't trust the kid in the living room where he might turn on the TV and learn from the news that Ed had lied about the game. The kid would find out soon enough that this was very real.

"Are you related to *my* daddy?" the little boy asked as he settled onto a chair at the old Formica table. His blue eyes wide, he stared at the pictures of his father and him and his mother plastered all over the walls. "Mommy says he has a big family."

"Yes, he does. And I guess that in a way I am related to him," Ed said as he took the box of hot chocolate packets out of the cupboard. He could at least make the little kid comfortable while he waited to implement the next phase of his plan. If only he could make himself comfortable with a damn strong drink.... "I'm your aunt Natalie's father."

The little boy peered through the doorway into the living room and then turned toward the open door of the bathroom off the hall. "Is Aunt Natalie here?"

"No." Natalie had never really been his. Her paternity had been denied and covered up so that Marie Kendall wouldn't lose what she'd valued most. Money. Image. Her looks.

In the end she'd lost them all. Just as her son Thad would. He had been the last of her children by Joseph Kendall, and although he hadn't joined the business, he was still the most like him.

Ruthless. Determined to keep what he considered his...even when it had really belonged to Ed.

Like Natalie.

And Marie.

But Ed wasn't as upset over losing them as he was over losing his son. His boy had stood by him through it all and had died trying to protect him. Ed hadn't deserved his boy's loyalty. He hadn't been a good father to Wade.

After Marie had refused to accept Ed's offer to leave Emily and build a life with her, Ed had quit Kendall. He'd started his own company, intent on making it even bigger than Joseph had. He hadn't. But he'd built a strong niche company, and in those war-torn countries, he'd learned what was really important.

Emily. She had always been so loving and supportive, uncomplaining when he was never around, never telling him how much their son had suffered. How much she had suffered. He'd intended to make it up to her that night, but then he and his family had run into the Kendalls at a holiday charity function.

He'd seen Natalie and known immediately she was his daughter…and what he'd been denied. He'd only intended to talk to Marie when he'd used his key to let himself into her house later that night. But things had gone so wrong.

Emily had never figured out what had happened. She'd claimed to understand that he had to keep traveling for his job. He had never been able to stop traveling, because he'd worried that even though another man had been convicted, he would eventually be caught. But the only one who'd figured out his guilt was his son, even though it had taken him years to piece it all together. And still Wade had stood by him.

He deserved to have his death avenged. Ed owed him that much since he'd never been there for his son, just as Thad Kendall had never been there for his son.

Ed drew in a deep breath and reached for the block of knives on the kitchen counter. It was just too bad that to avenge Wade, Ed would have to take the life of this sweet kid.

# *Chapter Twelve*

Caroline had thought her heart had hurt during Thad's callous goodbye speech. But she hadn't known how much a heart could rip apart until the day care director had called to report Mark missing, taken by an armed gunman.

She couldn't stop shaking. And it didn't help that she was here, at the Kendall mansion, where people had been murdered, perhaps by the same man who'd abducted her son and shot her friend.

While Thad had filled in his family on what had happened at the day care center, she had phoned Tammy and had been surprised her friend had even taken her call. But Tammy, being the friend she was, had been as concerned about Mark as she was her own wounded husband. Steve was still in surgery, having a bullet removed from his shoulder. The doctors had assured Tammy that the gunshot wound was not life-threatening. Steve Stehouwer would live.

But she had no such assurances about her son.

Strong arms wrapped around her, pulling her back against a chest in which a heart pounded as madly as hers did.

"We'll find him," Thad assured her.

She tugged free of his grasp and whirled on him. "How? You're not even certain who took him!"

His family, who had all gathered in the family room, grew quiet and watched her, probably afraid she was losing her mind. But what did she care? If she'd truly lost her son, what did losing her mind matter?

Ash, the only one of Thad's family she had previously met, approached them. The St. Louis PD detective said, "We have a lead on the man who murdered our parents."

"But why would he take Mark?" she asked. "Why would he come after *my* son?"

"Money," Craig Kendall, the man she'd seen at St. Luke's, remarked. "He may call us with a demand for ransom so that he can get to some country with no extradition."

He thought like a businessman—logically. She thought like a mother, and so did the woman who approached her. She had to be the aunt Thad had spoken of so lovingly. She folded Caroline into her arms as if she were one of the family.

"We'll pay whatever he asks," she promised. "We'll get our Mark back."

*Our.* They'd already claimed her son as a Kendall. She clutched at the woman's softness and warmth before pulling back.

Tears streamed down her face, but she couldn't fight them back any longer. "We don't know that this is about ransom or revenge," she pointed out. "We don't know the whole story because Thad won't tell us."

Instead of staring at her as if she'd lost her mind,

Thad's family was staring at him. All of them with the same suspicion and doubt that she'd harbored.

He shook his head. "We don't have time for this. I have calls to make—"

"To whom?" his oldest brother asked. "That mysterious woman who took her time getting the message to you that the man convicted of killing our parents was innocent? Who is she?"

"Who are *you?*" Caroline asked.

He shook his head, his phone clasped in his hand as he backed from the room.

His sister stopped him. "You told me who I really am," she reminded him. "Don't you think it's fair that we find out who you really are?"

Thad shook his head and groaned. "I can't."

"Our son is missing," Caroline said. "Maybe his kidnapping has to do with your parents' killer and maybe it has to do with whatever you're keeping from us."

"We can't help you unless we know everything," Detective Kendall said. "We might be wasting our time chasing down the wrong leads."

"I'll find that out after I make a couple of calls," Thad promised.

"To whom?" Caroline demanded to know. "Who are you calling?"

He closed his eyes, as if praying for divine intervention. Then finally he answered them all, "My superior in the State Department."

Natalie's fiancé nodded as if he had confirmation of something he'd already learned. And he wrapped his arms around Natalie, offering her the comfort Caroline had refused to accept from Thad.

She'd only wanted the truth. But now that she knew…her mind reeled from all the possibilities. "You work for the government?" she asked.

Thad nodded.

"And you've been doing this for years?"

"I was recruited out of college," he admitted, holding her gaze while his family reacted with gasps of surprise.

She suspected that was another lie. He hadn't been *recruited;* he had sought them out, offering up his life for his country.

Or for excitement.

Or for justice.…

"So have you made a lot of enemies over the years?" She had to know.

"Only if my cover was blown," he said. "And until recently I was certain that it had never been compromised. You all just became some of a very small group of people who know that I'm more than a photojournalist."

"What happened recently?" Ash asked, ever the detective.

"When I left midassignment to come back here, one of my associates was abducted," Thad said, his blue eyes darkening with regret and guilt. "Before he was murdered, he was tortured."

Could that be happening now to their son? Could someone be torturing him?

She gasped in horror, and her legs gave out, folding beneath her.

THAD WAS TOO FAR AWAY to catch Caroline before she hit the floor. She never lost consciousness, though, or her anger and resentment at him. When he reached out to help her up, she shrank back from him, as if unable to bear his touch, and got to her feet herself.

"I wish you never came back," she whispered at him.

He didn't blame her for hating him. At the moment he hated himself for putting their son in danger.

"If he never came back, Gray and I would be dead," Natalie defended him.

He shook his head at his sister, not wanting anyone to further upset Caroline. His phone rang, with the call he'd been waiting to have returned, but he hesitated to reach for it. Not wanting to leave Caroline alone.

"Take it," she ordered him. "If it'll help you find my son, take the damn call."

He clicked the phone on. "Kendall…"

"Still no chatter," Anya replied without greeting. "I don't believe you've been compromised."

"Someone stormed a day care center with a gun today and abducted my son," he told her, whether she cared or not.

She gasped. "I'm sorry."

"I don't need your sympathy. I need your help," he implored her. "I'm calling in every favor I've got coming. I need to find my son as soon as possible."

"I'll find out what I can from here," she promised, "and call back."

He clicked off the phone and turned to his family. "I want you all to do the same. Call in every favor you have coming."

Devin was already reaching for his phone, as was Gray and Ash. Aunt Angela reached for Caroline instead, wrapping her arm around her trembling body and offering her support.

"You need to lie down," his aunt told her, "and rest."

Caroline shook her head. "I can't…"

"You're going through the worst nightmare a parent can," she commiserated. "There's nothing anyone can do or say to comfort you. But you have to keep the faith that your son will come back to you. And when he does, you'll need to be strong."

Because the boy might be traumatized from what he'd seen.

Devin lifted his phone away from his ear. "Jolie pulled the old employee records from dead storage. She found Ed Turner's insurance applica—"

"Ed Turner?" Uncle Craig interrupted. "He hasn't worked at the company in decades. He quit long before your parents were murdered. He started up his own company. Hell, Devin, you've been trying to get your hands—"

"I didn't think it was him, either," Devin said. "But Aunt Angela put him on the list."

When her husband turned to her, Angela nodded. "I suspected back then…"

"But he was married, too. His wife just died."

"Not every man is as honorable as you are," Aunt Angela told her husband, her eyes warm with love for him.

"But what could Ed want with Thad's son?" Uncle Craig asked, his brow furrowed with confusion. "He has his own money."

"According to the records Jolie found," Devin said,

"he also had a son named Wade with a date of birth making him about a year older than you, Thad."

Uncle Craig sucked in a breath as he realized what Thad had long ago. This wasn't about money or even the past. At least not the two decades-old past. It was about revenge.

"The dentist is listed," Devin said, "so she's getting Rachel the information to verify dental records."

Thad was glad that his brothers had been as clever as he was and had fallen for smart, resourceful women. He turned toward Ash. "You got an address for Turner yet?"

"Too many of them," Ash said with a sigh. "The guy and his corporation own properties all over St. Louis and the surrounding areas. We have to run them all down."

"We need to hurry," he said.

He wasn't sure how much time his son had, if he had any left at all.


CAROLINE WASN'T LIKE THAD'S brothers' wife and fiancée. She wasn't a crime-scene tech or even all that computer savvy. She didn't know how to chase down leads to her son's whereabouts. She didn't have the slightest idea how to find her son. But she knew he wasn't at the Kendall estate.

And she hadn't wanted to be there, either.

Her son had gotten away from his kidnapper at the mall. What if he'd escaped him again and found someone to drive him home? He knew his address. So she held her breath as she opened the door, hoping he waited for her inside and would rush into her arms.

But her house was eerily quiet and empty. No Mark. She wasn't alone, though. Thad had insisted on driving her home.

No matter what she said to him or how coldly she treated him, he had been considerate and patient with her. Of course he was used to kidnappings and to violence. She hadn't been until his world had collided with hers.

"Aunt Angela was right," he said. Sliding his arm around her waist, he led her toward the stairs. "You should get some rest."

"How?" Her heart pounded erratically, and her legs shook.

He supported most of her weight up the stairs and down the short hall to her room.

"Do you have anything you can take that will help you sleep?" he asked, his blue eyes dark with concern for her as she dropped onto the edge of her bed.

She wasn't the one he needed to worry about; he needed to worry about their child.

"My son," she said. "I need Mark back in my arms. I won't sleep until he's home." Her voice cracked as emotion welled up inside her. "I want my son."

*But her baby was gone....*

"I'll bring him home to you," Thad promised.

"You don't even know for sure who has him," she reminded him. Sure, Ed Turner sounded like the most viable suspect, but because of Thad, there were so many. "You have so many enemies."

"I'm sorry."

She shook her head. "I know it's not your fault. You

were just doing your job. You didn't even know about Mark." She sucked in a breath. "So I blame myself."

He dropped to his knees in front of her, as if begging her forgiveness. "None of this was your fault," he said. "I should have stayed away. I had no right to try to be part of your lives, not with the life I've lived."

"You're a hero," she reminded him. "You saved your sister's life and her fiancé's. And you've probably saved countless other lives."

"There's only one life I'm worried about right now."

Their son's.

He cupped her face in his hands, so that their gazes met and held. "I will find him."

But would it be too late?

"Then go," she urged. He shouldn't be wasting his time with her. "Do whatever you have to do to track down the man who took our son."

"I don't want to leave you alone," he said.

"Mark needs you more than I do," she reminded him. He had skills that no one else in the St. Louis Police Department possessed, not even his brother.

He nodded and reached beneath his jacket and pulled out a gun. "I'm leaving you this."

She shuddered. "I don't want that."

"I won't leave you alone unless you keep it," he said.

She shook her head. "But I don't like guns."

"When we dated, I took you to the shooting range," he said, reminding her of the date she'd found so exciting and so unlike her usual routine.

"That was my first clue that you were more than just a photojournalist," she said. He'd been an expert shot and very familiar with the weapons.

"You were a natural," he said. "Do you remember what I showed you about how to take off the safety and aim?"

She nodded. She hadn't forgotten anything he'd taught her, but she still hesitated before reaching for it. "I really don't want to have a gun in the house with a child."

But the child wasn't there. And if Thad didn't leave to find him, Mark might never come home. So she grabbed the gun and immediately tucked it into the drawer of the bedside table.

"He'll be home again," Thad said as if he'd read her mind. "I'll bring him home to you."

Thad had never made her promises, not four years ago and not since he'd been back…until today. She didn't know if that meant he would be able to keep his promise, but at least she knew that he would try, that he would probably die trying.

She leaned forward and pressed a kiss to his lips. His breath shuddered out against her mouth, and he kissed her back.

She pulled back when she tasted tears. They were hers. She'd cried so many she was numb to them. But she brushed the moisture from his face and mouth and implored, "Be careful…."

She didn't want to lose them both, but a shiver raced down her spine with foreboding. And she knew their Christmas was going to be far from merry.

# Chapter Thirteen

His heart thudding in his chest, Thad studied the blowup of Ed Turner's DMV photo and compared it to the police artist sketch of the man who'd taken Mark. "It's definitely him."

"It's the guy the day care director described hanging around earlier. I should have called you about him, but he'd gone into the coffee shop, so they'd figured he'd just been waiting to meet someone." Ash, sitting in the driver's seat of the unmarked St. Louis PD cruiser, studied the house across the street from where he'd parked.

This neighborhood wasn't as nice or well kept as Caroline's. The houses were smaller, older, in various states of disrepair or totally abandoned. It was hard to tell which of the last two was Turner's house.

Was he there just living in squalor, or had he abandoned it all together?

"This doesn't make any sense," Ash said, shaking his head in confusion. "Of all the properties he owns—the high-rise condos or that three-story mansion near the country club, why would he be staying at this dump?"

"This was Wade Turner's last known address," Thad

reminded him. "And Wade Turner was the man I killed, right?"

"His dental records match those of the man you killed," Ash confirmed.

That was why Ed Turner had gone off the grid—he'd been grieving. "You said he's owned this house for a while."

"Property records show that he and his wife bought it when they were first married thirty-five years ago," Ash said with a glance at his laptop, which was balanced between his seat and Thad's. "Ed kept it even after they moved up. His son had been living in it for the past several years. Wade never really held down a job. With his mother slipping him his father's money, he hadn't needed one. He lived here for free and got enough money for drugs and alcohol."

"He had a problem with both?"

"Not enough to get him arrested, but enough for him to turn up as a person of interest from time to time."

"Until he turned up in the morgue."

"Ed never claimed his body. Are you sure he even noticed he was missing?" Ash wondered. "It sounds like they were estranged for a while."

"Wade was still his son," Thad said. "Ed would have recognized that picture from the ATM footage."

"It was grainy and hard to see—"

"Wade was his son, and I killed him," Thad said. "And that's why Ed Turner abducted my son. He wants an eye for an eye."

Which meant that Mark might already be dead. Thad reached for the door handle. He couldn't wait for the

Special Response Team that Ash had called in. He had to know now if his son was alive or dead.

His brother's hand grasped his shoulder. "You're not going anywhere."

"I'm going to bring my son home." He'd promised Caroline.

The fear and pain on her beautiful face haunted him. Her image had been burned on his mind for the past four years. But always when he'd thought about her, she had been smiling and happy. Not devastated like she was now.

"If Turner really is as dangerous as you think, you're going to get yourself killed," Ash said.

"You may want to wait for backup," Thad said, "but I don't need it."

On most of his assignments, he hadn't had it, and those assignments had usually gone smoother than when he'd had help.

"Even when backup gets here, you can't go in there with us," Ash said, acting more like a protective big brother than a detective.

"The hell I—"

"You're not authorized."

"One phone call and I'll be leading this investigation," Thad warned him. "I have more authority than you do. Hell, I have more authority than the whole St. Louis PD."

"More ego, too," Ash retorted.

"More at stake," Thad corrected him.

"Exactly," his brother agreed. "You're too involved."

"He's my son." And that may have already cost the little boy his life.

Ash glanced back where the SRT van was pulling up along the street, out of the line of vision of the house they were watching. He blew out a ragged breath and then dragged in a deep one. "They're here."

Thad wasn't so sure that was a good thing, a SWAT team storming the house. "Keep them back."

"Until I assess the situation," Ash said.

"I'll assess the situation." He had to get close enough to see inside, to see if his son lived.

Ash shook his head. "Let me do this for you. Stay out here."

Thad shook his head. "I can't do that." Even though his heart pounded erratically with fear over what they might find inside....

"Thad—"

"I've seen things," he reminded his brother. "You have no idea the things I've seen."

"I was over there, too." Ash reminded him of his deployment. "I've seen things. But if you're right about Turner, this—"

"Is wasting time." And he'd already done enough of that trying to convince everyone else that it didn't matter what facade Ed Turner showed the world: successful businessman, humanitarian, leader in lifesaving military communications—he was still a killer. He had brutally murdered two people in their beds twenty years ago. He had killed Thad's parents; he probably wouldn't hesitate to kill his son, too.

"Let's go." Shaking off Ash's hand on his arm, he threw open the door and, keeping below the other cars parked on the street, he headed toward the house.

Ash stayed close behind him, covering his back and

keeping as low as Thad did. The only sound he made was the command he whispered into the radio pinned to his shirt collar. "Stand down until I give the order."

Ash wouldn't be giving the order. Thad didn't need backup, not even his brother. All he needed was his son. He crept close to the house. The paint, which might have once been white, was now gray and peeling off the weathered wood. Icicles hung low from the eaves, dripping despite the cold temperatures, probably because there was no insulation in the attic. Or the walls.

If Mark was inside, he would be cold. And scared.

Thad rose just high enough to peer through a window. But newspapers had been taped over the glass. He couldn't see inside, not even a shadow or a flash of light. Maybe that was good, though, because then Turner couldn't see out, either.

"We need SRT," Ash said. "They have infrared and heat sensors. They can tell us if there's anyone inside."

The heat sensor only worked if the person was alive. So it wouldn't tell Thad everything he needed to know. He would only learn that with his own eyes. He walked away from the house, causing his brother to gasp and stare at in him surprise.

Thad needed that element of surprise. So after he'd walked a few strides away, he turned back and ran, hurling himself through that newspaper-covered window. Glass shattered and caught at his clothes and skin. He didn't feel any pain; he was totally focused on the room.

He swung his barrel toward the doorways, expecting Turner to rush inside with his gun barrel pressed to Mark's temple—if the child was still alive. But nothing moved inside the house. Not a creak or a curse. Then someone breathed—and it wasn't Thad. He was still holding his breath. The breath turned to a gasp and then a cry.

"Daddy!"

A little boy shifted out of the corner of the couch where he'd been cowering. He vaulted at Thad, throwing his arms around his neck.

Thad clasped him close with one arm while he kept his gun raised. More cautiously, Ash stepped through the window.

"Thank God," he murmured when he saw father and son.

"Where's the man?" Thad asked, not wanting his brother to step into a trap as he moved around, securing the house.

"My new friend, Ed?"

Bile rose in Thad's throat, but he nodded. "Where is Ed?"

A smile of anticipation curved Mark's little bow-shaped mouth. "He went to get Mommy for me."

"What?"

"He's going to bring her here, so me and her can be together," Mark explained. "Ed told me that you would come later, but you'd be late...like you were that day at the mall."

Turner had meant Thad would be too late—too late to save his family. He hugged the little boy tight, like he should have held Caroline.

He shouldn't have left her alone even with the gun. Caroline was too softhearted to use it, even to save herself.

Thad had known that, but he'd still left her alone, thinking she would be safer at her house than out looking for their son with him. His only hope was that the police cars patrolling her neighborhood stopped Ed before he broke into her home. He couldn't lose Caroline.

THE BLAST AND TINKLE of shattering glass snapped Caroline out of her daze of fear and concern for her son's safety. Still clutching his teddy bear, she jumped up from where she'd been sitting on Mark's bed, rushed toward the stairs and peered over the railing.

A man rolled across her living-room floor, toppling the Christmas tree before regaining his feet. He was an older man, probably nearly as old as Thad's uncle Craig. Like Craig Kendall, he was also very good-looking with blond hair and dark eyes. But beneath the handsome facade was a madness and rage that had a sense of foreboding racing across Caroline's skin.

He must have been the man she'd felt watching her and Mark. Was he the one who'd grabbed her son? She wanted to confront him, to yell at him and demand he tell her where Mark was.

But Mark wasn't with him. Did that mean her son had gotten away? Had Thad rescued him?

Because if the man had Mark, why would he have come for her? To kill her?

She swallowed a squeak of fear, but he must have heard her.

A gun clutched in his hand, he whirled toward the stairwell. And her. She grabbed a lamp from the hall table and hurled it down at him. The porcelain struck his shoulders, eliciting an oath from him as it cracked and broke.

He fired the gun, embedding the bullet in the wall behind her head. She screamed and ran for her bedroom. And the gun Thad had left her.

But could she use it?

She slammed her door and turned the lock, which was probably too flimsy to keep out anyone. So she rushed toward her dresser and pushed the heavy oak piece of furniture toward the door, which was already rattling under a pounding fist.

Then, sitting on the floor, she used just her legs and shoved the dresser against the door. But since she could move it, so could he. It wouldn't even take him as long or as much effort.

Her hand shaking, she reached for the bedside table and pulled out the gun. Because she was shaking so badly, she fumbled with the safety before getting it off.

But would she be able to get off a shot before he got her? The doorjamb splintered as the lock broke the wood. And then the door slammed into the back of the dresser.

Again and again, like an axe swinging at a log.

The piece of furniture rocked back and forth before finally, slowly, falling forward. The mirror struck the floor and shattered, sending a shower of glass flying at Caroline like confetti on New Year's Eve.

She doubted she would see New Year's, though, or even Christmas.

Unless she fired first.

So she raised the barrel of the gun toward the door and pressed her finger against the trigger.

## Chapter Fourteen

Each shot sent a bullet of fear through Thad's heart. He vaulted through the shattered picture window and staggered across the floor, stumbling over the fallen Christmas tree. Regaining his balance on all the broken glass and ornaments, he ran across the living room and up the steps to the second story.

To Caroline.

The trim around her bedroom door had splintered. Some pieces of wood lay on the floor in the hall while others had been pushed inside with the door. Fearful of what he might find—like at Turner's house—Thad edged closer to the opening.

But it wasn't open—not entirely. A turned-over dresser blocked half the doorway. Thad leaned in just as a bullet whizzed past his head and struck the wall behind him. He lifted his gun to fire back but, as he zeroed in on the shooter, he lowered the barrel. "Caroline!"

"Oh, my God!" she shrieked as she dropped her gun. "Did I shoot you? Are you all right?"

She climbed over the back of the dresser, reaching

for him. He knelt on the wood and clasped her tight in his arms.

"Are you all right?" he asked, pulling back to stare at her face. Nicks and cuts marred the silky perfection of her skin. "You're hurt."

She shook her head. "It was the glass from the mirror."

The mirror of the dresser she'd been strong and smart enough to push across the door, to buy herself some time to retrieve the gun.

He couldn't have been more proud of her.

"Is he gone?" she asked. "Did I shoot him?"

"He's not dead," he said, almost regretful that he'd found no body lying in the hall.

But Turner may have still been inside the house. Thad had left Ash outside, to guard what else mattered most to him.

He grabbed up his weapon again. "Stay here. I'm going to finish searching the house and then go back outside."

She reached out, clutching at him. "Don't leave me."

She wasn't talking about just physically. She didn't want Turner attacking him as he had her.

"I'll be right back," he promised her.

Unless Ed Turner waited somewhere in the house, ready to ambush him.

*HOW LONG HAD HE BEEN GONE?*

She hadn't heard any more shots, but she hadn't heard anything else, either. Just the eerie silence that had reigned before the glass shattered.

She lifted her head, straining for a noise, any noise.

And finally, she heard footfalls on the steps. Someone was coming back upstairs. She grabbed the gun again.

But she couldn't fire it and risk almost hitting the wrong person. Almost hitting someone she loved. Instead, she tucked the weapon back inside the drawer of the bedside table.

She was just heading toward the bathroom to lock herself inside there when she heard a soft voice. "What happened to the Christmas tree? Will Santa still be able to put presents under it?"

Thad carried their boy down the hall toward her. She ran to greet them, pulling Mark into her arms to squeeze his warm little body tight.

Her voice shaking with tears, she asked, "Are you all right, sweetheart?"

"I missed you, Mommy," he said, winding his arms around her neck. "My new friend, Ed, was going to come get you for me."

She shivered and not just because cold winter air blew through her broken picture window. "That man is not your friend, honey," she corrected him. "He's a stranger."

"Ed told me that he's Aunt Natalie's dad," Mark said, "and that makes him family."

And all Mark had wanted for Christmas. Even the shopping mall Santa had been surprised that he hadn't asked for a toy or a video game.

Thad patted his son's back. "That man didn't tell you the truth."

The little boy's blue eyes widened with shock.

Maybe Caroline shouldn't have protected him so much from the realities of the world.

"Ed lied?" Mark asked.

Thad uttered a ragged sigh. "Aunt Natalie's dad and mine died a long time ago."

She waited, worried that he might tell the little boy more than he was ready to learn about the world. But he stopped himself and met her gaze over Mark's head.

"And I need to go catch the man responsible for his death," he continued. But he was talking to her now, not their son.

She nodded in complete understanding.

"I searched the whole house before I took Mark from Ash and brought him inside. Turner isn't here. But I want to take the two of you to the estate," he said. "To make sure you'll be safe."

She shook her head. "He's been through too much already."

"Exactly."

"It's getting late," she said. Afternoon had slipped into evening. Her son had been gone too long. "He'll sleep better in his own bed."

"But the window—"

"Can be repaired tonight." Being a single mom and home owner, she'd made certain to find a trusty handyman long ago.

"But what about security?"

"Is the estate any more secure?" she asked. "It's been broken into, too." Twice. But she didn't need to remind him of that.

He sighed again. "You're right. There's only one way to guarantee the security of the people I love." He leaned forward and pressed a kiss to Mark's forehead.

Despite the excitement he'd had that day, the little boy's eyes were already drifting closed.

Then Thad kissed her, too, brushing his lips across hers. None of the danger she and her son had gone through was really his fault, yet she held on to her resentment against him. It was the only way to protect her heart from breaking when he intended to put himself in danger to apprehend their son's kidnapper.

When he pulled back, hurt flashed in his eyes that she hadn't responded to his kiss. "I'm sorry," he said, "about everything. I don't blame you for being mad at me. I'm mad at myself. I thought for sure that I shook whoever might have followed me, but instead I led him right here—" his chest rose with an agitated breath "—to you and Mark."

She opened her mouth, ready to absolve him. But before she could, he continued, "I'll do what I should have the day after Mark was grabbed at the mall. I'll make sure the St. Louis PD has a unit in the driveway until Turner's caught."

"Done," Ash assured them as he climbed the stairs. "And we'll get someone here to fix your window."

"Thank you," she said to Detective Kendall. But her gratitude was for Thad because he'd brought her son home just as he had promised.

Now if only she could get him to promise to bring himself safely home to her.

But this man, Turner, may have gotten away with murder twenty years ago, if he was the one responsible for Thad's parents' deaths. So she knew Thad would not rest until the man had finally been brought to justice.

Her arms aching with the weight of her soundly

sleeping son, she turned for his bedroom. The brothers talked behind her.

"We have units sitting on Turner's house, too," Ash said. "In case he goes back, thinking the boy's still there."

"This guy is good," Thad said. "He's been looking over his shoulder for twenty years, worried that his past would finally catch up with him. He's not going to walk into a trap. I suspect that he even got training…where I got training, when he was setting up those defense contracts."

"I don't care how damn good he is. He won't get away again," Ash said, his voice gruff with anger.

"No, he won't," Thad said. "He doesn't intend to."

"What do you mean?"

"I'll meet you downstairs," Thad said, dismissing his brother to follow Caroline into Mark's room. "I can't believe he's out."

Thad pulled back the blankets for her to lay Mark onto his bed. She slipped off his boots and pulled the blankets back up to his chin, which was damp from the drool trailing out of the corner of his open mouth.

"Kids are resilient," she assured him. She'd seen some of her students bounce back from tragedies. "And thankfully he's too young to really understand what happened."

In case they were going to discuss what happened, she walked from her son's room and, when Thad followed her into the hall, pulled his door shut. She hated losing sight of him for even that minute, but Thad had thoroughly checked the house before bringing their son inside. So the bogeyman wasn't waiting in his closet, ready to grab him the minute she stepped away.

If only she really believed that.

She needed to get rid of the other danger to her son now. So she walked the short distance down the hall to her room, stepped over her dresser and retrieved the gun from her bedside table. Careful not to point it at him again, she extended the handle toward Thad.

Instead of taking it, he busied himself with righting her dresser and pushing it back where it had been.

"The department people need to clean up the glass in here," he remarked. "Or you're going to get hurt."

It was too late for that.

"I'm more worried about me or Mark getting hurt if I keep this gun in the house," she said, hating the weight and coldness of the weapon in her hand.

"But if you insist on staying here, you'll need that for protection."

She shook her head.

"You must have scared off Turner with it," he pointed out.

"But I nearly shot you."

"It's not like I didn't have it coming," he said with a halfhearted grin.

"Just take it," she urged him. "I don't want it in the house with Mark." She'd heard too many stories about what happened when guns were left around curious children.

"I didn't scare him…with what I told him about Turner?" Thad asked as he finally grabbed the handle of the gun.

She shook her head. "He needs to know the man is not his friend."

Because she understood what Thad's brother did not—Ed Turner was not done with them. Maybe she should have kept the gun.

But the thought of Mark getting a hold of it…

She shuddered. She had nearly lost him once, and she wouldn't survive if something happened to her son. Or Thad.

She stared at him, committing his every handsome feature to memory. She worried that when he left her this time, he would never be coming back.

Thad met her gaze, as if he were ready to flinch at what he'd see there. "I don't blame you for hating me. I hate myself for putting you two in danger."

Tears burned her eyes, so she shut them to clear away the sting. And when she opened them, Thad was gone. He wouldn't hear her words, but she uttered them anyway. "I don't hate you."

She just loved him too much to lose him again.

TURNER WASN'T SURPRISED to find police cars parked along his street. They were unmarked, but by just being late models, they stuck out like sore thumbs among the rust buckets parked in front of the run-down houses. He should have maintained the house better. Simply keeping it hadn't been enough to honor Emily.

But that was all he'd ever done. Kept her but never really taken care of her. It wasn't surprising that when she'd finally gone to the doctor, she had been sick too long for treatment. He'd loved her. But, just like this house, he'd ignored her.

Because she hadn't been as pretty or charming or vivacious as Marie Kendall. And he had been a bewitched fool instead of a man.

Joseph and Marie had been so rich and beautiful and powerful. They had reminded him of the characters Tom and Daisy from *The Great Gatsby*. And just like Tom and Daisy, they had been careless people. Joseph hadn't cared whom he'd used to build his company, destroying other businesses to build his. And Marie hadn't cared whom she'd hurt in her endless quest for attention. She'd destroyed marriages and families and neglected her own children.

He recited aloud a quote from the book. "They were careless people, Tom and Daisy—they smashed up things and creatures and then retreated back into their money or their vast carelessness, or whatever it was that kept them together, and let other people clean up the mess they had made." Twenty years ago, Ed had cleaned up their mess when he'd killed them, and he'd saved their children and future victims from their vast carelessness.

And how had Thad Kendall repaid him? By killing his son.

"Wade…"

Poor Wade. The kid had never had a chance. He'd never had a father. Ed had been too obsessed with building his company, with trying to prove to Marie Kendall that he could be every bit as rich and successful as Joseph.

He could have never built his company big enough or his houses opulent enough to impress Marie, though. Or for her to let him claim his daughter.…

Emily hadn't cared about the money Ed had made or all the houses Ed had built. She had always loved this first one best. She had always loved Ed best.

Maybe that was why, of all the condos and homes Wade could have lived in, he had chosen his mother's favorite house. He had been a good son to his mother. And in the end, he had been a good son to Ed even though Ed had never given his son what he'd deserved from his father.

He'd never given him love or attention.

Now it was too late. But Ed had made him a promise. Justice. He had promised to avenge his death, and this time Ed would not fail his son. He'd gotten away with murder before. He probably wouldn't this time, but he didn't care anymore. He had nothing left to care about, and soon, neither would Thad Kendall.

# *Chapter Fifteen*

Thad had commandeered the St. Louis PD interrogation room for his personal interviews. He'd talked to everyone he'd been able to round up who'd ever known or spoken to or just passed Ed Turner on the damn street.

*Ruthless businessman.*

*Generous philanthropist.*

*Inventive genius.*

*Loving husband.*

*Supportive father.*

Those were the statements he hadn't bothered to write down, having already committed them to memory. Along with every other thing he had learned about Ed Turner in the past twelve hours. But those statements were superficial, from people who'd really never known Ed Turner at all.

Just as so many people had really never known Thad Kendall. Except for Caroline. She knew him.

And Ed's recently deceased, long-suffering wife of thirty-five years had known Turner best. Thad hadn't been able to bring her into the interrogation room. But he'd found the next best thing in the house where Mark had been held.

Her diaries. She had recorded all her hopes and fears. She'd known everything about her husband, even why he was an alcoholic.

"We've got all his usual bars and liquor stores staked out," Ash said, pressing his fist over his mouth to stanch a yawn. He had been awake all night, too, at Thad's side for every interview, probably because he hadn't trusted his younger brother to conduct them without resorting to torture.

But in the end it had come down to what they'd read, not what they'd heard. Ash tapped the cover of the journal he'd just finished. "Eventually he'll run out of whatever liquor he had with him," Ash said, "and he'll go for more."

Thad shook his head. His gut told him that Ed Turner had quit drinking…the day Thad shot and killed his son. Otherwise he wouldn't have been clearheaded enough to follow a spy without being detected and to figure out what mattered most to Thad.

His heart clutched at the image he'd burned into his mind—Mark with his arms wound tight around his mother's neck and Caroline clinging to the baby she'd thought lost to her forever.

Because of Thad.

He really wouldn't blame her if she hated him. He hated himself for putting them in danger. "You're sure they're safe?"

As he had every other time Thad had asked him, Ash assured him, "I have my best men sitting on her house. They won't let Turner get to your son or your…" He peered up at Thad, who was too agitated to sit down.

"What is Caroline to you? Just the mother of your child?"

"What is Rachel to you?"

"The love of my life," Ash answered automatically and from his heart.

Thad rubbed his hands over his face, which was rough with stubble. "That's what Caroline is to me. It's what she was four years ago."

"But you never brought her around. You never mentioned her."

"I knew I had to leave her." And introducing her to the family, and knowing how she would have instantly become a part of it, would have made it impossible for him to do that. "It was the hardest thing I've ever had to do."

"But you're planning on doing it again," Ash reminded him. "You're planning on leaving her and your son."

"I have no choice."

"You have a choice. Hell, you're a Kendall. You have a lot of choices. You could work anywhere in St. Louis—local television stations. Hell, national stations. At Kendall Communications. Or even here," Ash said, his voice deep with emotion, "with me."

Thad smiled, moved that his brother would make such an offer. "I thought I had too much ego for you to want to work with me."

"I could beat it out of you," Ash replied with a quick and cocky grin, "just like I did when we were kids."

Thad was surprised to find a grin on his own lips. "Why do I have a feeling that we'd both be visiting Uncle Craig's office a lot if we worked together?"

Ash shuddered. "You were never *summoned* as often as Devin and I were. Don't understand why Dev wanted to work there."

"I do," Thad admitted.

Ash laughed.

"No. I'm serious."

"Why? Because Dad built the company?"

Having been only eleven when Joseph Kendall had been murdered, Thad hadn't idolized his father like his brothers had. He'd idolized Uncle Craig instead. "Because some of those advances our family company has made in communications have saved lives."

"You're talking spy techie stuff."

Thad nodded. "And military. We could use some of that kind of equipment now to track down Ed Turner. Hell, we need *his* stuff to do that. His is better, and that's why we keep losing contracts to him."

Ash chuckled. "You're usually half a world away, but you keep up on the family business better than I do and I live down the street from the office."

"I'm more concerned about where Turner is right now." They'd found where he'd been staying last; they had units going past his other properties. Where the hell was he?

Frustration gnawed at him. He would not be able to sleep or eat or even rest until Ed Turner was at the very least behind bars, at the most six feet under with his stalker son.

"You don't need the special equipment," Ash said. "Your interviews got us everything we need to know to track down Ed Turner. We really could use you in the department, even if you just gave classes on interrogation techniques."

"You wouldn't let me use all the techniques I know," Thad reminded him.

"You didn't need them." Ash laughed. "Maybe you do suck because we actually just needed Emily Turner's diaries. From reading those, I know where we'll find Ed Turner."

Thad shook his head, unconvinced that Turner was still drinking. Something as traumatic as losing a son could cause a sober man to drink. And it could cause a drunk to sober up.

"Don't you remember what she'd written?" Ash asked. "About how, if Ed was actually in town, he would ruin the boy's holiday because he'd tie on the drunk of all drunks on Christmas Eve." He glanced at his watch. "It's Christmas Eve now."

*Christmas Eve.*

"I know where Turner is," he said. "And he's not at a bar or liquor store."

Ash tensed. "The estate? I put a patrol there, too, just in case he returned to the scene again."

No, Turner intended to create a new scene. For Thad.

CAROLINE SLEPT ON THE EDGE of Mark's single-size mattress, her arms wrapped tight around her son. Or she tried to sleep.

She was caught somewhere in that point between light sleep and being fully awake. Probably because Mark was restless, his elbows and feet jabbing into her as he moved in his sleep.

Kids were resilient. But her little man had been

through an awful lot that he wasn't mature enough to process.

She would talk to the school psychologist about having Mark meet with a professional or giving Caroline the tools to help her son herself. After what had happened, she was unlikely to let Mark out of her sight for a while.

Now a shiver chased down her spine and not just because Mark had stolen all the blankets but because she had that odd sensation of being watched. The police officers were outside, parked in her driveway as she'd learned from his brother that Thad had been every night since Mark had nearly been abducted from the mall.

That was probably why Ed Turner had decided to take Mark from the day care. He'd known then that it would be easier than getting past Thad, who would die for his son.

And for her…

Had he? Was that why she had that odd feeling?

Then suddenly she knew why—because a cold barrel was pressed against her temple.

"Don't scream," a man advised her. "Don't even move."

Despite his warning, she moved slightly, trying to cover Mark with her body.

"Where's that gun?" he asked, pressing the barrel harder against her temple.

She swallowed hard, choking down her nerves and fear. "I—I gave it back to Thad."

Her voice, or Turner's, awakened Mark, who murmured then rubbed at his eyes.

"Shh…" She soothed her son. "Go back to sleep."

"It's nearly morning," Turner said, gesturing toward where light snuck around the edges of the shade on Mark's window. "And he must know what today is. After all, he is a Kendall."

She would have shaken her head but his gun held it still. "He's an Emerson, not a Kendall."

Turner laughed. "I don't care what his last name is. The kid is definitely a Kendall and definitely Thad Kendall's son."

"Hurting him won't bring your son back, Mr. Turner," she said.

"Thad made sure my boy could never come back," he said, his voice gruff with bitterness and anguish. The man might have been a killer, but he'd also been a father. And that father was grieving.

"Thad was only protecting his family," she reminded him. "Your son was trying to kill his sister."

Ed shook his head. "Wade figured everything out, you know. He finally understood why I'd done everything I had." He expelled a shaky sigh. "Why I'd failed him and his mother so much…"

"He loved you," she said, grasping at straws. She needed to keep him talking, needed to distract him so she could figure out how to save Mark. "He was trying to protect you from being arrested."

Ed sighed. "Yes, he was a good boy."

"I'm a good boy," Mark murmured sleepily.

"You are," Turner agreed. "It's just too bad…"

"You don't have to do this," Caroline said. "Please, don't do this."

"My daddy says you're not my friend," Mark said as he fully awakened and noticed the man standing over his bed, holding a gun on his mother. "And you're not just playing."

"No," Turner admitted almost regretfully. "I'm not just playing."

And no matter what Caroline said, she doubted he would change his mind from carrying out his revenge on Thad. He wanted Thad to suffer as much as he was suffering.

She regretted now not telling Thad earlier about Mark. He had missed all the important milestones the boy had already passed. He had missed so much, and now he would never have the chance to make up for what he'd missed.

And she would never have the chance to tell him how much she had loved him and would always love him... even after she was gone.

BLOOD COVERED THEIR FACES.

No matter how much carnage he'd seen in war, Thad knew he would never forget this sight—never get out of his mind finding bloodied bodies on Christmas Eve.

His hand shook as he reached out to check for a pulse. The skin was already cold, as cold as the blood now running through Thad's veins.

He lifted his cell phone to his mouth. It was on, his connection open to Ash, who'd been driving too slow and carefully. So Thad had lost him. "I'm sorry. Your guys are dead."

The police officers were slumped inside their car, one lying over the dash, the other over the steering wheel. Turner was definitely not drinking, not when he was able to move as quickly and dangerously as he had.

He had definitely done more than just sell his equipment to soldiers and spies; he'd demonstrated how to use it himself.

He was exactly like Thad, more dangerous than he seemed.

Ash's curse crackled in the phone. "Wait for me and SRT."

"No."

"We're only a couple minutes out—"

"That'll be too late."

If it wasn't already....

If the same scene didn't await Thad inside the house.

"Don't you dare go in there," Ash said, his voice sharp with anger and fear. "It's a trap."

"I know."

And if Mark and Caroline were already gone, he didn't particularly care.

# Chapter Sixteen

The policemen were dead. If they weren't, they would have tried to rescue her and Mark. But Caroline and Mark had been alone with the gunman, the killer, for a while now.

She hadn't been able to keep him talking. They had all fallen silent some time ago, Mark nodding off to sleep again in her arms as she sat in the living room next to the fallen Christmas tree.

But Ed Turner hadn't shot them yet. He was waiting. For Thad.

"I'm a teacher," she said. "The most popular teacher at my elementary school." She wasn't bragging; she was trying to get him to know her, so that it wouldn't be as easy for him to shoot her as it had been for him to shoot the policemen who'd been guarding her and Mark. "My kids keep coming back to visit me. They threw me a baby shower when I was pregnant with Mark. I was alone when I had him, and I raised him alone for the first three years of his life. He means everything to me."

"And you mean everything to him," Turner assured her with an almost sympathetic smile. "When he was at my house, he talked about his daddy, but he wanted to be with his mommy."

Tears stung her eyes and tickled her nose. But she couldn't give in to them and risk succumbing to hysteria. He would probably shoot her then just to keep her quiet. And she would leave her son at the mercy of the madman.

"He was a good boy at your house," she said with all the certainty as if she had been there, too. "He always minds his manners and is considerate of other people."

"He was very good," Turner admitted. "He said *please* and *thank you* and even *may* instead of *can*. He's a smart kid."

"Very smart," she said with more than maternal pride—with an educator's assessment. "My second-graders aren't as polite and mature as Mark. He'll grow up to be a fine young man."

Turner's sympathy turned to pity now. And he shook his head. "No, he won't. But the two of you will be together, just like you both wanted."

She tried to suppress it, but a cry of dismay slipped through her lips. Mark shifted in her arms, reacting to the noise and her fear.

"I won't make you suffer," Turner promised.

"No, you just want to make me suffer," Thad remarked as he passed through the archway between the kitchen and living room.

She hadn't seen him. But Turner must have, because he stood far enough behind the foyer wall that Thad would not have been able to shoot him. Turner would have been able to shoot her and Mark, though.

"We've been waiting for you," Turner said with an

edge of frustration. "You took your damn sweet time getting here."

"Sorry about that," Thad said conversationally, as if he was used to guns and violence and death.

But then Caroline reminded herself that he *was* used to all those things.

"Were you waiting for your brother and SWAT to back you up again?" Ed asked. "They won't get in here fast enough to save them."

"Or you," Thad agreed. "But that's your plan, too."

"What?" His dark eyes narrowed as if he mentally tried to assess how much of his plan Thad had figured out.

"You want to kill yourself," Thad clarified.

Turner grinned and shook his head. "No, I want you to do it."

Thad nodded. "Death by cop."

"You're not a cop."

"No," he agreed. "But I'm not a reporter, either."

"Spy?"

Thad nodded. "I became one because of you."

That startled Turner enough to turn more fully toward Thad and away from her and Mark. She understood now what Thad was trying to do, distract Turner enough for her and Mark to get out of the line of fire.

While he stepped into it…while he gave up his life for hers.

She wanted to tell him now what she should have earlier. She didn't hate him at all. She loved him. But if he was successful, she would never get the chance.

Mark would never get to really know his father, either. But, as the little boy was awake now, and frozen with fear, he would forever remember the image of his father dying right in front of him.

He was too young now to understand the sacrifice his father was willing to make. He would only remember that Santa hadn't brought him what he'd wanted for Christmas this year. Instead he'd taken away the only chance of the boy ever having a family.

WHILE TURNER WAS FOCUSED ON HIM, Thad was focused on everything else. Ash and the SRT had arrived outside and were creeping toward the house. But they wouldn't burst inside until Ash heard the go word through the open cell connection.

And he wouldn't get the go word until Caroline and Mark were able to take some kind of cover. The fallen Christmas tree wouldn't protect them. But if Caroline could somehow flip over the couch and get herself and Mark behind it...

She wouldn't meet his gaze for him to try to convey the message to her. Was she still so angry with him that she couldn't stand to look at him? But then she was more focused on their son than on him. She had wrapped her arms tight around Mark, as if to shield his body. And she'd also covered his eyes and ears as if to shield his mind.

Turner laughed. "You're smooth, Kendall. I'll give you that, but you're not smart enough to fool me. Do you think I'd actually believe I had any influence on *your* life?"

"You, more than anyone else, has," Thad replied. And he realized as he said it that he spoke the truth.

"When you killed my parents, you destroyed my childhood."

"Your parents did that," Turner said. "They weren't who you must have made them out to be in your mind. You idolized memories tainted by the way the media portrayed them."

"The media did romanticize them," Thad said.

"So you have no idea what they were really like," Turner insisted, as if he was trying to justify killing them. "You were much better off with your aunt and uncle."

"Yes," Thad readily agreed. "Aunt Angela and Uncle Craig were wonderful guardians to us. But you'd already done your damage that Christmas Eve you murdered my parents in their beds."

"I did you a favor when I killed Joseph and Marie," Turner said almost desperately. "I protected you from *them*. They didn't care who they hurt," Turner said in defense of his actions. "They would have hurt you, your brothers and *Natalie*—my daughter."

Thad nodded. "Probably. But they never would have hurt us as much as you had."

"I never laid a hand on any of you. I just went into Natalie's room. But after what I'd done, after losing my temper with Joseph and Marie, I knew I could never tell her I was her father." He glanced down at his hand, as if still seeing their blood on it.

That was what he would have seen every time he'd tried to see Natalie.

"And no matter how much success I'd earned," he said, "the Kendalls would always have *more*."

"More?"

"More money. More influence. More stuff."

"None of that mattered to us," Thad insisted.

Turner uttered a bitter laugh. "Tell Wade that. Oh, you can't…because you killed him." He turned back toward Caroline and Mark.

"You think we cared anything about the stuff?" Thad asked. "You ruined Christmas for us. You didn't just take away our parents. You took away hope and wonder and joy. For the past twenty years not one of us ever had a *merry* Christmas."

He had Turner's attention again. But he cared less about distracting him than about telling him everything that Thad had just suddenly realized himself. "You gave us nightmares. Natalie used to wake up nearly every night with them, screaming over the memories she was only able to suppress when she was awake. When she was asleep, the blond-haired bogeyman with the dark eyes—" how had no one ever realized that it was Ed Turner she'd seen that night in her room? "—would come back, and this time he would take Uncle Craig and Aunt Angela and me and Devin and Thad. He would take everything away from her."

"I—I left her there because I didn't want that," Ed said, as if he'd made a great sacrifice in not kidnapping his own daughter.

"You want to make me suffer now," Thad reminded him, "because I saved her from your son. I saved your daughter's life, and you want to take revenge on me for that?"

Turner gasped as Thad's words finally penetrated his rage and madness to the brilliant mind of the man who'd invented top-secret communications for the State Department. "Oh, my God…"

"You would rather have sweet Natalie, who you had already made suffer for twenty years, lose what little happiness she had just managed to finally find in her life?"

"No," Turner sputtered, "I—I didn't want her to suffer."

Thad shook his head as disgust overwhelmed him. "I became a spy because I hadn't been able to save my parents that night, because I hadn't been able to protect my family from the utter devastation of *your* careless actions."

"No." Turner shook his head. "It wasn't about that. Your parents only cared about money and status. Your mother would have affairs just for attention, to make herself feel desirable and special and to make your father jealous. She never really had any intention of leaving him. Not because she loved him but because she loved being his wife. She loved the money and the prestige of being Mrs. Joseph Kendall. She just used me."

But he had obviously fallen deeply in love with Marie Kendall.

"She did use you," Thad brutally agreed. He had no defense for his mother's actions. "She didn't care about you at all. You were just a means to an end."

"I left Kendall Communications," Turner said, "and started my own company. I was going to prove to her that I could be a better man than your father. That I could be richer and more successful. But while I was gone building my company, Joseph built his even bigger. And I realized that no matter what I did, I would never be enough for Marie."

"No," Thad said. "But you were enough for Emily."

Turner met his gaze, and grief filled his dark eyes. "Emily…"

"We found her diaries in the house. She loved you. She knew everything. And she loved you." He didn't dare look away from Turner, but he wanted to glance at Caroline, to see if she could ever love him like Emily Turner had loved Ed.

Unconditionally. No matter the monster he'd been. No matter where he'd been.

"I realized that, too," Ed said. "I never deserved her. I came home that Christmas, and I wanted to start over with her and Wade. Emily had worked on some charity event—it was *The Nutcracker* ballet. She and Wade and I attended."

"We were there." He remembered jerking at his tie and scuffing his shoes. And his mother being mad that he and his brothers weren't behaving like little gentlemen. She'd wanted everyone to think they were the perfect family. Why did they have to act like animals? Why couldn't they act the perfect little princess like Natalie?

"I know," Ed said gravely. "I saw all of you. I saw *Natalie*. And I knew she was mine. And your mother had never had the decency to tell me that I had a daughter."

Caroline choked on a small cry of alarm and guilt. But she wasn't at all like his mother. The situation was entirely different.

But Thad didn't dare try to reassure her with even a

glance much less a word. For the moment Turner had forgotten all about her and Mark.

But to save them, Thad had to remind the man that they were there.

"So you were pissed off and you killed her," Thad said. "Because you were mad and probably drunk. And you wanted revenge. Just like now."

Turner shook his head, but he wasn't able to voice a denial.

"You're not threatening my family for justice," Thad insisted, "because justice was done when I killed your son and saved your daughter. Killing my son and the woman I love won't be justice. It'll just be murder."

He uttered a heavy sigh of pity. "And that makes you the most careless person of all. A vengeful killer."

PANIC QUICKENED TURNER'S PULSE as the guilt rushed back over him. After twenty years of living with the burden, he had finally fought it off only for Thad Kendall's words to settle the weight back onto his shoulders.

He wasn't that kind of man, or Emily wouldn't have loved him like she had for as long as she had.

He shook his head in denial. "You're wrong. It's not about revenge."

"It's not about justice, either," Kendall said. "Not unless you wanted your son to kill your daughter. Is that what you wanted?"

His stomach churned as the truth rose to the top. "No." To him she would always be the sweet little girl who'd looked like a princess that night at the ballet and an angel that night as she lay sleeping and he came to her room.

"I had to kill him," Kendall insisted. "It was the only way to save Natalie's life because he was determined to end it."

"That was my fault," Ed admitted. "I wasn't a real father to him. I was never around—I was off trying to build my company." Trying to be Joseph Kendall. "I left him and his mother alone so much. Then after she died and he found her diaries…"

His breath shuddered out as he remembered the final confrontation with his son. At the cemetery after everyone else had left, Wade had verbally and even physically assaulted him. Ed had let him get in the one blow, knowing he deserved it. But he'd stopped him and tried to hold him, had tried to apologize and explain…just as he'd been trying to explain to Thad. "He blamed me for breaking his mother's heart. Hell, I think he blamed me for her cancer." And maybe that had been Ed's fault. If he'd been home more, if he'd taken better care of her… Wade had been right to blame him. "He hated me."

"He wouldn't have tried to protect you had he really hated you," Kendall argued. "Despite everything, he loved you."

"I gave him no reason to love me," Ed said, the misery eating at him. His hand began to shake as finally he succumbed to the effects of alcohol withdrawal. He'd started drinking even before that Christmas Eve. He'd started drinking when Marie had refused his offer to leave Emily.

But he had control. He could handle it. Just a little shot in his coffee in the morning. A drink at lunch, just enough to take the edge of his anger and his regrets.

"How long has it been since you've had a drink?"

Thad asked. Of course he would notice Ed's shakes; the guy didn't miss much.

If Ed hadn't stopped drinking, he never would have kept up let alone gotten the jump on Kendall. He'd known from that single kill shot that the man was more than just a photojournalist. Just as Ed had been more than a communications company owner. He was a killer, too.

"I haven't been drinking since that night they showed Wade's picture on the news," he admitted. "Even from that grainy security cam footage, I recognized my son. I knew it was him." Probably more because of the sick feeling in his gut than that horrible security still photo.

"He used to be a good kid," Ed defended his boy. "He was smart, too. I think he always knew I was guilty. He woke up that night I came home from killing your parents. He thought I was Santa Claus…until he saw the blood."

Kendall shuddered.

"Yours wasn't the only Christmas I ruined," Ed pointed out. Maybe because he hadn't been sober long enough, he hadn't realized before everything he'd taken from the Kendall children. Not just their parents, however sorry excuses they'd been for a mother and a father. He had taken away their childhoods, just as he had taken away Wade's.

"He was only eleven," Thad reminded him. "He would have been too young to figure out what happened. He didn't know then that Natalie was his sister, did he?"

"No," Ed replied. "I couldn't have told him that. And

when that other man was arrested for the Christmas Eve Murders, I think he forgot all about that night."

"Until that man was cleared of the conviction."

He nodded. "That was around the same time his mother died, and he found her diaries. Then he put it all together and realized what I had done twenty years ago, that Natalie was mine."

"He hadn't wanted just to kill her, though," Thad said. "He had wanted to hide your guilt."

Ed groaned as the pain overwhelmed him. "No one could hide my guilt. I wasn't ever able to even drink it away. I can't go on like this. And I can't let my son die alone."

He lifted his gun. But he was too much a coward to pull the trigger himself. Or he would have committed suicide years ago. All he had to do was point his gun at Thad Kendall's family.

Even though Thad Kendall had already figured out Ed's plan, he wouldn't take the risk that Ed might actually shoot his son and the woman he loved. He put his finger on the trigger and waited, hoping Kendall wouldn't make him press it before he fired the first shot.

# Chapter Seventeen

The gunshot echoed through the living room. Then the room exploded, bodies catapulting through windows and doors. Guns drawn and pointed.

Caroline wrapped her arms tighter around Mark and hoped he wasn't able to see or hear anything. Only Ed Turner's hand bled, his gun lying on the floor beneath him. Thad had shot only his hand, which had caused Turner to drop his gun. Despite all the reasons he had to hate and want revenge for his parents' murders and his son's kidnapping, he hadn't killed the man.

She stared up at him, stunned by his action and his compassion. He had stepped between the killer and the lawmen, protecting him with his own body.

"It's over," he told them all, staring first at her, then the SRT members and lastly at his brother. Ash gripped his gun tightly, its barrel trained on Ed Turner's head. "It's over, Ash."

His breath shuddering out in a ragged sigh, the detective lowered his weapon. He forced his gaze from his parents' killer to his nephew and Caroline. "Are you both all right?"

She nodded, her throat too choked with fear and tears to reply.

"I'll bring in the paramedics to check you out," Ash said.

"No, we're fine," she finally managed to assure him.

"Ed needs medical treatment," Thad said. He had turned back to the man, checking his injury himself. No doubt he had experienced treating gunshot wounds in some of the areas he'd been.

But how many had he treated that he'd actually inflicted?

"Why didn't you kill me?" Turner asked. "Because it was what I wanted?"

Thad turned to her and Mark then. And she knew it was because of them. He hadn't wanted to kill a man in front of his son, not even to protect his son.

She couldn't believe she had once had doubts about his ability to be a parent. He was a better one than she could ever hope to be. She needed to tell him that and so much more.

But he turned away from her again and told his brother, "Get her and Mark out of here. Take them to the estate."

She glanced around at the broken windows and doors and the Christmas tree she would never be able to salvage by morning.

Cuffs were already being slapped on Turner's wrists despite his injury. He wouldn't get free again; he was no longer a threat.

As if Ed Turner had seen her lingering fear, the older, broken man spoke to her. "I'm sorry."

She couldn't absolve him of his sins. She could only

gather up her son in her arms and follow his uncle out to a waiting patrol car. She glanced back at Thad, hoping it wasn't the last time she'd see him.

Now that his parents' killer would finally be brought to justice, would he head back to one of those countries where he thought they needed him?

Ash caught her backward glance. "I won't let him leave."

"You can't keep him here unless he wants to stay," she said. And that was why she hadn't told him about her love the last time they were together. It was also why she'd fought so hard against falling for him again.

"WHY ARE YOU HERE?" Turner asked as he met Thad's gaze through the holding cell bars.

Thad wasn't really certain himself, except that something had drawn him back to his parents' killer. Despite everything they had said to each other at Caroline's house, it felt as if they'd left too much unsaid, too.

Maybe it was the reporter in him that had Thad wanting answers to more questions. Maybe he'd lived the cover too long. What had made Ed Turner the monster—Marie Kendall's rejection or what he'd done in order to build his wealth and power enough to impress her?

"You're on suicide watch," he remarked.

Ed shrugged. "We both know I'm not going to kill myself. Or I would have done it long ago. I should have done it long ago."

"We all have our reasons for doing what we do," he said with a weary sigh. "What are your reasons, do you think?"

"I didn't kill myself because of Emily," he said. "I never deserved her love or her loyalty. I never returned it. But I couldn't do that…." He sucked in a shaky breath.

"Why did you kill my parents?"

"I explained all that to you already," Ed said, confusion on his face.

Thad nodded. "You did tell me why. I guess what I really want to know is *how*."

Ed shuddered. "No one needs to know the details of how their parents were murdered."

Thad actually already knew them. He'd read the police files long ago. "I mean *how* did you do it? How did you become the kind of man who could kill?"

"I think you know," Ed said. "And that's why you're here. You're worried that because we might have done some of the same things in the same places that you're like me."

The guy was so smart. How had his life fallen so far apart? Because he'd lost the love he'd thought he wanted without ever appreciating the love he'd already had?

"We did things we had to do over there," Ed reminded him. "To save our own lives and others' lives."

Thad sighed. "We all find ways to justify our actions."

"What's your justification for being here instead of with your family?" Ed asked wistfully.

Thad suspected that the man wished he could live his whole life over again.

"Fear," Thad admitted. "Fear that I've already

screwed up my chance at happiness." Fear that he didn't deserve that happiness at all.

Ed's lips curved into a faint smile. "So what am I, your confidant now?"

"My mission." He wanted more from Ed Turner than just answers.

"I've been that for too long," Ed said. "You let me affect your life for too much of your life."

"Yes," Thad agreed. "So you're going to do the right thing."

"I don't intend to profess my innocence. I want to do the time," he said, "for all my crimes." He shuddered and rubbed a shaking hand over his face. "I can't believe I hurt so many people."

So had Thad, without even realizing he had. Like Ed Turner, he had justified his actions as being for the greater good. How much was he really like Ed Turner?

"It's time for me to face the truth," Ed said, "without alcohol, without blaming anyone else for what I've done."

Thad breathed a sigh of relief that his family would be spared a long, drawn-out trial.

"Thank you for helping me do that," Turner said. "And don't worry—" he waited until Thad met his gaze "—you're nothing like me."

That was the question, the *fear,* that had brought Thad to the jail instead of home to his family.

"I thought you were," Turner said. "The way you killed Wade. And in all those news interviews, I saw no real guilt on your face. You had totally justified what you'd done. But you were right—it was justified."

Or had he done what Ed Turner had been doing the past twenty years.

"But if you were really a killer, if you really had that darkness inside you that I have, you would have killed me today."

Thad chuckled. "It was what you wanted."

"But you said that wasn't why you didn't kill me."

"I had time to take the shot and the lighting to see your hand," Thad explained. "It wasn't like the night that I shot Wade. It was dark that night and there was so much smoke. And I knew I'd only get one shot." So he'd taken the kill shot.

"You may have had the light and the time today, but you had every reason to want to kill me," Ed said. "I'm the man who killed your parents, the one who terrorized your son and the woman you love. You wouldn't even have to have the darkness inside you to justify killing me. No one would have questioned your reasoning for taking me out with a kill shot." He laughed. "Hell, they would have applauded you, probably even given you a medal."

"If I'd killed you," Thad said, "it wouldn't have been for a medal. It would have been for vengeance." And Caroline would have known it and never forgiven him for killing a man in front of their son. Thad wanted to be a better man for her, a good father to Mark.

"See, you're not like me at all," Ed said. "I gave you something."

"Turner Connections?" he asked with a laugh.

Ed sighed. "No, I've already turned that over to Natalie."

"She'll refuse it."

"Then you can have it. Fold it into Kendall Communications like your brother's been trying to do."

"Don't expect Natalie to come see you," he warned him.

"I've put her on the list of people I refuse to see," Ed said. "I took too much away from her. Affected too much of her past. I just want her to focus on her future."

Thad nodded in agreement.

"You need to do the same," Ed said. "Now get out of here. Go be with your family."

After being gone for so many years, physically and emotionally, Thad wasn't sure he even knew how to do that.

As if Turner could read his mind, he said, "It's Christmas. It's the time for miracles."

Thad glanced at his watch. It wasn't Christmas yet. He had a few more hours until midnight, a few more hours to figure out how to make his miracle happen.

*HE WAS GONE.*

Panic pressed on her chest, stealing away Caroline's breath. She had thought they would be safe here, with Turner behind bars. But the bed where she'd tucked Mark in less than an hour ago was now empty. In fact, the blankets were so smooth it looked as if he'd never slept at all.

Resisting the urge to give in to her panic and utter a scream, she pressed her hand over her mouth and hurried from the room. If she checked every room, she would wake up the others. Pretty much every Kendall had met her and Mark when Ash had brought them to the estate.

Except Thad.

She didn't even know if he'd come home yet. Or if he even intended to.

She could wake up any of the others, though, and they would help her search for her son. But she wanted to check one place first, just in case she was overreacting.

She rushed down the stairwell and through the two-story foyer. She stopped, her mind frazzled as she tried to remember again what was where. The house was so big. Hell, it wasn't a house at all. Nothing with double stairwells and two separate wings of bedrooms could be considered a mere house. The ceilings were so high that noises echoed.

Christmas music, something she never expected to hear in the Kendall household, drifted down the hall. And a deep voice was pitched low, rumbling in a one-sided conversation.

She followed the noises to the family room. The Christmas tree rose to the pitch of the cathedral ceiling. Its twinkling lights reflected back from the wall of glass behind it and cast a beautiful glow across the man and the boy who sat on the couch near the tree. She had thought she might find her son here, drawn back to the tree with which he'd been so awed earlier. She'd never expected to find Thad beneath the tree, too. Mark was cuddled up on his lap, their heads bowed close together over the book father read to son.

Caroline's heart warmed and swelled in her chest. She had to clasp her arms around herself so that she wouldn't throw her arms around them both and never let go. Mark wasn't the only one who'd wanted this for Christmas: family.

He had just been the only one hopeful enough to believe Santa could bring him what he wanted. Caroline had stopped believing in Santa long ago. But not as long ago as Thad.

He finished the story with a flourish of affected voices and special effects. Mark giggled in delight. And Caroline clapped.

"Mommy!" Mark exclaimed. "Daddy was just reading me a story."

"I found him down here by the tree," Thad explained.

"It's so pretty," Mark said with a happy sigh as he snuggled into the corner of the couch where he'd piled pillows and blankets. "Can I sleep down here under it?"

Panic fluttered in her chest again.

"He's safe," Thad assured her. "The whole family's here tonight."

She was surprised that any of them would want to be here tonight of all nights: the twentieth anniversary of their parents' murders. But they had been there when she and Mark arrived, and then they'd decided to spend Christmas Eve together.

But for Thad.

"They keep coming down to check on him," he said, gesturing toward the plate of cookies and milk that had been left on the coffee table for Mark instead of Santa.

"They're going to spoil him," she said.

"Is that going to be a problem?" he asked, studying her face with genuine concern that she might not be comfortable with his family embracing Mark so fully.

She glanced at her son, who was already drifting off to sleep as he stared up at the tree. "No. I think it's wonderful that he got what he wanted for Christmas."

She leaned down to press a kiss to Mark's forehead. Then she tapped a finger on the book Thad had been reading. "'The Night Before Christmas'?"

"Would you rather I read him something else?" he asked, lifting a brow.

"You can read him whatever you want. You saved us tonight," she said. "And you saved Edward Turner, too."

"Too many people have already died," he said with a weary sigh.

She wondered when he'd last slept. She reached for his hand and tugged him to his feet. "It's Christmas now," she said, noticing that it was after midnight.

"Did Santa bring you what you wanted?" he asked.

"Not yet." But she led him down the hall to the stairs and then up to the suite that was his. She'd been shown to this suite earlier but had refused to assume that Thad would want her staying with him. So she and Mark were staying down the hall in a guest suite.

Except now neither of them intended to stay in there. Mark was asleep downstairs. Thad's family would watch over him. And she intended to sleep here, with Thad. She reached for the buttons on his shirt, sliding them open so that the material parted and fell away from his chest.

"I'm not Mark," he said, his voice rough as his eyes lit with passion. "I don't need your help."

She froze with her hands raised up between them. "I know," she said. Her son had been the last thing on her mind as she'd bared Thad's heavily muscled chest. "You don't need anyone."

He shook his head, and then he wrapped his hands around her waist, pulling her close to him. "I need you...."

She didn't wait for whatever else he had to say, and he looked as if he intended to say more. She'd heard what she needed, that she was needed. Sliding her arms around his neck, she pressed her mouth against his and kissed him in a way that would leave no doubt that she needed him, too.

Thad's lips parted on a groan, and he deepened the kiss, sliding his tongue into her mouth. Her pulse pounded as desire overwhelmed her. She wasn't the only one losing control.

Thad's hands shook as he fumbled with the belt of her robe and pushed the soft fleece from her shoulders. She hadn't dressed for seduction; as a single mother, she never did. But Thad acted as if her simple cotton nightgown was a see-through negligee. His pupils dilated, his eyes darkening with passion.

"You are so beautiful." The words came out in a sexy rasp.

And for the first time in a long time, Caroline felt beautiful. Acting the seductress, she slowly released the buttons and parted the fabric so that it slid off her shoulders and fell atop the robe.

Thad sucked in a sharp breath. "*So* damn beautiful…"

He was the beautiful one with the lamplight gleaming on the hard muscles of his bare chest and arms. She had to open her mouth to breathe as he literally stole her breath away. Then his lips pressed to hers again, kissing her as if he never intended to stop.

She never wanted him to stop. Never wanted him to leave…but tonight was only about tonight. Not tomorrow, even though dawn was beginning to lighten the sky outside his windows. He acted as if he had all night. He took his time taking off the last of their clothes. Took his time touching her…everywhere.

And kissing every inch of her skin. Her knees weak, she dropped onto his bed, and he followed her down. His body covered hers, slick skin sliding over slick skin.

After kissing her lips, his mouth slid down her cheek, into the hollow below her jaw. She shivered at the delicious sensation. But he moved lower, sliding his lips across her collarbone and over the slope of her breasts. She arched, silently begging him for more. He gave her more, his lips closing over the nipple.

She whimpered as the passion intensified and pressure built inside her. Then his fingers were there, sliding into her, and she arched against his hand. But it wasn't enough, even as she came, to release the most intense pressure.

She reached for him, closing her hands around the length of him. He pulsed and shuddered in her grasp. "Caroline…"

"Take me, Thad…." She was already his. She had always been his.

"I—I don't have any protection."

She didn't care. He had given her the most precious gift the last time he'd left her; she would be blessed if he left her another.

She parted her legs and arched her hips and guided

him to her core. As if his control snapped, he thrust inside her, joining their bodies. Caroline clung to him, wrapping her legs tight around his waist and her arms tight around his shoulders.

Muscles strained along his neck and in his shoulders and arms as he braced himself above her. He stared down at her, his eyes full of awe and something more.

Something she dared not trust in case she was only imagining it. So she closed her eyes and clutched him close. She met his every thrust, taking him deeper and deeper into her body and her heart. Every time she'd thought she couldn't love him any more, she learned to love him more.

The pressure wound tighter, the exquisite pain of it nearly tearing her apart before she shattered. Pleasure, even more intense than the pressure, overwhelmed her. She had never known anything as powerful or as profound.

Thad tensed and joined her in ecstasy, her name on his lips as he buried his face in her neck and his body deep in hers. He clutched her close, keeping them joined, as he rolled to his side and carried her with him, tight in his arms. As if he never intended to let her go.

As if he never intended to leave.

"Caroline," he began, as if he was coming back to all those words she'd seen earlier in his gaze as he'd stared at her.

But she was too much a coward to hear them now, when she was more vulnerable and more in love than she had ever been with him, so she closed her eyes. And she pretended to sleep.

When Christmas came, she would learn if Santa had brought her what she wanted…or if he intended to take it—and Thad—away from her again.

# Chapter Eighteen

*She was gone.*

And Thad had only himself to blame for waking up to an empty bed. He should have told her what she deserved to hear, what she had deserved to hear from him four years ago.

That he loved her. That he couldn't leave her and Mark ever again.

He had dressed and rushed downstairs to tell her those words and had found the house full of people, everyone who mattered to him, except for *her*.

"She's coming back," Aunt Angela said as she pressed a mug of coffee into his hand. "She only went to check on her friend's husband."

"You saw her?"

Aunt Angela smiled. "This morning, when she left. You were still sleeping." And from the twinkle in his aunt's eyes, she knew how Caroline had known he was still sleeping.

She'd been in his arms all night, or what had been left of the night when he'd finally fallen asleep.

"You had to know she was coming back," his aunt

persisted as she pointed to the little boy who sat on Uncle Craig's lap. "She would never leave him here."

He grinned at his son. "No, she wouldn't."

"She was going to stop off to get his gifts from their house and bring them back here," Ash said as he and Rachel joined Thad and Aunt Angela. "She couldn't bring them yesterday and risk him finding out the truth about Santa."

Rachel patted his hands, which as always, covered her belly. "I'd say Santa is very real this year."

"Santa Claus brought you something, Daddy!" Mark exclaimed, wriggling out of Craig's lap to run over to where *Santa* stood by the tree.

At the sight of former navy SEAL Grayson Scott in a Santa suit complete with padded belly and snowy-white beard, Thad choked on his sip of coffee laughing. Gray was a great addition to the Kendall family, so loving and protective of Natalie that he would do anything for her. *Anything*.

Just as Thad would do for Caroline, if the stubborn woman would give him the chance to prove it to her. He glanced toward the door to see if she'd returned. But Mark grabbed his hand and pressed the package into it.

"Maybe you should wait for Caroline," Aunt Angela suggested, "if she got you that present."

Thad shook his head. "It's definitely not her handwriting. She writes like an elementary school teacher." Not like an impatient man, which was what the scrawl of his name reminded Thad.

"That handwriting doesn't belong to either of your brothers," Aunt Angela remarked. "Gray—I mean, Santa?"

He shook his head. "Not mine. If you don't recognize it, Thad, maybe you shouldn't open it."

Thad wasn't surprised where the navy SEAL's thoughts had gone. His forayed there, too, wondering yet if his true identity had been revealed after he'd walked off that last mission to come home. But when he inspected the gold-foil-wrapped package, he realized it was a book.

"*The Great Gatsby.* It looks old."

He glanced inside. "First edition."

Ed Turner hadn't just ransacked his suite the day he'd broken into the estate. He'd left him a gift under the tree, one he'd probably thought he would have no further use for if he'd managed to manipulate Thad into killing him.

"Who's it from?" Ash asked as he studied his face.

Thad shook his head, unwilling to ruin the first happy Christmas morning the Kendalls had had in twenty years. The gift didn't bother him, but it might bother the others. "Just an old acquaintance."

Bored with the book, Mark went back to the couch and the game Uncle Craig had been playing with him. He crawled into his lap as naturally as if he'd known the man his entire life.

Aunt Angela squeezed Thad's hand. "He's such a sweet boy and exactly what we've needed around here again. Children."

"We know what we're having," Ash said, raising his voice to draw everyone's attention.

Aunt Angela's eyes lit with excitement. To her, news like this was far more thrilling than opening any present. "Really?"

"We're going to have a baby boy," Rachel announced.

Mark clapped. "Good! Boys rule. Girls drool."

"You're lucky your mother isn't here to hear that," Thad warned his son, but he couldn't keep the smile from his face. He slapped his brother's back. "That's great, you two. Congratulations."

Ash nodded, his green eyes bright. He reached out for Aunt Angela, catching her hands in both of his now. "We're going to name him Connor."

For the son she and Uncle Craig had lost way too young.

Tears glimmered in her warm brown eyes, and Uncle Craig hugged Mark tight. "That's wonderful," he said. "A beautiful gift...just like children are."

Thad gazed around the room at his family. He had never seen them as happy on any other Christmas, not even the ones before his parents had been killed. Only he, missing Caroline, and Natalie, were not completely happy.

He joined his sister where she stood by the windows, staring out onto the snow-covered patio. "Hey, Nat..." He wrapped an arm around her shoulders. "What are you doing over here by yourself?"

*Santa* had been watching her, too, his gaze full of concern. He started across the room, but Aunt Angela caught him, thrusting a tray of cookies at him. He was already family, but their aunt was giving the siblings a moment like so many they'd stolen over the years as Devin and Ash joined them.

"What's going on, little sister?" Devin asked. He

must have also noticed how she'd distanced herself from them, as if she was now an outsider.

"I'm sorry," she said, glancing over her shoulder at Mark, who jumped up and down next to Gray, trying to reach a cookie. Her fiancé lifted the boy easily and held him as naturally as if he was already a father himself. "It's my fault all these horrible things happened."

"It damn well isn't!" Devin corrected her.

"I caused it," she said. "It all happened because of me." She turned to Thad. "That's why your son was kidnapped." She shuddered. "What if you hadn't been able to save him and Caroline? How much different would today be?"

"Miserable," he admitted. "But I still wouldn't blame you for any of it. It would be like my blaming Mark for what happened. You had no control over what our mother did, or what Ed Turner did."

She sucked in a deep breath and nodded. "I know that. I do." She lifted her shoulders as if finally relieving herself of the burden of guilt she'd carried needlessly. "He's not my father, you know."

"We know," Ash assured her. "You are one hundred percent our sister. You always have been and you always will be a Kendall."

Her quick grin flashed. "Well, at least until I become Mrs. Grayson Scott in a few months."

Thad reached into his pocket for the gift he hadn't yet placed under the tree because the person he wanted to give it to wasn't there. But then he turned away from the window and caught sight of her across the room.

She had returned, carrying her own bag of gifts as if she were Santa Claus. But there was nothing masculine about her red sweater, black skirt and tall leather boots, or all the generous curves he'd kissed and caressed just hours ago.

Their gazes met and held, and his temperature rose at just the memory of her touch, of her taste. He started forward to close the distance between them.

But Uncle Craig stood up and clinked a champagne flute with a spoon. Instead of passing out cookies, Aunt Angela was now moving around with a tray of drinks.

The siblings moved back to the middle of the room and gathered around the man who'd been their rock for so many years. Each accepted a glass of champagne, ready to celebrate whatever he deemed worthy of celebration, which, today, was so much.

"I have an announcement to make," he said. He stopped Aunt Angela, taking the tray from her and pressing a drink into her hand. "It's your present, actually."

"My present?" She lifted her fingers to the diamond pendant he'd bought her.

"Not that," he said. "Your real present, if you think you can handle it."

She narrowed her eyes with suspicion. "What are you talking about?"

"Time," he said. "After everything we've been through the past four months, I've realized how little of it we actually have. So I don't want to waste another minute apart from you, my sweet wife."

She blinked back tears at his compliment and the depth of love for her on his face.

He turned toward the rest of them now. "I'm officially announcing my retirement from Kendall Communications."

Devin lifted his glass. "I understand your reasons," he said as he glanced down at his fiancée, whose hand he held in his free one. "But I don't think I can run the company alone."

Uncle Craig laughed. "We both know that's not true. You've done more with that company than I have, and you can take it even further on your own."

Devin shook his head. "Not on my own." He turned to Thad now. "I need help to take it in the direction I want to go. Are you interested in a job, little brother?"

"I need him at SLPD," Ash interrupted, as if their little brother was a toy the two former rivals used to fight over.

Thad suspected he could do more good at Kendall Communications. But before he could answer, he had to ask a question of his own.

CAROLINE HELD HER BREATH, waiting for Thad's answer just like the rest of his family did. Was he going to stay? Would he give up being a spy to become part of his family's company?

To become a family man?

"Mark," he said to his son, "bring your mother over here. She's the only one who hasn't opened a present yet."

Heat rushed to her face, and she shook her head. "This isn't the time," she protested even as Mark, surprisingly strong for his size, tugged her toward the Christmas tree and Thad. "Everyone's waiting for your answer."

"And I'm waiting for yours," he said, and he pulled a small box from his pocket.

Her heart began to pound out its own version of "Jingle Bells." "I don't understand."

He dropped to one knee in front of her and his entire family.

"What did Santa bring Mommy?" Mark asked his aunt, who lifted him up in her arms.

"Diamonds," Natalie replied with a lusty sigh as Thad opened the box to reveal a solitaire on a delicate band of interlaced gold and silver.

"Looks like tinsel," Mark said in delight. "It's pretty."

It was beautiful, but Caroline didn't care about the jewelry. She cared about the man.

He stared up at her, his blue eyes full of hope and promise and love. Now she no longer feared what he wanted to tell her; she kicked herself for not letting him ask the night before. But somehow it was fitting that he propose here, on Christmas morning in front of their son and their family and the twinkling tree.

"I love you, Caroline Emerson," he said. "I have loved you for years. Leaving you was the hardest thing I've ever had to do. And I've done a lot of hard things over the years. I thought of you every day, wondering what you were doing and if I'd forever lost my chance with you."

Choked with emotion, she could only shake her head. There had never been anyone else for her. There never could be anyone in her heart but Thad Kendall.

"I never want to leave you again," he said. "I want to spend the rest of my life making up for the hurt I caused you. I want to spend the rest of my life giving you the love and devotion you deserve…if you'll have me."

Caroline's heart pounded harder at the look on his handsome face. She'd never seen it on him before: uncertainty. He didn't know how much she'd wanted this, how much she'd wanted him.

"Marry me, Caroline," he implored her. "Please, let me be your husband."

She threw her arms around his neck with such force she nearly knocked him backward into the tree. "I love you, Thad."

He kissed her.

But then one of his brothers pointed out, "She didn't say yes yet."

"Do you blame her?" Natalie asked. "He's kind of a flight risk."

"Not anymore," he promised them all. "I'm going to take that job at Kendall Communications. I'm going to be a nine-to-five company man."

Devin snorted. "Good luck getting those hours."

"Are you sure?" Caroline asked. "Don't give up anything for me. I'll marry you if you work at Kendall or at the police department or even if you feel you have to go back—"

He pressed his finger over her lips as he rose up from his knee and hugged her close. "I'll never go back. I've done what I can over there. I can do more good at Kendall and at home with you and Mark."

She smiled. "I would like a little girl."

"Good thing you're retiring," Angela said to her husband as she leaned against his side. "We're going to be very busy babysitting."

"Very busy," he agreed. And the man who had run a multimillion-dollar corporation sounded delighted at the thought of playing with grandkids. He and his wife were more than uncle and aunt or guardians to the Kendall siblings—they were their real parents.

Thad slid the engagement ring onto Caroline's finger. The diamond and metal twinkled nearly as brightly as the tree, or as his eyes as he stared at her. "Thank you for giving me exactly what I wanted for Christmas," he told her. "Your love."

"Santa brought me what I wanted, too," Mark said, wriggling down from his aunt's arms to hurl himself at her and Thad. His father lifted him up so that he snuggled between them. "A family."

Thad kissed his forehead. "Santa did good this year," he said, and he glanced around the room at his loved ones. "We all got what he wanted."

Love and happiness. There were no greater Christmas blessings.

\* \* \* \* \*

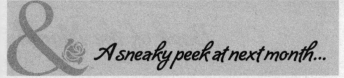

*A sneaky peek at next month...*

# INTRIGUE...

**BREATHTAKING ROMANTIC SUSPENSE**

*My wish list for next month's titles...*

**In stores from 21st December 2012:**

❏ Grayson – Delores Fossen

& Dade – Delores Fossen

❏ Breathless Encounter – Cindy Dees

& Switched – HelenKay Dimon

❏ Cavanaugh's Surrender – Marie Ferrarella

& Montana Midwife – Cassie Miles

❏ Colton Destiny – Justine Davis

**Available at WHSmith, Tesco, Asda, Eason, Amazon and Apple**

*Just can't wait?*

# Special Offers

Every month we put together collections and longer reads written by your favourite authors.

Here are some of next month's highlights— and don't miss our fabulous discount online!

On sale 21st December

On sale 4th January

On sale 4th January

## Save 20% on all Special Releases

Find out more at
**www.millsandboon.co.uk/specialreleases**

*Visit us Online*

0113/ST/MB398